image comics presents

THE WALKING DEAD™

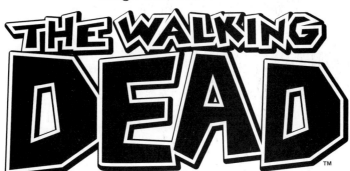

ROBERT KIRKMAN
CREATOR, WRITER, LETTERER

CHARLIE ADLARD
PENCILER, INKER

CLIFF RATHBURN
GRAY TONES

TONY MOORE
COVER

For SKYBOUND ENTERTAINMENT

Robert Kirkman - CEO
J.J. Didde - President
Sean Mackiewicz - Editorial Director
Shawn Kirkham - Director of Business Development
Helen Leigh - Office Manager
Brandon West - Inventory Control
Feldman Public Relations LA - Public Relations

For international rights inquiries,
please contact: foreign@skybound.com

WWW.SKYBOUND.COM

IMAGE COMICS, INC.
Robert Kirkman - chief operating officer
Erik Larsen - chief financial officer
Todd McFarlane - president
Marc Silvestri - chief executive officer
Jim Valentino - vice-president

Eric Stephenson - publisher
Ron Richards - director of business development
Jennifer de Guzman - pr & marketing director
Branwyn Bigglestone - accounts manager
Emily Miller - accounting assistant
Jamie Parreno - marketing assistant
Jenna Savage - administrative assistant
Kevin Yuen - digital rights coordinator
Jonathan Chan - production manager
Drew Gill - art director
Tyler Shainline - print manager
Monica Garcia - production artist
Vincent Kukua - production artist
Jana Cook - production artist
www.imagecomics.com

THE WALKING DEAD, VOL. 3: SAFETY BEHIND BARS. Eighth Printing. Published by Image Comics, Inc. Office of publication: 2001 Center Street, 6th Floor, Berkeley, CA 94704. Copyright © 2013 Robert Kirkman, LLC. All rights reserved. Originally published in single magazine format as THE WALKING DEAD #13-18. THE WALKING DEAD™ (including all prominent characters featured in this issue), its logo and all character likenesses are trademarks of Robert Kirkman, LLC, unless otherwise noted. Image Comics® and its logos are registered trademarks of Image Comics, Inc. No part of this publication may be reproduced or transmitted, in any form or by any means (except for short excerpts for review purposes) without the express written permission of Image Comics, Inc. All names, characters, events and locales in this publication are entirely fictional. Any resemblance to actual persons (living and/or dead), events or places, without satiric intent, is coincidental. For information regarding the CPSIA on this printed material call: 203-595-3636 and provide reference # RICH – 478948.

PRINTED IN USA

ISBN: 978-1-58240-805-7

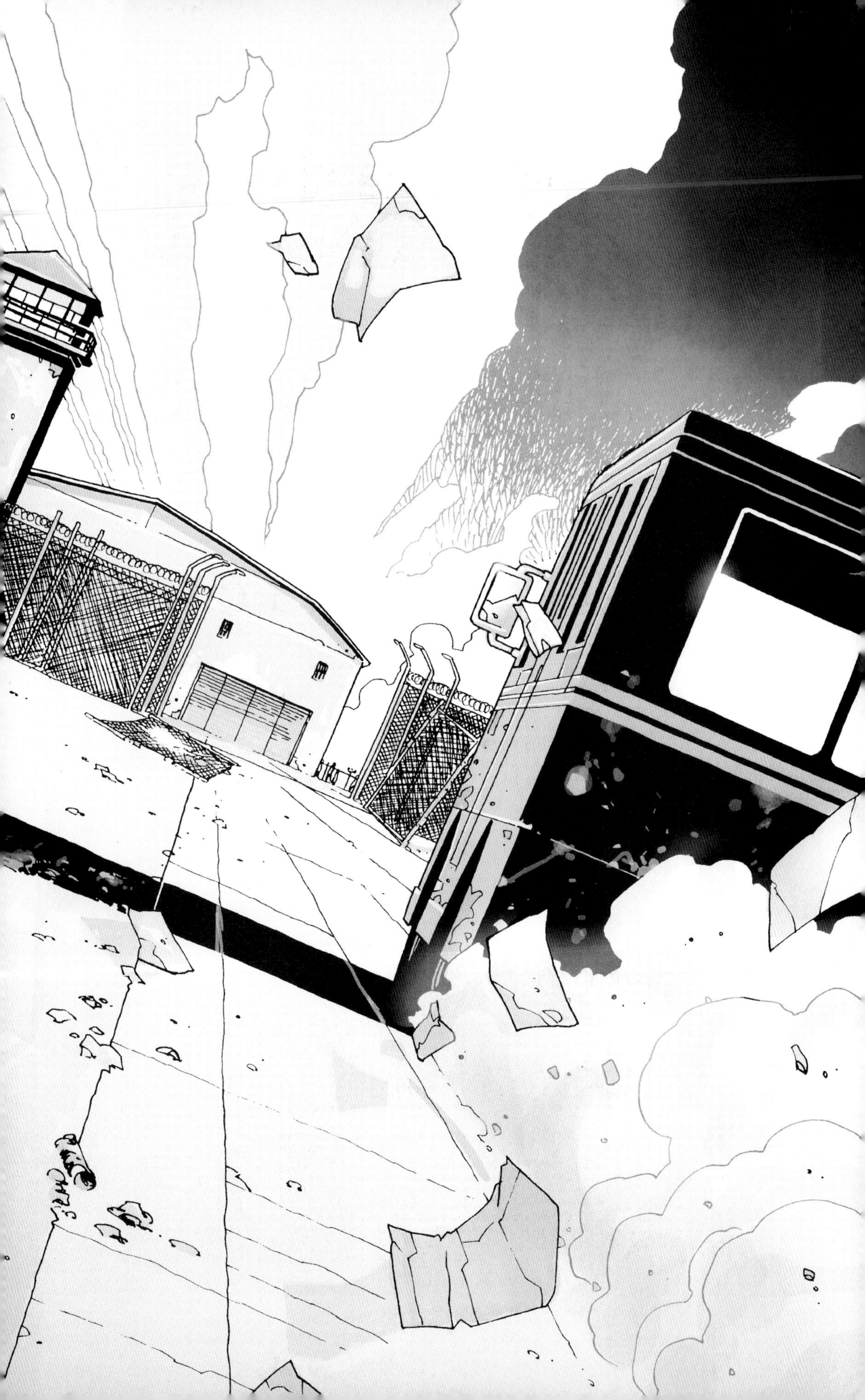

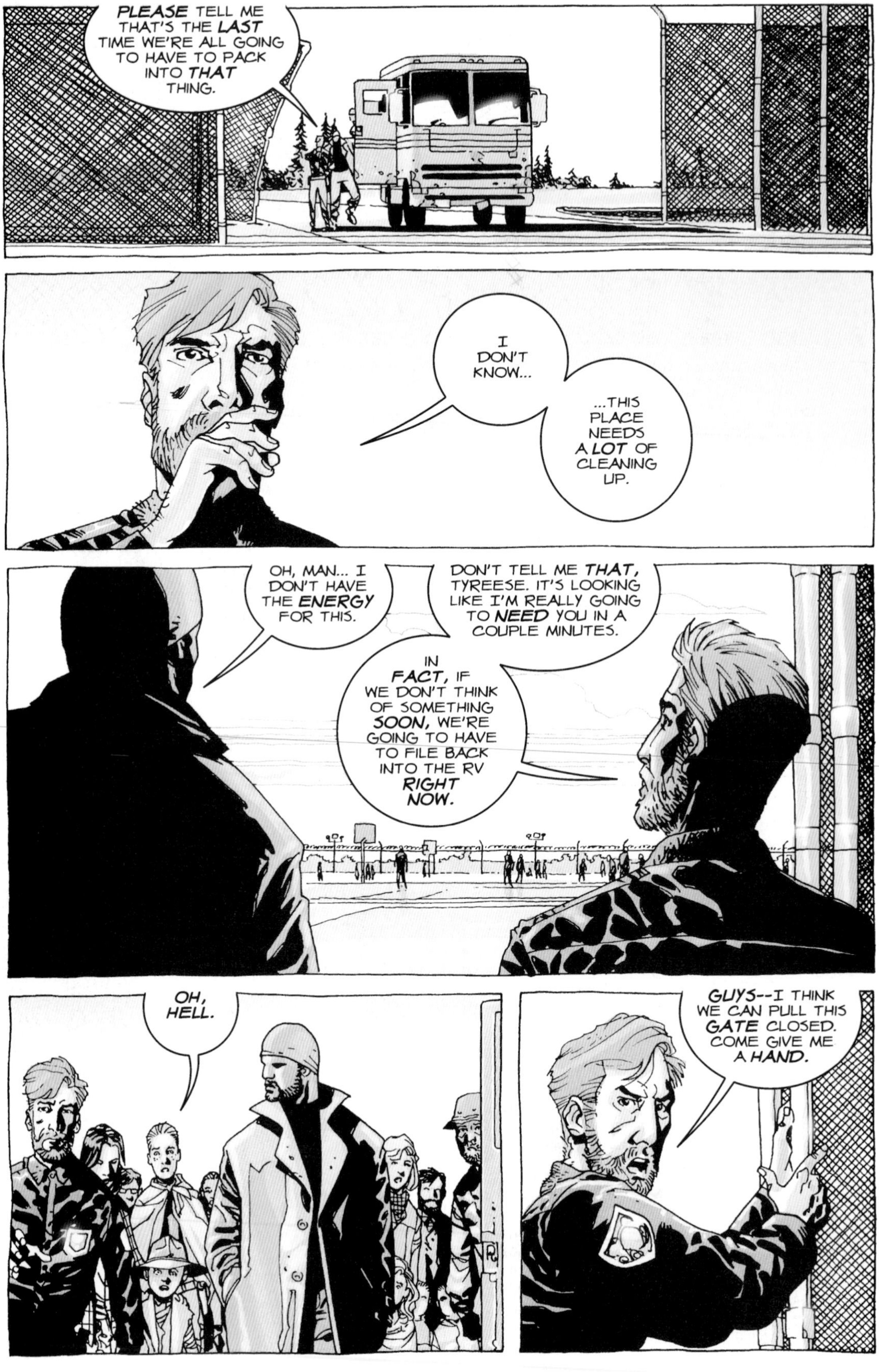
PLEASE TELL ME THAT'S THE LAST TIME WE'RE ALL GOING TO HAVE TO PACK INTO THAT THING.
I DON'T KNOW...
...THIS PLACE NEEDS A LOT OF CLEANING UP.
OH, MAN... I DON'T HAVE THE ENERGY FOR THIS.
DON'T TELL ME THAT, TYREESE. IT'S LOOKING LIKE I'M REALLY GOING TO NEED YOU IN A COUPLE MINUTES.
IN FACT, IF WE DON'T THINK OF SOMETHING SOON, WE'RE GOING TO HAVE TO FILE BACK INTO THE RV RIGHT NOW.
OH, HELL.
GUYS--I THINK WE CAN PULL THIS GATE CLOSED. COME GIVE ME A HAND.

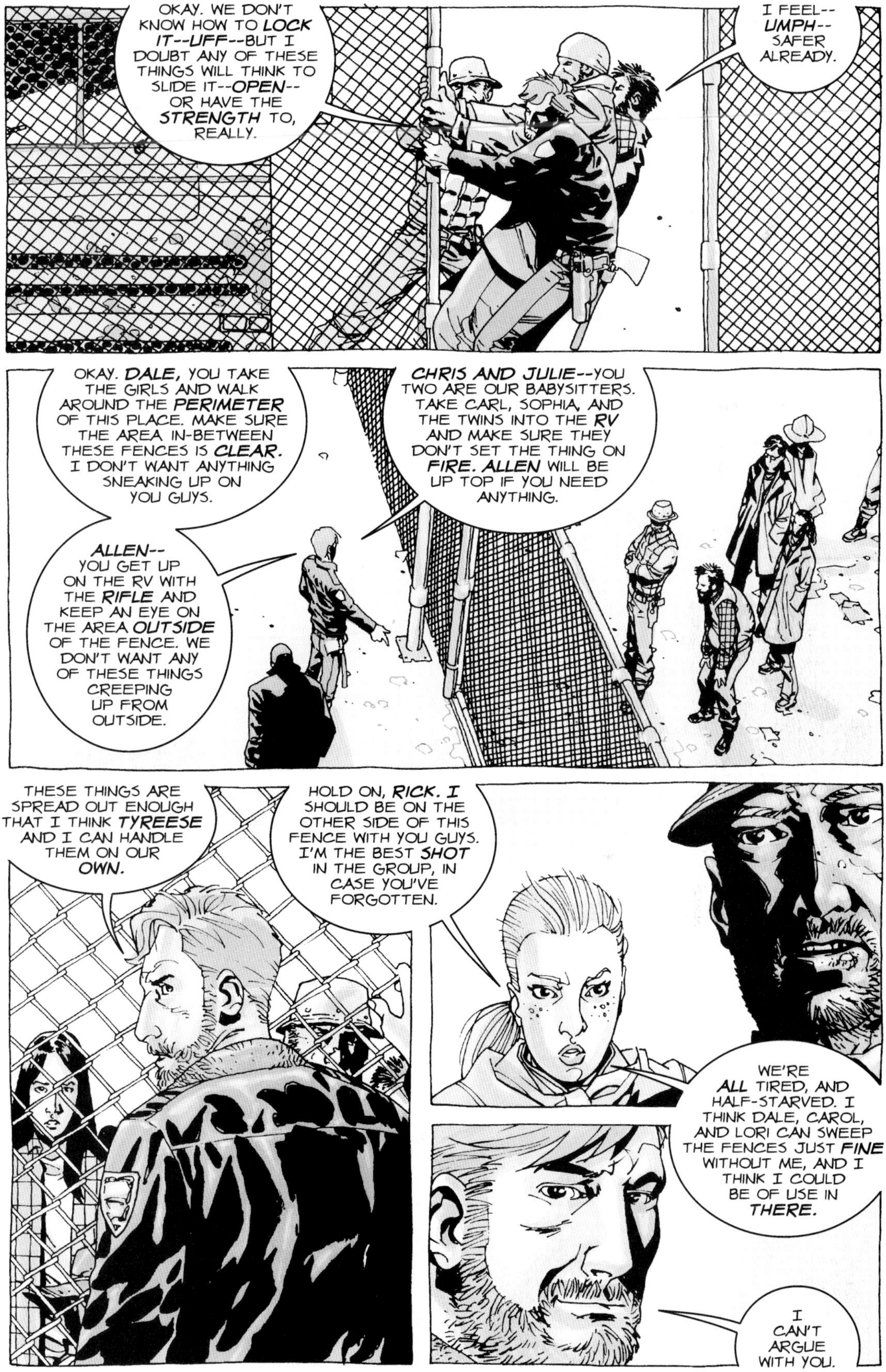

OKAY. WE DON'T KNOW HOW TO LOCK IT--UFF--BUT I DOUBT ANY OF THESE THINGS WILL THINK TO SLIDE IT--OPEN--OR HAVE THE STRENGTH TO, REALLY.
I FEEL--UMPH--SAFER ALREADY.
OKAY. DALE, YOU TAKE THE GIRLS AND WALK AROUND THE PERIMETER OF THIS PLACE. MAKE SURE THE AREA IN-BETWEEN THESE FENCES IS CLEAR. I DON'T WANT ANYTHING SNEAKING UP ON YOU GUYS.
ALLEN--YOU GET UP ON THE RV WITH THE RIFLE AND KEEP AN EYE ON THE AREA OUTSIDE OF THE FENCE. WE DON'T WANT ANY OF THESE THINGS CREEPING UP FROM OUTSIDE.
CHRIS AND JULIE--YOU TWO ARE OUR BABYSITTERS. TAKE CARL, SOPHIA, AND THE TWINS INTO THE RV AND MAKE SURE THEY DON'T SET THE THING ON FIRE. ALLEN WILL BE UP TOP IF YOU NEED ANYTHING.
THESE THINGS ARE SPREAD OUT ENOUGH THAT I THINK TYREESE AND I CAN HANDLE THEM ON OUR OWN.
HOLD ON, RICK. I SHOULD BE ON THE OTHER SIDE OF THIS FENCE WITH YOU GUYS. I'M THE BEST SHOT IN THE GROUP, IN CASE YOU'VE FORGOTTEN.
WE'RE ALL TIRED, AND HALF-STARVED. I THINK DALE, CAROL, AND LORI CAN SWEEP THE FENCES JUST FINE WITHOUT ME, AND I THINK I COULD BE OF USE IN THERE.
I CAN'T ARGUE WITH YOU.

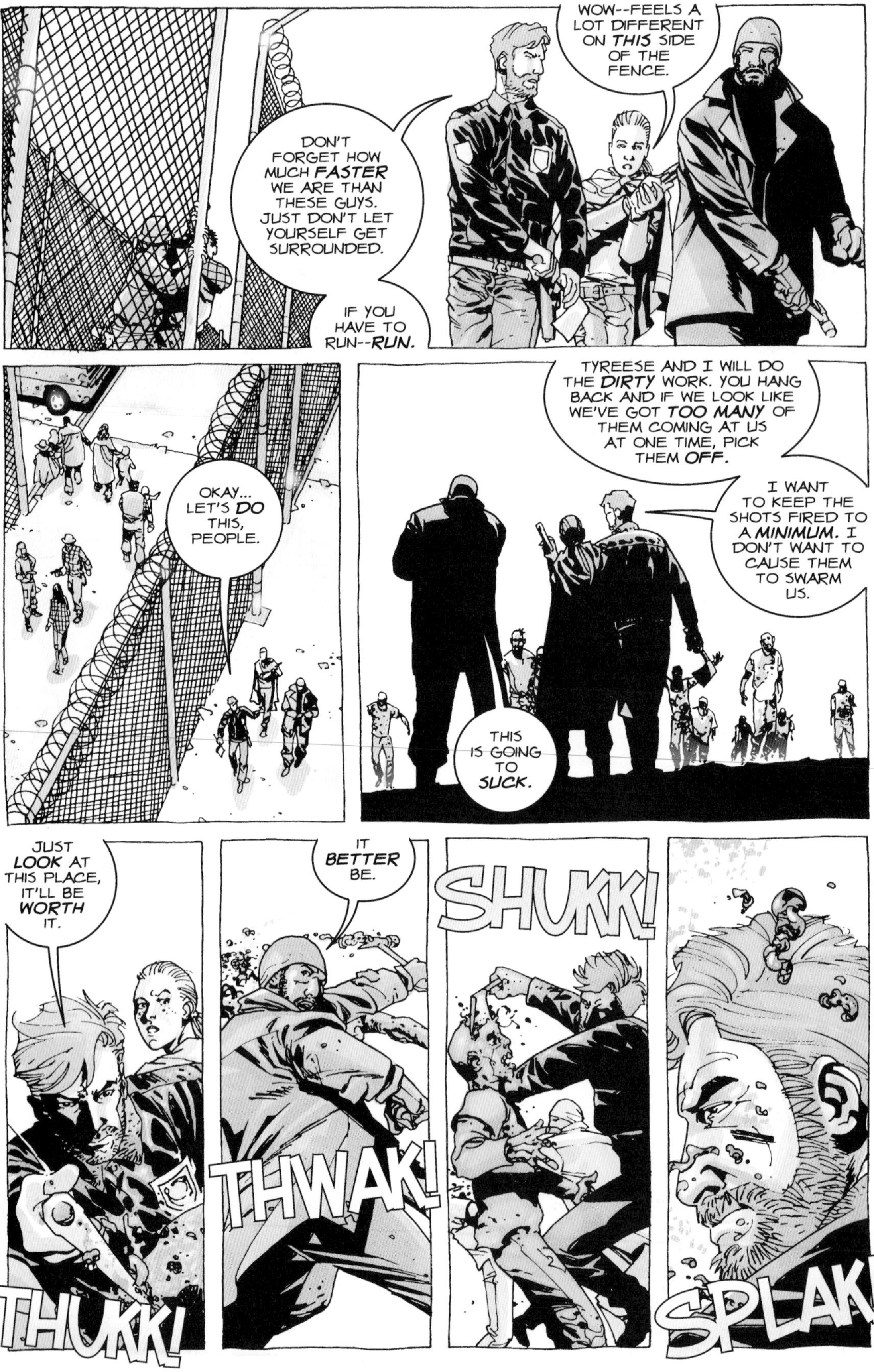
WOW--FEELS A LOT DIFFERENT ON THIS SIDE OF THE FENCE.
DON'T FORGET HOW MUCH FASTER WE ARE THAN THESE GUYS. JUST DON'T LET YOURSELF GET SURROUNDED.
IF YOU HAVE TO RUN--RUN.
OKAY... LET'S DO THIS, PEOPLE.
TYREESE AND I WILL DO THE DIRTY WORK. YOU HANG BACK AND IF WE LOOK LIKE WE'VE GOT TOO MANY OF THEM COMING AT US AT ONE TIME, PICK THEM OFF.
I WANT TO KEEP THE SHOTS FIRED TO A MINIMUM. I DON'T WANT TO CAUSE THEM TO SWARM US.
THIS IS GOING TO SUCK.
JUST LOOK AT THIS PLACE, IT'LL BE WORTH IT.
THUKK!
IT BETTER BE.
THWAK!
SHUKK!
SPLAK!

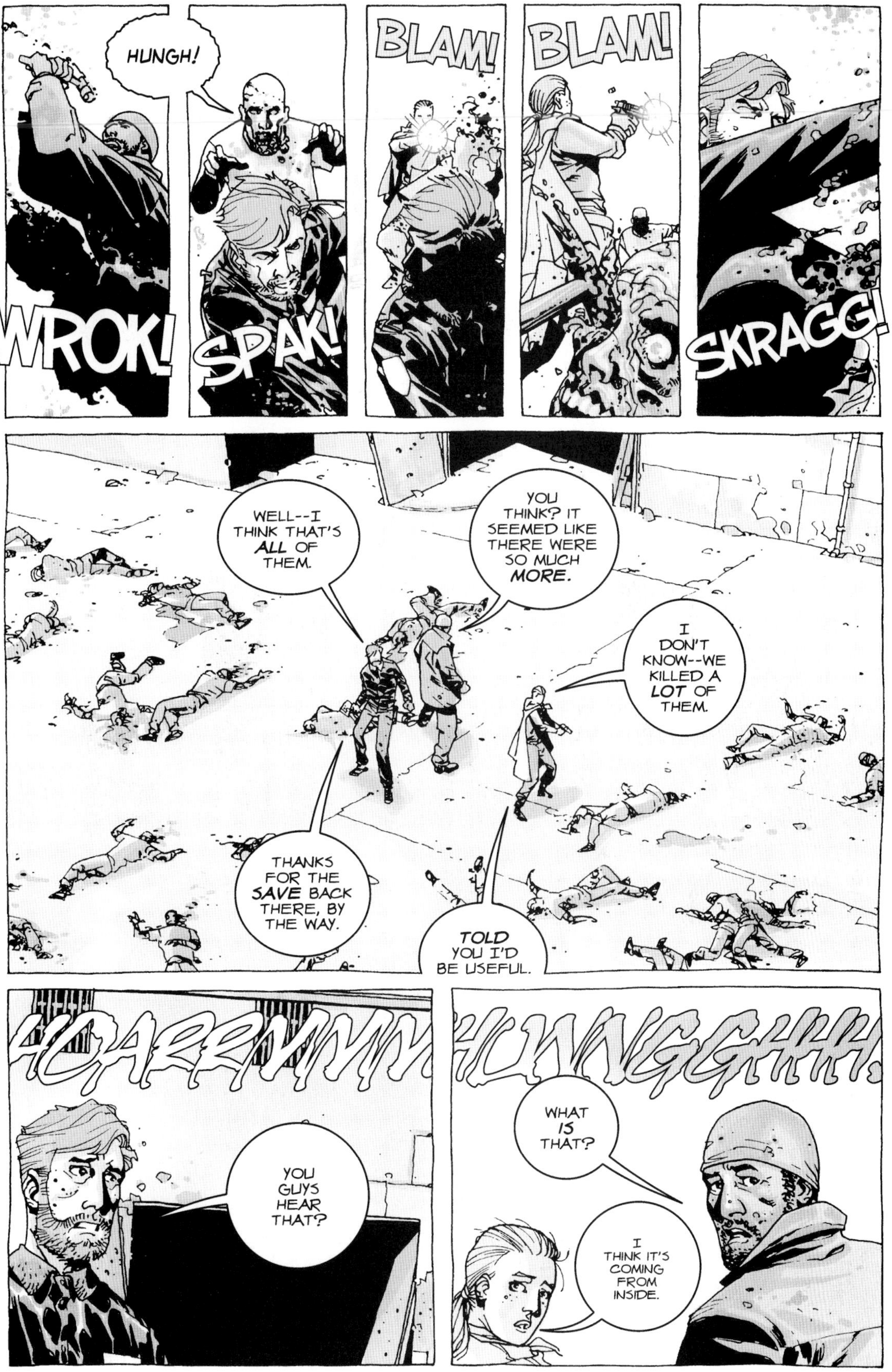
WROK!
HUNGH!
SPAK!
BLAM!
BLAM!
SKRAGG!
WELL--I THINK THAT'S ALL OF THEM.
YOU THINK? IT SEEMED LIKE THERE WERE SO MUCH MORE.
I DON'T KNOW--WE KILLED A LOT OF THEM.
THANKS FOR THE SAVE BACK THERE, BY THE WAY.
TOLD YOU I'D BE USEFUL.
HOARRMMMMHUNNGGHHH!
YOU GUYS HEAR THAT?
WHAT IS THAT?
I THINK IT'S COMING FROM INSIDE.

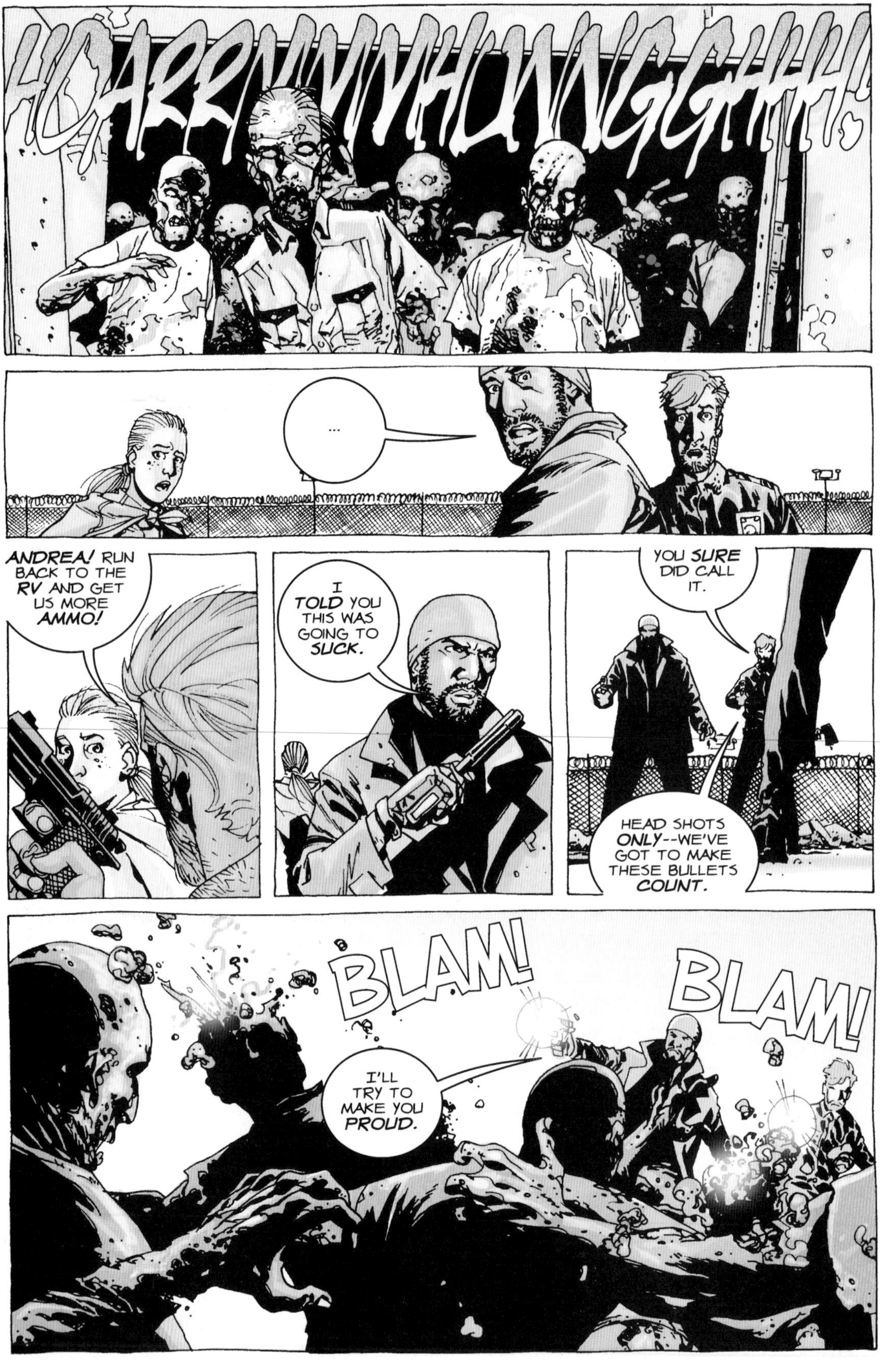
HGARRRMMMHUNNGGHHH!
...
ANDREA! RUN BACK TO THE RV AND GET US MORE AMMO!
I TOLD YOU THIS WAS GOING TO SUCK.
YOU SURE DID CALL IT.
HEAD SHOTS ONLY--WE'VE GOT TO MAKE THESE BULLETS COUNT.
BLAM!
BLAM!
I'LL TRY TO MAKE YOU PROUD.

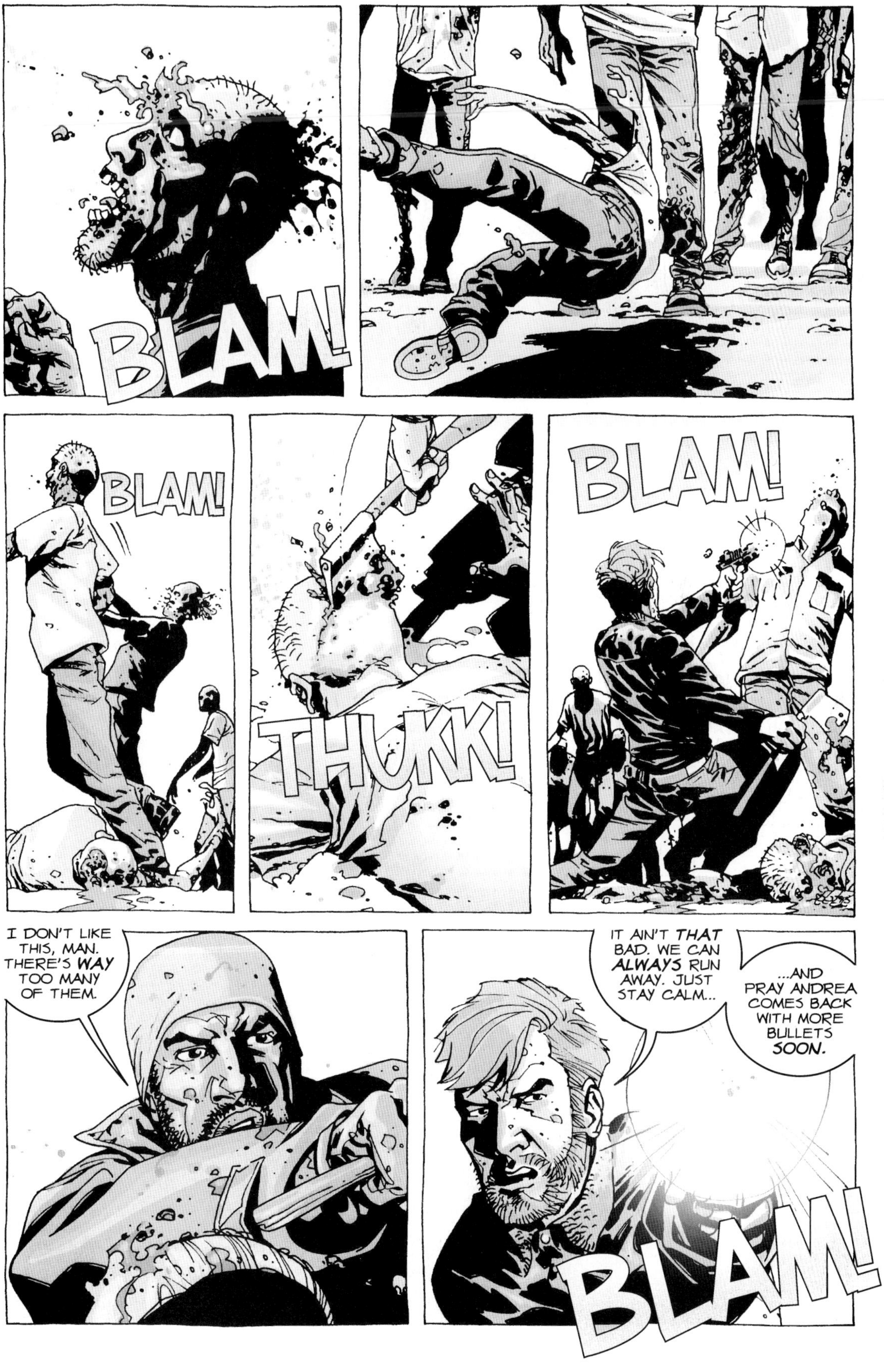
BLAM!
BLAM!
THUKK!
BLAM!
I DON'T LIKE THIS, MAN. THERE'S WAY TOO MANY OF THEM.
IT AIN'T THAT BAD. WE CAN ALWAYS RUN AWAY. JUST STAY CALM...
...AND PRAY ANDREA COMES BACK WITH MORE BULLETS SOON.
BLAM!

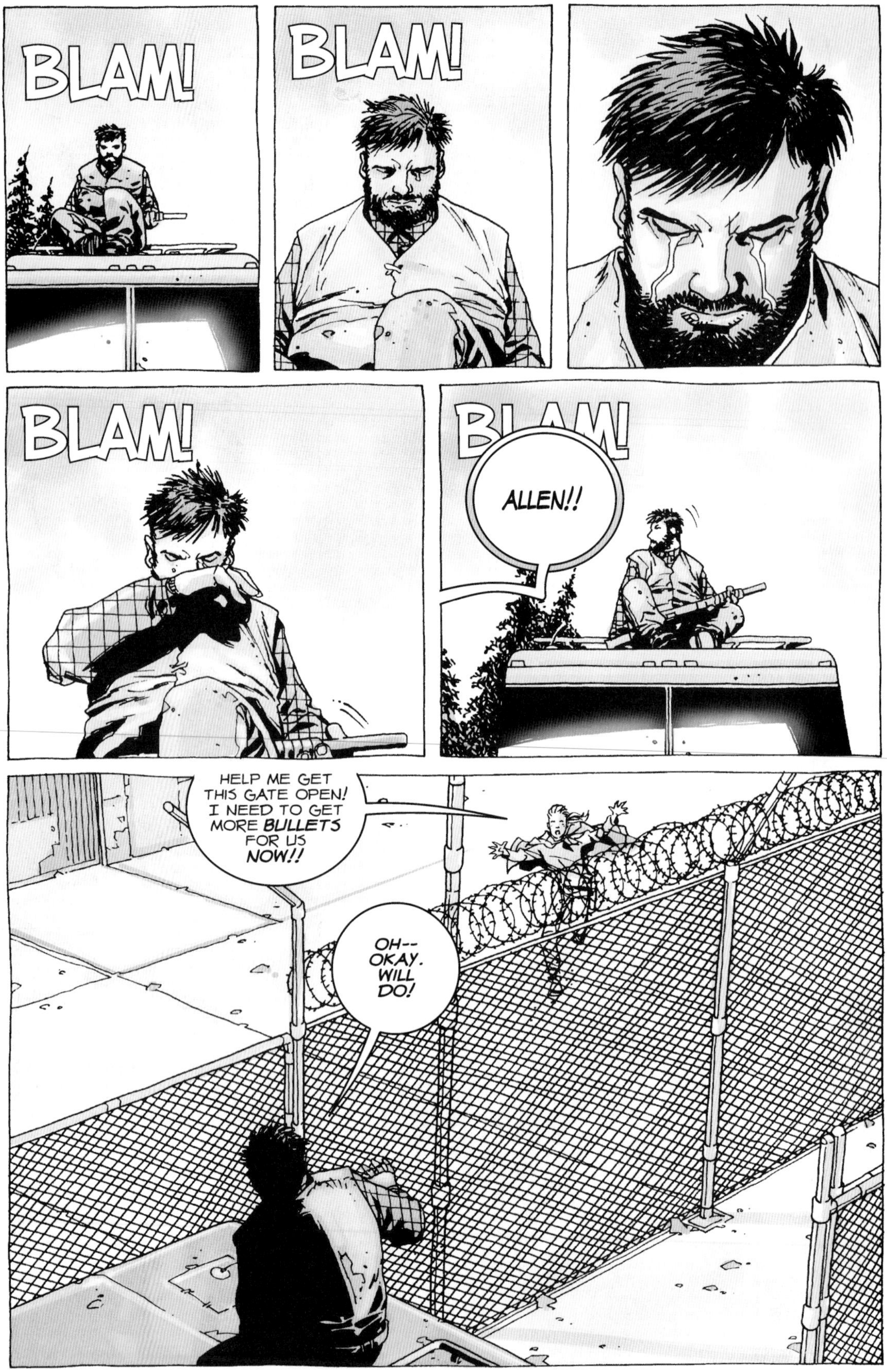
BLAM!
BLAM!
BLAM!
BLAM!
ALLEN!!
HELP ME GET THIS GATE OPEN! I NEED TO GET MORE BULLETS FOR US NOW!!
OH-- OKAY. WILL DO!

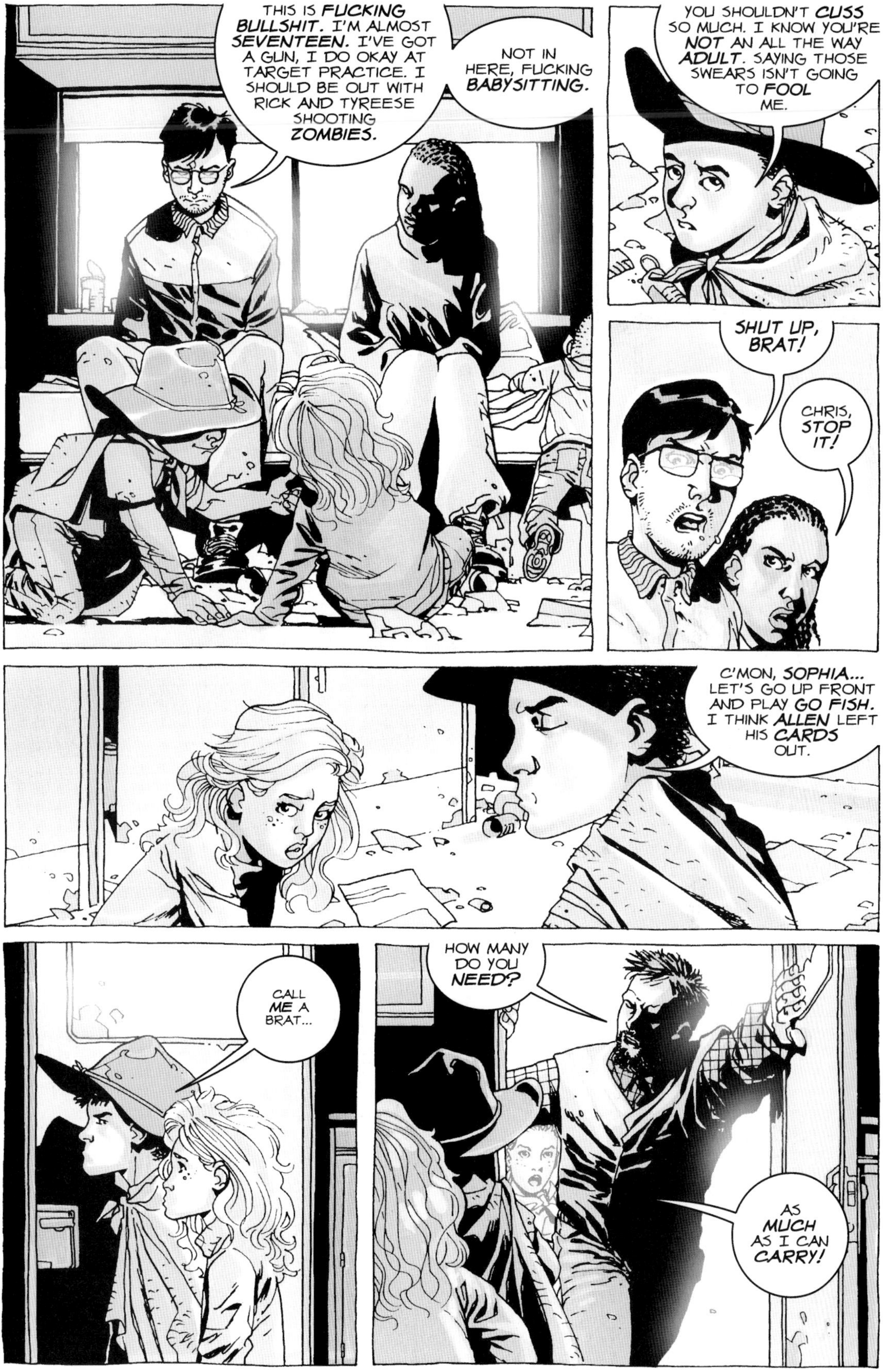
THIS IS FUCKING BULLSHIT. I'M ALMOST SEVENTEEN. I'VE GOT A GUN, I DO OKAY AT TARGET PRACTICE. I SHOULD BE OUT WITH RICK AND TYREESE SHOOTING ZOMBIES.
NOT IN HERE, FUCKING BABYSITTING.
YOU SHOULDN'T CUSS SO MUCH. I KNOW YOU'RE NOT AN ALL THE WAY ADULT. SAYING THOSE SWEARS ISN'T GOING TO FOOL ME.
SHUT UP, BRAT!
CHRIS, STOP IT!
C'MON, SOPHIA... LET'S GO UP FRONT AND PLAY GO FISH. I THINK ALLEN LEFT HIS CARDS OUT.
CALL ME A BRAT...
HOW MANY DO YOU NEED?
AS MUCH AS I CAN CARRY!

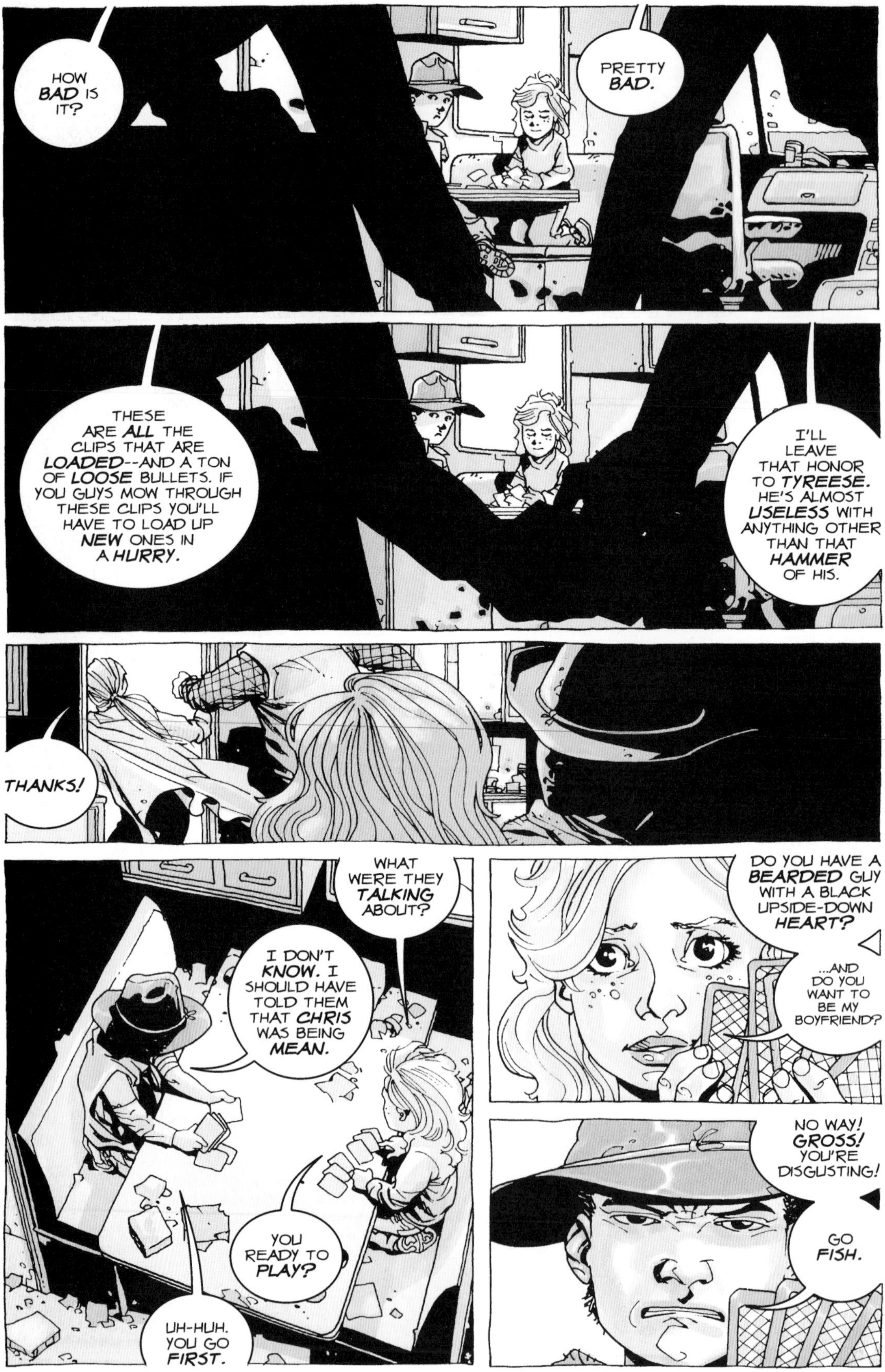

HOW BAD IS IT?
PRETTY BAD.
THESE ARE ALL THE CLIPS THAT ARE LOADED--AND A TON OF LOOSE BULLETS. IF YOU GUYS MOW THROUGH THESE CLIPS YOU'LL HAVE TO LOAD UP NEW ONES IN A HURRY.
I'LL LEAVE THAT HONOR TO TYREESE. HE'S ALMOST USELESS WITH ANYTHING OTHER THAN THAT HAMMER OF HIS.
THANKS!
WHAT WERE THEY TALKING ABOUT?
I DON'T KNOW. I SHOULD HAVE TOLD THEM THAT CHRIS WAS BEING MEAN.
YOU READY TO PLAY?
UH-HUH. YOU GO FIRST.
DO YOU HAVE A BEARDED GUY WITH A BLACK UPSIDE-DOWN HEART?
...AND DO YOU WANT TO BE MY BOYFRIEND?
NO WAY! GROSS! YOU'RE DISGUSTING!
GO FISH.

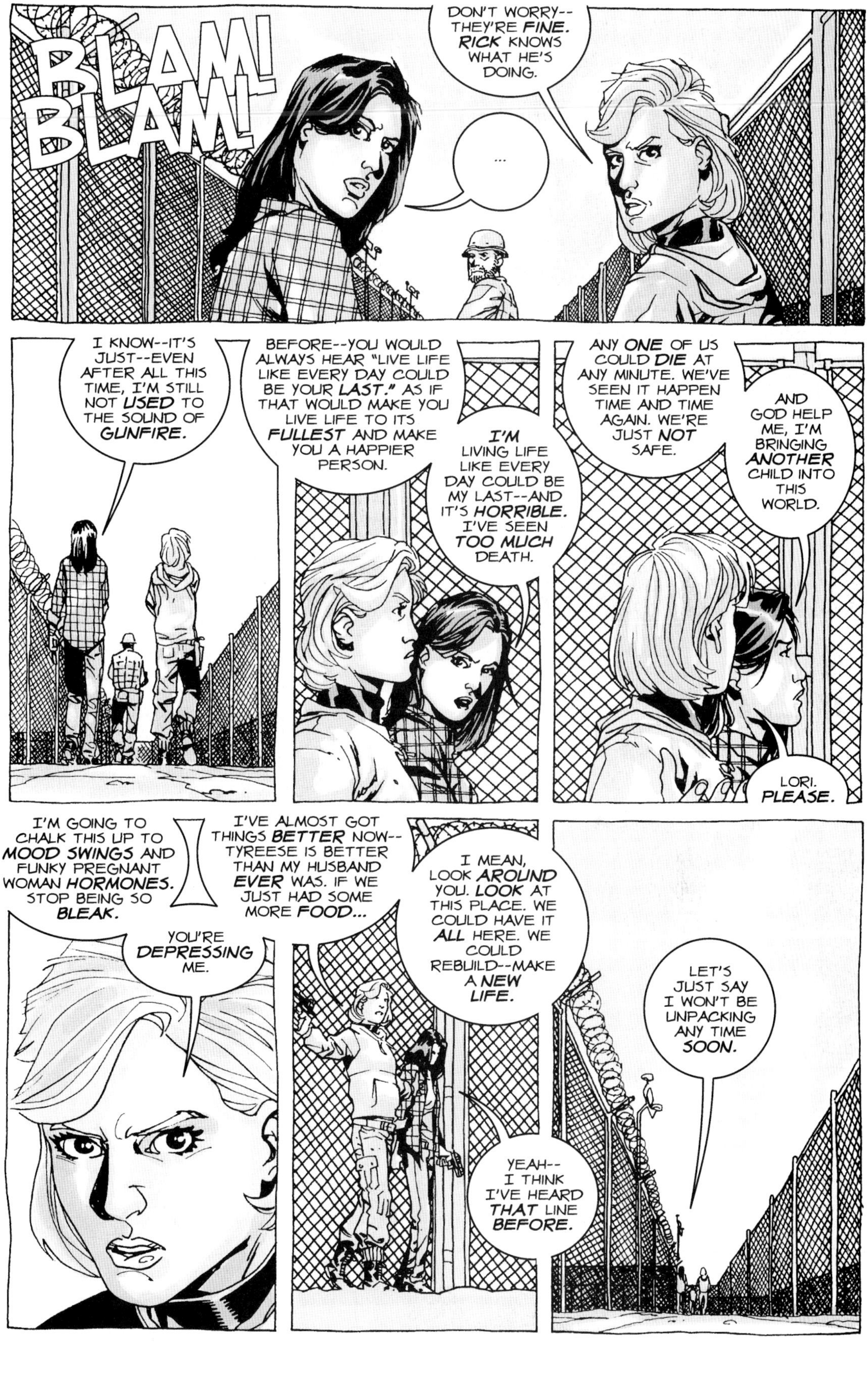
BLAM! BLAM!
DON'T WORRY-- THEY'RE FINE. RICK KNOWS WHAT HE'S DOING.
...
I KNOW--IT'S JUST--EVEN AFTER ALL THIS TIME, I'M STILL NOT USED TO THE SOUND OF GUNFIRE.
BEFORE--YOU WOULD ALWAYS HEAR "LIVE LIFE LIKE EVERY DAY COULD BE YOUR LAST." AS IF THAT WOULD MAKE YOU LIVE LIFE TO ITS FULLEST AND MAKE YOU A HAPPIER PERSON.
I'M LIVING LIFE LIKE EVERY DAY COULD BE MY LAST--AND IT'S HORRIBLE. I'VE SEEN TOO MUCH DEATH.
ANY ONE OF US COULD DIE AT ANY MINUTE. WE'VE SEEN IT HAPPEN TIME AND TIME AGAIN. WE'RE JUST NOT SAFE.
AND GOD HELP ME, I'M BRINGING ANOTHER CHILD INTO THIS WORLD.
LORI. PLEASE.
I'M GOING TO CHALK THIS UP TO MOOD SWINGS AND FUNKY PREGNANT WOMAN HORMONES. STOP BEING SO BLEAK.
YOU'RE DEPRESSING ME.
I'VE ALMOST GOT THINGS BETTER NOW-- TYREESE IS BETTER THAN MY HUSBAND EVER WAS. IF WE JUST HAD SOME MORE FOOD...
I MEAN, LOOK AROUND YOU. LOOK AT THIS PLACE. WE COULD HAVE IT ALL HERE. WE COULD REBUILD--MAKE A NEW LIFE.
YEAH-- I THINK I'VE HEARD THAT LINE BEFORE.
LET'S JUST SAY I WON'T BE UNPACKING ANY TIME SOON.

BLAM!

BLAM!

I GOT ANOTHER CLIP LOADED! WHO WANTS IT?!

I'LL TAKE IT!

THIS KEEPS UP LIKE *THIS*-- WE'RE GOING TO *RUN* OUT!

I THINK WE'VE LUCKED OUT-- *LOOK.*

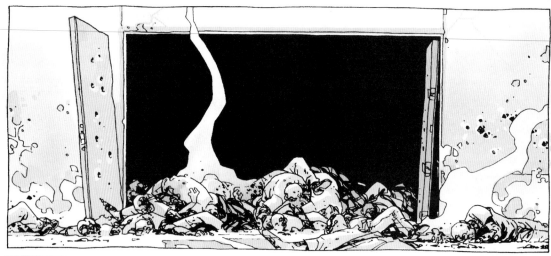

YOU THINK THAT'S *ALL* OF THEM?

IT'D BE *NICE.*

ONE WAY TO FIND OUT--

BLAM!

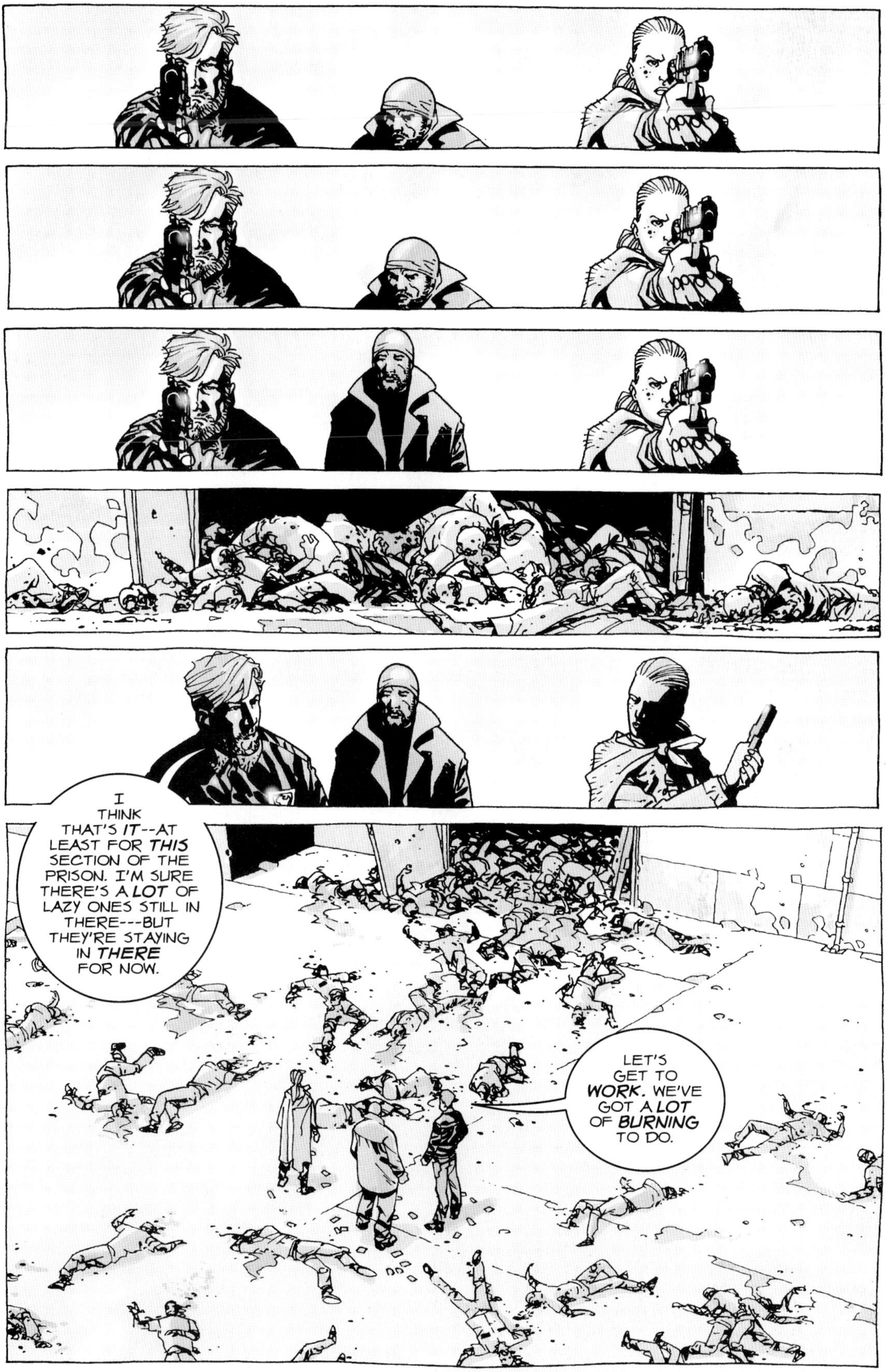
I THINK THAT'S IT--AT LEAST FOR THIS SECTION OF THE PRISON. I'M SURE THERE'S A LOT OF LAZY ONES STILL IN THERE---BUT THEY'RE STAYING IN THERE FOR NOW.
LET'S GET TO WORK. WE'VE GOT A LOT OF BURNING TO DO.

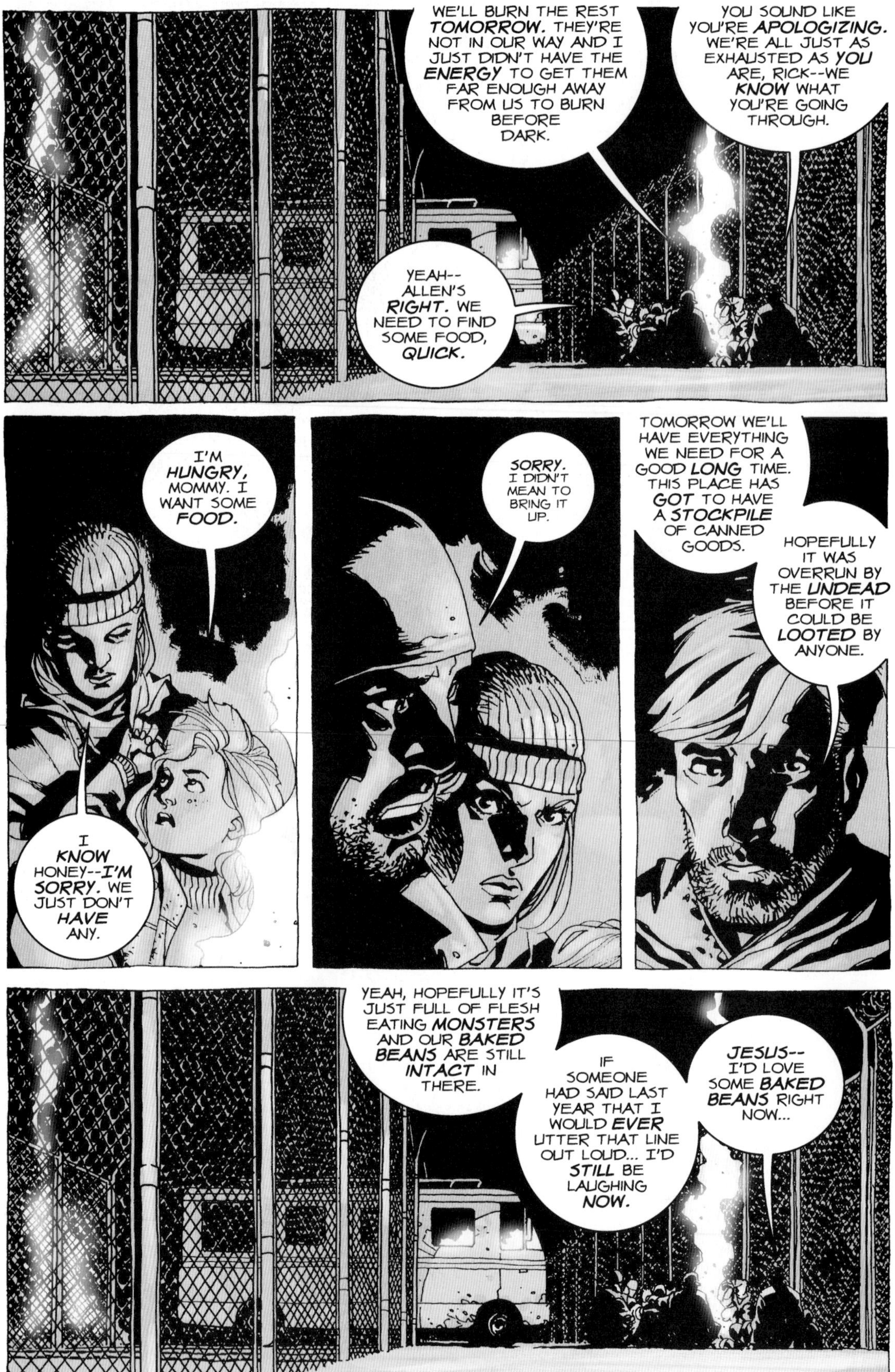
WE'LL BURN THE REST TOMORROW. THEY'RE NOT IN OUR WAY AND I JUST DIDN'T HAVE THE ENERGY TO GET THEM FAR ENOUGH AWAY FROM US TO BURN BEFORE DARK.
YOU SOUND LIKE YOU'RE APOLOGIZING. WE'RE ALL JUST AS EXHAUSTED AS YOU ARE, RICK--WE KNOW WHAT YOU'RE GOING THROUGH.
YEAH-- ALLEN'S RIGHT. WE NEED TO FIND SOME FOOD, QUICK.
I'M HUNGRY, MOMMY. I WANT SOME FOOD.
I KNOW HONEY--I'M SORRY. WE JUST DON'T HAVE ANY.
SORRY. I DIDN'T MEAN TO BRING IT UP.
TOMORROW WE'LL HAVE EVERYTHING WE NEED FOR A GOOD LONG TIME. THIS PLACE HAS GOT TO HAVE A STOCKPILE OF CANNED GOODS.
HOPEFULLY IT WAS OVERRUN BY THE UNDEAD BEFORE IT COULD BE LOOTED BY ANYONE.
YEAH, HOPEFULLY IT'S JUST FULL OF FLESH EATING MONSTERS AND OUR BAKED BEANS ARE STILL INTACT IN THERE.
IF SOMEONE HAD SAID LAST YEAR THAT I WOULD EVER UTTER THAT LINE OUT LOUD... I'D STILL BE LAUGHING NOW.
JESUS-- I'D LOVE SOME BAKED BEANS RIGHT NOW...

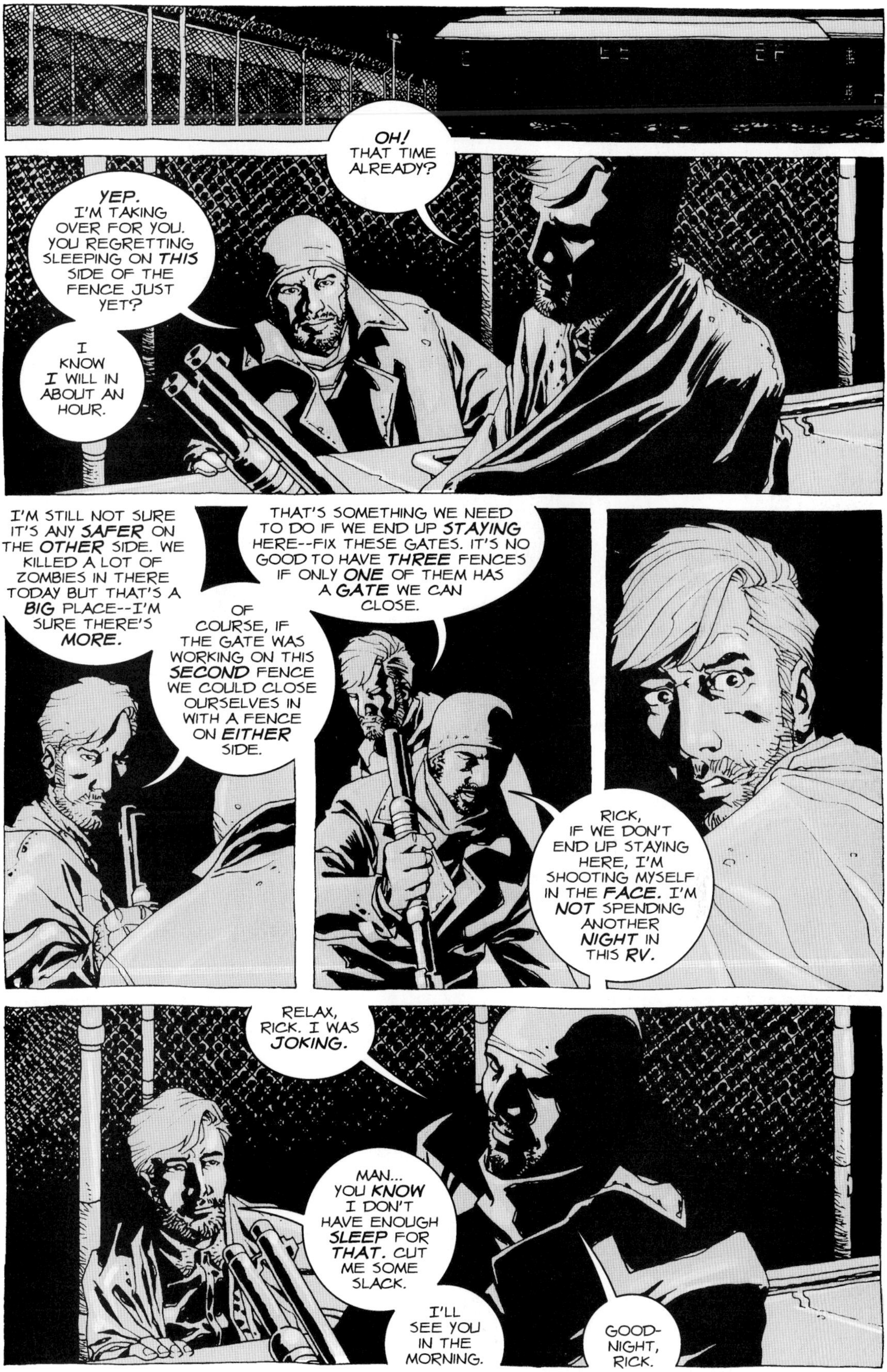
OH! THAT TIME ALREADY?
YEP. I'M TAKING OVER FOR YOU. YOU REGRETTING SLEEPING ON THIS SIDE OF THE FENCE JUST YET?
I KNOW I WILL IN ABOUT AN HOUR.
I'M STILL NOT SURE IT'S ANY SAFER ON THE OTHER SIDE. WE KILLED A LOT OF ZOMBIES IN THERE TODAY BUT THAT'S A BIG PLACE--I'M SURE THERE'S MORE.
OF COURSE, IF THE GATE WAS WORKING ON THIS SECOND FENCE WE COULD CLOSE OURSELVES IN WITH A FENCE ON EITHER SIDE.
THAT'S SOMETHING WE NEED TO DO IF WE END UP STAYING HERE--FIX THESE GATES. IT'S NO GOOD TO HAVE THREE FENCES IF ONLY ONE OF THEM HAS A GATE WE CAN CLOSE.
RICK, IF WE DON'T END UP STAYING HERE, I'M SHOOTING MYSELF IN THE FACE. I'M NOT SPENDING ANOTHER NIGHT IN THIS RV.
RELAX, RICK. I WAS JOKING.
MAN... YOU KNOW I DON'T HAVE ENOUGH SLEEP FOR THAT. CUT ME SOME SLACK.
I'LL SEE YOU IN THE MORNING.
GOOD-NIGHT, RICK.

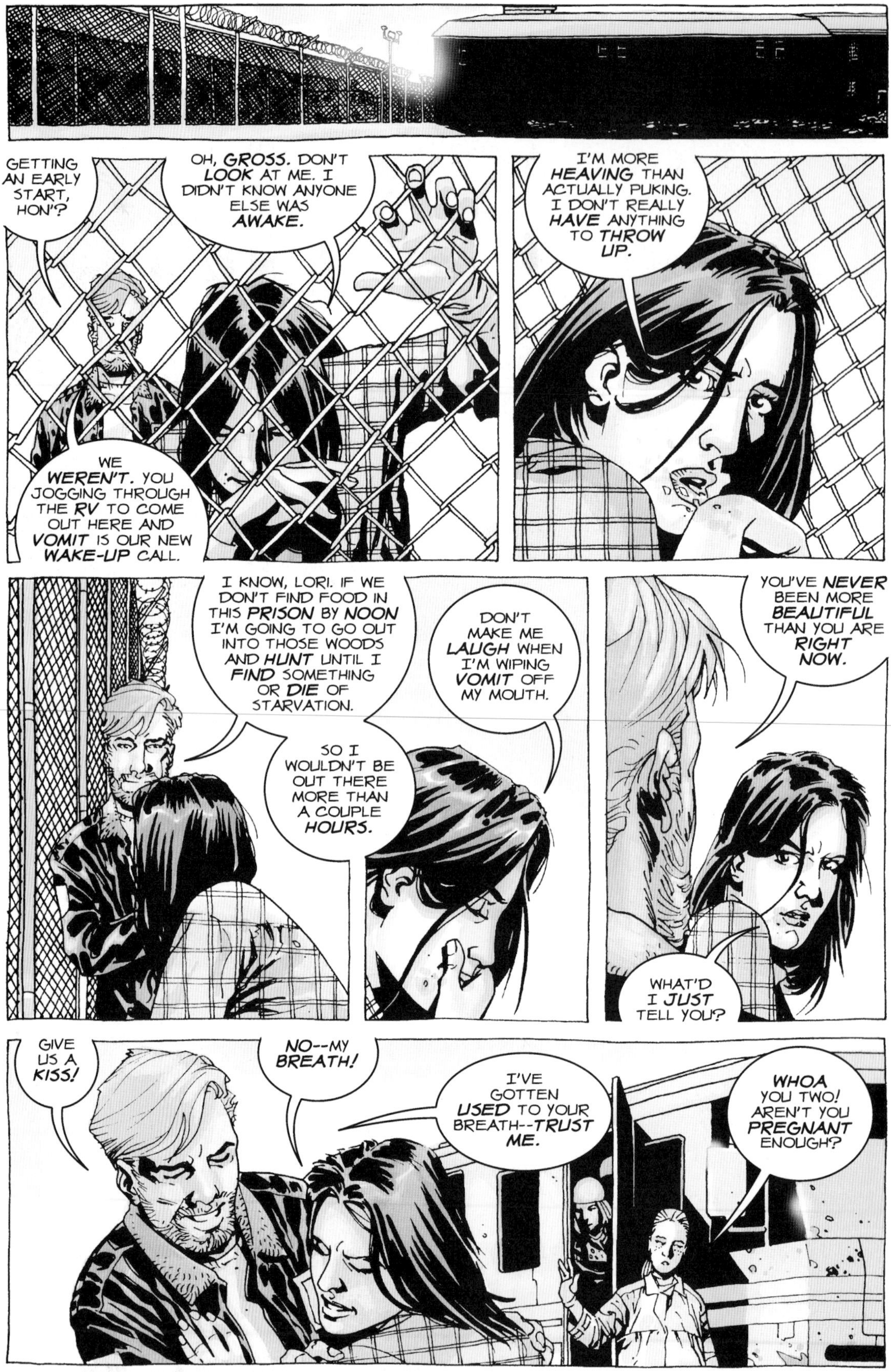

GETTING AN EARLY START, HON'?
OH, GROSS. DON'T LOOK AT ME. I DIDN'T KNOW ANYONE ELSE WAS AWAKE.
WE WEREN'T. YOU JOGGING THROUGH THE RV TO COME OUT HERE AND VOMIT IS OUR NEW WAKE-UP CALL.
I'M MORE HEAVING THAN ACTUALLY PUKING. I DON'T REALLY HAVE ANYTHING TO THROW UP.
I KNOW, LORI. IF WE DON'T FIND FOOD IN THIS PRISON BY NOON I'M GOING TO GO OUT INTO THOSE WOODS AND HUNT UNTIL I FIND SOMETHING OR DIE OF STARVATION.
SO I WOULDN'T BE OUT THERE MORE THAN A COUPLE HOURS.
DON'T MAKE ME LAUGH WHEN I'M WIPING VOMIT OFF MY MOUTH.
YOU'VE NEVER BEEN MORE BEAUTIFUL THAN YOU ARE RIGHT NOW.
WHAT'D I JUST TELL YOU?
GIVE US A KISS!
NO--MY BREATH!
I'VE GOTTEN USED TO YOUR BREATH--TRUST ME.
WHOA YOU TWO! AREN'T YOU PREGNANT ENOUGH?

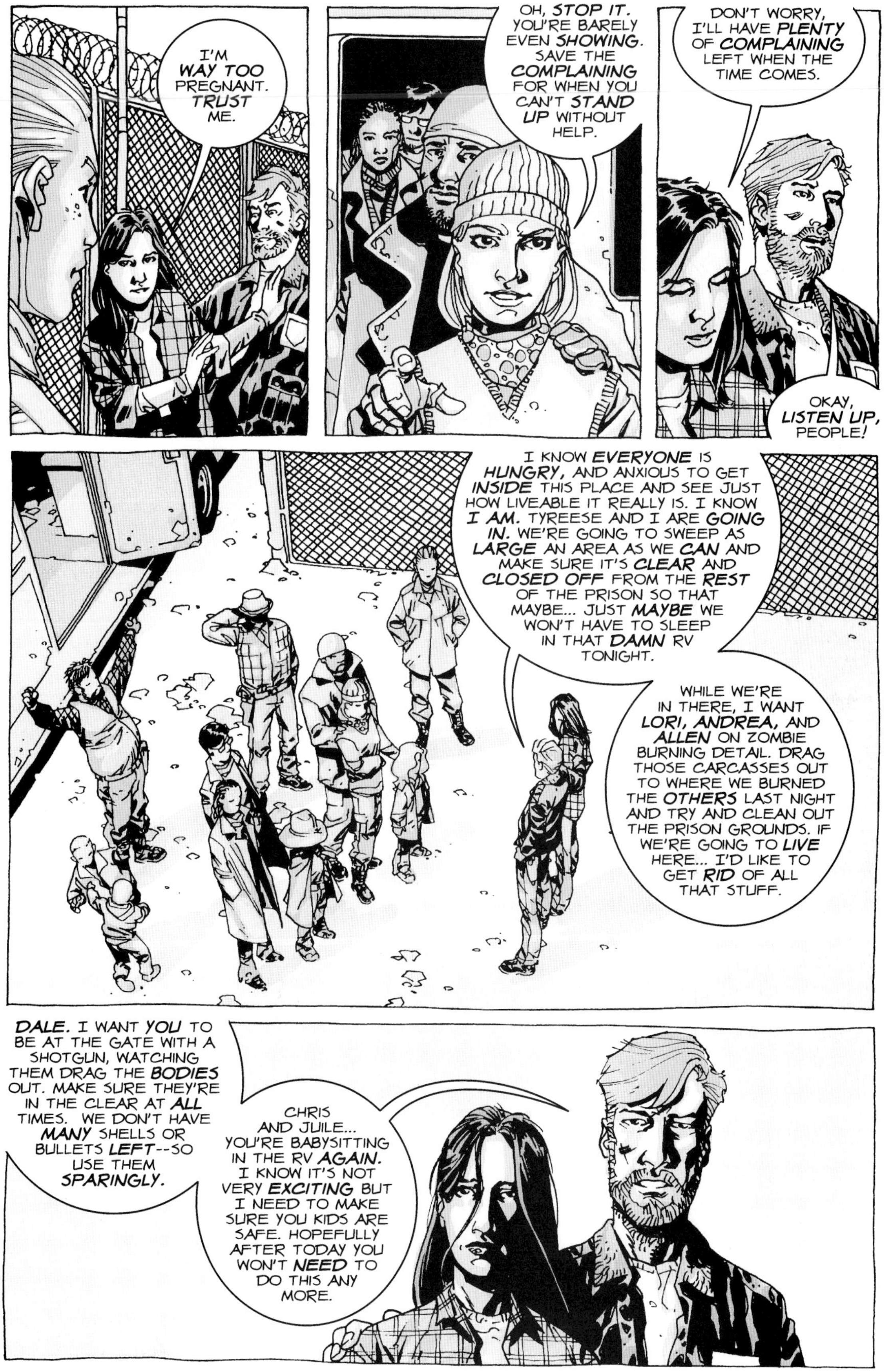
I'M WAY TOO PREGNANT. TRUST ME.
OH, STOP IT. YOU'RE BARELY EVEN SHOWING. SAVE THE COMPLAINING FOR WHEN YOU CAN'T STAND UP WITHOUT HELP.
DON'T WORRY, I'LL HAVE PLENTY OF COMPLAINING LEFT WHEN THE TIME COMES.
OKAY, LISTEN UP, PEOPLE!
I KNOW EVERYONE IS HUNGRY, AND ANXIOUS TO GET INSIDE THIS PLACE AND SEE JUST HOW LIVEABLE IT REALLY IS. I KNOW I AM. TYREESE AND I ARE GOING IN. WE'RE GOING TO SWEEP AS LARGE AN AREA AS WE CAN AND MAKE SURE IT'S CLEAR AND CLOSED OFF FROM THE REST OF THE PRISON SO THAT MAYBE... JUST MAYBE WE WON'T HAVE TO SLEEP IN THAT DAMN RV TONIGHT.
WHILE WE'RE IN THERE, I WANT LORI, ANDREA, AND ALLEN ON ZOMBIE BURNING DETAIL. DRAG THOSE CARCASSES OUT TO WHERE WE BURNED THE OTHERS LAST NIGHT AND TRY AND CLEAN OUT THE PRISON GROUNDS. IF WE'RE GOING TO LIVE HERE... I'D LIKE TO GET RID OF ALL THAT STUFF.
DALE. I WANT YOU TO BE AT THE GATE WITH A SHOTGUN, WATCHING THEM DRAG THE BODIES OUT. MAKE SURE THEY'RE IN THE CLEAR AT ALL TIMES. WE DON'T HAVE MANY SHELLS OR BULLETS LEFT--SO USE THEM SPARINGLY.
CHRIS AND JUILE... YOU'RE BABYSITTING IN THE RV AGAIN. I KNOW IT'S NOT VERY EXCITING BUT I NEED TO MAKE SURE YOU KIDS ARE SAFE. HOPEFULLY AFTER TODAY YOU WON'T NEED TO DO THIS ANY MORE.

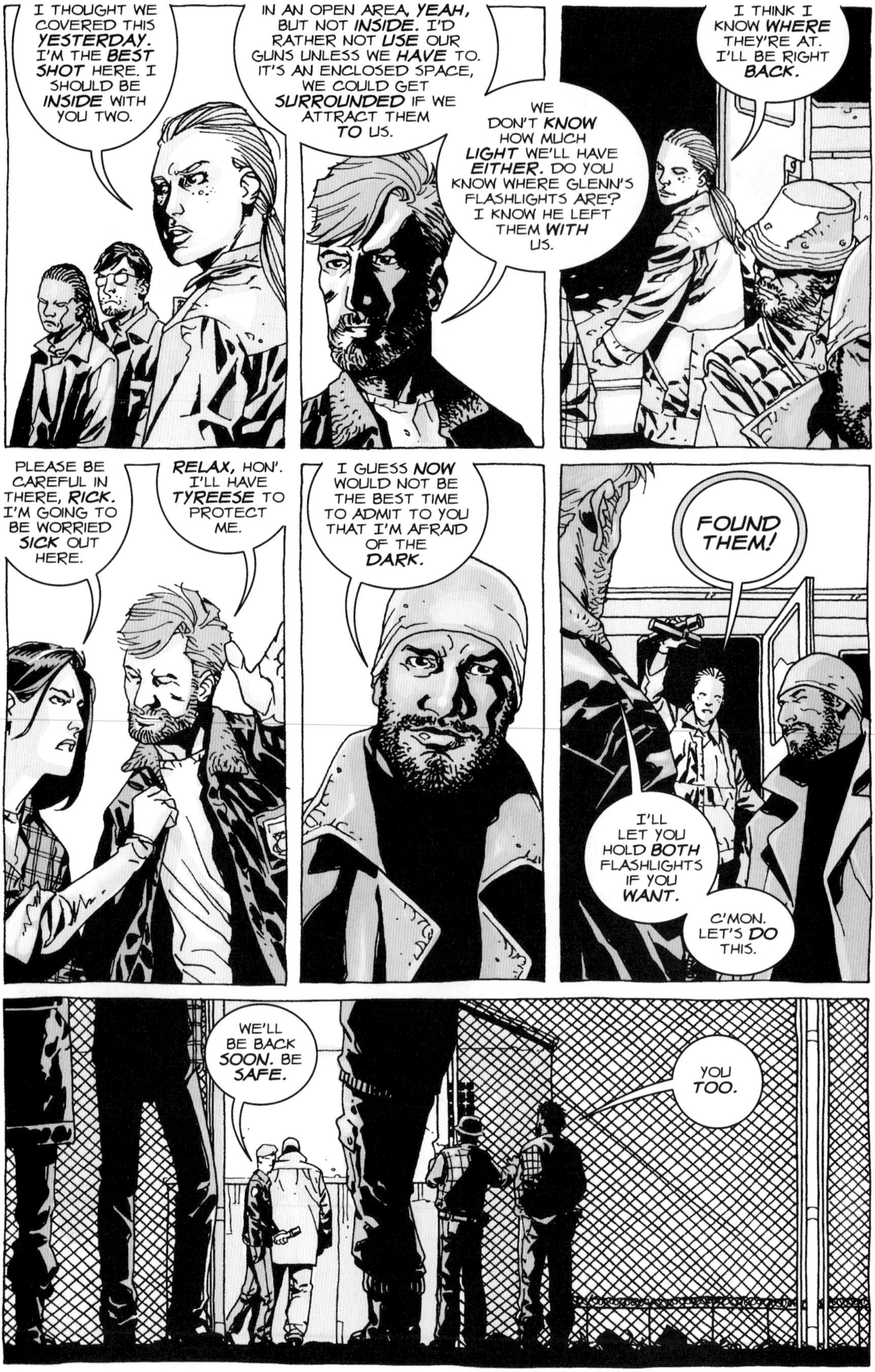
I THOUGHT WE COVERED THIS YESTERDAY. I'M THE BEST SHOT HERE. I SHOULD BE INSIDE WITH YOU TWO.
IN AN OPEN AREA, YEAH, BUT NOT INSIDE. I'D RATHER NOT USE OUR GUNS UNLESS WE HAVE TO. IT'S AN ENCLOSED SPACE, WE COULD GET SURROUNDED IF WE ATTRACT THEM TO US.
WE DON'T KNOW HOW MUCH LIGHT WE'LL HAVE EITHER. DO YOU KNOW WHERE GLENN'S FLASHLIGHTS ARE? I KNOW HE LEFT THEM WITH US.
I THINK I KNOW WHERE THEY'RE AT. I'LL BE RIGHT BACK.
PLEASE BE CAREFUL IN THERE, RICK. I'M GOING TO BE WORRIED SICK OUT HERE.
RELAX, HON'. I'LL HAVE TYREESE TO PROTECT ME.
I GUESS NOW WOULD NOT BE THE BEST TIME TO ADMIT TO YOU THAT I'M AFRAID OF THE DARK.
FOUND THEM!
I'LL LET YOU HOLD BOTH FLASHLIGHTS IF YOU WANT.
C'MON. LET'S DO THIS.
WE'LL BE BACK SOON. BE SAFE.
YOU TOO.

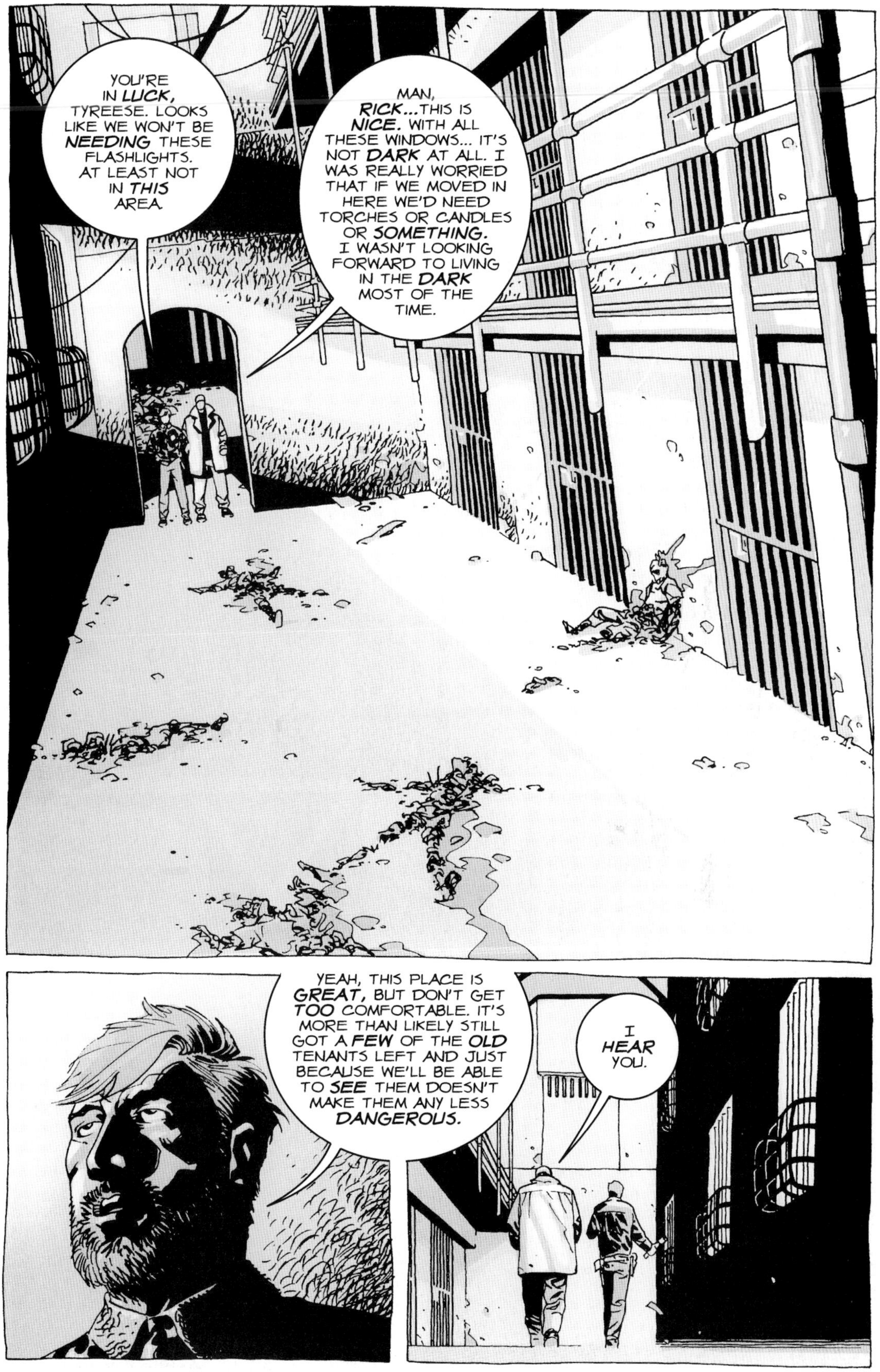
YOU'RE IN LUCK, TYREESE. LOOKS LIKE WE WON'T BE NEEDING THESE FLASHLIGHTS. AT LEAST NOT IN THIS AREA.
MAN, RICK...THIS IS NICE. WITH ALL THESE WINDOWS... IT'S NOT DARK AT ALL. I WAS REALLY WORRIED THAT IF WE MOVED IN HERE WE'D NEED TORCHES OR CANDLES OR SOMETHING. I WASN'T LOOKING FORWARD TO LIVING IN THE DARK MOST OF THE TIME.
YEAH, THIS PLACE IS GREAT, BUT DON'T GET TOO COMFORTABLE. IT'S MORE THAN LIKELY STILL GOT A FEW OF THE OLD TENANTS LEFT AND JUST BECAUSE WE'LL BE ABLE TO SEE THEM DOESN'T MAKE THEM ANY LESS DANGEROUS.
I HEAR YOU.

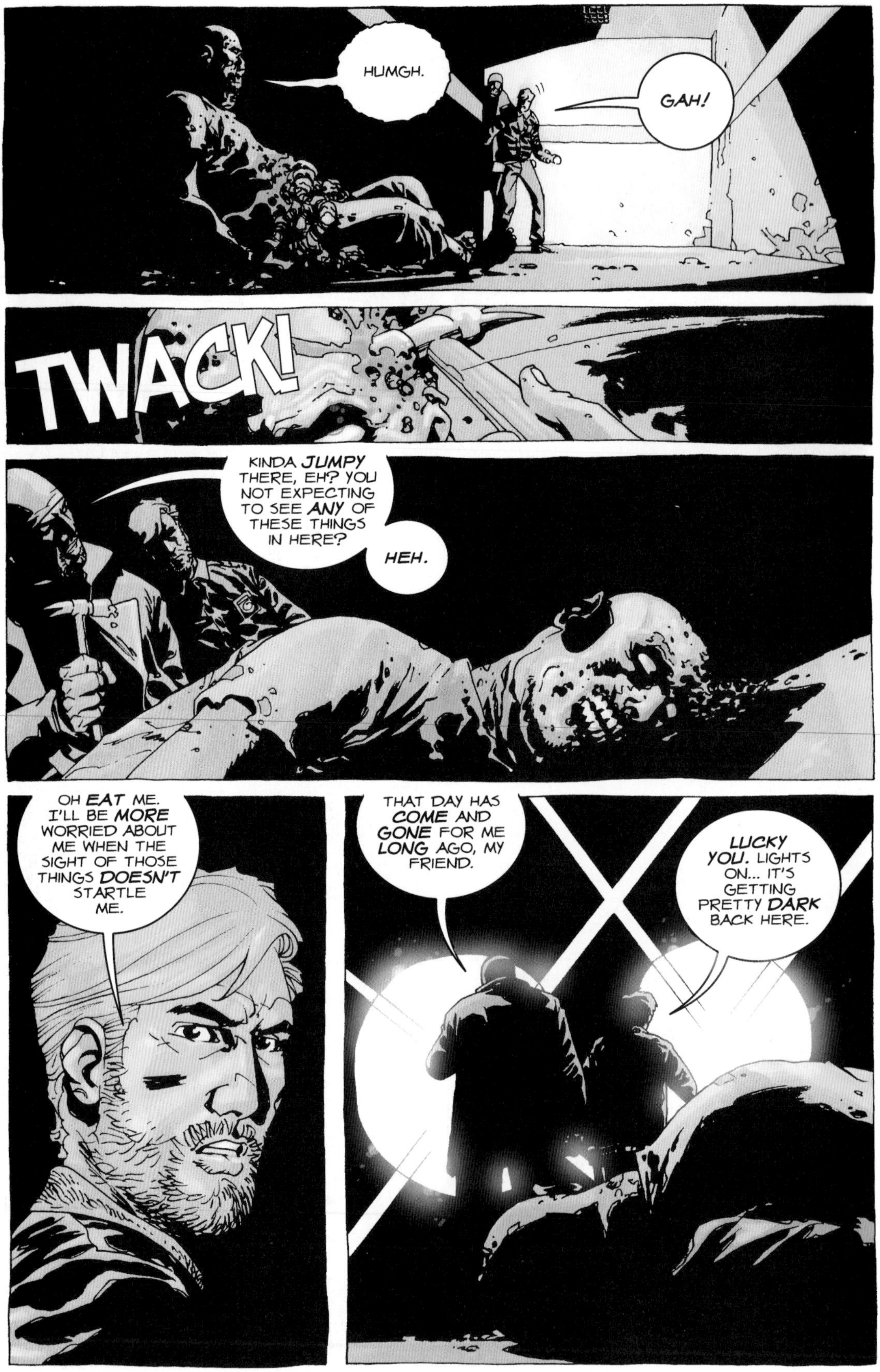
HUMGH.
GAH!
TWACK!
KINDA JUMPY THERE, EH? YOU NOT EXPECTING TO SEE ANY OF THESE THINGS IN HERE?
HEH.
OH EAT ME. I'LL BE MORE WORRIED ABOUT ME WHEN THE SIGHT OF THOSE THINGS DOESN'T STARTLE ME.
THAT DAY HAS COME AND GONE FOR ME LONG AGO, MY FRIEND.
LUCKY YOU. LIGHTS ON... IT'S GETTING PRETTY DARK BACK HERE.

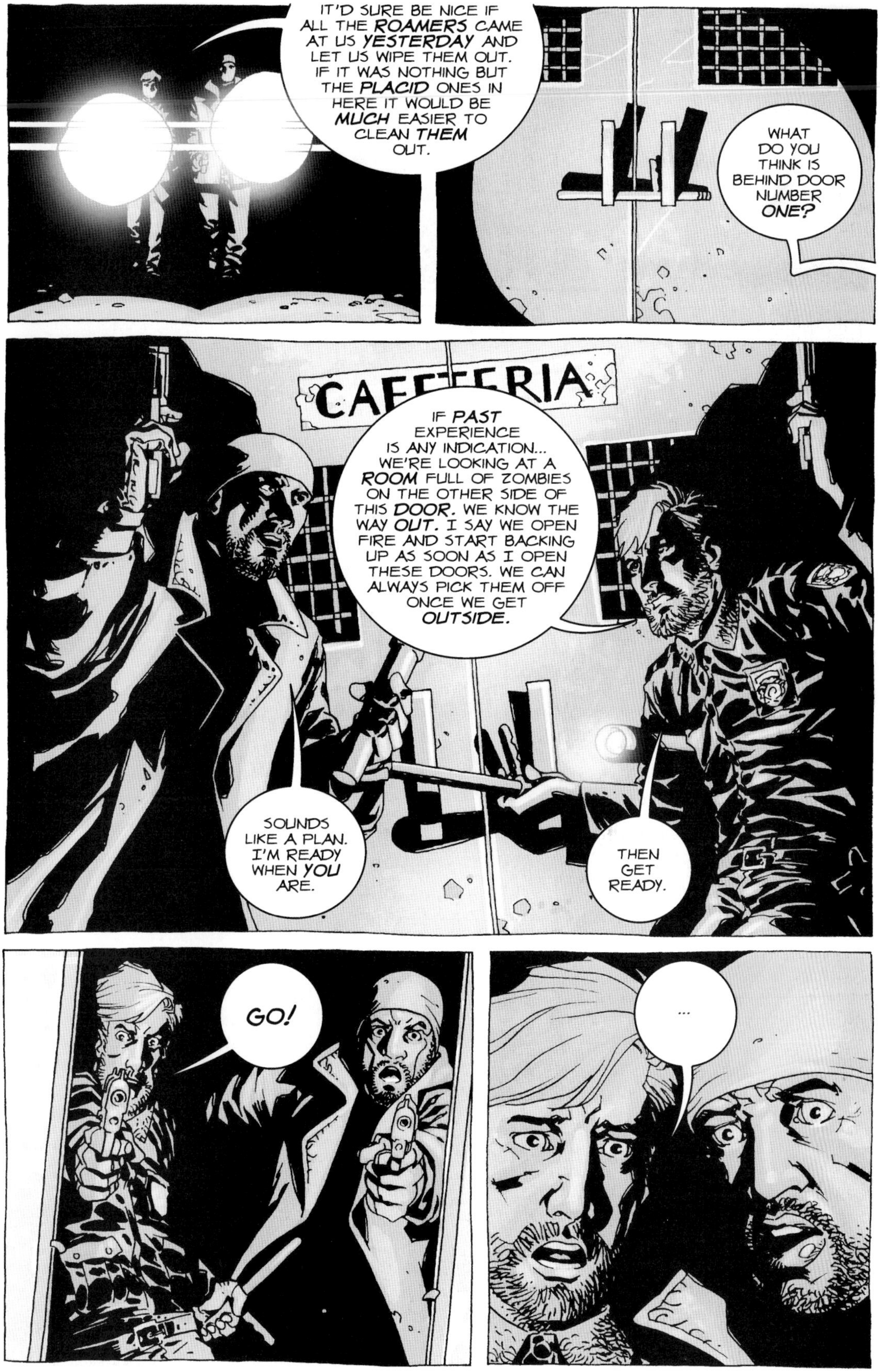
IT'D SURE BE NICE IF ALL THE ROAMERS CAME AT US YESTERDAY AND LET US WIPE THEM OUT. IF IT WAS NOTHING BUT THE PLACID ONES IN HERE IT WOULD BE MUCH EASIER TO CLEAN THEM OUT.
WHAT DO YOU THINK IS BEHIND DOOR NUMBER ONE?
CAFETERIA
IF PAST EXPERIENCE IS ANY INDICATION... WE'RE LOOKING AT A ROOM FULL OF ZOMBIES ON THE OTHER SIDE OF THIS DOOR. WE KNOW THE WAY OUT. I SAY WE OPEN FIRE AND START BACKING UP AS SOON AS I OPEN THESE DOORS. WE CAN ALWAYS PICK THEM OFF ONCE WE GET OUTSIDE.
SOUNDS LIKE A PLAN. I'M READY WHEN YOU ARE.
THEN GET READY.
GO!
...

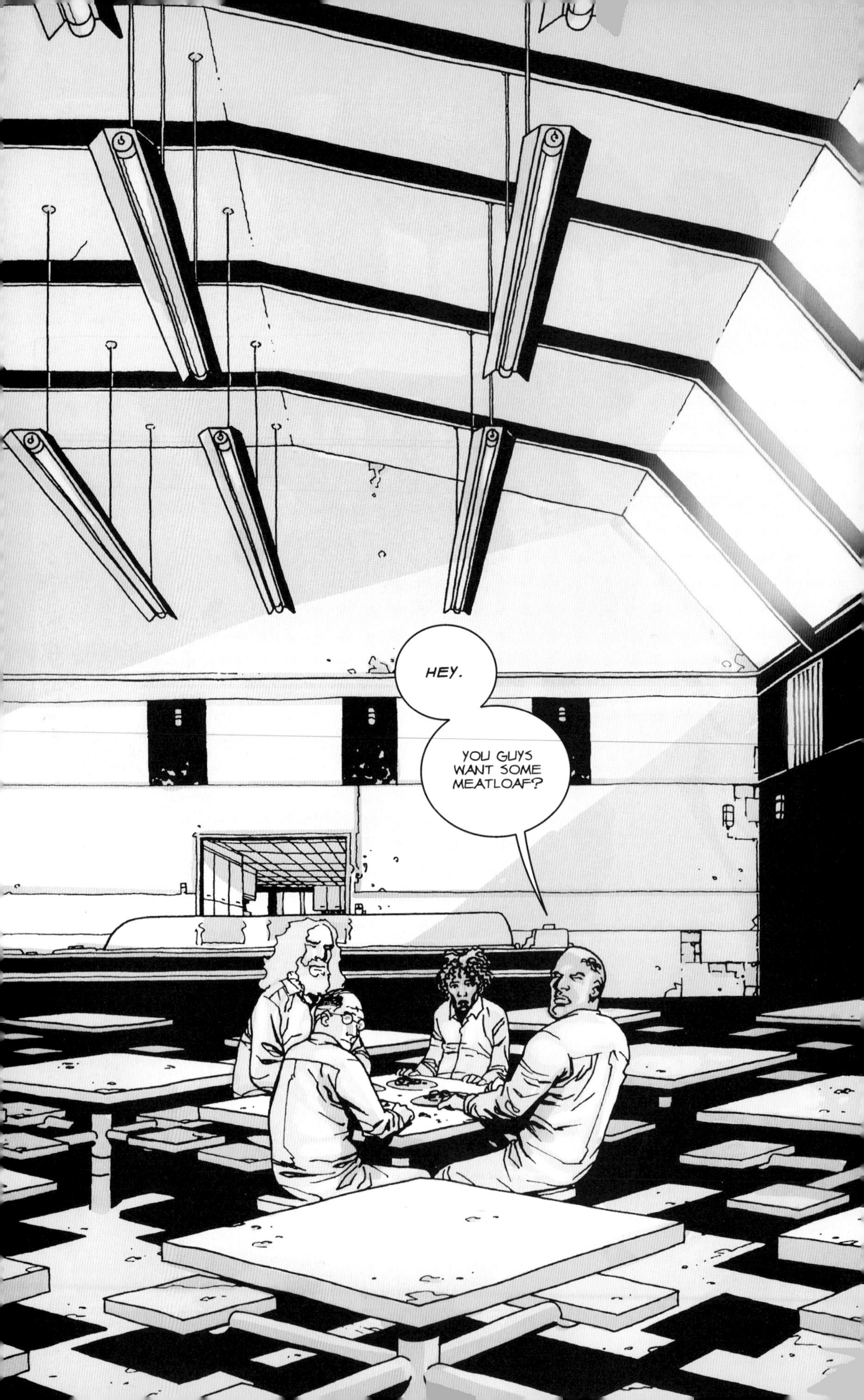
HEY.
YOU GUYS WANT SOME MEATLOAF?

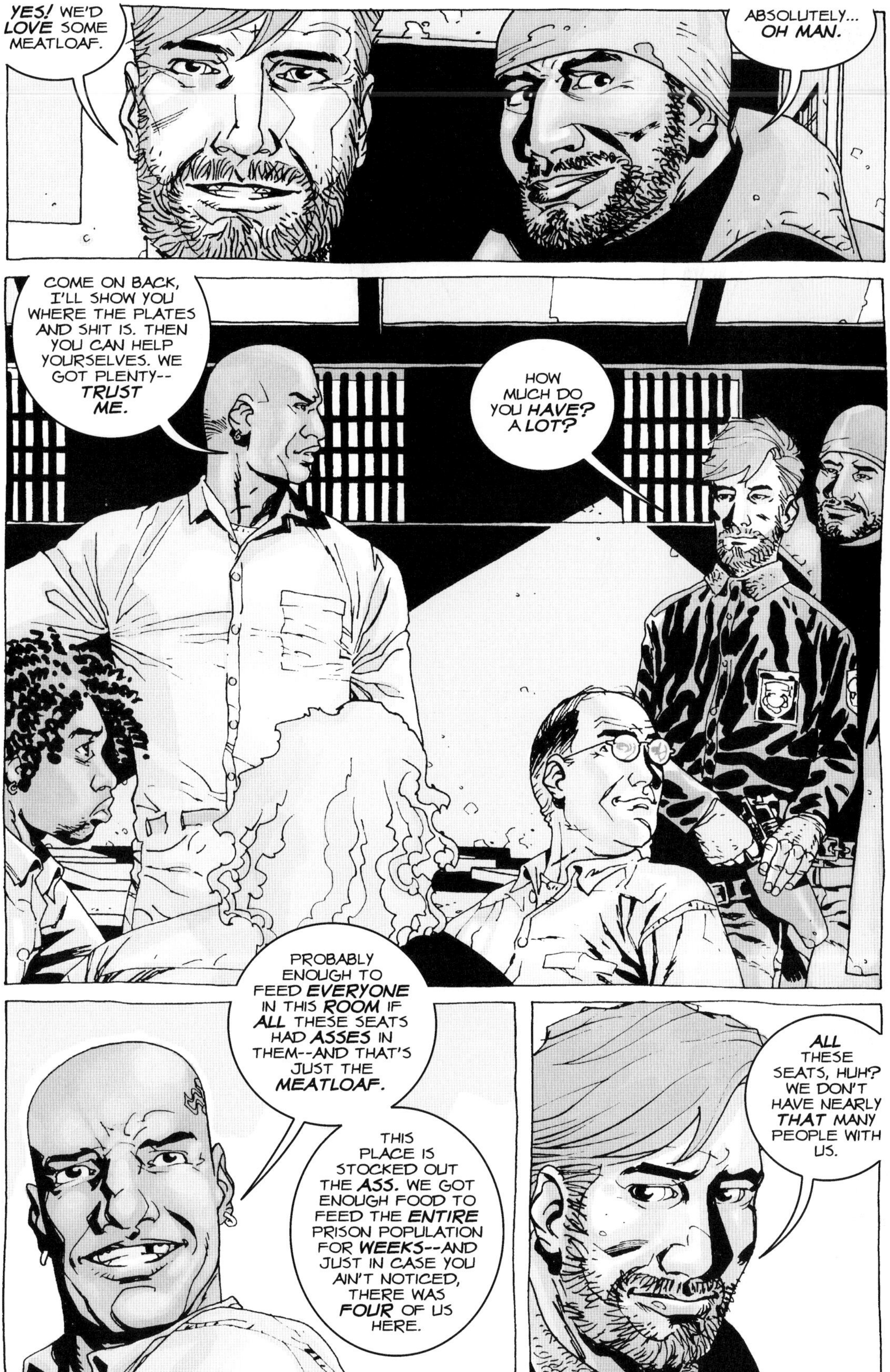
YES! WE'D LOVE SOME MEATLOAF.
ABSOLUTELY... OH MAN.
COME ON BACK, I'LL SHOW YOU WHERE THE PLATES AND SHIT IS. THEN YOU CAN HELP YOURSELVES. WE GOT PLENTY-- TRUST ME.
HOW MUCH DO YOU HAVE? A LOT?
PROBABLY ENOUGH TO FEED EVERYONE IN THIS ROOM IF ALL THESE SEATS HAD ASSES IN THEM--AND THAT'S JUST THE MEATLOAF.
THIS PLACE IS STOCKED OUT THE ASS. WE GOT ENOUGH FOOD TO FEED THE ENTIRE PRISON POPULATION FOR WEEKS--AND JUST IN CASE YOU AIN'T NOTICED, THERE WAS FOUR OF US HERE.
ALL THESE SEATS, HUH? WE DON'T HAVE NEARLY THAT MANY PEOPLE WITH US.

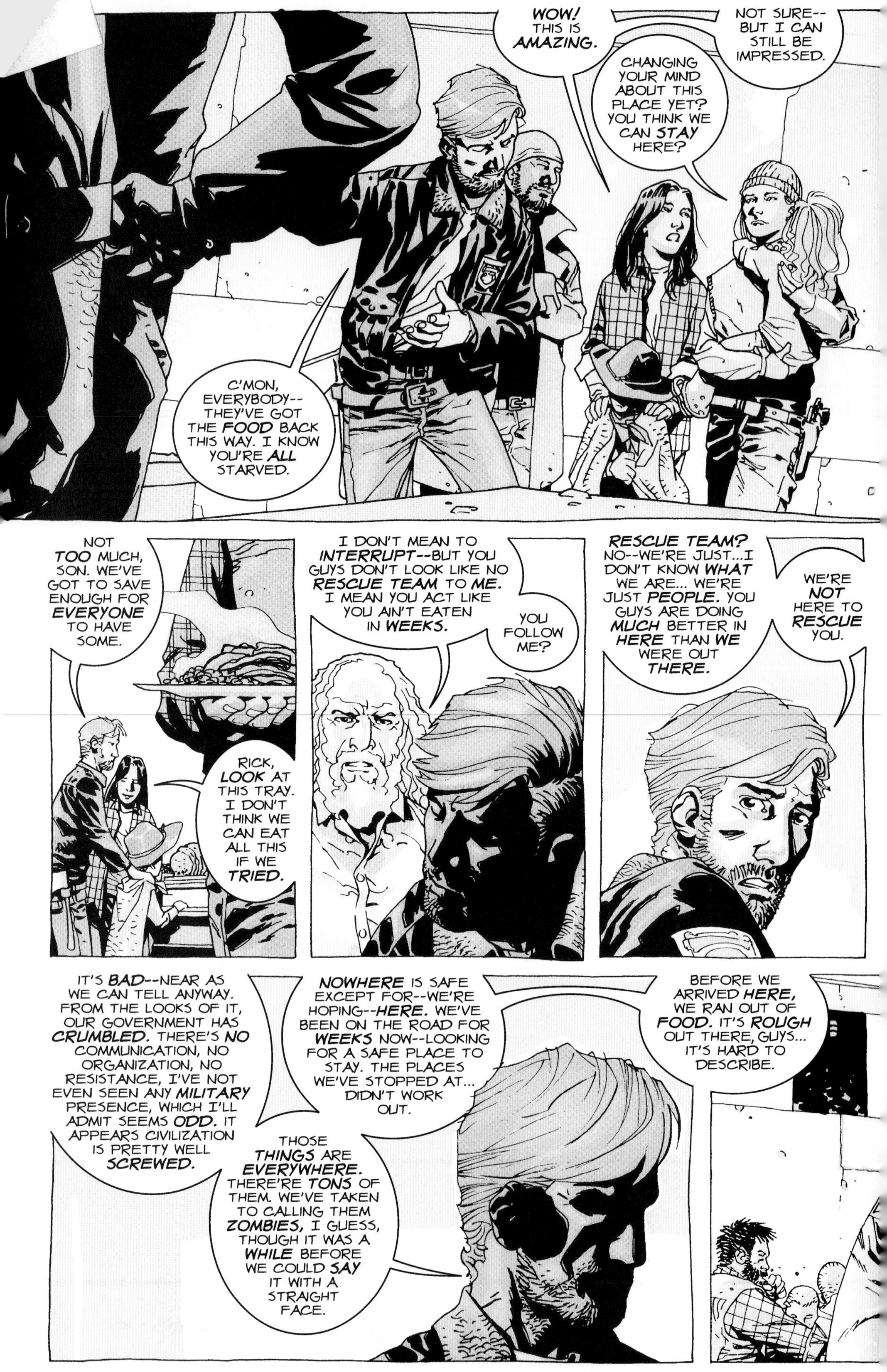
WOW! THIS IS AMAZING.
NOT SURE-- BUT I CAN STILL BE IMPRESSED.
CHANGING YOUR MIND ABOUT THIS PLACE YET? YOU THINK WE CAN STAY HERE?
C'MON, EVERYBODY-- THEY'VE GOT THE FOOD BACK THIS WAY. I KNOW YOU'RE ALL STARVED.
NOT TOO MUCH, SON. WE'VE GOT TO SAVE ENOUGH FOR EVERYONE TO HAVE SOME.
RICK, LOOK AT THIS TRAY. I DON'T THINK WE CAN EAT ALL THIS IF WE TRIED.
I DON'T MEAN TO INTERRUPT--BUT YOU GUYS DON'T LOOK LIKE NO RESCUE TEAM TO ME. I MEAN YOU ACT LIKE YOU AIN'T EATEN IN WEEKS.
YOU FOLLOW ME?
RESCUE TEAM? NO--WE'RE JUST...I DON'T KNOW WHAT WE ARE... WE'RE JUST PEOPLE. YOU GUYS ARE DOING MUCH BETTER IN HERE THAN WE WERE OUT THERE.
WE'RE NOT HERE TO RESCUE YOU.
IT'S BAD--NEAR AS WE CAN TELL ANYWAY. FROM THE LOOKS OF IT, OUR GOVERNMENT HAS CRUMBLED. THERE'S NO COMMUNICATION, NO ORGANIZATION, NO RESISTANCE, I'VE NOT EVEN SEEN ANY MILITARY PRESENCE, WHICH I'LL ADMIT SEEMS ODD. IT APPEARS CIVILIZATION IS PRETTY WELL SCREWED.
NOWHERE IS SAFE EXCEPT FOR--WE'RE HOPING--HERE. WE'VE BEEN ON THE ROAD FOR WEEKS NOW--LOOKING FOR A SAFE PLACE TO STAY. THE PLACES WE'VE STOPPED AT... DIDN'T WORK OUT.
THOSE THINGS ARE EVERYWHERE. THERE'RE TONS OF THEM. WE'VE TAKEN TO CALLING THEM ZOMBIES, I GUESS, THOUGH IT WAS A WHILE BEFORE WE COULD SAY IT WITH A STRAIGHT FACE.
BEFORE WE ARRIVED HERE, WE RAN OUT OF FOOD. IT'S ROUGH OUT THERE, GUYS... IT'S HARD TO DESCRIBE.

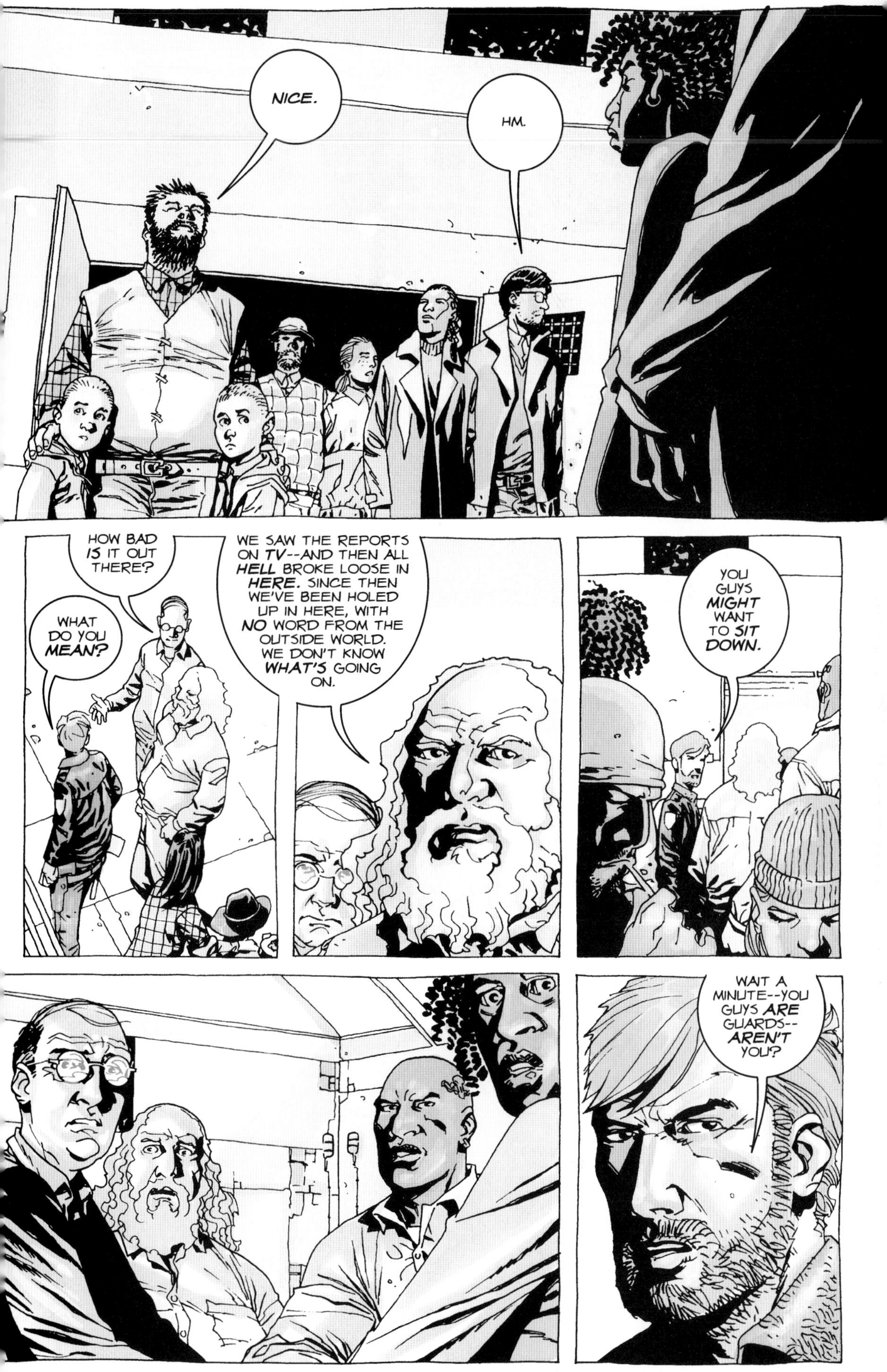
NICE.
HM.
HOW BAD IS IT OUT THERE?
WHAT DO YOU MEAN?
WE SAW THE REPORTS ON TV--AND THEN ALL HELL BROKE LOOSE IN HERE. SINCE THEN WE'VE BEEN HOLED UP IN HERE, WITH NO WORD FROM THE OUTSIDE WORLD. WE DON'T KNOW WHAT'S GOING ON.
YOU GUYS MIGHT WANT TO SIT DOWN.
WAIT A MINUTE--YOU GUYS ARE GUARDS--AREN'T YOU?

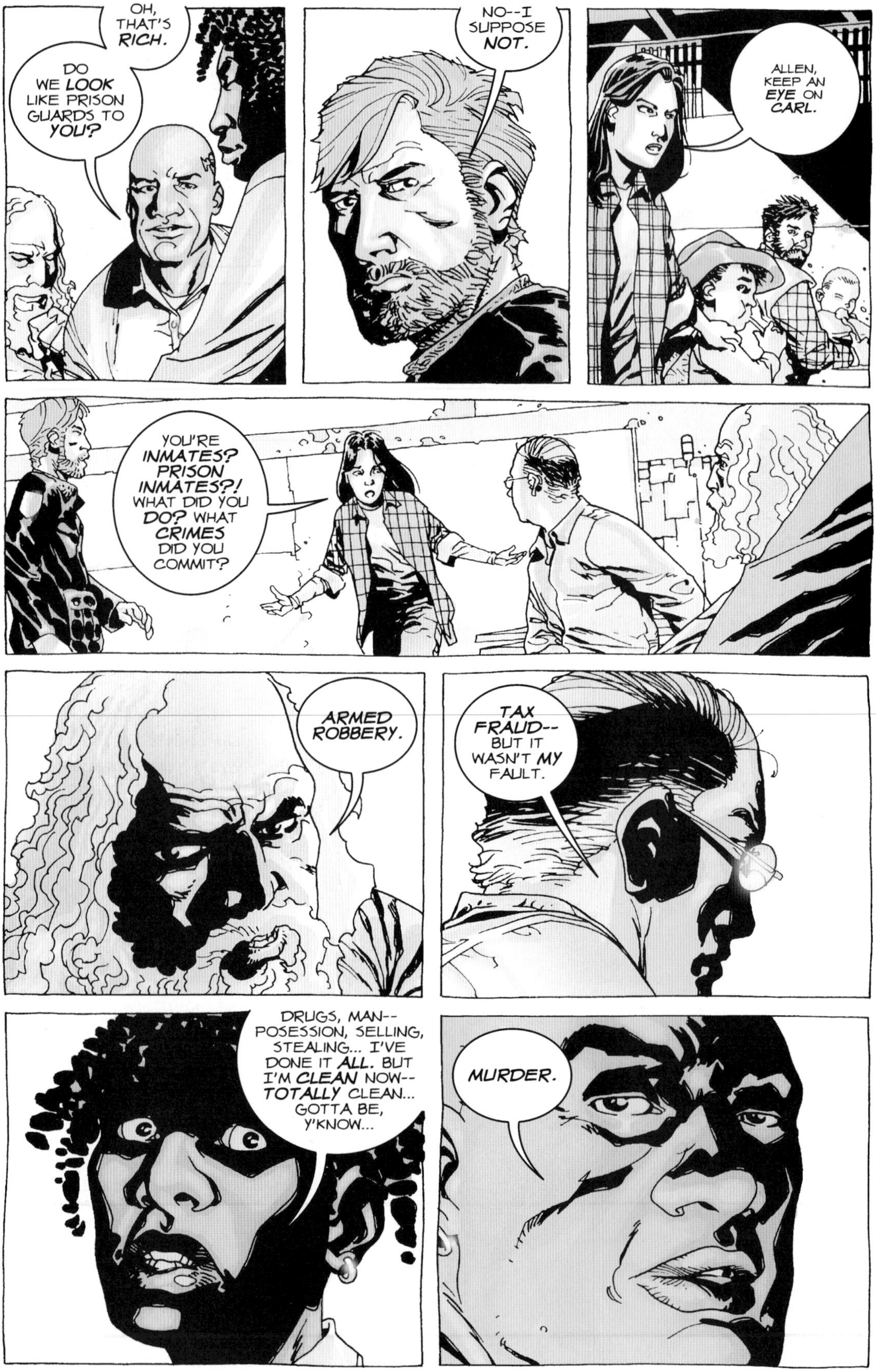
OH, THAT'S RICH.
DO WE LOOK LIKE PRISON GUARDS TO YOU?
NO--I SUPPOSE NOT.
ALLEN, KEEP AN EYE ON CARL.
YOU'RE INMATES? PRISON INMATES?! WHAT DID YOU DO? WHAT CRIMES DID YOU COMMIT?
ARMED ROBBERY.
TAX FRAUD-- BUT IT WASN'T MY FAULT.
DRUGS, MAN-- POSESSION, SELLING, STEALING... I'VE DONE IT ALL. BUT I'M CLEAN NOW-- TOTALLY CLEAN... GOTTA BE, Y'KNOW...
MURDER.

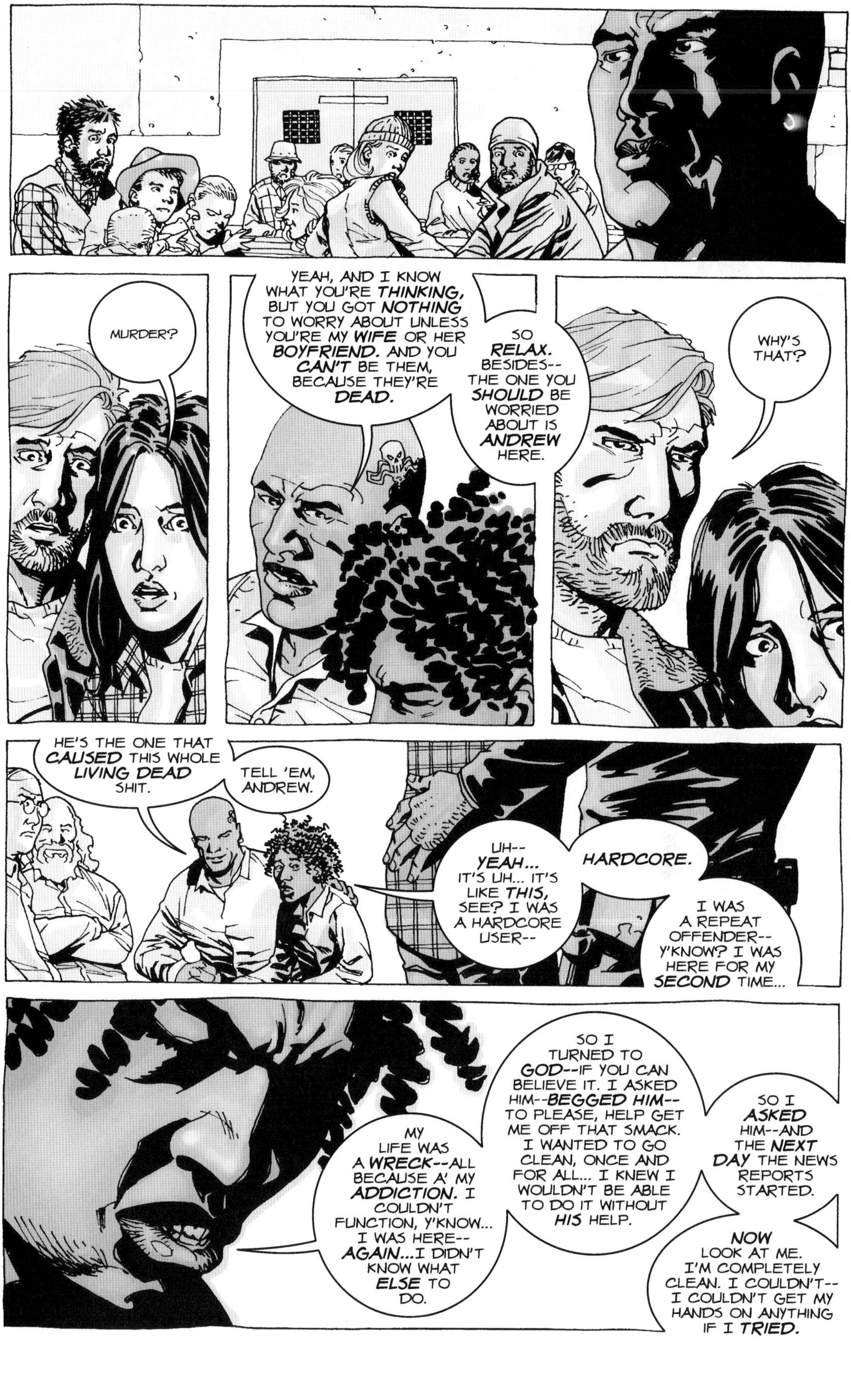
MURDER?
YEAH, AND I KNOW WHAT YOU'RE THINKING, BUT YOU GOT NOTHING TO WORRY ABOUT UNLESS YOU'RE MY WIFE OR HER BOYFRIEND. AND YOU CAN'T BE THEM, BECAUSE THEY'RE DEAD.
SO RELAX. BESIDES-- THE ONE YOU SHOULD BE WORRIED ABOUT IS ANDREW HERE.
WHY'S THAT?
HE'S THE ONE THAT CAUSED THIS WHOLE LIVING DEAD SHIT.
TELL 'EM, ANDREW.
UH-- YEAH... IT'S UH... IT'S LIKE THIS, SEE? I WAS A HARDCORE USER--
HARDCORE.
I WAS A REPEAT OFFENDER-- Y'KNOW? I WAS HERE FOR MY SECOND TIME...
MY LIFE WAS A WRECK--ALL BECAUSE A' MY ADDICTION. I COULDN'T FUNCTION, Y'KNOW... I WAS HERE-- AGAIN...I DIDN'T KNOW WHAT ELSE TO DO.
SO I TURNED TO GOD--IF YOU CAN BELIEVE IT. I ASKED HIM--BEGGED HIM-- TO PLEASE, HELP GET ME OFF THAT SMACK. I WANTED TO GO CLEAN, ONCE AND FOR ALL... I KNEW I WOULDN'T BE ABLE TO DO IT WITHOUT HIS HELP.
SO I ASKED HIM--AND THE NEXT DAY THE NEWS REPORTS STARTED.
NOW LOOK AT ME. I'M COMPLETELY CLEAN. I COULDN'T-- I COULDN'T GET MY HANDS ON ANYTHING IF I TRIED.

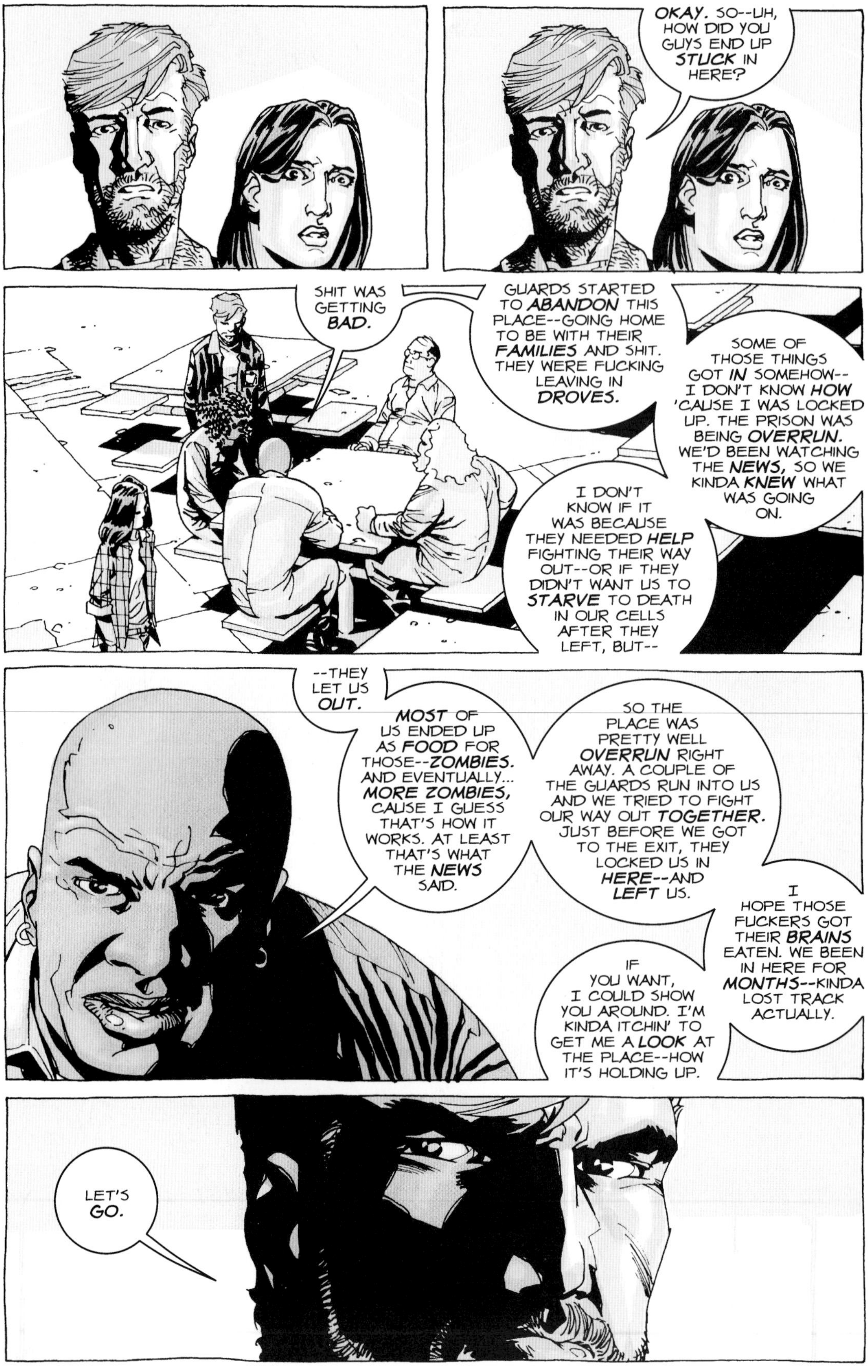
OKAY. SO--UH, HOW DID YOU GUYS END UP STUCK IN HERE?
SHIT WAS GETTING BAD.
GUARDS STARTED TO ABANDON THIS PLACE--GOING HOME TO BE WITH THEIR FAMILIES AND SHIT. THEY WERE FUCKING LEAVING IN DROVES.
SOME OF THOSE THINGS GOT IN SOMEHOW-- I DON'T KNOW HOW 'CAUSE I WAS LOCKED UP. THE PRISON WAS BEING OVERRUN. WE'D BEEN WATCHING THE NEWS, SO WE KINDA KNEW WHAT WAS GOING ON.
I DON'T KNOW IF IT WAS BECAUSE THEY NEEDED HELP FIGHTING THEIR WAY OUT--OR IF THEY DIDN'T WANT US TO STARVE TO DEATH IN OUR CELLS AFTER THEY LEFT, BUT--
--THEY LET US OUT.
MOST OF US ENDED UP AS FOOD FOR THOSE--ZOMBIES. AND EVENTUALLY... MORE ZOMBIES, CAUSE I GUESS THAT'S HOW IT WORKS. AT LEAST THAT'S WHAT THE NEWS SAID.
SO THE PLACE WAS PRETTY WELL OVERRUN RIGHT AWAY. A COUPLE OF THE GUARDS RUN INTO US AND WE TRIED TO FIGHT OUR WAY OUT TOGETHER. JUST BEFORE WE GOT TO THE EXIT, THEY LOCKED US IN HERE--AND LEFT US.
I HOPE THOSE FUCKERS GOT THEIR BRAINS EATEN. WE BEEN IN HERE FOR MONTHS--KINDA LOST TRACK ACTUALLY.
IF YOU WANT, I COULD SHOW YOU AROUND. I'M KINDA ITCHIN' TO GET ME A LOOK AT THE PLACE--HOW IT'S HOLDING UP.
LET'S GO.

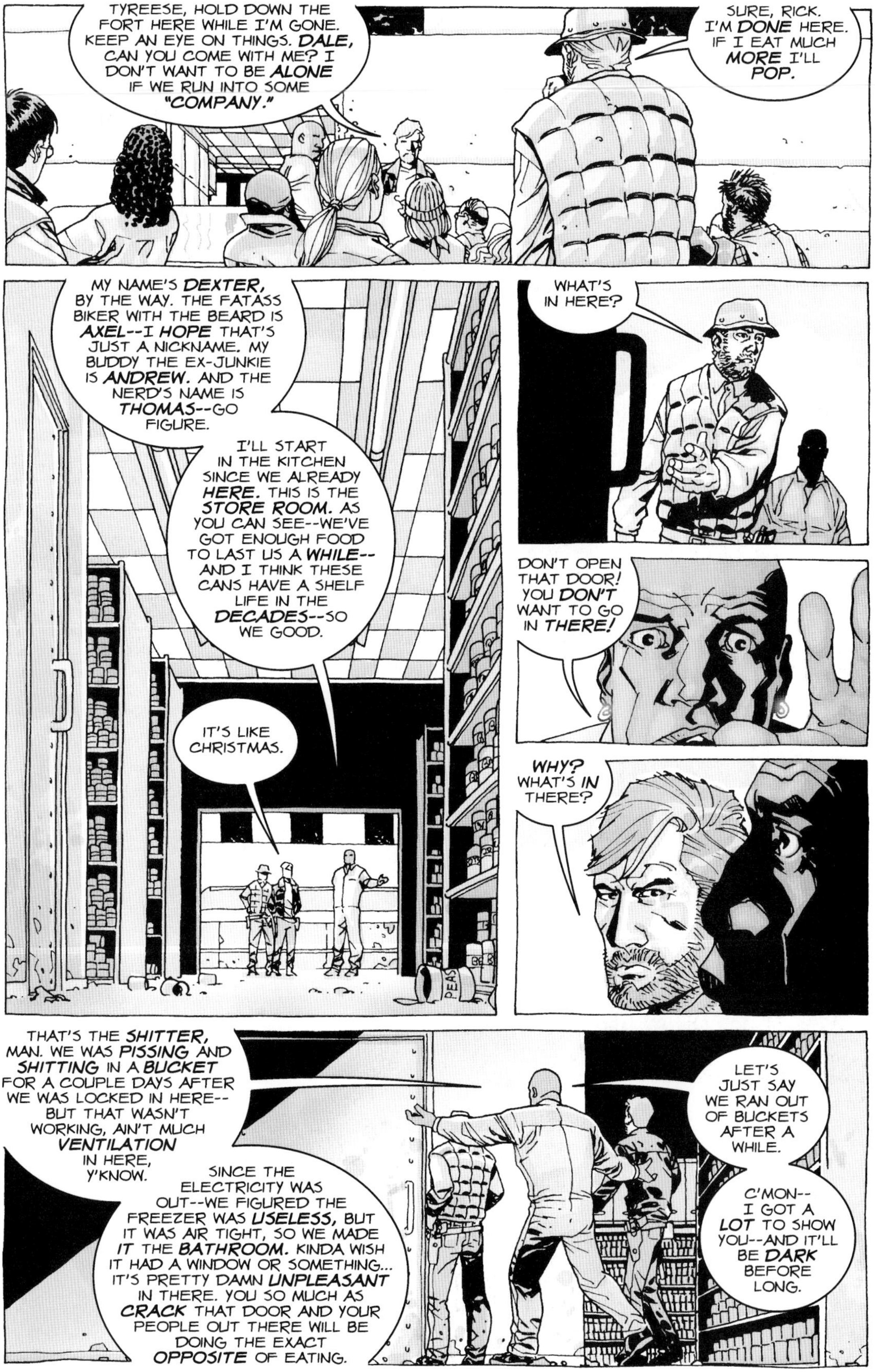

TYREESE, HOLD DOWN THE FORT HERE WHILE I'M GONE. KEEP AN EYE ON THINGS. DALE, CAN YOU COME WITH ME? I DON'T WANT TO BE ALONE IF WE RUN INTO SOME "COMPANY."
SURE, RICK. I'M DONE HERE. IF I EAT MUCH MORE I'LL POP.
MY NAME'S DEXTER, BY THE WAY. THE FATASS BIKER WITH THE BEARD IS AXEL--I HOPE THAT'S JUST A NICKNAME. MY BUDDY THE EX-JUNKIE IS ANDREW. AND THE NERD'S NAME IS THOMAS--GO FIGURE.
I'LL START IN THE KITCHEN SINCE WE ALREADY HERE. THIS IS THE STORE ROOM. AS YOU CAN SEE--WE'VE GOT ENOUGH FOOD TO LAST US A WHILE--AND I THINK THESE CANS HAVE A SHELF LIFE IN THE DECADES--SO WE GOOD.
IT'S LIKE CHRISTMAS.
PEAS
WHAT'S IN HERE?
DON'T OPEN THAT DOOR! YOU DON'T WANT TO GO IN THERE!
WHY? WHAT'S IN THERE?
THAT'S THE SHITTER, MAN. WE WAS PISSING AND SHITTING IN A BUCKET FOR A COUPLE DAYS AFTER WE WAS LOCKED IN HERE--BUT THAT WASN'T WORKING, AIN'T MUCH VENTILATION IN HERE, Y'KNOW.
SINCE THE ELECTRICITY WAS OUT--WE FIGURED THE FREEZER WAS USELESS, BUT IT WAS AIR TIGHT, SO WE MADE IT THE BATHROOM. KINDA WISH IT HAD A WINDOW OR SOMETHING... IT'S PRETTY DAMN UNPLEASANT IN THERE. YOU SO MUCH AS CRACK THAT DOOR AND YOUR PEOPLE OUT THERE WILL BE DOING THE EXACT OPPOSITE OF EATING.
LET'S JUST SAY WE RAN OUT OF BUCKETS AFTER A WHILE.
C'MON--I GOT A LOT TO SHOW YOU--AND IT'LL BE DARK BEFORE LONG.

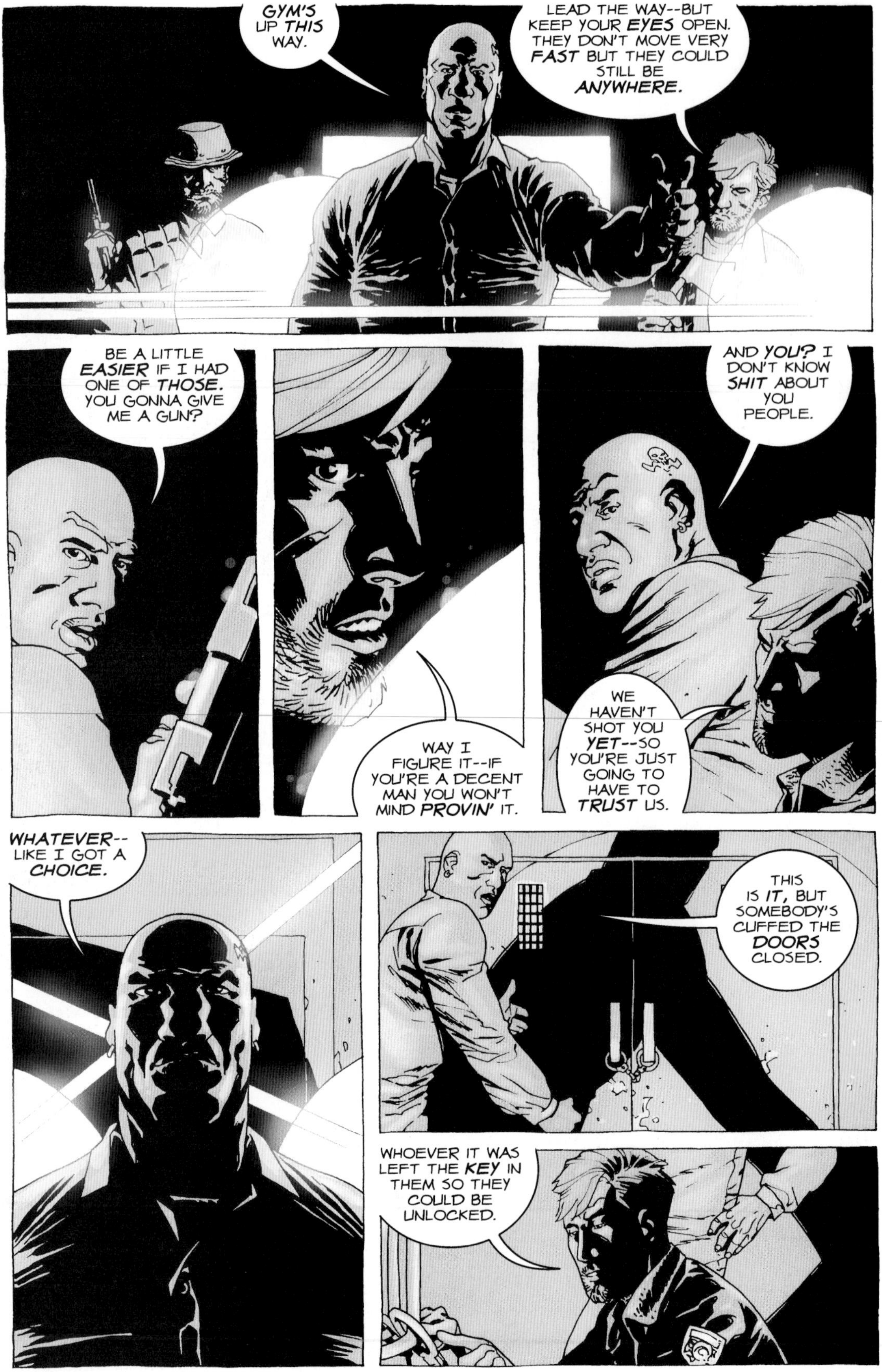
GYM'S UP THIS WAY.
LEAD THE WAY--BUT KEEP YOUR EYES OPEN. THEY DON'T MOVE VERY FAST BUT THEY COULD STILL BE ANYWHERE.
BE A LITTLE EASIER IF I HAD ONE OF THOSE. YOU GONNA GIVE ME A GUN?
WAY I FIGURE IT--IF YOU'RE A DECENT MAN YOU WON'T MIND PROVIN' IT.
AND YOU? I DON'T KNOW SHIT ABOUT YOU PEOPLE.
WE HAVEN'T SHOT YOU YET--SO YOU'RE JUST GOING TO HAVE TO TRUST US.
WHATEVER-- LIKE I GOT A CHOICE.
THIS IS IT, BUT SOMEBODY'S CUFFED THE DOORS CLOSED.
WHOEVER IT WAS LEFT THE KEY IN THEM SO THEY COULD BE UNLOCKED.

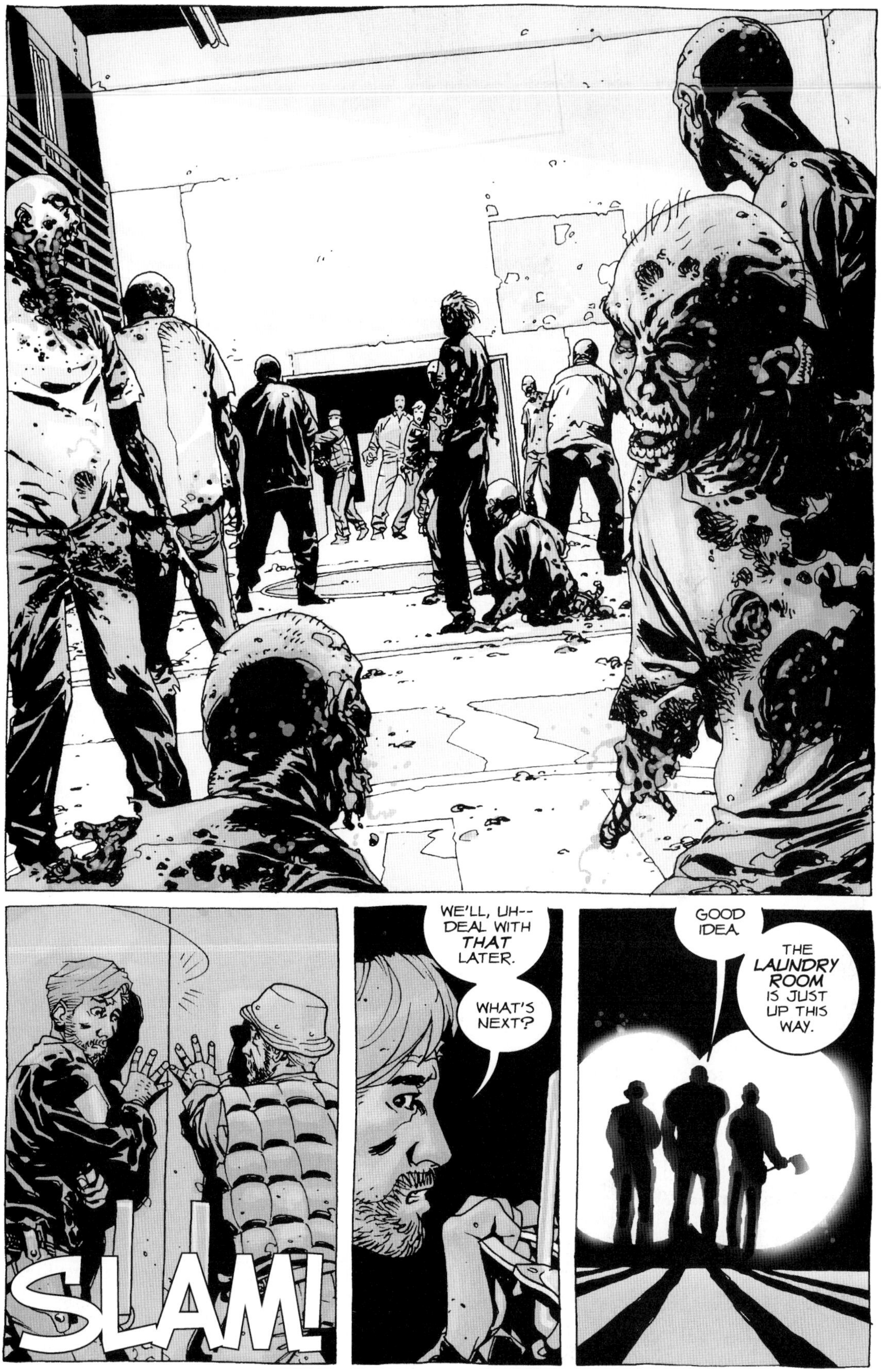
SLAM!
WE'LL, UH--
DEAL WITH *THAT* LATER.
WHAT'S NEXT?
GOOD IDEA.
THE *LAUNDRY ROOM* IS JUST UP THIS WAY.

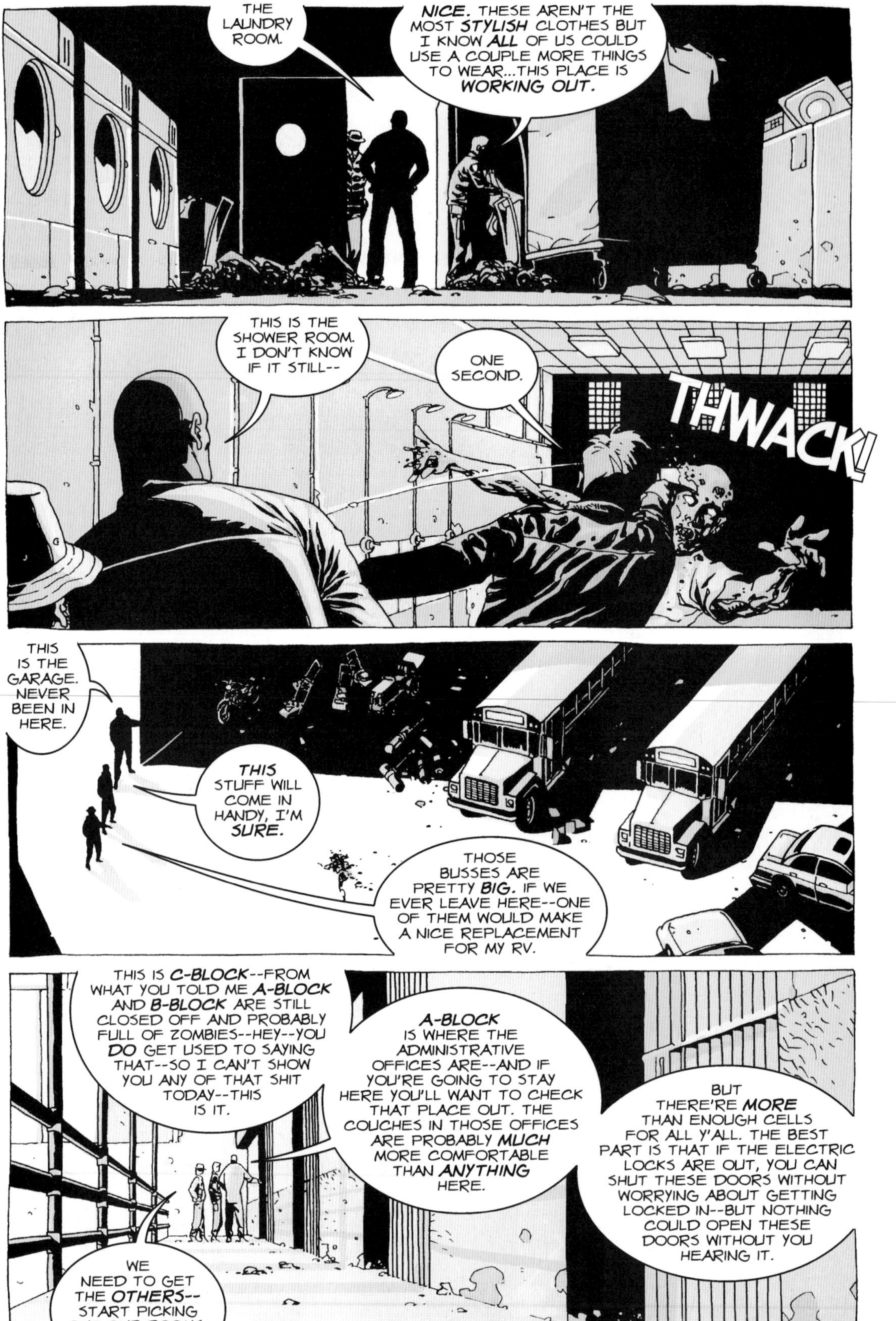

THE LAUNDRY ROOM.
NICE. THESE AREN'T THE MOST STYLISH CLOTHES BUT I KNOW ALL OF US COULD USE A COUPLE MORE THINGS TO WEAR...THIS PLACE IS WORKING OUT.
THIS IS THE SHOWER ROOM. I DON'T KNOW IF IT STILL--
ONE SECOND.
THWACK!
THIS IS THE GARAGE. NEVER BEEN IN HERE.
THIS STUFF WILL COME IN HANDY, I'M SURE.
THOSE BUSSES ARE PRETTY BIG. IF WE EVER LEAVE HERE--ONE OF THEM WOULD MAKE A NICE REPLACEMENT FOR MY RV.
THIS IS C-BLOCK--FROM WHAT YOU TOLD ME A-BLOCK AND B-BLOCK ARE STILL CLOSED OFF AND PROBABLY FULL OF ZOMBIES--HEY--YOU DO GET USED TO SAYING THAT--SO I CAN'T SHOW YOU ANY OF THAT SHIT TODAY--THIS IS IT.
A-BLOCK IS WHERE THE ADMINISTRATIVE OFFICES ARE--AND IF YOU'RE GOING TO STAY HERE YOU'LL WANT TO CHECK THAT PLACE OUT. THE COUCHES IN THOSE OFFICES ARE PROBABLY MUCH MORE COMFORTABLE THAN ANYTHING HERE.
BUT THERE'RE MORE THAN ENOUGH CELLS FOR ALL Y'ALL. THE BEST PART IS THAT IF THE ELECTRIC LOCKS ARE OUT, YOU CAN SHUT THESE DOORS WITHOUT WORRYING ABOUT GETTING LOCKED IN--BUT NOTHING COULD OPEN THESE DOORS WITHOUT YOU HEARING IT.
WE NEED TO GET THE OTHERS--START PICKING OUT OUR ROOMS.

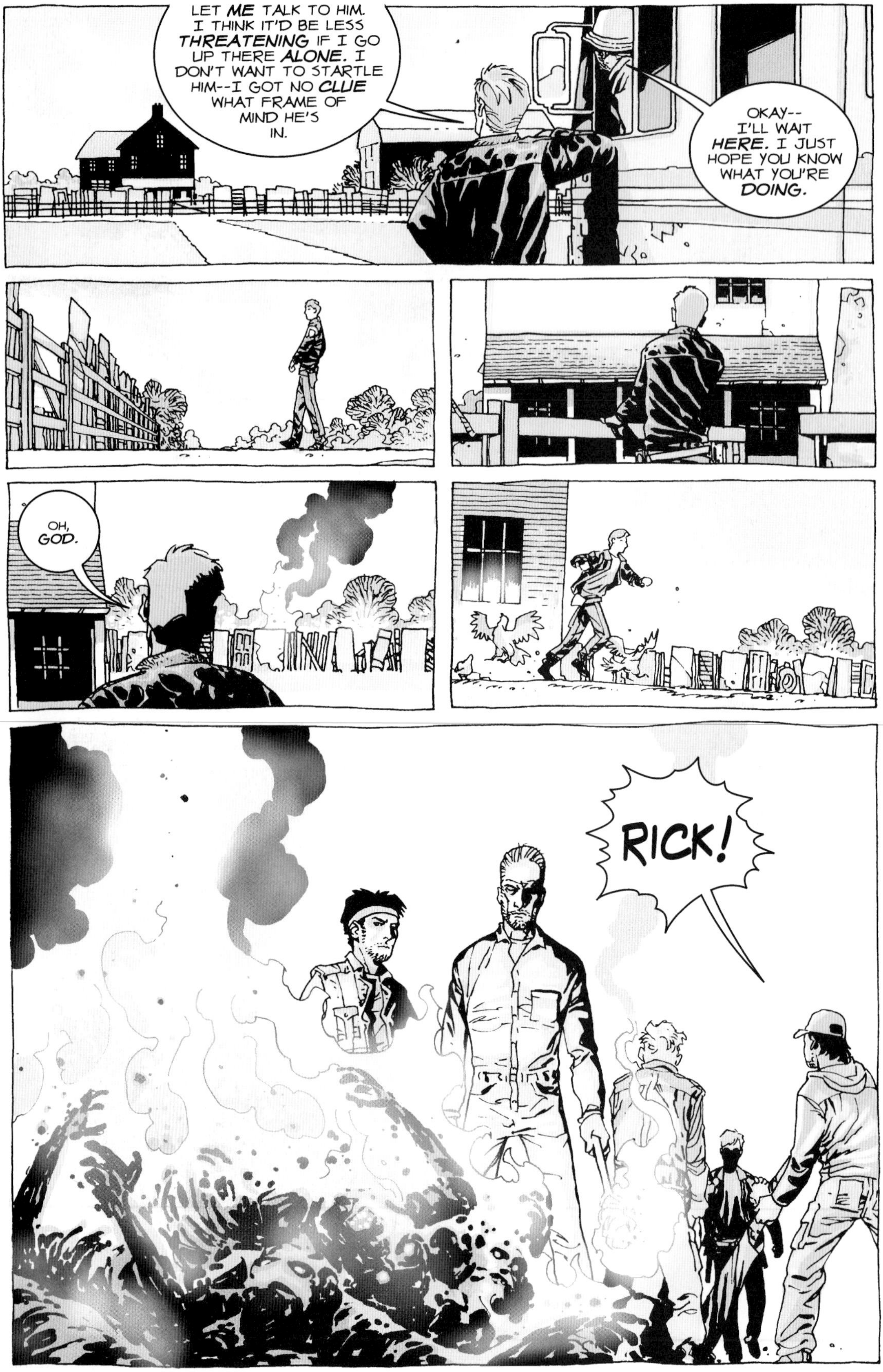
LET ME TALK TO HIM. I THINK IT'D BE LESS THREATENING IF I GO UP THERE ALONE. I DON'T WANT TO STARTLE HIM--I GOT NO CLUE WHAT FRAME OF MIND HE'S IN.
OKAY-- I'LL WAIT HERE. I JUST HOPE YOU KNOW WHAT YOU'RE DOING.
OH, GOD.
RICK!

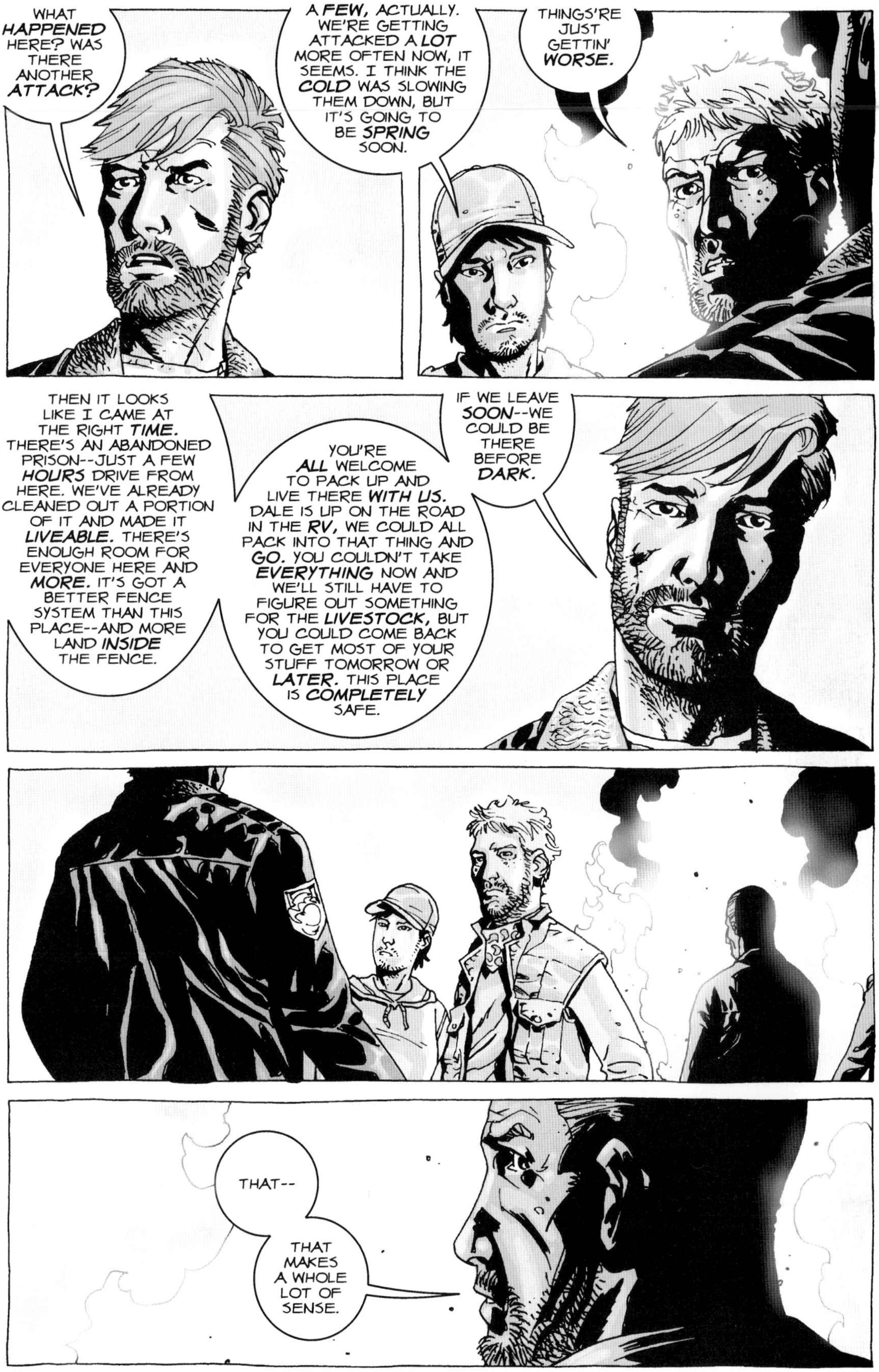
WHAT HAPPENED HERE? WAS THERE ANOTHER ATTACK?
A FEW, ACTUALLY. WE'RE GETTING ATTACKED A LOT MORE OFTEN NOW, IT SEEMS. I THINK THE COLD WAS SLOWING THEM DOWN, BUT IT'S GOING TO BE SPRING SOON.
THINGS'RE JUST GETTIN' WORSE.
THEN IT LOOKS LIKE I CAME AT THE RIGHT TIME. THERE'S AN ABANDONED PRISON--JUST A FEW HOURS DRIVE FROM HERE. WE'VE ALREADY CLEANED OUT A PORTION OF IT AND MADE IT LIVEABLE. THERE'S ENOUGH ROOM FOR EVERYONE HERE AND MORE. IT'S GOT A BETTER FENCE SYSTEM THAN THIS PLACE--AND MORE LAND INSIDE THE FENCE.
YOU'RE ALL WELCOME TO PACK UP AND LIVE THERE WITH US. DALE IS UP ON THE ROAD IN THE RV, WE COULD ALL PACK INTO THAT THING AND GO. YOU COULDN'T TAKE EVERYTHING NOW AND WE'LL STILL HAVE TO FIGURE OUT SOMETHING FOR THE LIVESTOCK, BUT YOU COULD COME BACK TO GET MOST OF YOUR STUFF TOMORROW OR LATER. THIS PLACE IS COMPLETELY SAFE.
IF WE LEAVE SOON--WE COULD BE THERE BEFORE DARK.
THAT--
THAT MAKES A WHOLE LOT OF SENSE.

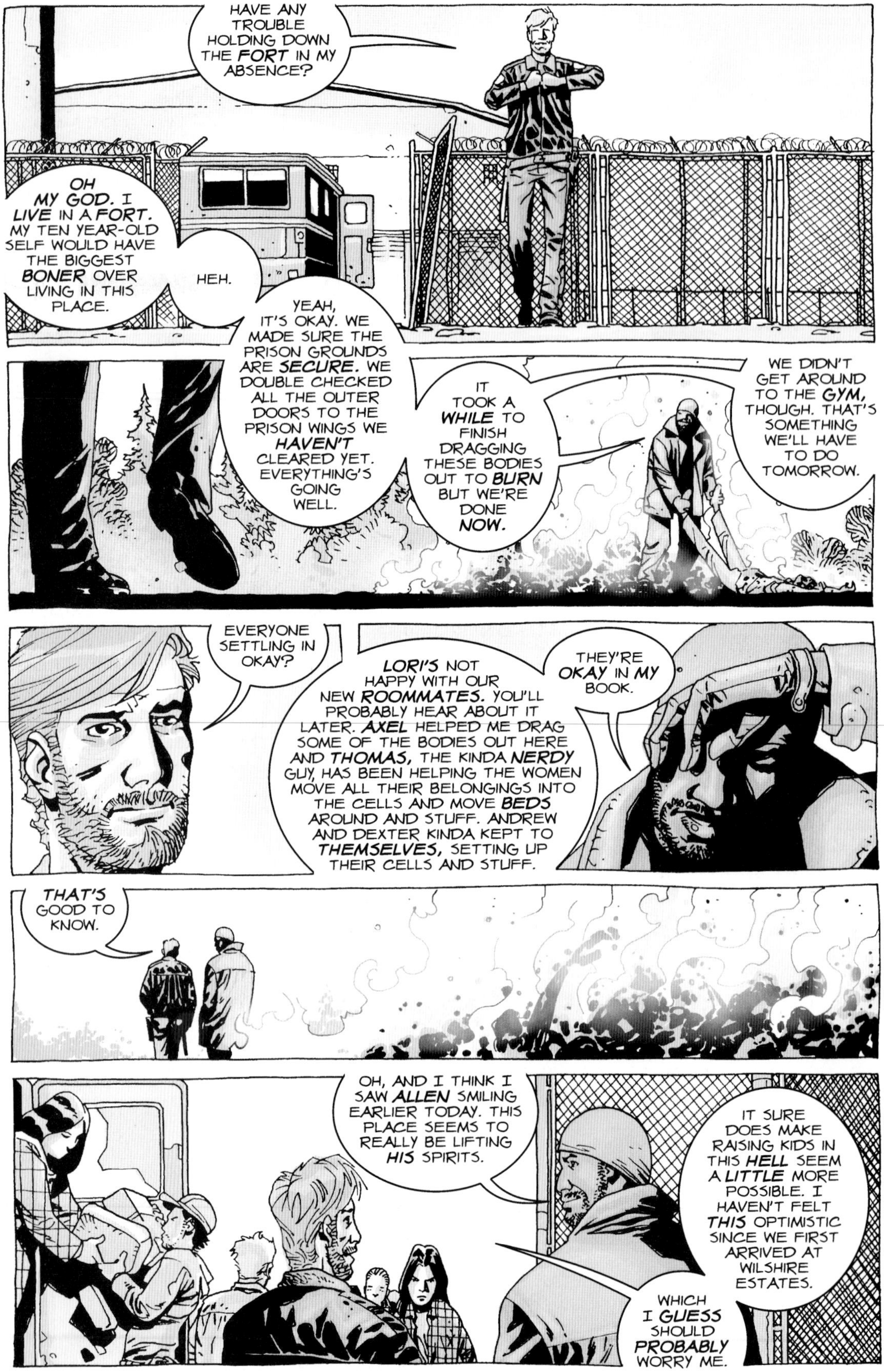
HAVE ANY TROUBLE HOLDING DOWN THE FORT IN MY ABSENCE?
OH MY GOD. I LIVE IN A FORT. MY TEN YEAR-OLD SELF WOULD HAVE THE BIGGEST BONER OVER LIVING IN THIS PLACE.
HEH.
YEAH, IT'S OKAY. WE MADE SURE THE PRISON GROUNDS ARE SECURE. WE DOUBLE CHECKED ALL THE OUTER DOORS TO THE PRISON WINGS WE HAVEN'T CLEARED YET. EVERYTHING'S GOING WELL.
IT TOOK A WHILE TO FINISH DRAGGING THESE BODIES OUT TO BURN BUT WE'RE DONE NOW.
WE DIDN'T GET AROUND TO THE GYM, THOUGH. THAT'S SOMETHING WE'LL HAVE TO DO TOMORROW.
EVERYONE SETTLING IN OKAY?
LORI'S NOT HAPPY WITH OUR NEW ROOMMATES. YOU'LL PROBABLY HEAR ABOUT IT LATER. AXEL HELPED ME DRAG SOME OF THE BODIES OUT HERE AND THOMAS, THE KINDA NERDY GUY, HAS BEEN HELPING THE WOMEN MOVE ALL THEIR BELONGINGS INTO THE CELLS AND MOVE BEDS AROUND AND STUFF. ANDREW AND DEXTER KINDA KEPT TO THEMSELVES, SETTING UP THEIR CELLS AND STUFF.
THEY'RE OKAY IN MY BOOK.
THAT'S GOOD TO KNOW.
OH, AND I THINK I SAW ALLEN SMILING EARLIER TODAY. THIS PLACE SEEMS TO REALLY BE LIFTING HIS SPIRITS.
IT SURE DOES MAKE RAISING KIDS IN THIS HELL SEEM A LITTLE MORE POSSIBLE. I HAVEN'T FELT THIS OPTIMISTIC SINCE WE FIRST ARRIVED AT WILSHIRE ESTATES.
WHICH I GUESS SHOULD PROBABLY WORRY ME.

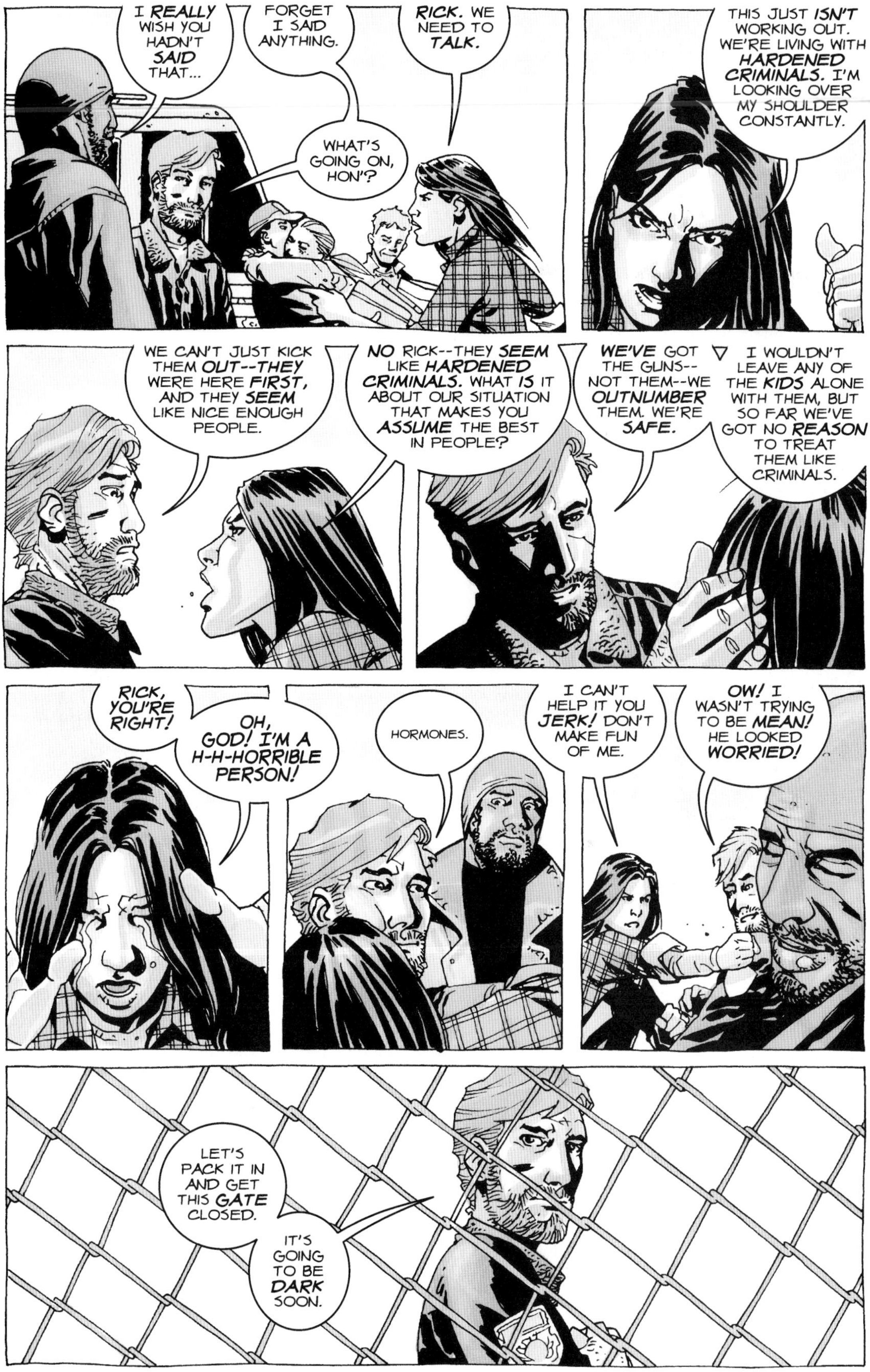
I REALLY WISH YOU HADN'T SAID THAT...
FORGET I SAID ANYTHING.
WHAT'S GOING ON, HON'?
RICK. WE NEED TO TALK.
THIS JUST ISN'T WORKING OUT. WE'RE LIVING WITH HARDENED CRIMINALS. I'M LOOKING OVER MY SHOULDER CONSTANTLY.
WE CAN'T JUST KICK THEM OUT--THEY WERE HERE FIRST, AND THEY SEEM LIKE NICE ENOUGH PEOPLE.
NO RICK--THEY SEEM LIKE HARDENED CRIMINALS. WHAT IS IT ABOUT OUR SITUATION THAT MAKES YOU ASSUME THE BEST IN PEOPLE?
WE'VE GOT THE GUNS--NOT THEM--WE OUTNUMBER THEM. WE'RE SAFE.
I WOULDN'T LEAVE ANY OF THE KIDS ALONE WITH THEM, BUT SO FAR WE'VE GOT NO REASON TO TREAT THEM LIKE CRIMINALS.
RICK, YOU'RE RIGHT!
OH, GOD! I'M A H-H-HORRIBLE PERSON!
HORMONES.
I CAN'T HELP IT YOU JERK! DON'T MAKE FUN OF ME.
OW! I WASN'T TRYING TO BE MEAN! HE LOOKED WORRIED!
LET'S PACK IT IN AND GET THIS GATE CLOSED.
IT'S GOING TO BE DARK SOON.

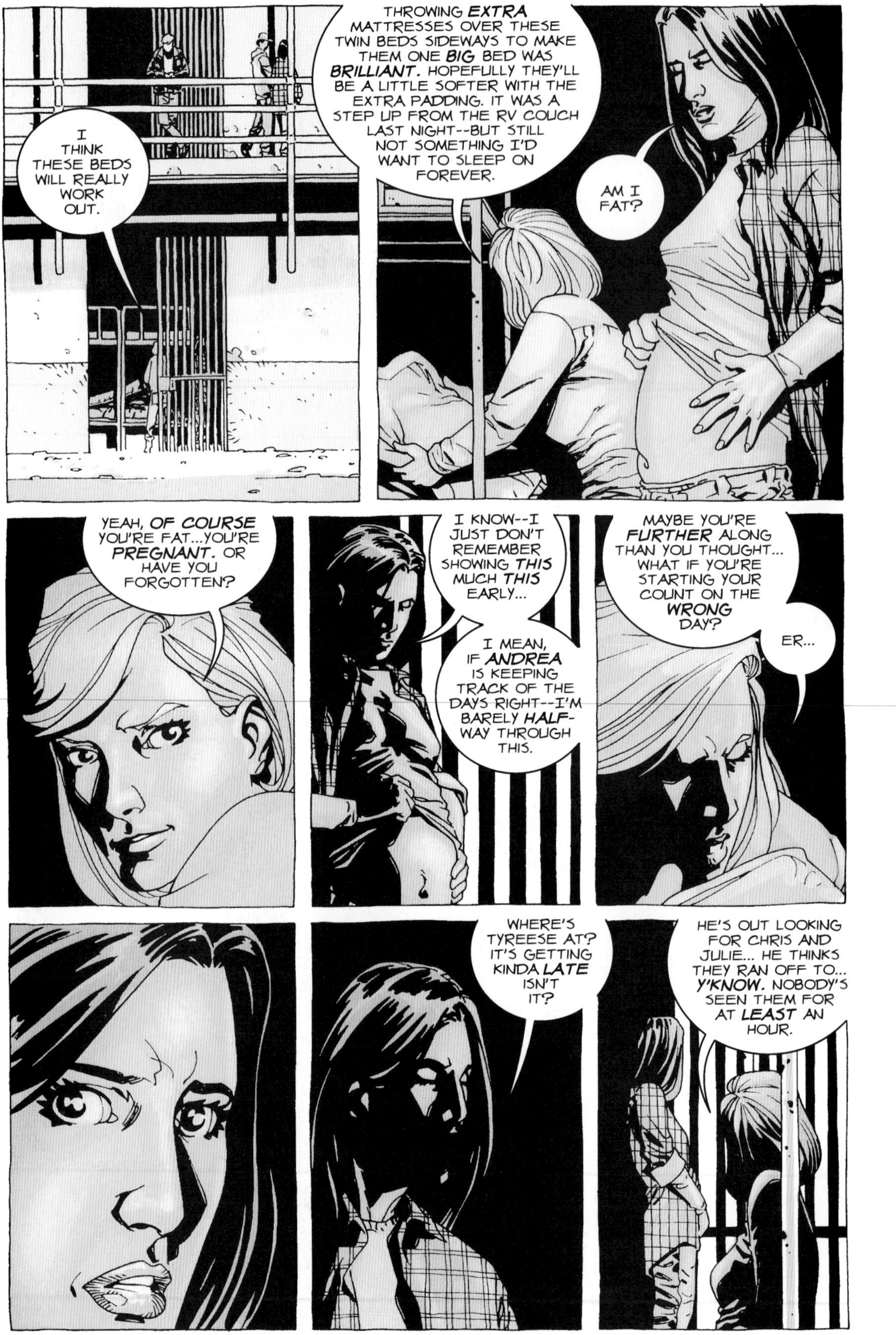
I THINK THESE BEDS WILL REALLY WORK OUT.
THROWING EXTRA MATTRESSES OVER THESE TWIN BEDS SIDEWAYS TO MAKE THEM ONE BIG BED WAS BRILLIANT. HOPEFULLY THEY'LL BE A LITTLE SOFTER WITH THE EXTRA PADDING. IT WAS A STEP UP FROM THE RV COUCH LAST NIGHT--BUT STILL NOT SOMETHING I'D WANT TO SLEEP ON FOREVER.
AM I FAT?
YEAH, OF COURSE YOU'RE FAT...YOU'RE PREGNANT. OR HAVE YOU FORGOTTEN?
I KNOW--I JUST DON'T REMEMBER SHOWING THIS MUCH THIS EARLY...
I MEAN, IF ANDREA IS KEEPING TRACK OF THE DAYS RIGHT--I'M BARELY HALF-WAY THROUGH THIS.
MAYBE YOU'RE FURTHER ALONG THAN YOU THOUGHT... WHAT IF YOU'RE STARTING YOUR COUNT ON THE WRONG DAY?
ER...
WHERE'S TYREESE AT? IT'S GETTING KINDA LATE ISN'T IT?
HE'S OUT LOOKING FOR CHRIS AND JULIE... HE THINKS THEY RAN OFF TO... Y'KNOW. NOBODY'S SEEN THEM FOR AT LEAST AN HOUR.

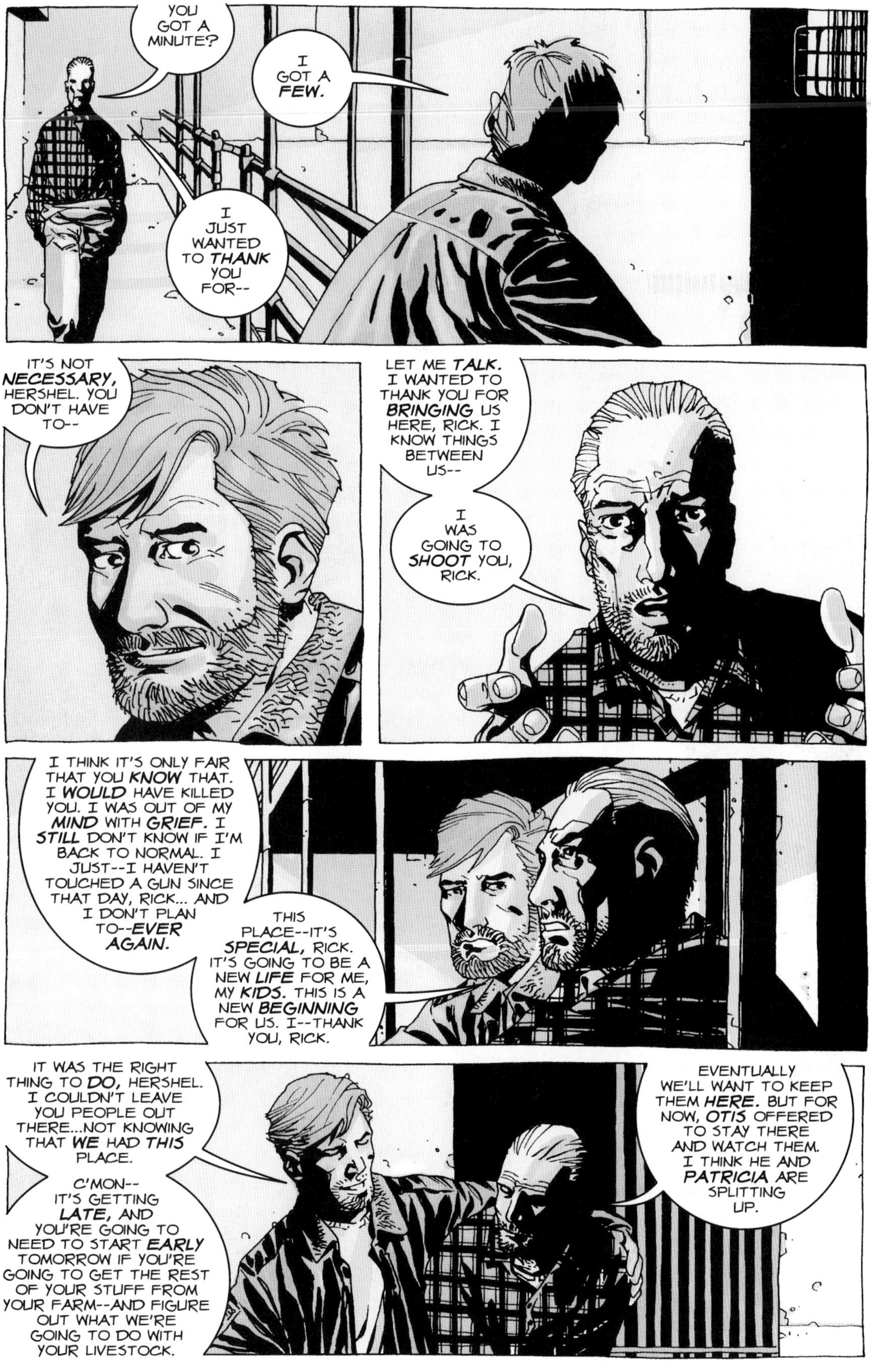

YOU GOT A MINUTE?
I GOT A FEW.
I JUST WANTED TO THANK YOU FOR--
IT'S NOT NECESSARY, HERSHEL. YOU DON'T HAVE TO--
LET ME TALK. I WANTED TO THANK YOU FOR BRINGING US HERE, RICK. I KNOW THINGS BETWEEN US--
I WAS GOING TO SHOOT YOU, RICK.
I THINK IT'S ONLY FAIR THAT YOU KNOW THAT. I WOULD HAVE KILLED YOU. I WAS OUT OF MY MIND WITH GRIEF. I STILL DON'T KNOW IF I'M BACK TO NORMAL. I JUST--I HAVEN'T TOUCHED A GUN SINCE THAT DAY, RICK... AND I DON'T PLAN TO--EVER AGAIN.
THIS PLACE--IT'S SPECIAL, RICK. IT'S GOING TO BE A NEW LIFE FOR ME, MY KIDS. THIS IS A NEW BEGINNING FOR US. I--THANK YOU, RICK.
IT WAS THE RIGHT THING TO DO, HERSHEL. I COULDN'T LEAVE YOU PEOPLE OUT THERE...NOT KNOWING THAT WE HAD THIS PLACE.
C'MON-- IT'S GETTING LATE, AND YOU'RE GOING TO NEED TO START EARLY TOMORROW IF YOU'RE GOING TO GET THE REST OF YOUR STUFF FROM YOUR FARM--AND FIGURE OUT WHAT WE'RE GOING TO DO WITH YOUR LIVESTOCK.
EVENTUALLY WE'LL WANT TO KEEP THEM HERE. BUT FOR NOW, OTIS OFFERED TO STAY THERE AND WATCH THEM. I THINK HE AND PATRICIA ARE SPLITTING UP.

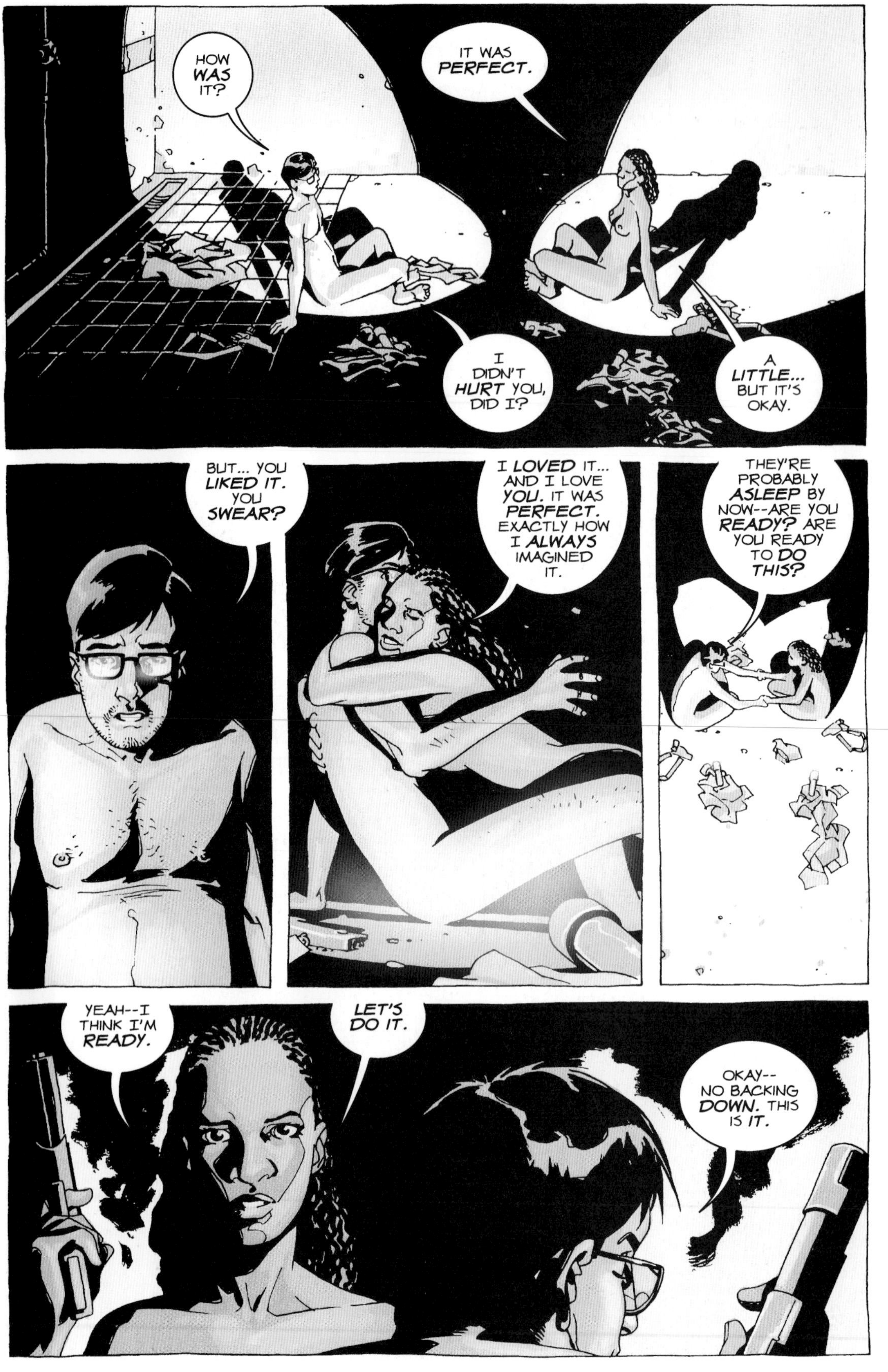
HOW WAS IT?
IT WAS PERFECT.
I DIDN'T HURT YOU, DID I?
A LITTLE... BUT IT'S OKAY.
BUT... YOU LIKED IT. YOU SWEAR?
I LOVED IT... AND I LOVE YOU. IT WAS PERFECT. EXACTLY HOW I ALWAYS IMAGINED IT.
THEY'RE PROBABLY ASLEEP BY NOW--ARE YOU READY? ARE YOU READY TO DO THIS?
YEAH--I THINK I'M READY.
LET'S DO IT.
OKAY-- NO BACKING DOWN. THIS IS IT.

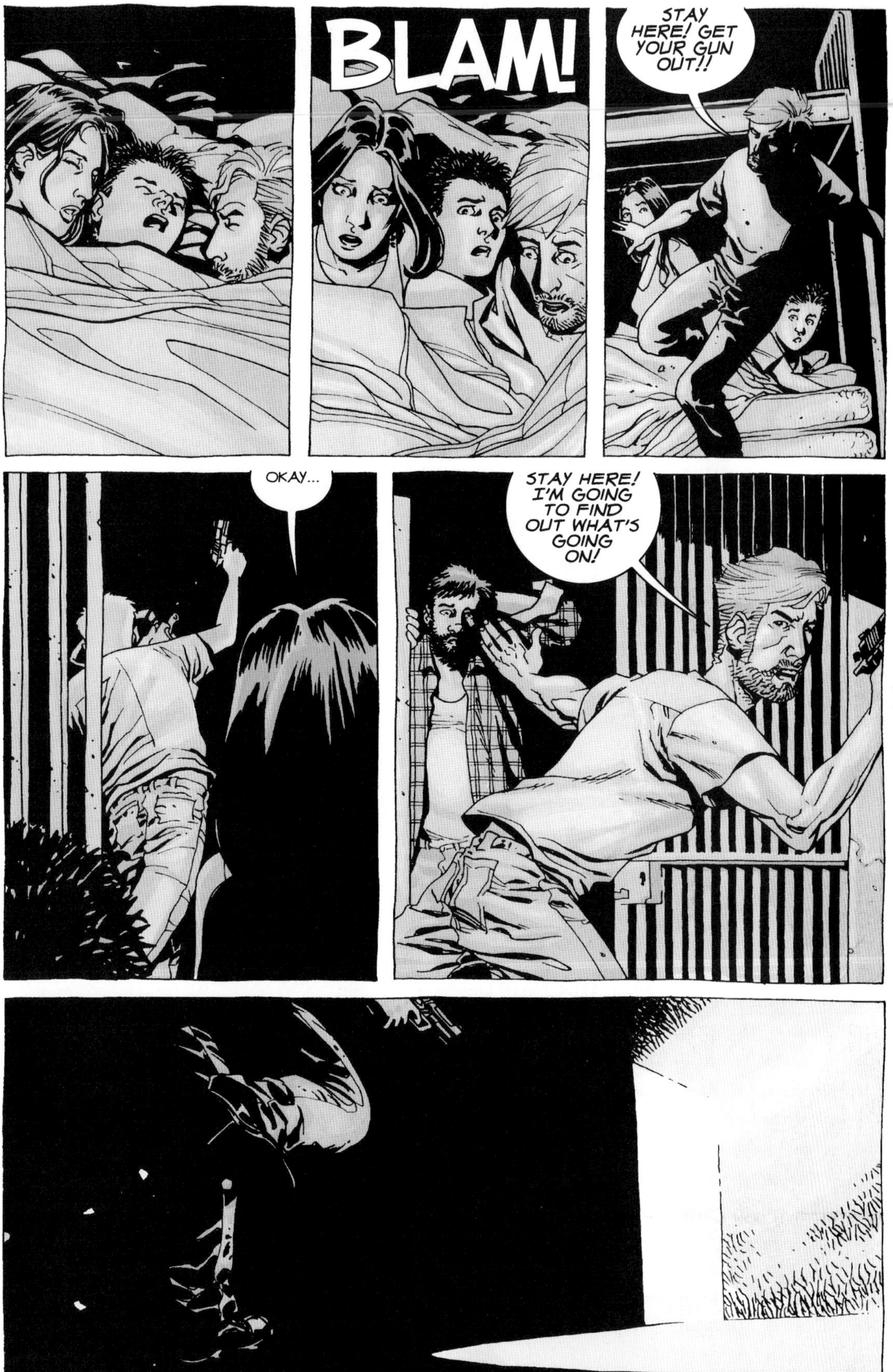
BLAM!
STAY HERE! GET YOUR GUN OUT!!
OKAY...
STAY HERE! I'M GOING TO FIND OUT WHAT'S GOING ON!

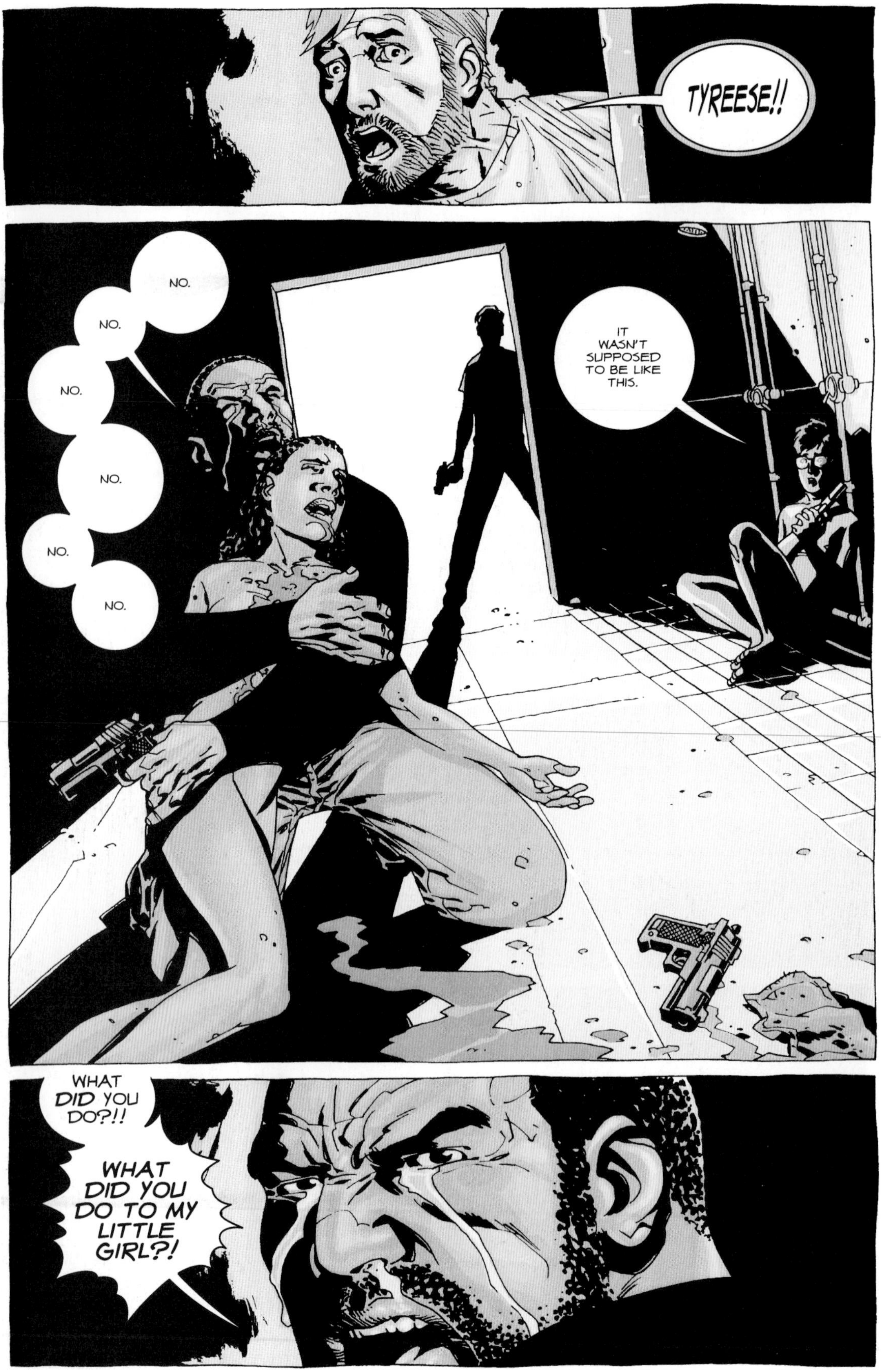
TYREESE!!
NO.
NO.
NO.
NO.
NO.
NO.
IT WASN'T SUPPOSED TO BE LIKE THIS.
WHAT DID YOU DO?!!
WHAT DID YOU DO TO MY LITTLE GIRL?!

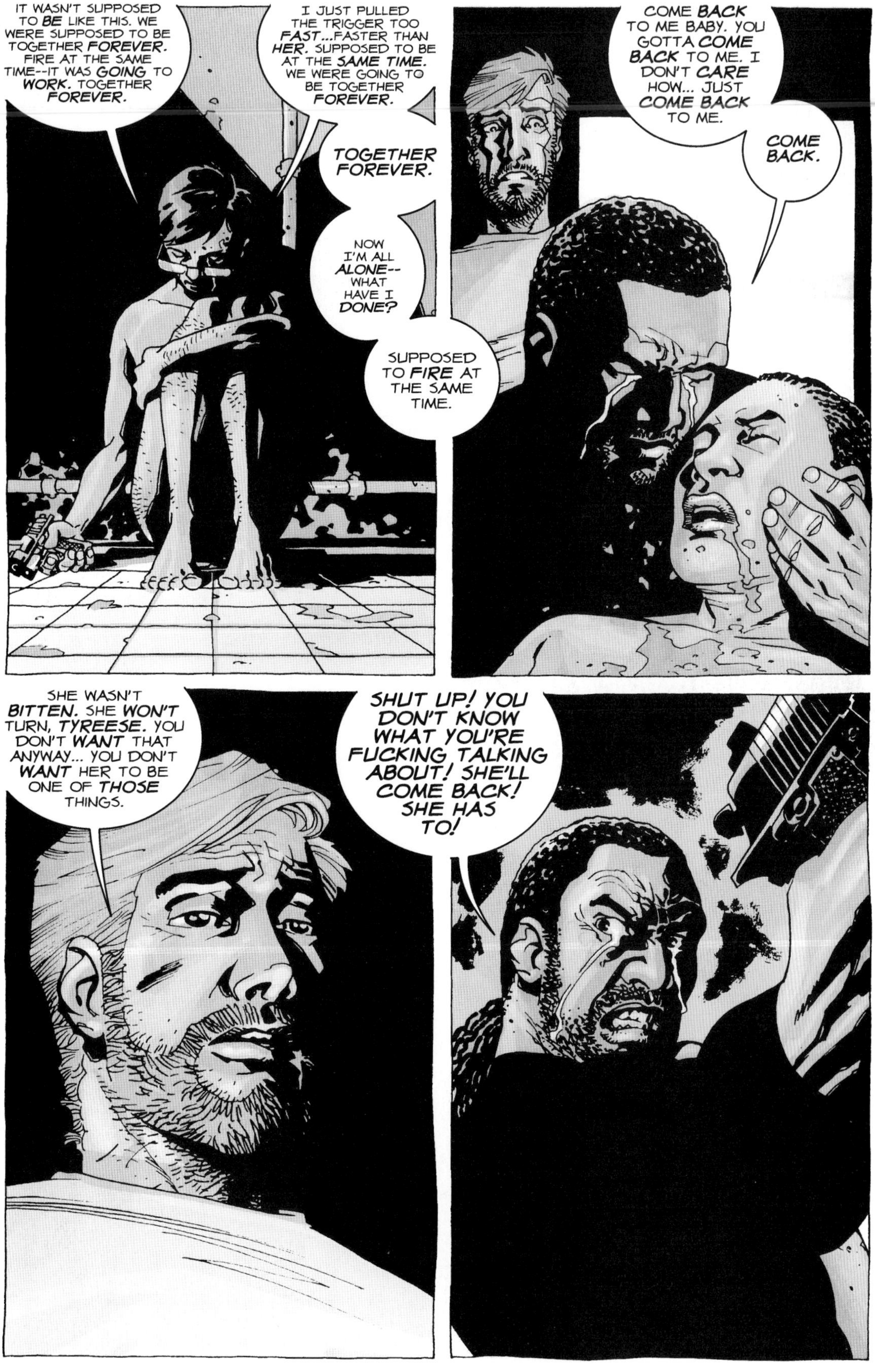
IT WASN'T SUPPOSED TO BE LIKE THIS. WE WERE SUPPOSED TO BE TOGETHER FOREVER. FIRE AT THE SAME TIME--IT WAS GOING TO WORK. TOGETHER FOREVER.
I JUST PULLED THE TRIGGER TOO FAST...FASTER THAN HER. SUPPOSED TO BE AT THE SAME TIME. WE WERE GOING TO BE TOGETHER FOREVER.
TOGETHER FOREVER.
NOW I'M ALL ALONE--WHAT HAVE I DONE?
SUPPOSED TO FIRE AT THE SAME TIME.
COME BACK TO ME BABY. YOU GOTTA COME BACK TO ME. I DON'T CARE HOW... JUST COME BACK TO ME.
COME BACK.
SHE WASN'T BITTEN. SHE WON'T TURN, TYREESE. YOU DON'T WANT THAT ANYWAY... YOU DON'T WANT HER TO BE ONE OF THOSE THINGS.
SHUT UP! YOU DON'T KNOW WHAT YOU'RE FUCKING TALKING ABOUT! SHE'LL COME BACK! SHE HAS TO!

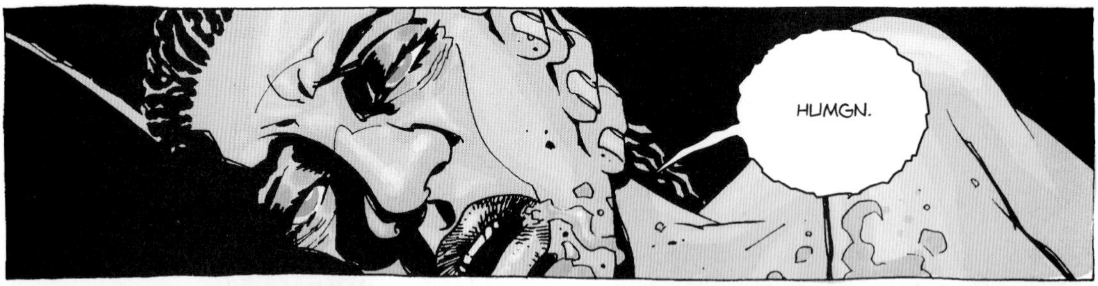
HUMGN.

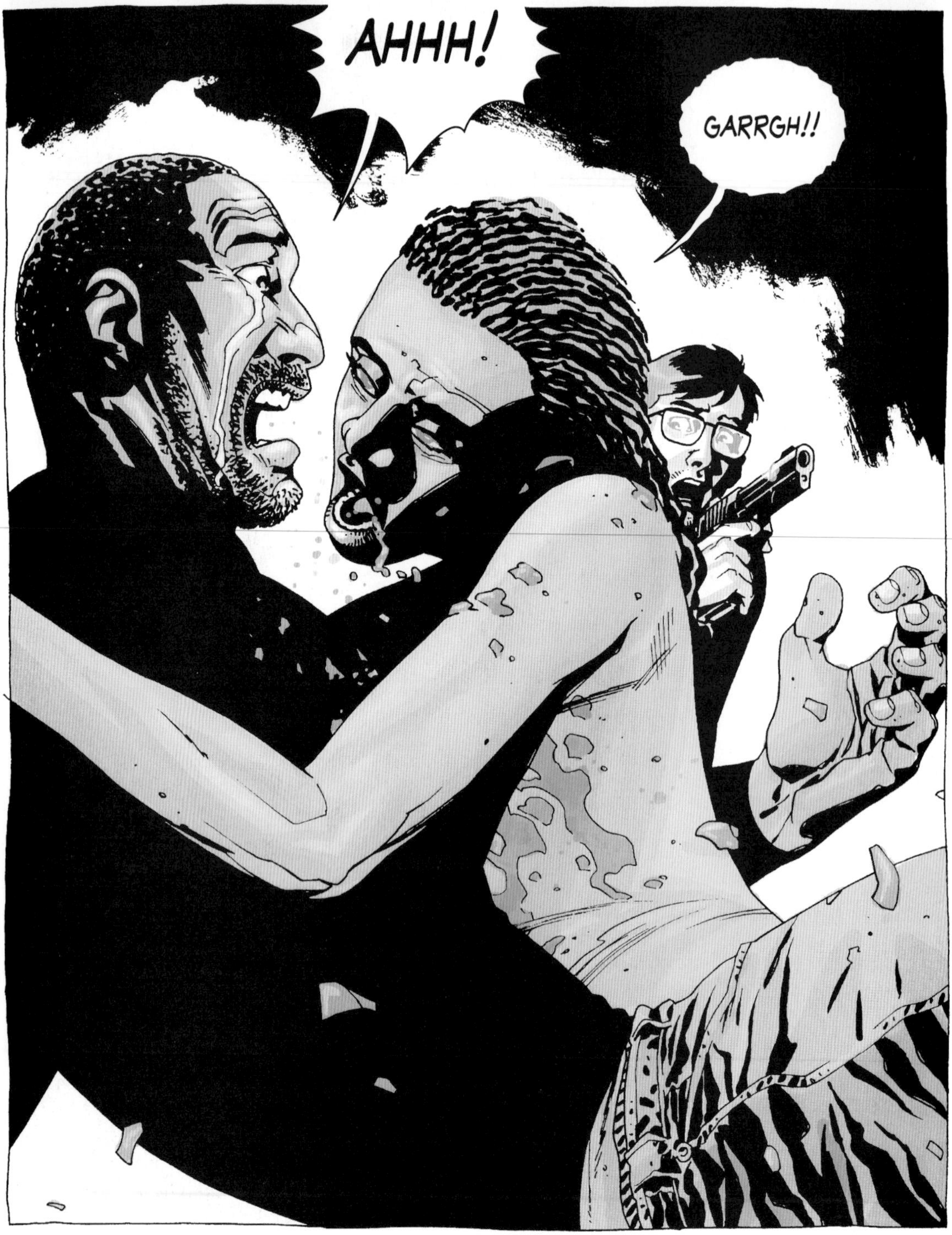
AHHH!
GARRGH!!

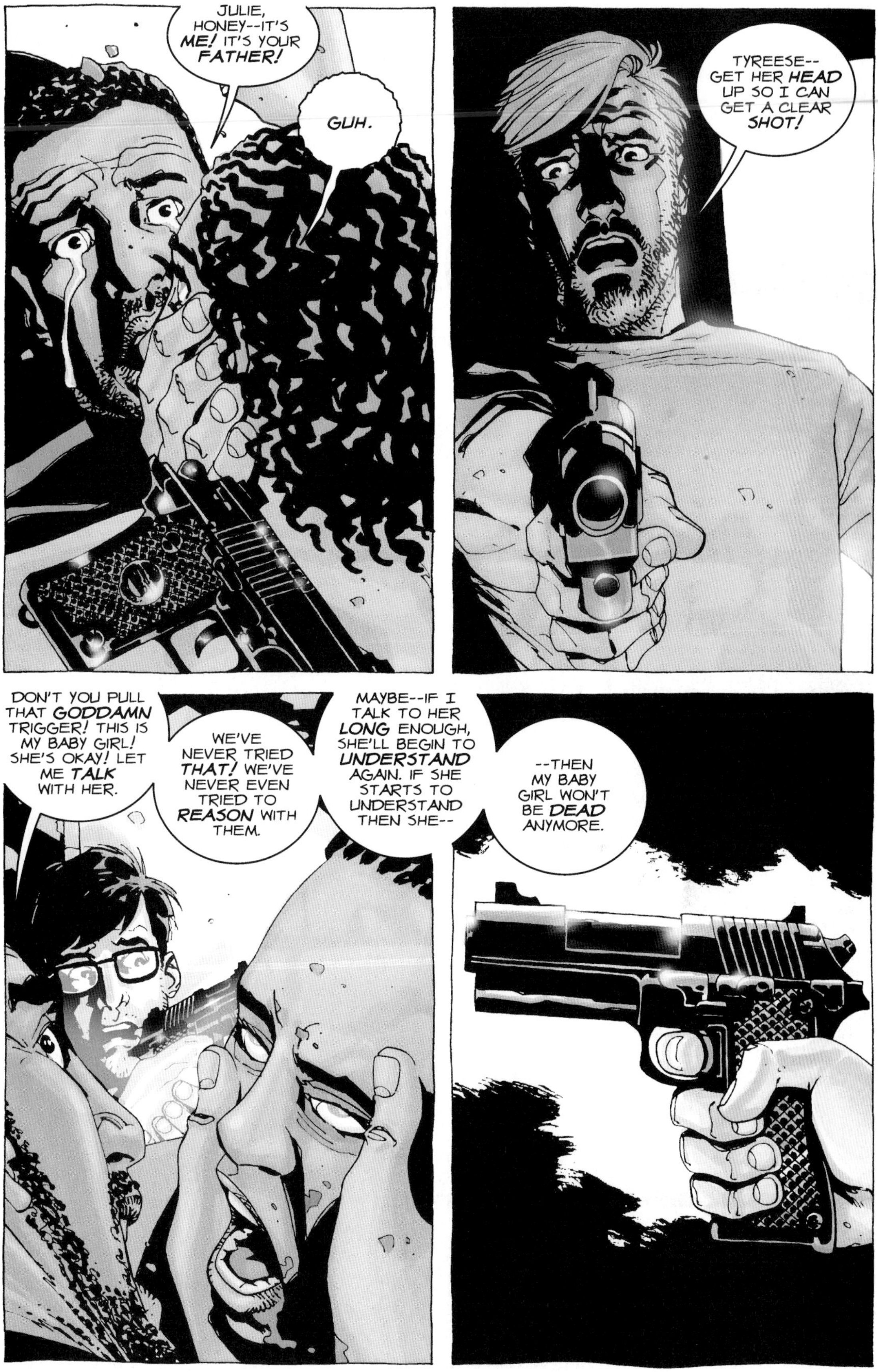
JULIE, HONEY--IT'S ME! IT'S YOUR FATHER!
GUH.
TYREESE-- GET HER HEAD UP SO I CAN GET A CLEAR SHOT!
DON'T YOU PULL THAT GODDAMN TRIGGER! THIS IS MY BABY GIRL! SHE'S OKAY! LET ME TALK WITH HER.
WE'VE NEVER TRIED THAT! WE'VE NEVER EVEN TRIED TO REASON WITH THEM.
MAYBE--IF I TALK TO HER LONG ENOUGH, SHE'LL BEGIN TO UNDERSTAND AGAIN. IF SHE STARTS TO UNDERSTAND THEN SHE--
--THEN MY BABY GIRL WON'T BE DEAD ANYMORE.

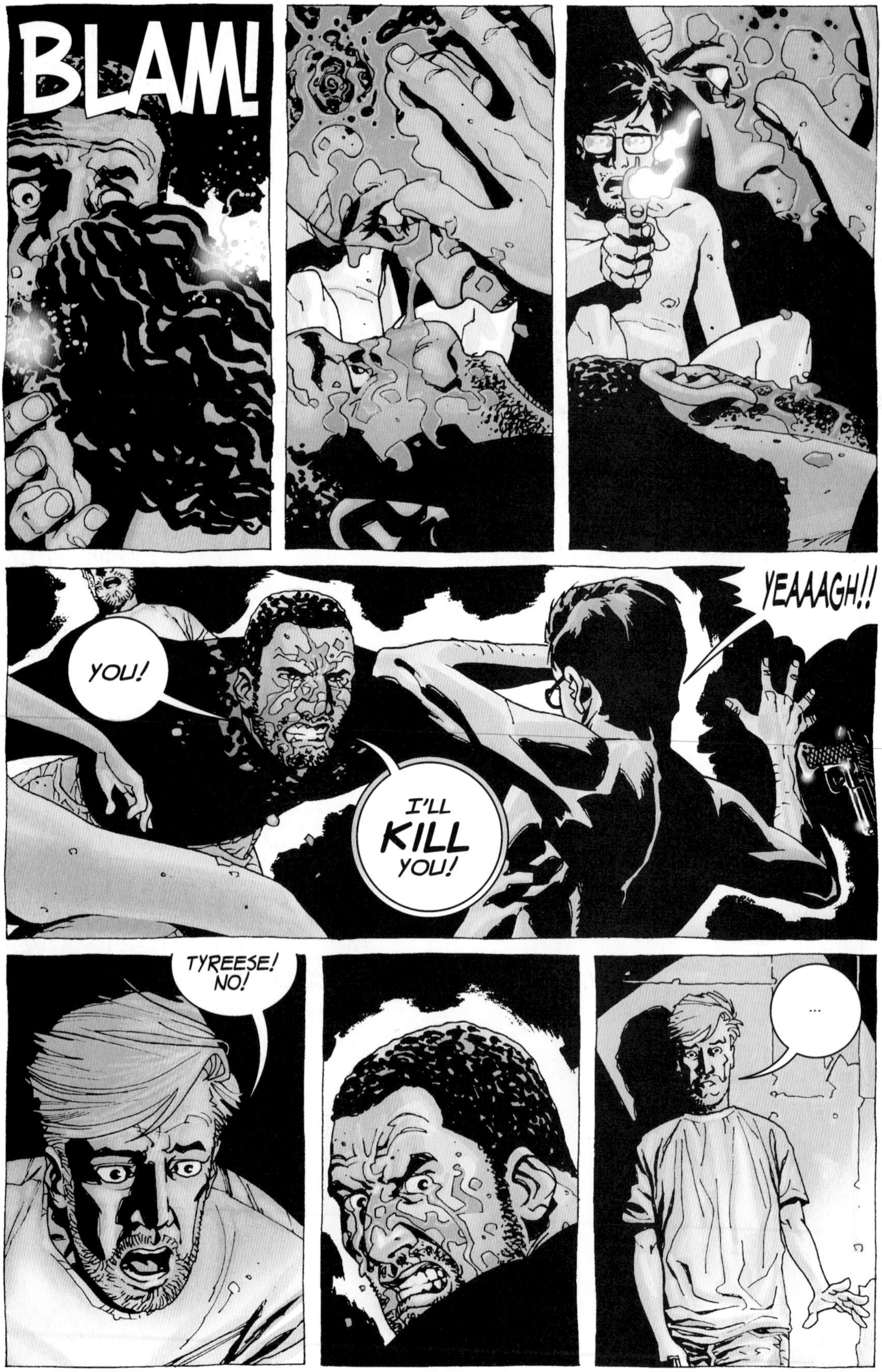
BLAM!
YOU!
I'LL KILL YOU!
YEAAAGH!!
TYREESE! NO!
...

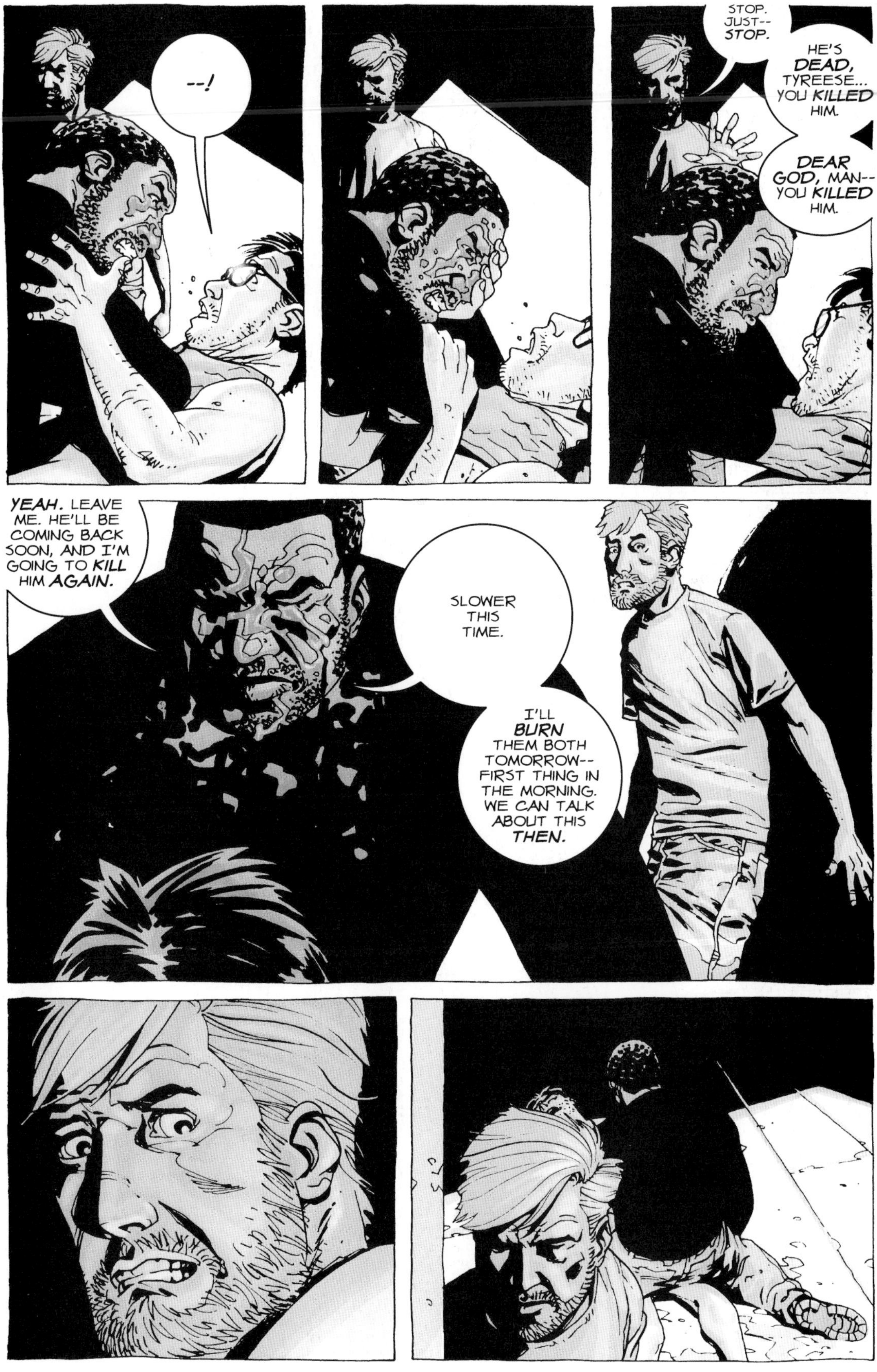

--!
STOP. JUST-- STOP.
HE'S DEAD, TYREESE... YOU KILLED HIM.
DEAR GOD, MAN-- YOU KILLED HIM.
YEAH. LEAVE ME. HE'LL BE COMING BACK SOON, AND I'M GOING TO KILL HIM AGAIN.
SLOWER THIS TIME.
I'LL BURN THEM BOTH TOMORROW-- FIRST THING IN THE MORNING. WE CAN TALK ABOUT THIS THEN.

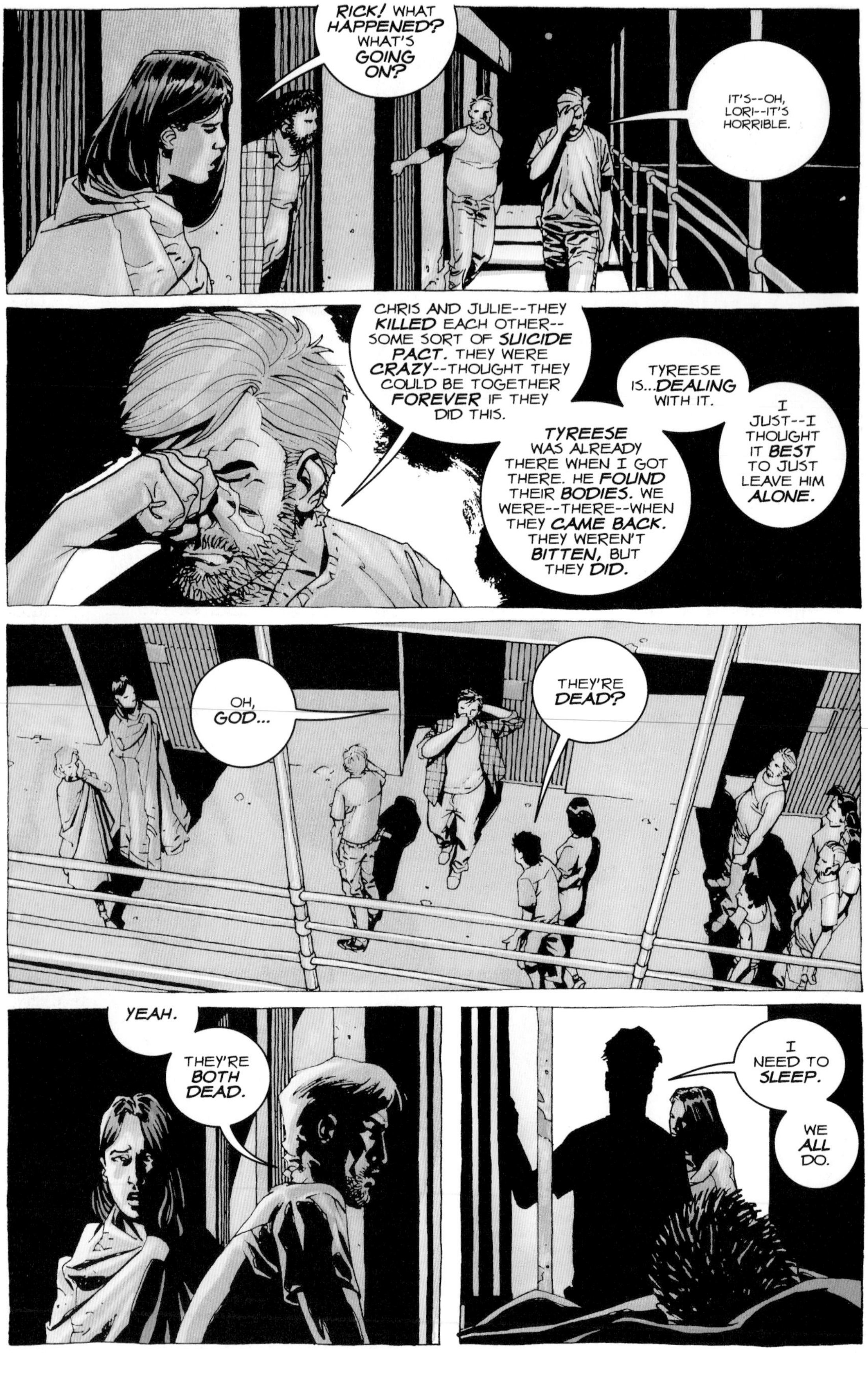
RICK! WHAT HAPPENED? WHAT'S GOING ON?
IT'S--OH, LORI--IT'S HORRIBLE.
CHRIS AND JULIE--THEY KILLED EACH OTHER--SOME SORT OF SUICIDE PACT. THEY WERE CRAZY--THOUGHT THEY COULD BE TOGETHER FOREVER IF THEY DID THIS.
TYREESE WAS ALREADY THERE WHEN I GOT THERE. HE FOUND THEIR BODIES. WE WERE--THERE--WHEN THEY CAME BACK. THEY WEREN'T BITTEN, BUT THEY DID.
TYREESE IS...DEALING WITH IT.
I JUST--I THOUGHT IT BEST TO JUST LEAVE HIM ALONE.
OH, GOD...
THEY'RE DEAD?
YEAH.
THEY'RE BOTH DEAD.
I NEED TO SLEEP.
WE ALL DO.

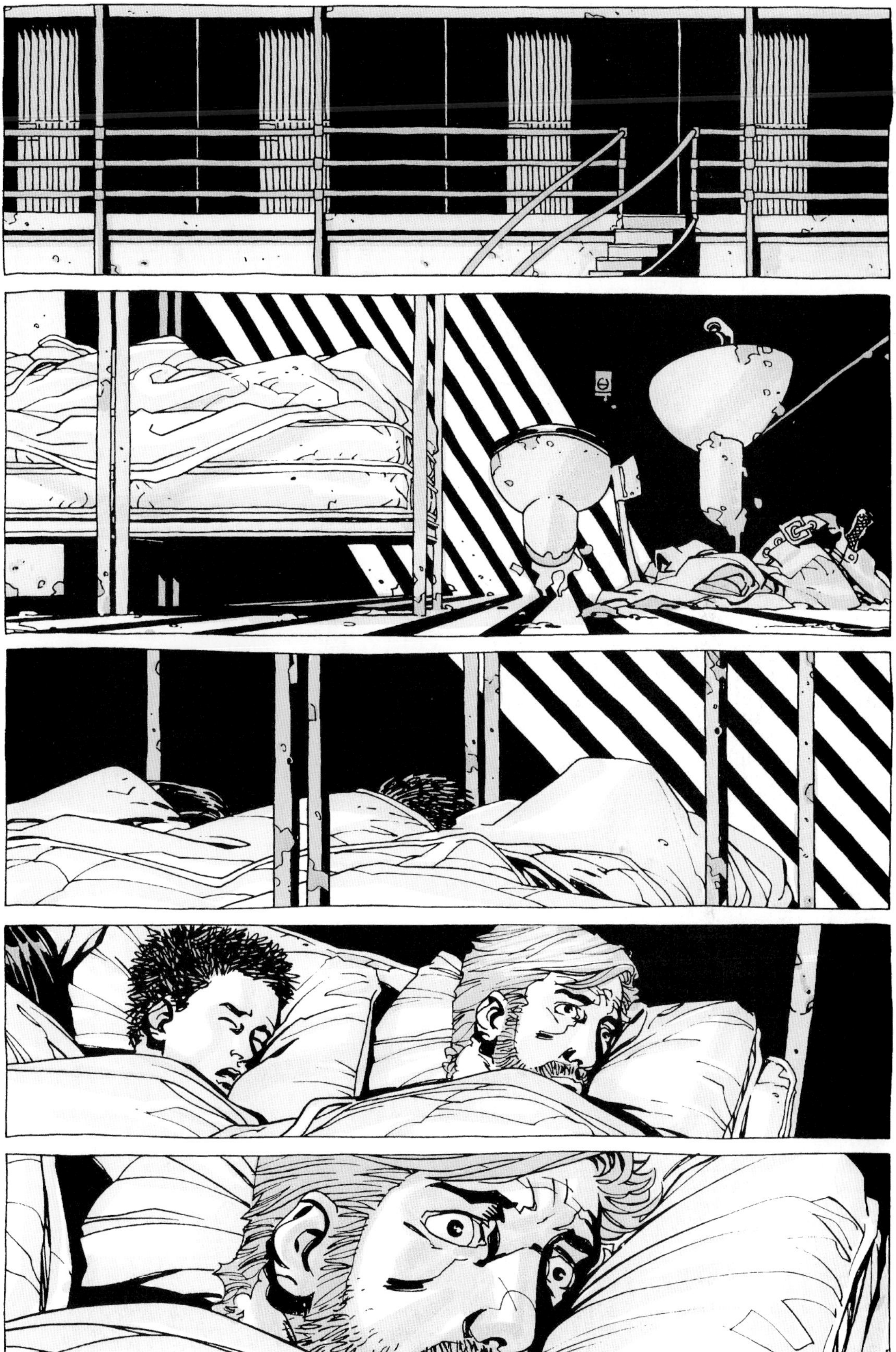

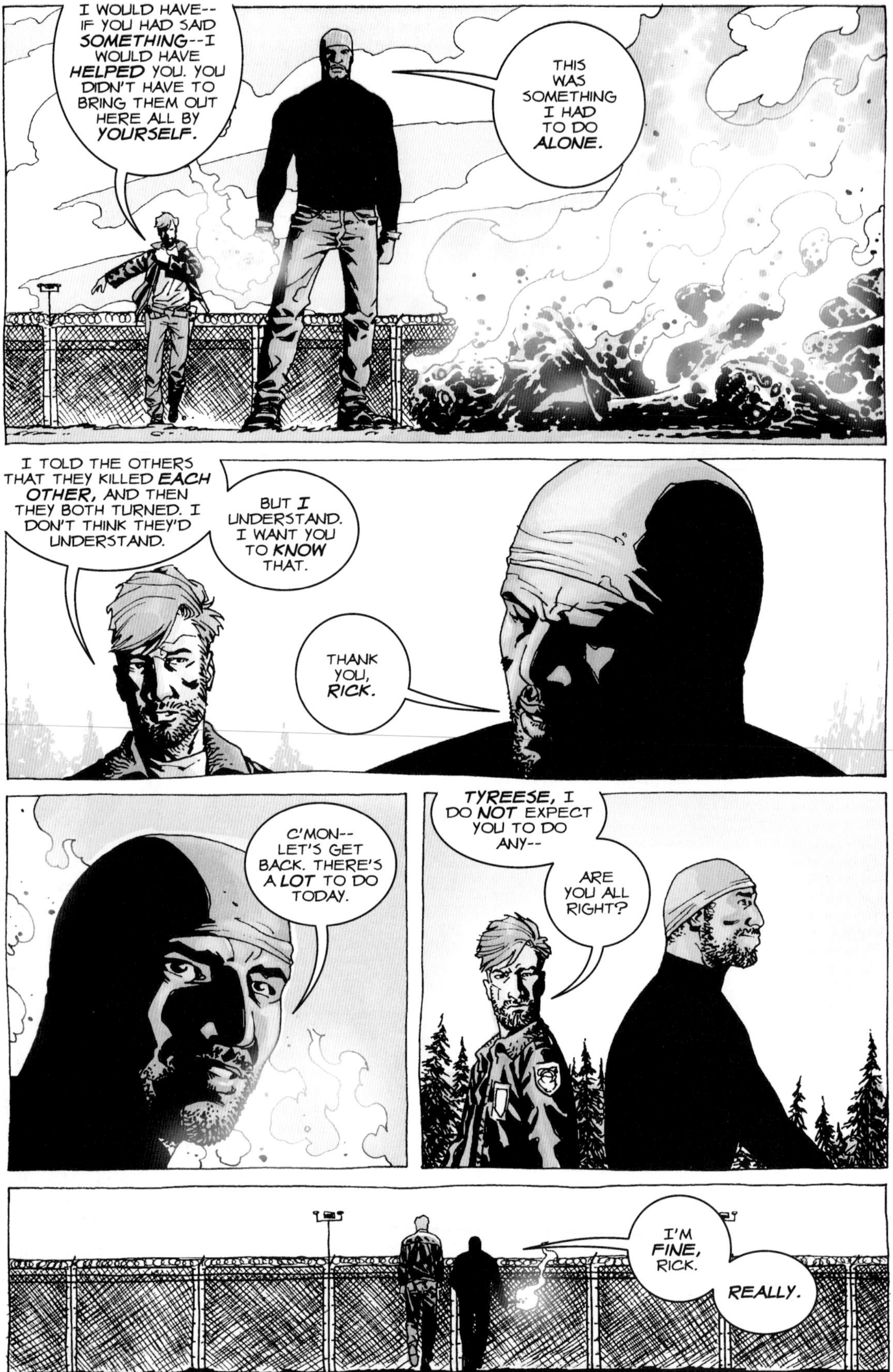
I WOULD HAVE-- IF YOU HAD SAID SOMETHING--I WOULD HAVE HELPED YOU. YOU DIDN'T HAVE TO BRING THEM OUT HERE ALL BY YOURSELF.
THIS WAS SOMETHING I HAD TO DO ALONE.
I TOLD THE OTHERS THAT THEY KILLED EACH OTHER, AND THEN THEY BOTH TURNED. I DON'T THINK THEY'D UNDERSTAND.
BUT I UNDERSTAND. I WANT YOU TO KNOW THAT.
THANK YOU, RICK.
C'MON-- LET'S GET BACK. THERE'S A LOT TO DO TODAY.
TYREESE, I DO NOT EXPECT YOU TO DO ANY--
ARE YOU ALL RIGHT?
I'M FINE, RICK.
REALLY.

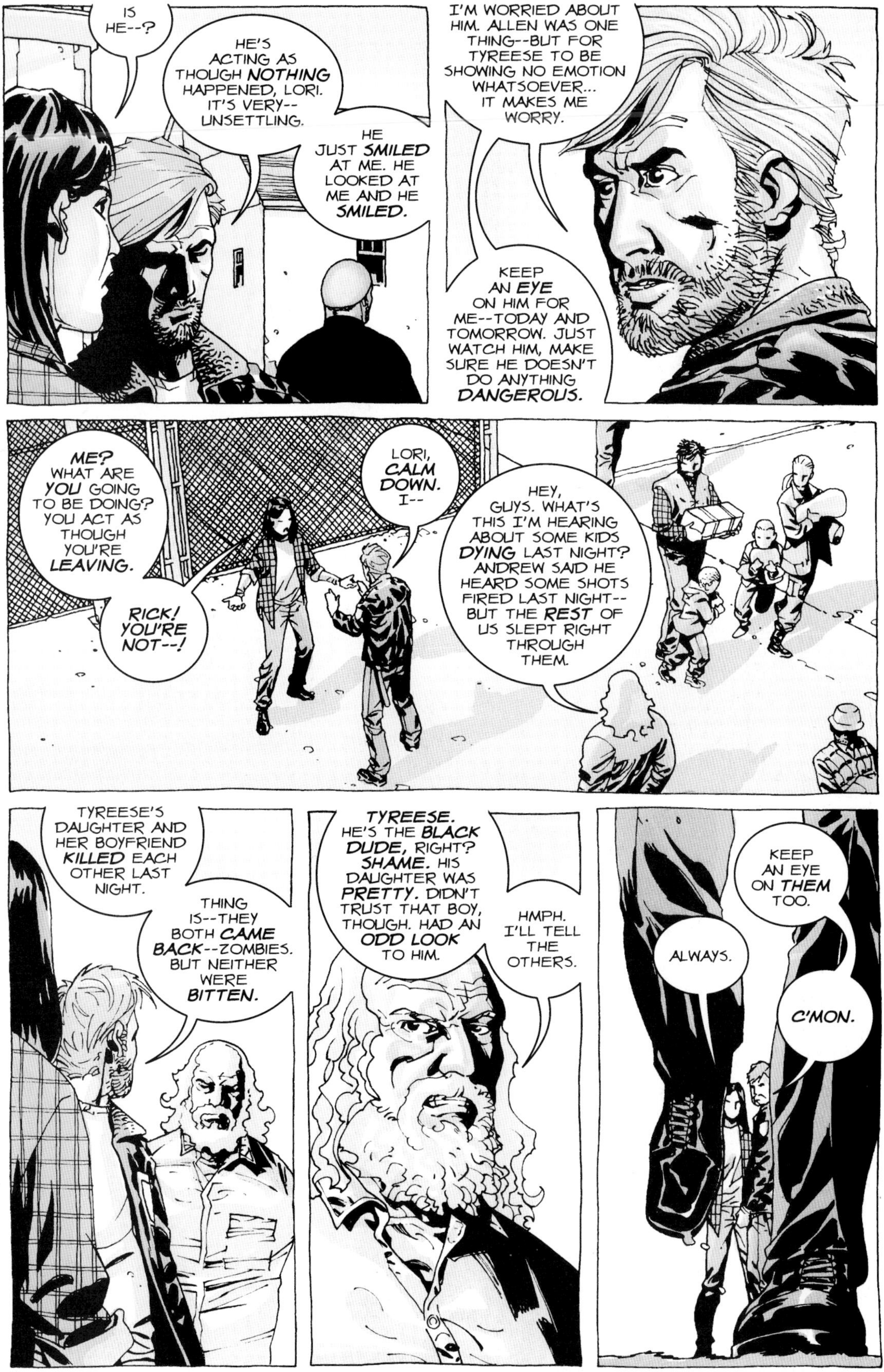

IS HE--?
HE'S ACTING AS THOUGH NOTHING HAPPENED, LORI. IT'S VERY-- UNSETTLING.
HE JUST SMILED AT ME. HE LOOKED AT ME AND HE SMILED.
I'M WORRIED ABOUT HIM. ALLEN WAS ONE THING--BUT FOR TYREESE TO BE SHOWING NO EMOTION WHATSOEVER... IT MAKES ME WORRY.
KEEP AN EYE ON HIM FOR ME--TODAY AND TOMORROW. JUST WATCH HIM, MAKE SURE HE DOESN'T DO ANYTHING DANGEROUS.
ME? WHAT ARE YOU GOING TO BE DOING? YOU ACT AS THOUGH YOU'RE LEAVING.
RICK! YOU'RE NOT--!
LORI, CALM DOWN. I--
HEY, GUYS. WHAT'S THIS I'M HEARING ABOUT SOME KIDS DYING LAST NIGHT? ANDREW SAID HE HEARD SOME SHOTS FIRED LAST NIGHT--BUT THE REST OF US SLEPT RIGHT THROUGH THEM.
TYREESE'S DAUGHTER AND HER BOYFRIEND KILLED EACH OTHER LAST NIGHT.
THING IS--THEY BOTH CAME BACK--ZOMBIES. BUT NEITHER WERE BITTEN.
TYREESE. HE'S THE BLACK DUDE, RIGHT? SHAME. HIS DAUGHTER WAS PRETTY. DIDN'T TRUST THAT BOY, THOUGH. HAD AN ODD LOOK TO HIM.
HMPH. I'LL TELL THE OTHERS.
KEEP AN EYE ON THEM TOO.
ALWAYS.
C'MON.

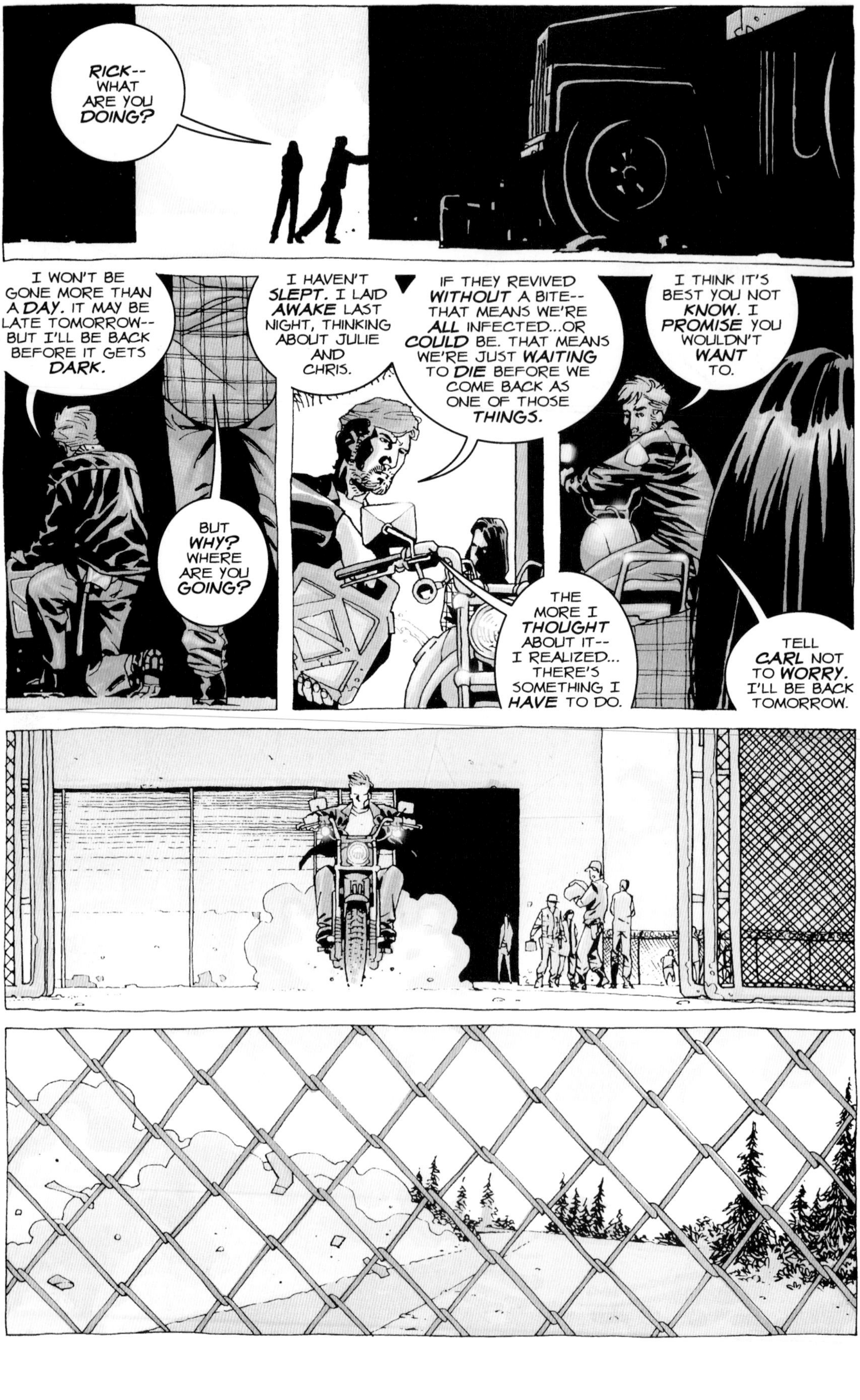
RICK-- WHAT ARE YOU DOING?
I WON'T BE GONE MORE THAN A DAY. IT MAY BE LATE TOMORROW-- BUT I'LL BE BACK BEFORE IT GETS DARK.
BUT WHY? WHERE ARE YOU GOING?
I HAVEN'T SLEPT. I LAID AWAKE LAST NIGHT, THINKING ABOUT JULIE AND CHRIS.
IF THEY REVIVED WITHOUT A BITE-- THAT MEANS WE'RE ALL INFECTED...OR COULD BE. THAT MEANS WE'RE JUST WAITING TO DIE BEFORE WE COME BACK AS ONE OF THOSE THINGS.
THE MORE I THOUGHT ABOUT IT-- I REALIZED... THERE'S SOMETHING I HAVE TO DO.
I THINK IT'S BEST YOU NOT KNOW. I PROMISE YOU WOULDN'T WANT TO.
TELL CARL NOT TO WORRY. I'LL BE BACK TOMORROW.

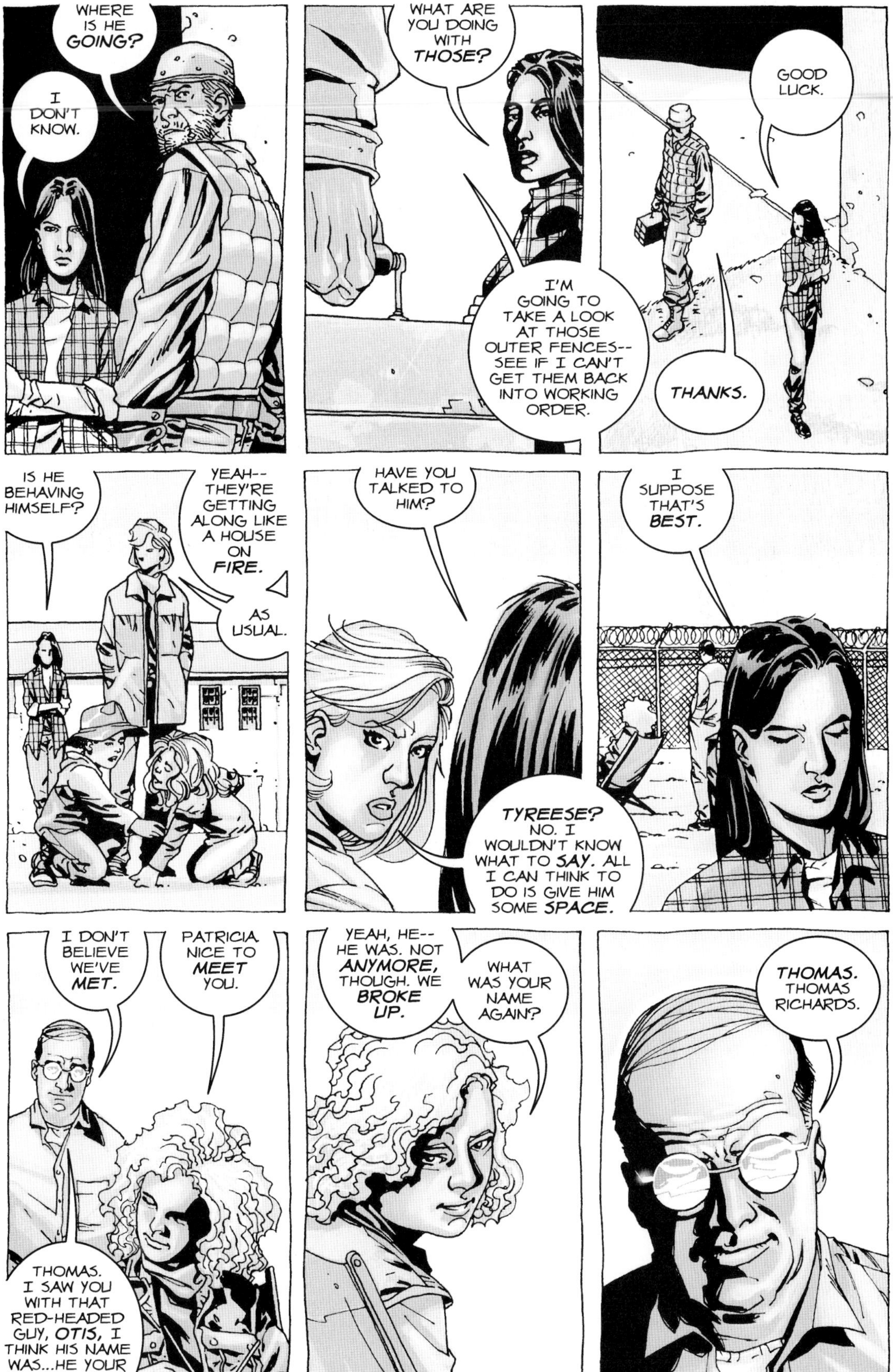
WHERE IS HE GOING?
I DON'T KNOW.
WHAT ARE YOU DOING WITH THOSE?
I'M GOING TO TAKE A LOOK AT THOSE OUTER FENCES-- SEE IF I CAN'T GET THEM BACK INTO WORKING ORDER.
GOOD LUCK.
THANKS.
IS HE BEHAVING HIMSELF?
YEAH-- THEY'RE GETTING ALONG LIKE A HOUSE ON FIRE.
AS USUAL.
HAVE YOU TALKED TO HIM?
TYREESE? NO. I WOULDN'T KNOW WHAT TO SAY. ALL I CAN THINK TO DO IS GIVE HIM SOME SPACE.
I SUPPOSE THAT'S BEST.
I DON'T BELIEVE WE'VE MET.
PATRICIA. NICE TO MEET YOU.
THOMAS. I SAW YOU WITH THAT RED-HEADED GUY, OTIS, I THINK HIS NAME WAS...HE YOUR BOYFRIEND?
YEAH, HE-- HE WAS. NOT ANYMORE, THOUGH. WE BROKE UP.
WHAT WAS YOUR NAME AGAIN?
THOMAS. THOMAS RICHARDS.

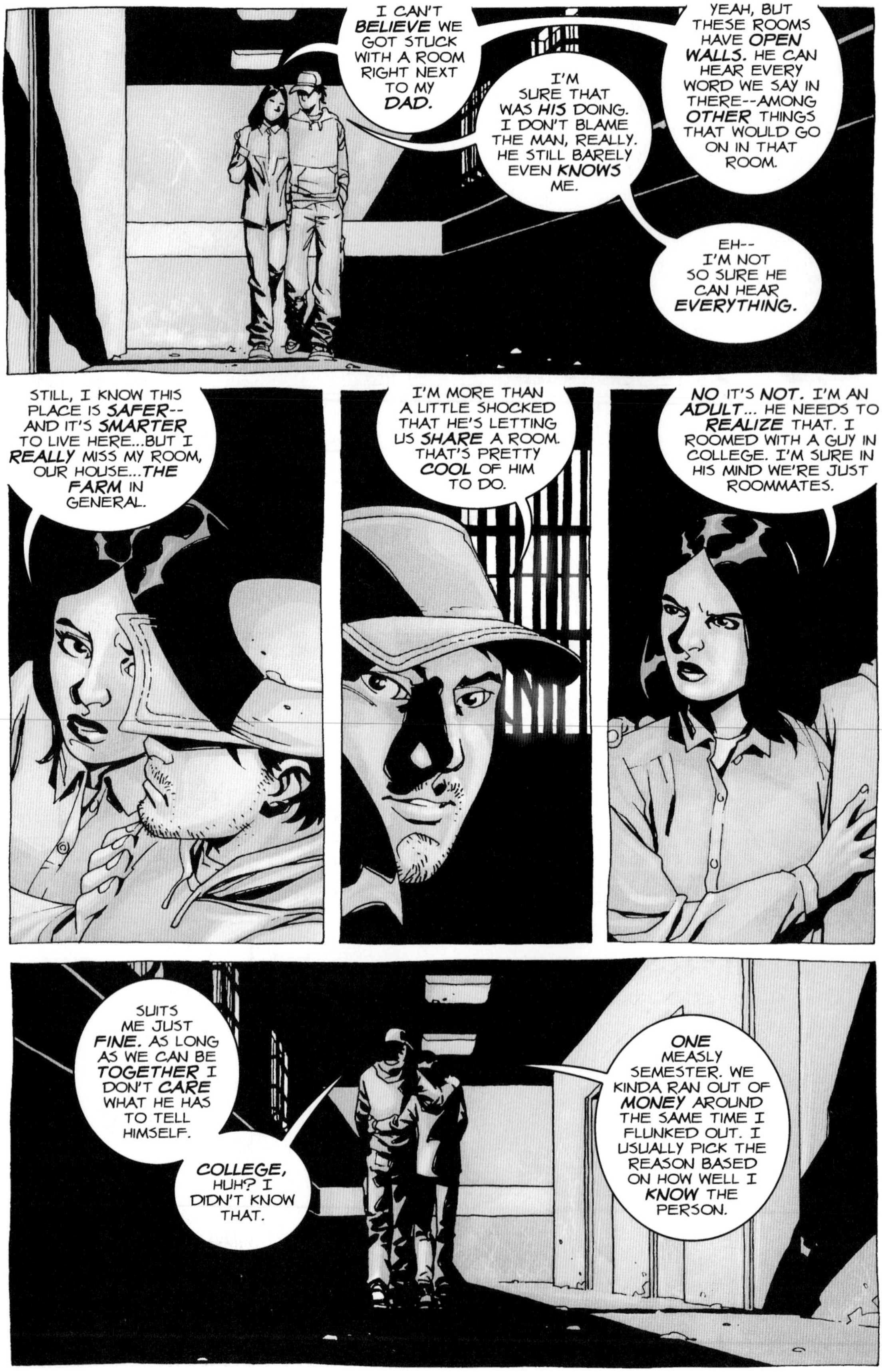
I CAN'T BELIEVE WE GOT STUCK WITH A ROOM RIGHT NEXT TO MY DAD.
I'M SURE THAT WAS HIS DOING. I DON'T BLAME THE MAN, REALLY. HE STILL BARELY EVEN KNOWS ME.
YEAH, BUT THESE ROOMS HAVE OPEN WALLS. HE CAN HEAR EVERY WORD WE SAY IN THERE--AMONG OTHER THINGS THAT WOULD GO ON IN THAT ROOM.
EH-- I'M NOT SO SURE HE CAN HEAR EVERYTHING.
STILL, I KNOW THIS PLACE IS SAFER-- AND IT'S SMARTER TO LIVE HERE...BUT I REALLY MISS MY ROOM, OUR HOUSE...THE FARM IN GENERAL.
I'M MORE THAN A LITTLE SHOCKED THAT HE'S LETTING US SHARE A ROOM. THAT'S PRETTY COOL OF HIM TO DO.
NO IT'S NOT. I'M AN ADULT... HE NEEDS TO REALIZE THAT. I ROOMED WITH A GUY IN COLLEGE. I'M SURE IN HIS MIND WE'RE JUST ROOMMATES.
SUITS ME JUST FINE. AS LONG AS WE CAN BE TOGETHER I DON'T CARE WHAT HE HAS TO TELL HIMSELF.
COLLEGE, HUH? I DIDN'T KNOW THAT.
ONE MEASLY SEMESTER. WE KINDA RAN OUT OF MONEY AROUND THE SAME TIME I FLUNKED OUT. I USUALLY PICK THE REASON BASED ON HOW WELL I KNOW THE PERSON.

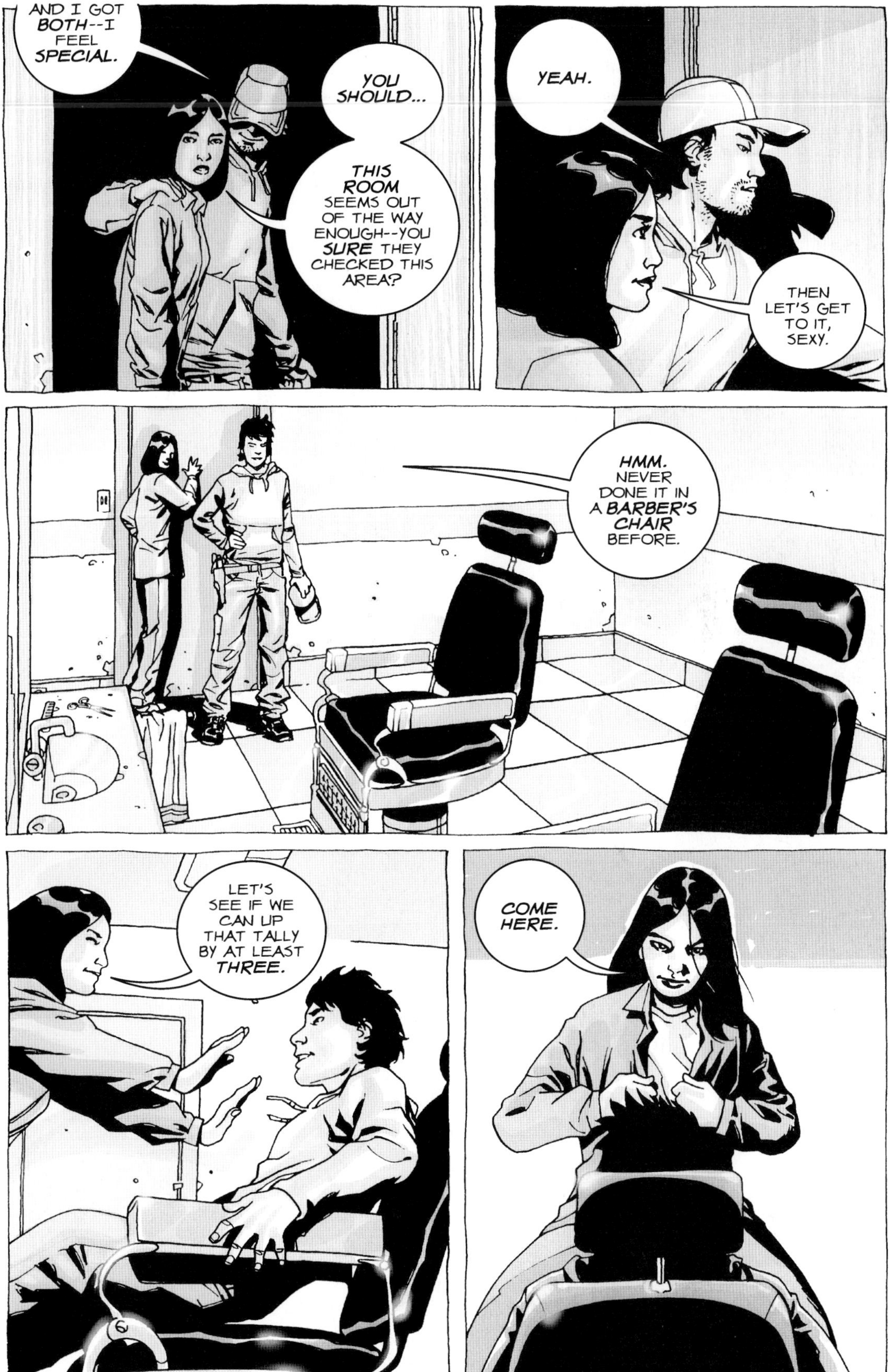
AND I GOT BOTH--I FEEL SPECIAL.
YOU SHOULD...
THIS ROOM SEEMS OUT OF THE WAY ENOUGH--YOU SURE THEY CHECKED THIS AREA?
YEAH.
THEN LET'S GET TO IT, SEXY.
HMM. NEVER DONE IT IN A BARBER'S CHAIR BEFORE.
LET'S SEE IF WE CAN UP THAT TALLY BY AT LEAST THREE.
COME HERE.

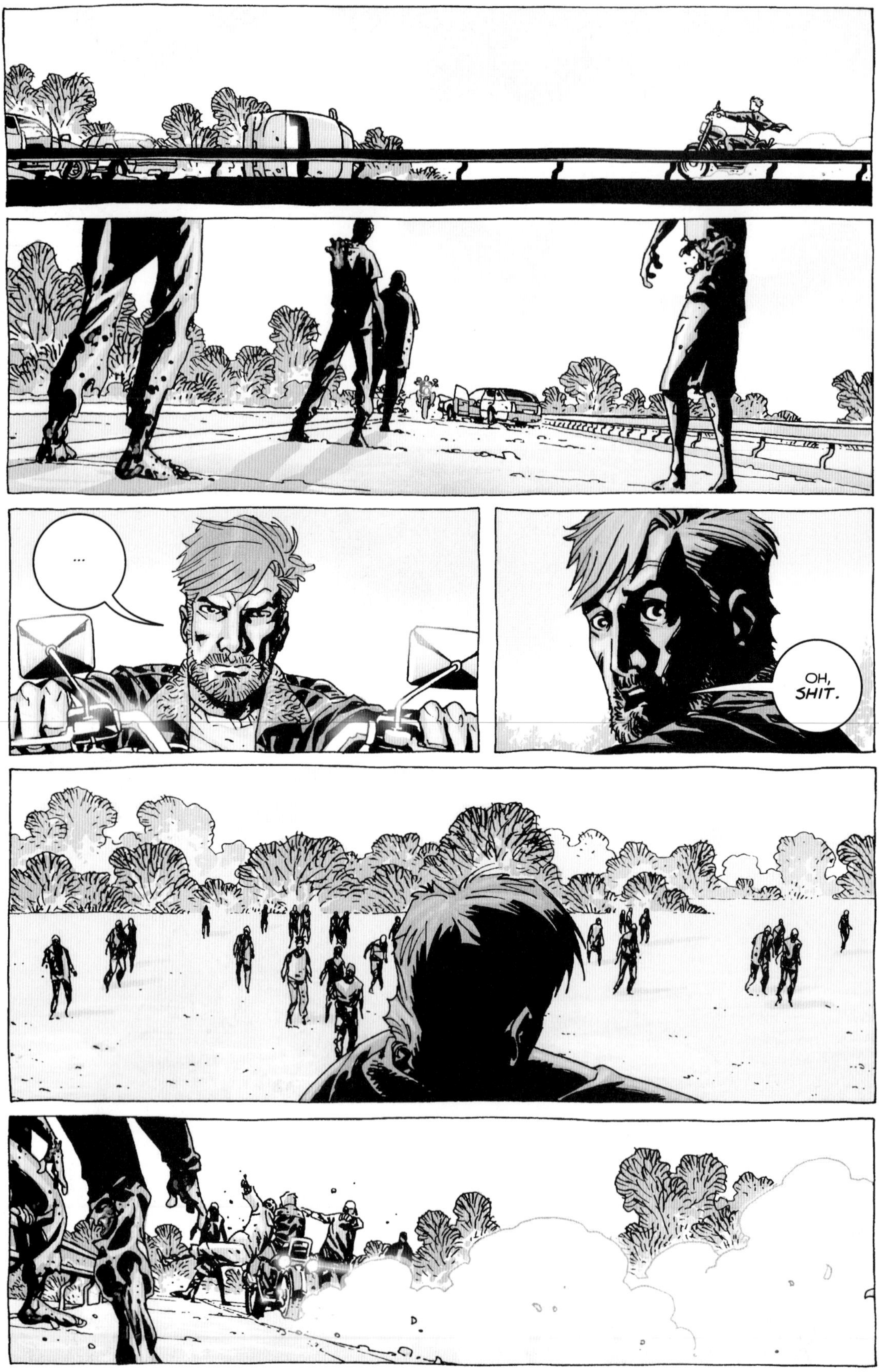
...
OH, SHIT.

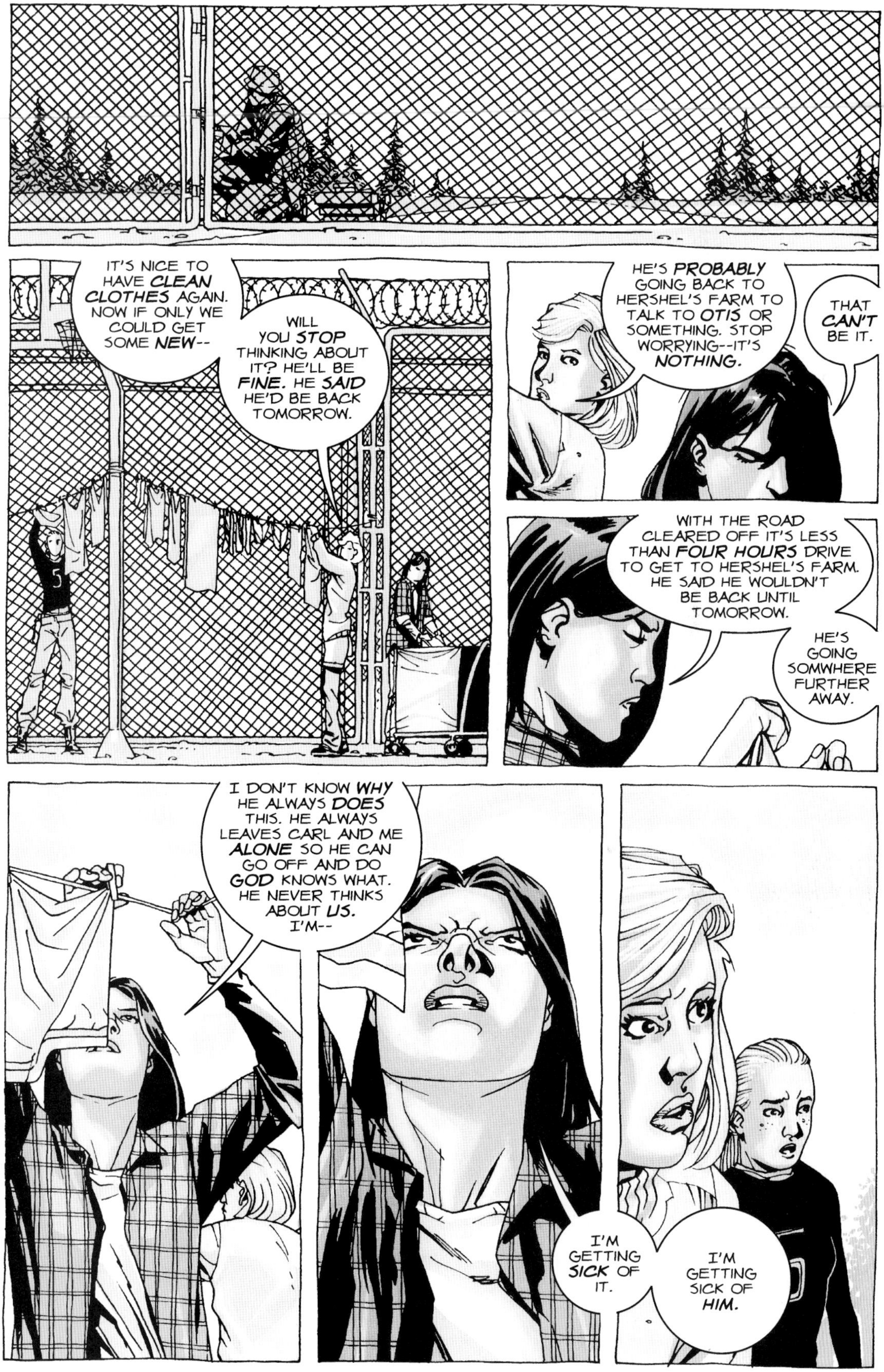

IT'S NICE TO HAVE CLEAN CLOTHES AGAIN. NOW IF ONLY WE COULD GET SOME NEW--
WILL YOU STOP THINKING ABOUT IT? HE'LL BE FINE. HE SAID HE'D BE BACK TOMORROW.
HE'S PROBABLY GOING BACK TO HERSHEL'S FARM TO TALK TO OTIS OR SOMETHING. STOP WORRYING--IT'S NOTHING.
THAT CAN'T BE IT.
WITH THE ROAD CLEARED OFF IT'S LESS THAN FOUR HOURS DRIVE TO GET TO HERSHEL'S FARM. HE SAID HE WOULDN'T BE BACK UNTIL TOMORROW.
HE'S GOING SOMWHERE FURTHER AWAY.
I DON'T KNOW WHY HE ALWAYS DOES THIS. HE ALWAYS LEAVES CARL AND ME ALONE SO HE CAN GO OFF AND DO GOD KNOWS WHAT. HE NEVER THINKS ABOUT US. I'M--
I'M GETTING SICK OF IT.
I'M GETTING SICK OF HIM.

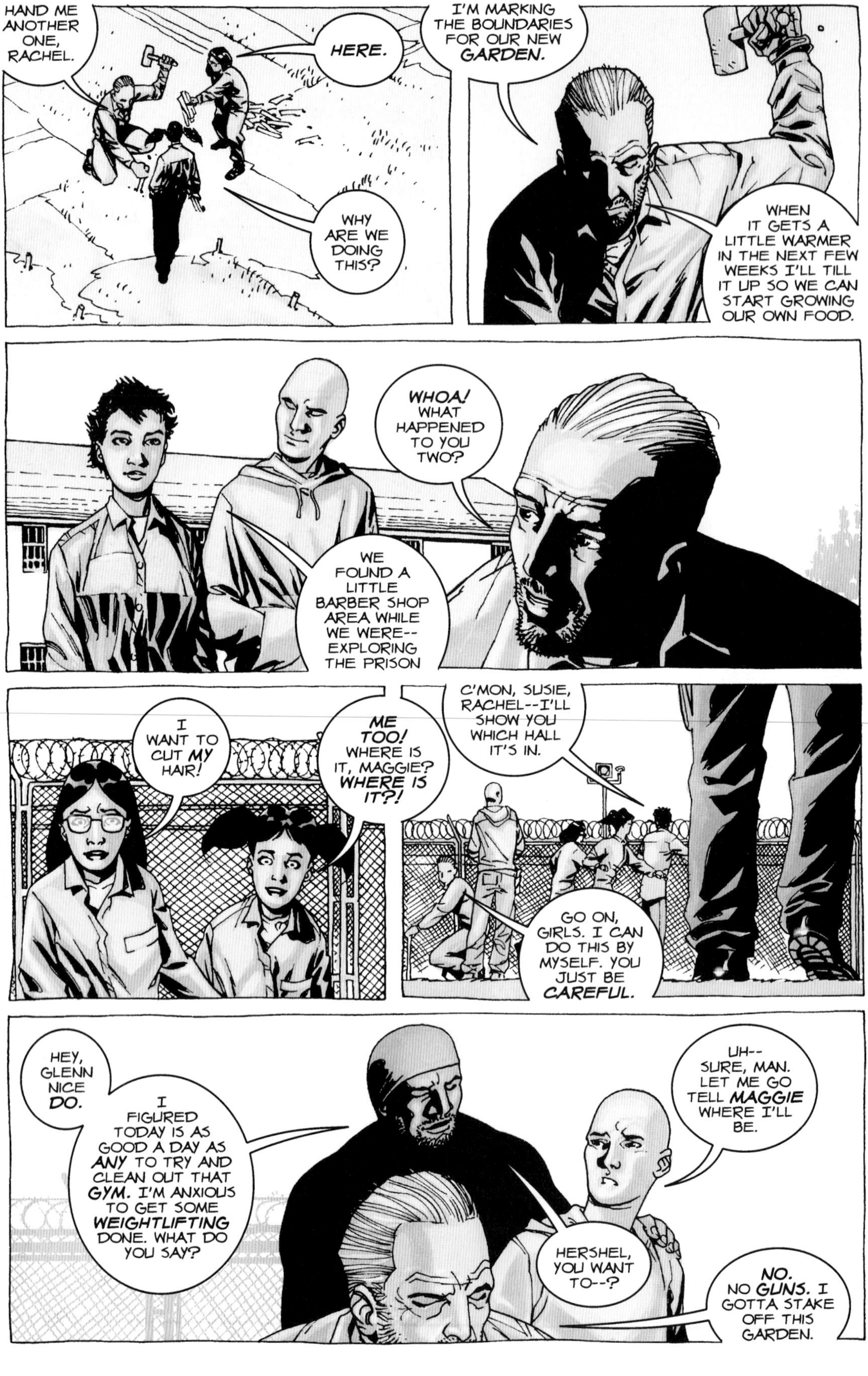
HAND ME ANOTHER ONE, RACHEL.
HERE.
WHY ARE WE DOING THIS?
I'M MARKING THE BOUNDARIES FOR OUR NEW GARDEN.
WHEN IT GETS A LITTLE WARMER IN THE NEXT FEW WEEKS I'LL TILL IT UP SO WE CAN START GROWING OUR OWN FOOD.
WHOA! WHAT HAPPENED TO YOU TWO?
WE FOUND A LITTLE BARBER SHOP AREA WHILE WE WERE-- EXPLORING THE PRISON
I WANT TO CUT MY HAIR!
ME TOO! WHERE IS IT, MAGGIE? WHERE IS IT?!
C'MON, SUSIE, RACHEL--I'LL SHOW YOU WHICH HALL IT'S IN.
GO ON, GIRLS. I CAN DO THIS BY MYSELF. YOU JUST BE CAREFUL.
HEY, GLENN NICE DO.
I FIGURED TODAY IS AS GOOD A DAY AS ANY TO TRY AND CLEAN OUT THAT GYM. I'M ANXIOUS TO GET SOME WEIGHTLIFTING DONE. WHAT DO YOU SAY?
UH-- SURE, MAN. LET ME GO TELL MAGGIE WHERE I'LL BE.
HERSHEL, YOU WANT TO--?
NO. NO GUNS. I GOTTA STAKE OFF THIS GARDEN.

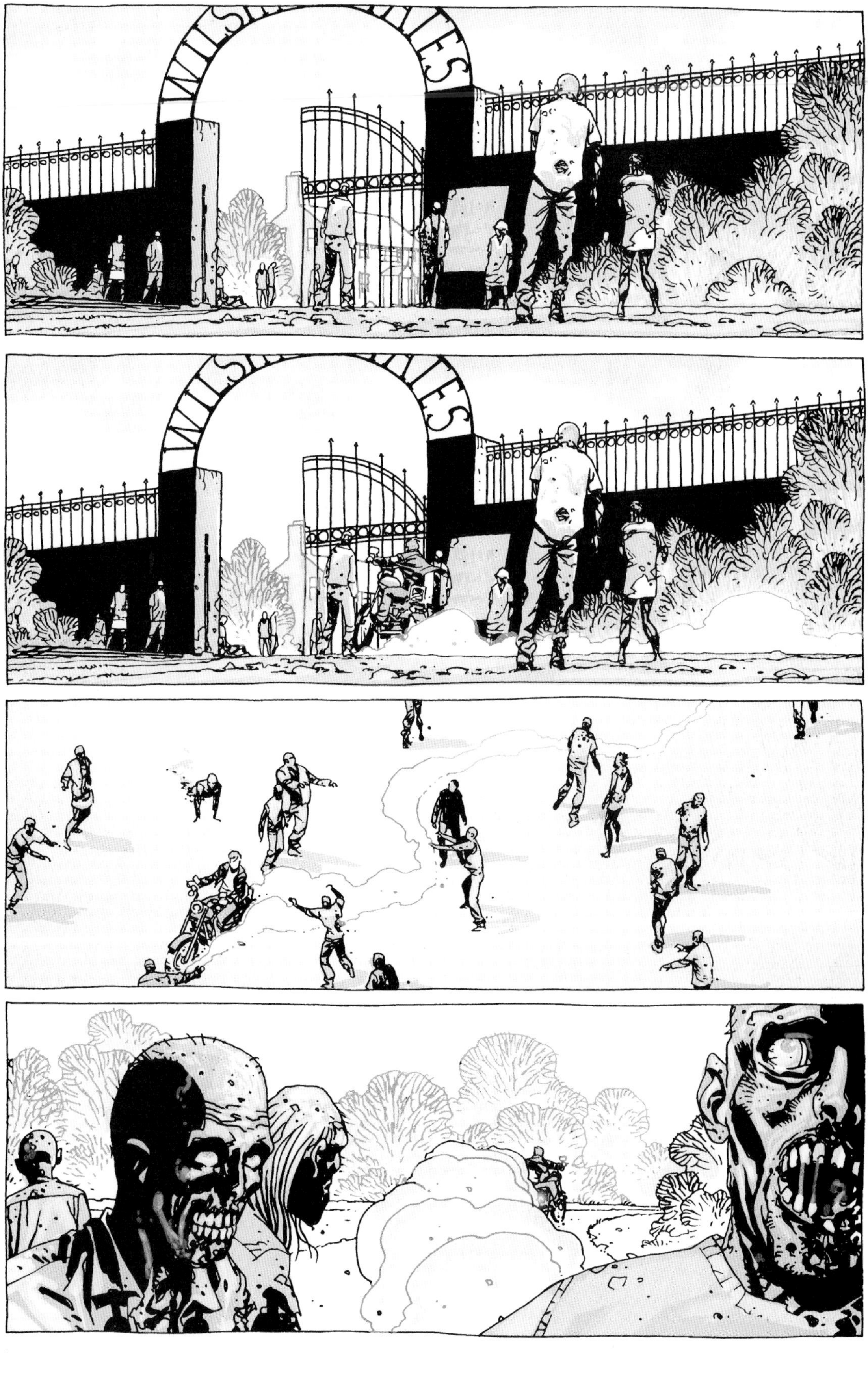

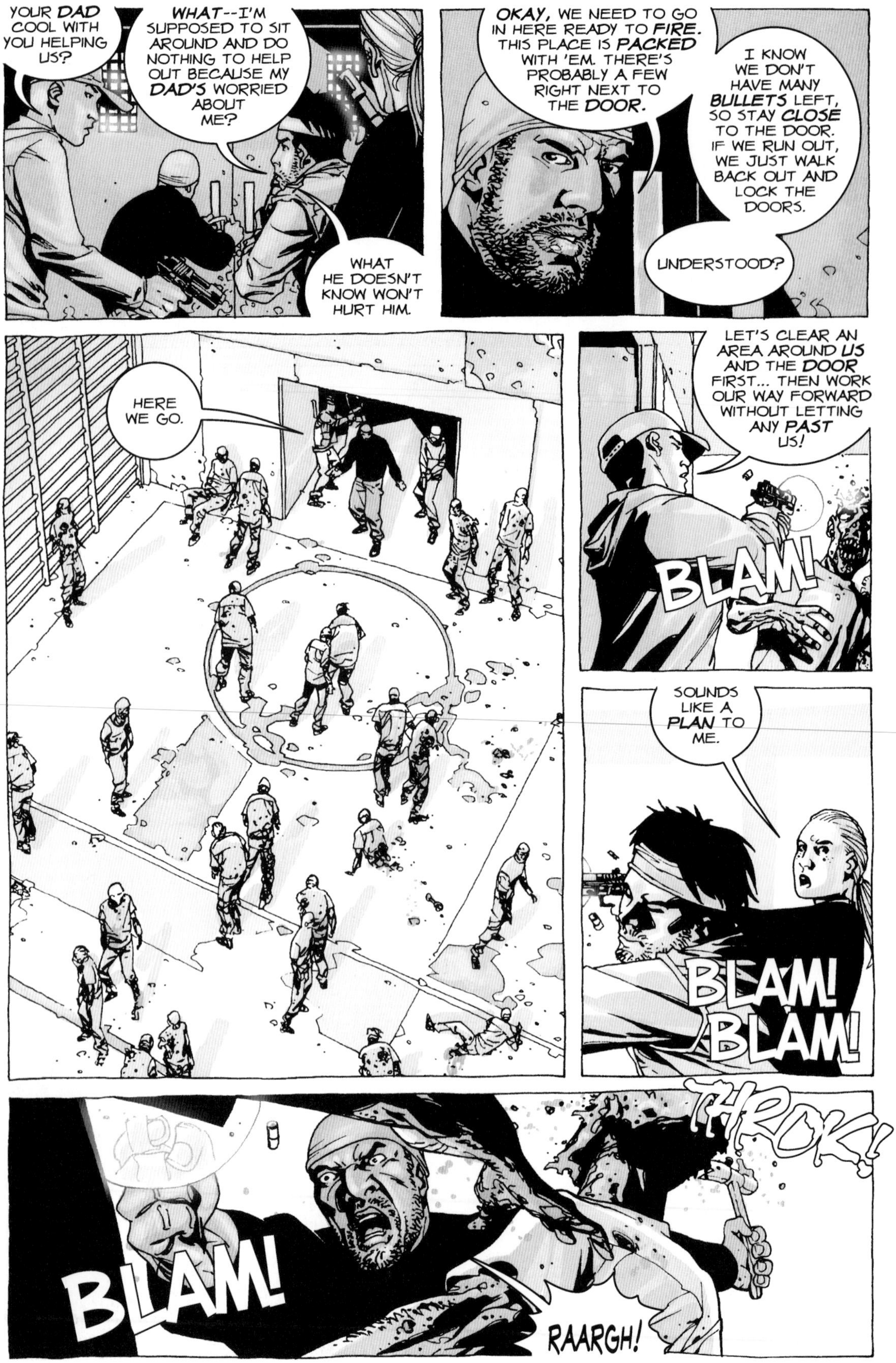
YOUR DAD COOL WITH YOU HELPING US?
WHAT--I'M SUPPOSED TO SIT AROUND AND DO NOTHING TO HELP OUT BECAUSE MY DAD'S WORRIED ABOUT ME?
WHAT HE DOESN'T KNOW WON'T HURT HIM.
OKAY, WE NEED TO GO IN HERE READY TO FIRE. THIS PLACE IS PACKED WITH 'EM. THERE'S PROBABLY A FEW RIGHT NEXT TO THE DOOR.
I KNOW WE DON'T HAVE MANY BULLETS LEFT, SO STAY CLOSE TO THE DOOR. IF WE RUN OUT, WE JUST WALK BACK OUT AND LOCK THE DOORS.
UNDERSTOOD?
HERE WE GO.
LET'S CLEAR AN AREA AROUND US AND THE DOOR FIRST... THEN WORK OUR WAY FORWARD WITHOUT LETTING ANY PAST US!
BLAM!
SOUNDS LIKE A PLAN TO ME.
BLAM!
BLAM!
THOK!
BLAM!
RAARGH!

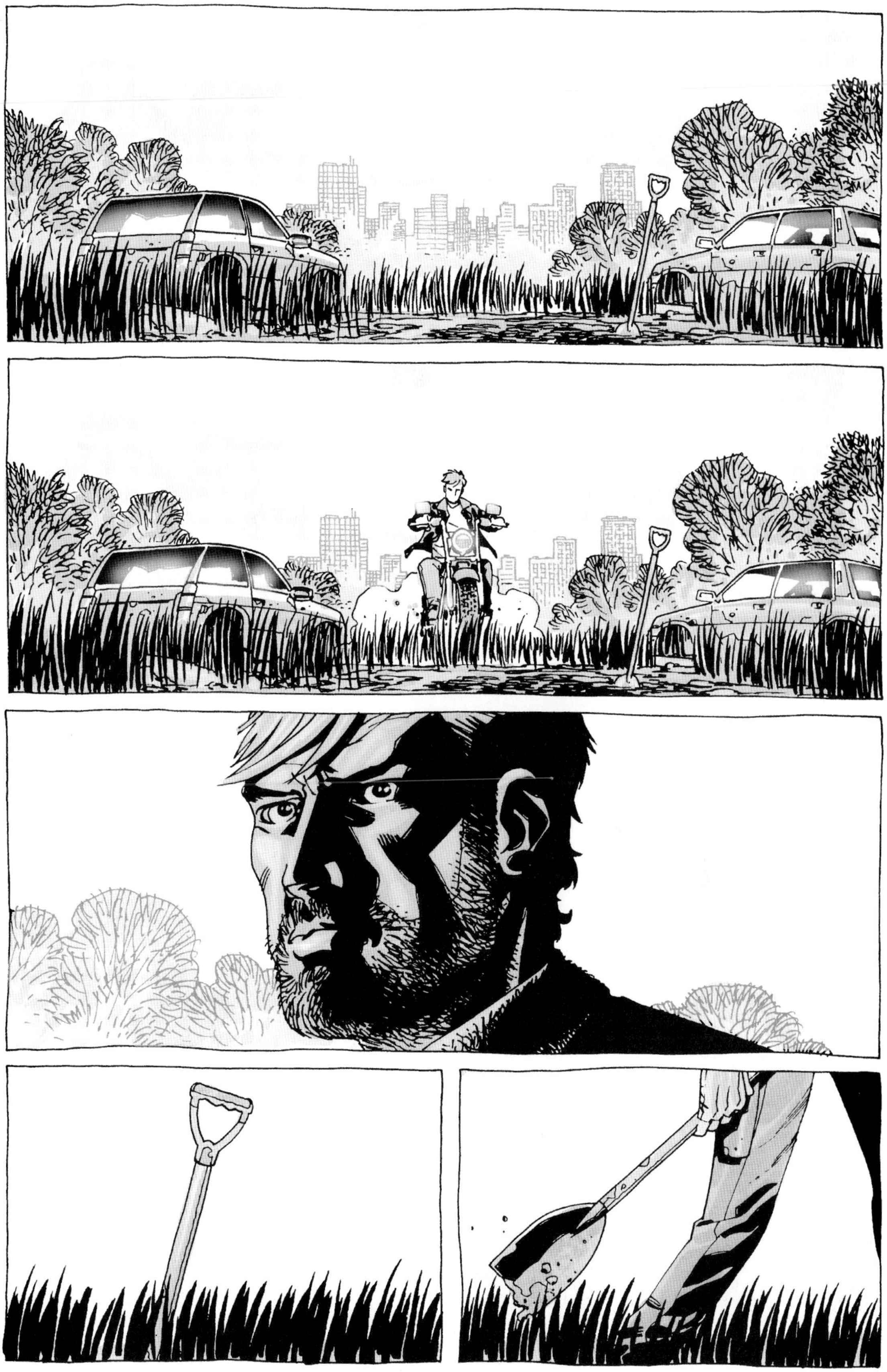

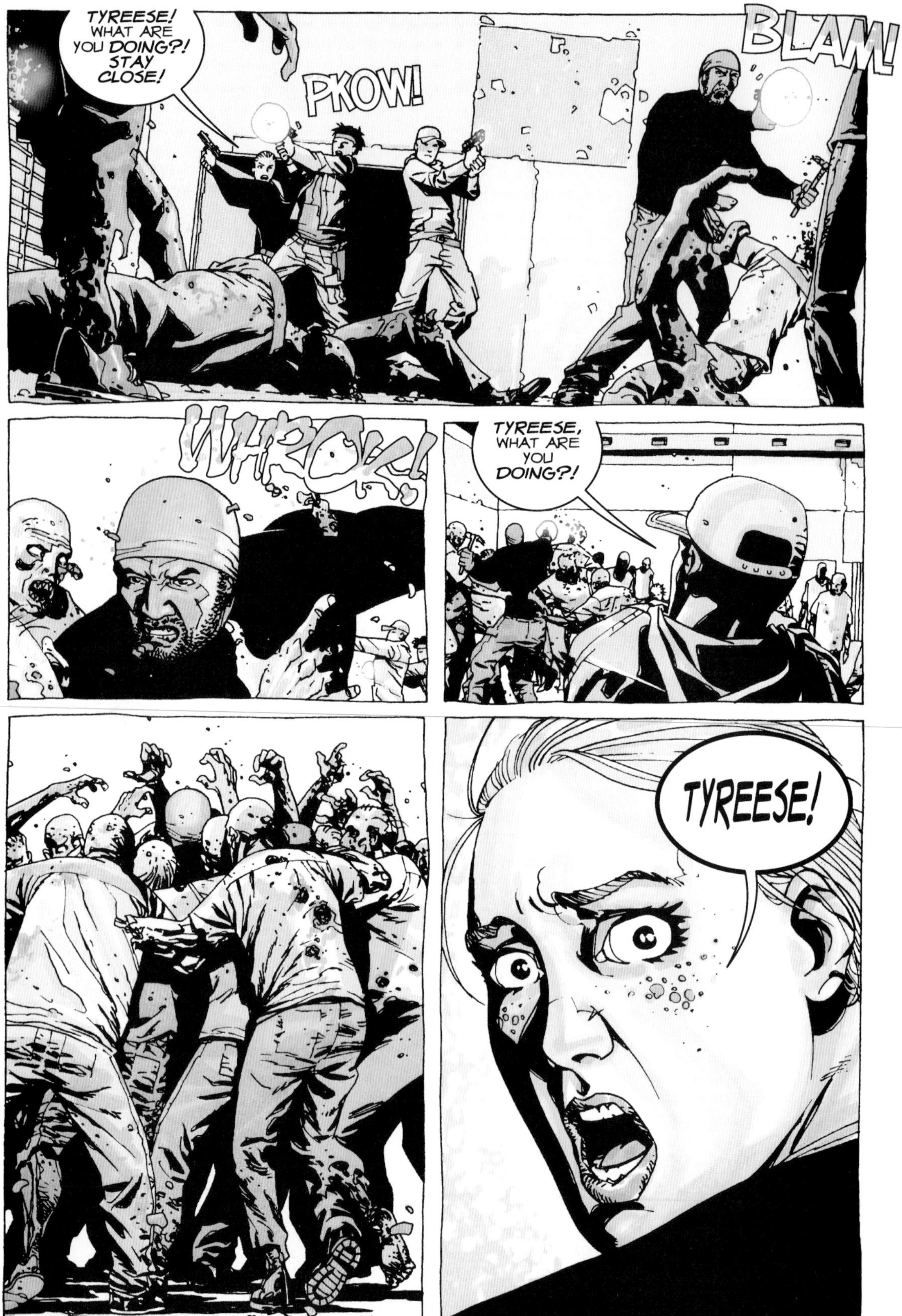
TYREESE! WHAT ARE YOU DOING?! STAY CLOSE!
PKOW!
BLAM!
WHROK!
TYREESE, WHAT ARE YOU DOING?!
TYREESE!

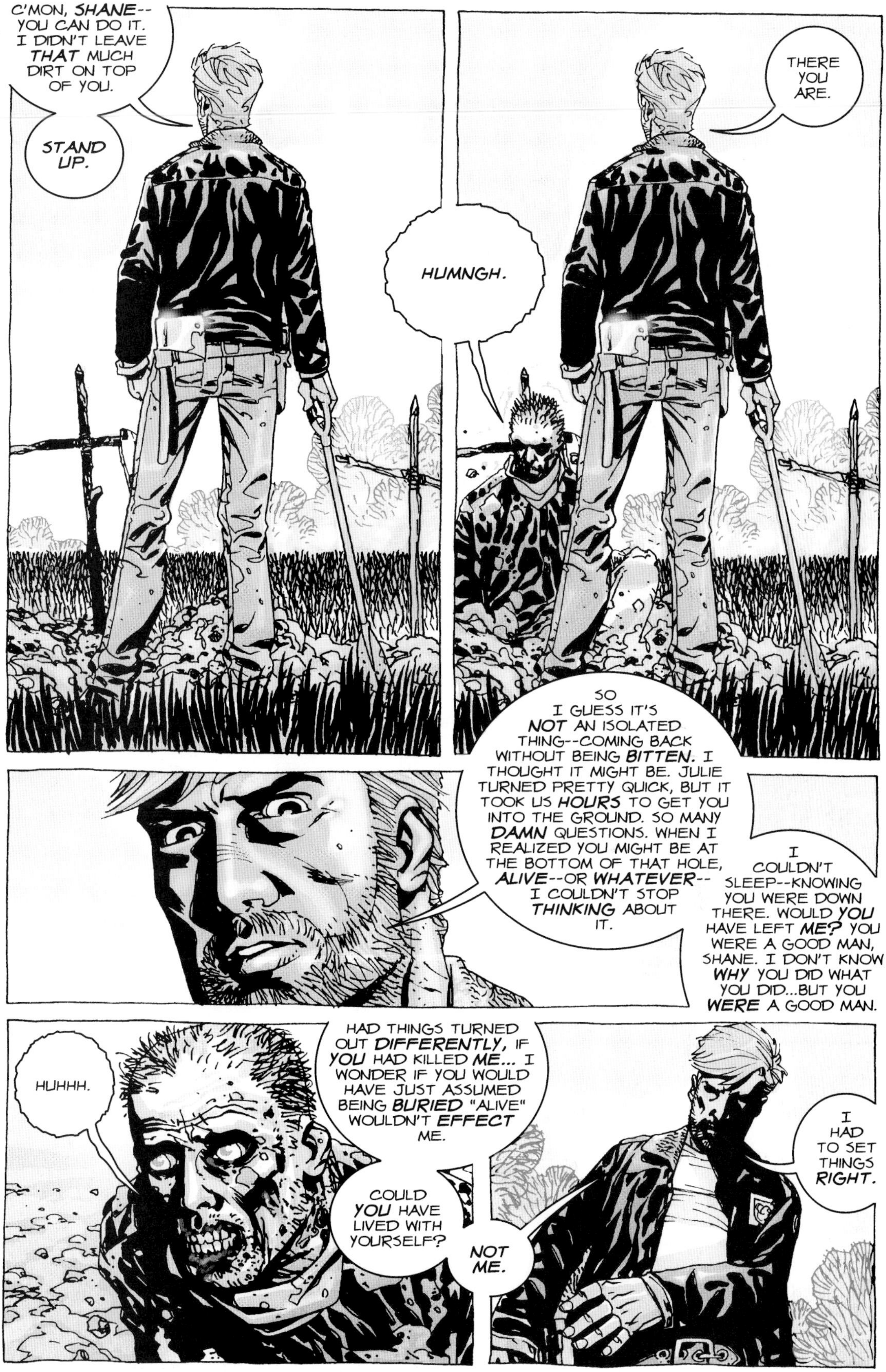
C'MON, SHANE--YOU CAN DO IT. I DIDN'T LEAVE THAT MUCH DIRT ON TOP OF YOU.
STAND UP.
THERE YOU ARE.
HUMNGH.
SO I GUESS IT'S NOT AN ISOLATED THING--COMING BACK WITHOUT BEING BITTEN. I THOUGHT IT MIGHT BE. JULIE TURNED PRETTY QUICK, BUT IT TOOK US HOURS TO GET YOU INTO THE GROUND. SO MANY DAMN QUESTIONS. WHEN I REALIZED YOU MIGHT BE AT THE BOTTOM OF THAT HOLE, ALIVE--OR WHATEVER--I COULDN'T STOP THINKING ABOUT IT.
I COULDN'T SLEEP--KNOWING YOU WERE DOWN THERE. WOULD YOU HAVE LEFT ME? YOU WERE A GOOD MAN, SHANE. I DON'T KNOW WHY YOU DID WHAT YOU DID...BUT YOU WERE A GOOD MAN.
HUHHH.
HAD THINGS TURNED OUT DIFFERENTLY, IF YOU HAD KILLED ME... I WONDER IF YOU WOULD HAVE JUST ASSUMED BEING BURIED "ALIVE" WOULDN'T EFFECT ME.
COULD YOU HAVE LIVED WITH YOURSELF?
NOT ME.
I HAD TO SET THINGS RIGHT.

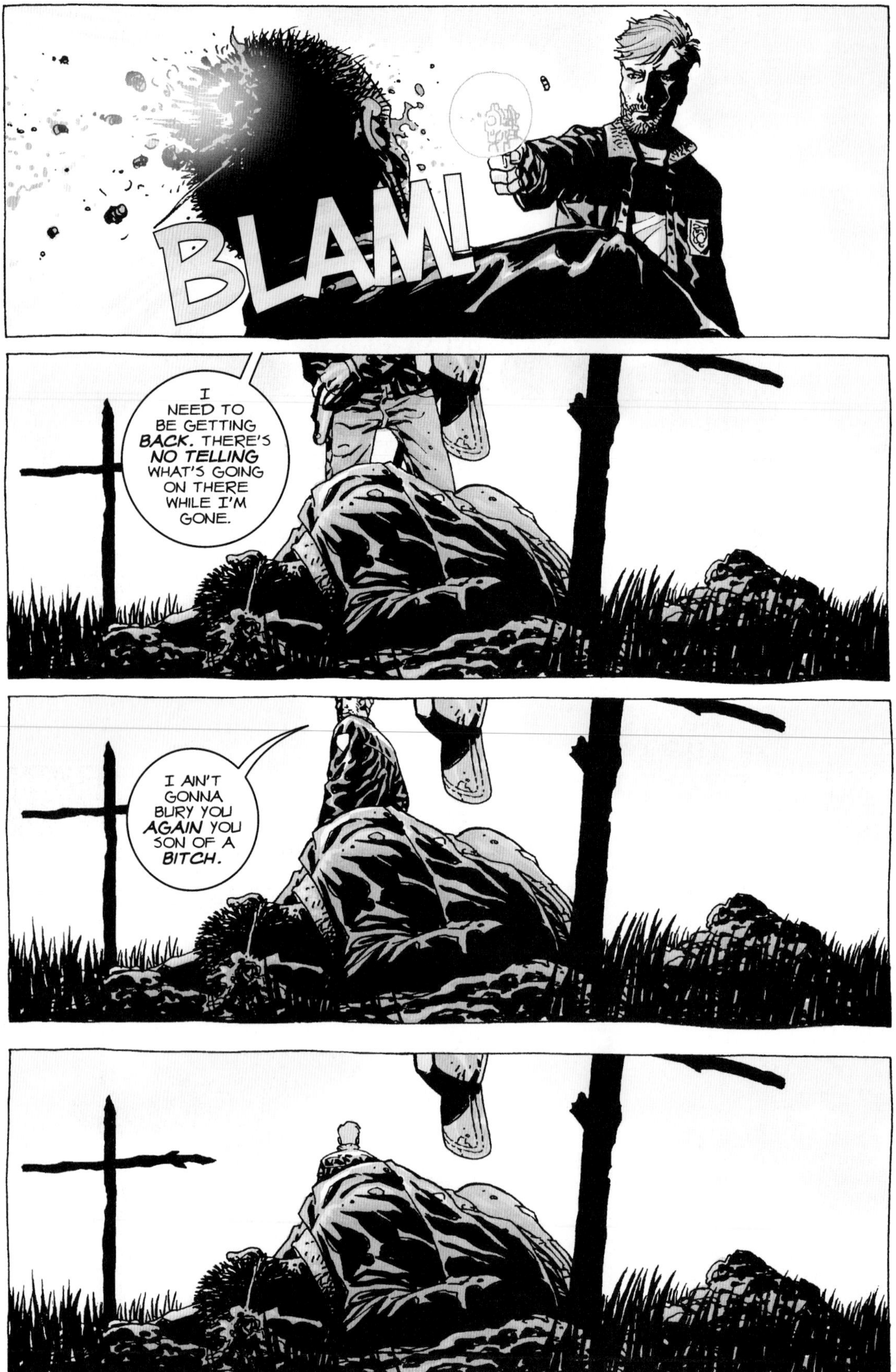
BLAM!
I NEED TO BE GETTING BACK. THERE'S NO TELLING WHAT'S GOING ON THERE WHILE I'M GONE.
I AIN'T GONNA BURY YOU AGAIN YOU SON OF A BITCH.

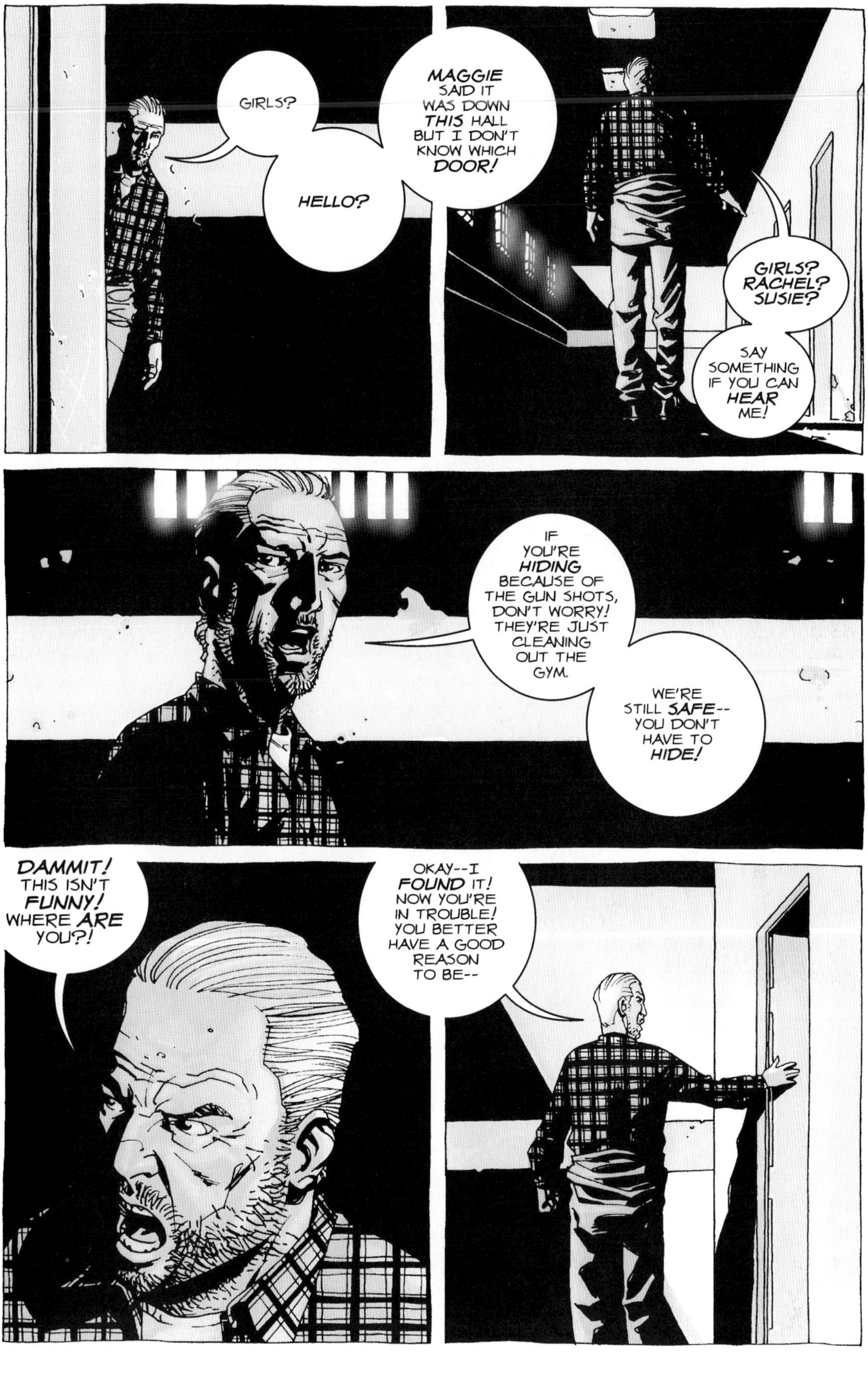
GIRLS?
HELLO?
MAGGIE SAID IT WAS DOWN THIS HALL BUT I DON'T KNOW WHICH DOOR!
GIRLS? RACHEL? SUSIE?
SAY SOMETHING IF YOU CAN HEAR ME!
IF YOU'RE HIDING BECAUSE OF THE GUN SHOTS, DON'T WORRY! THEY'RE JUST CLEANING OUT THE GYM.
WE'RE STILL SAFE-- YOU DON'T HAVE TO HIDE!
DAMMIT! THIS ISN'T FUNNY! WHERE ARE YOU?!
OKAY--I FOUND IT! NOW YOU'RE IN TROUBLE! YOU BETTER HAVE A GOOD REASON TO BE--

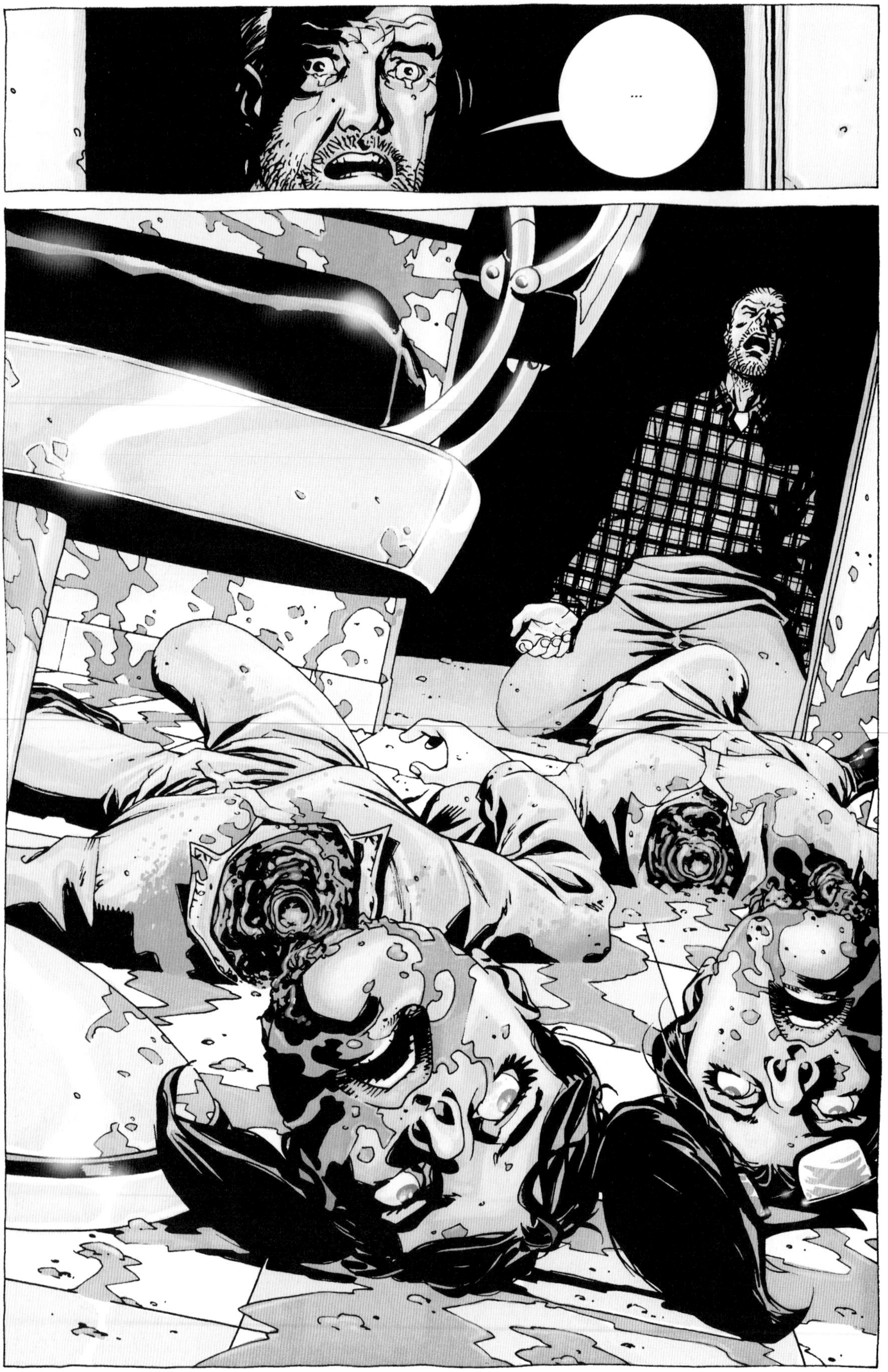
...

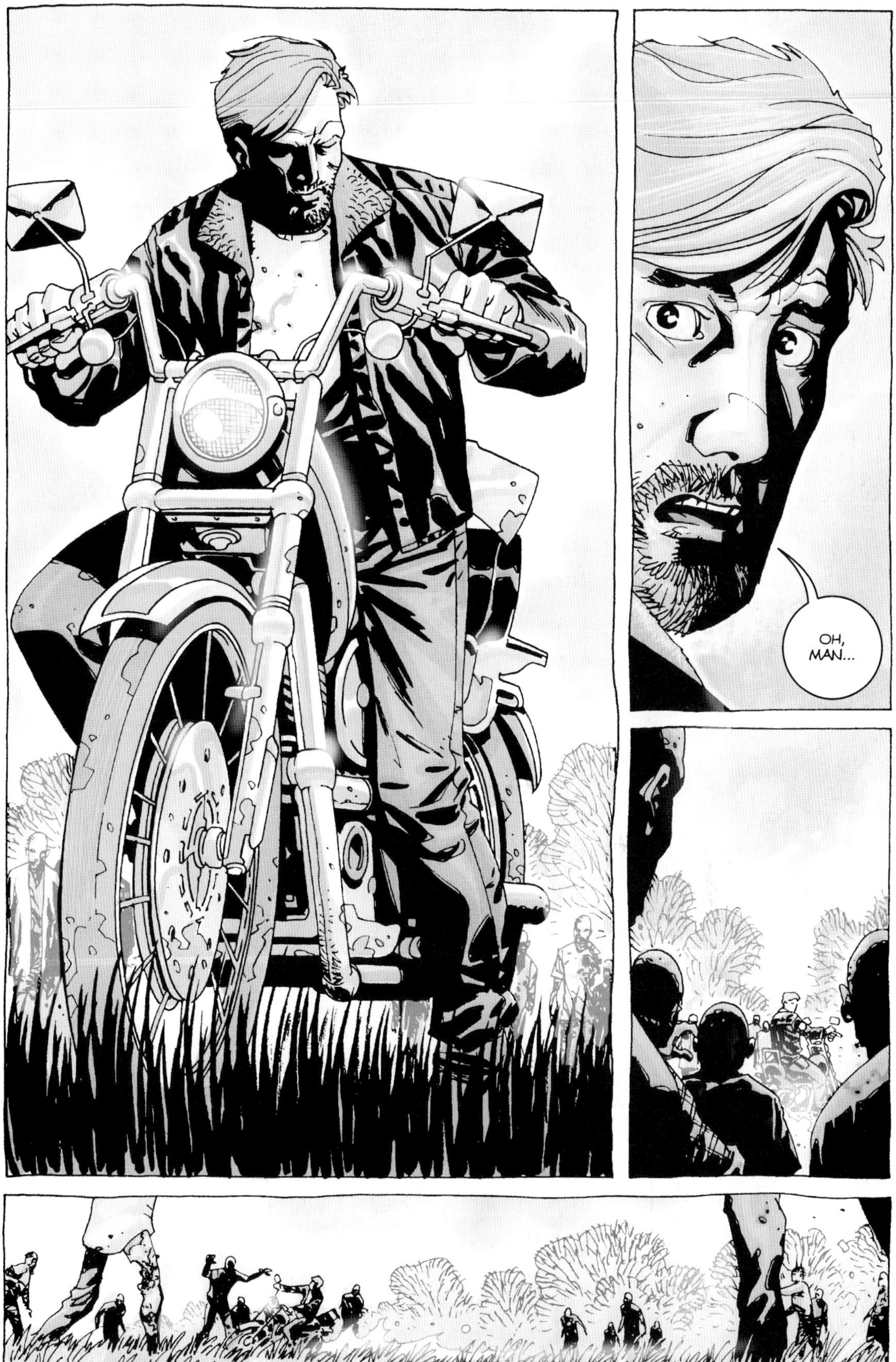
OH,
MAN...

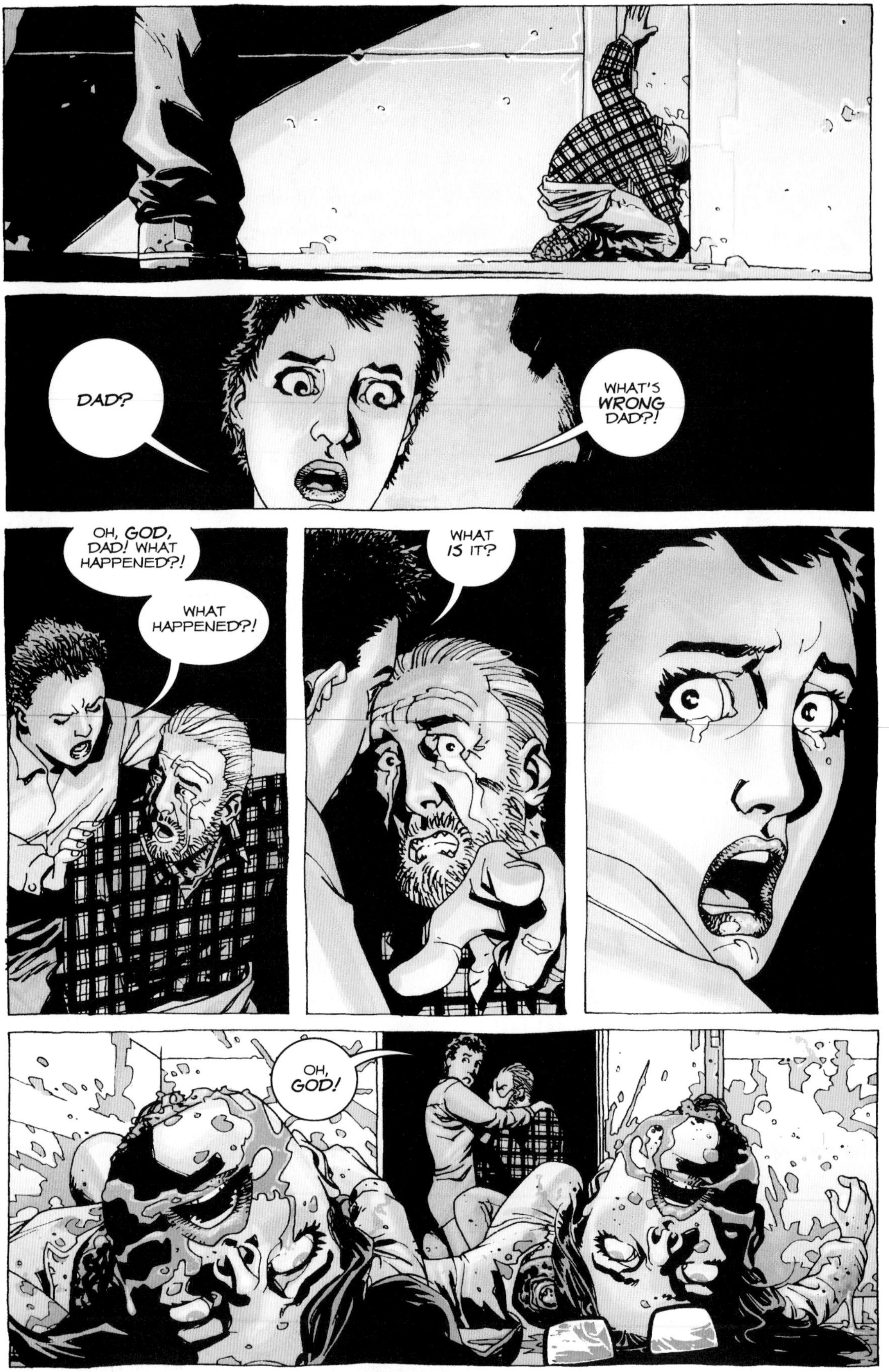
DAD?
WHAT'S WRONG DAD?!
OH, GOD, DAD! WHAT HAPPENED?!
WHAT HAPPENED?!
WHAT IS IT?
OH, GOD!

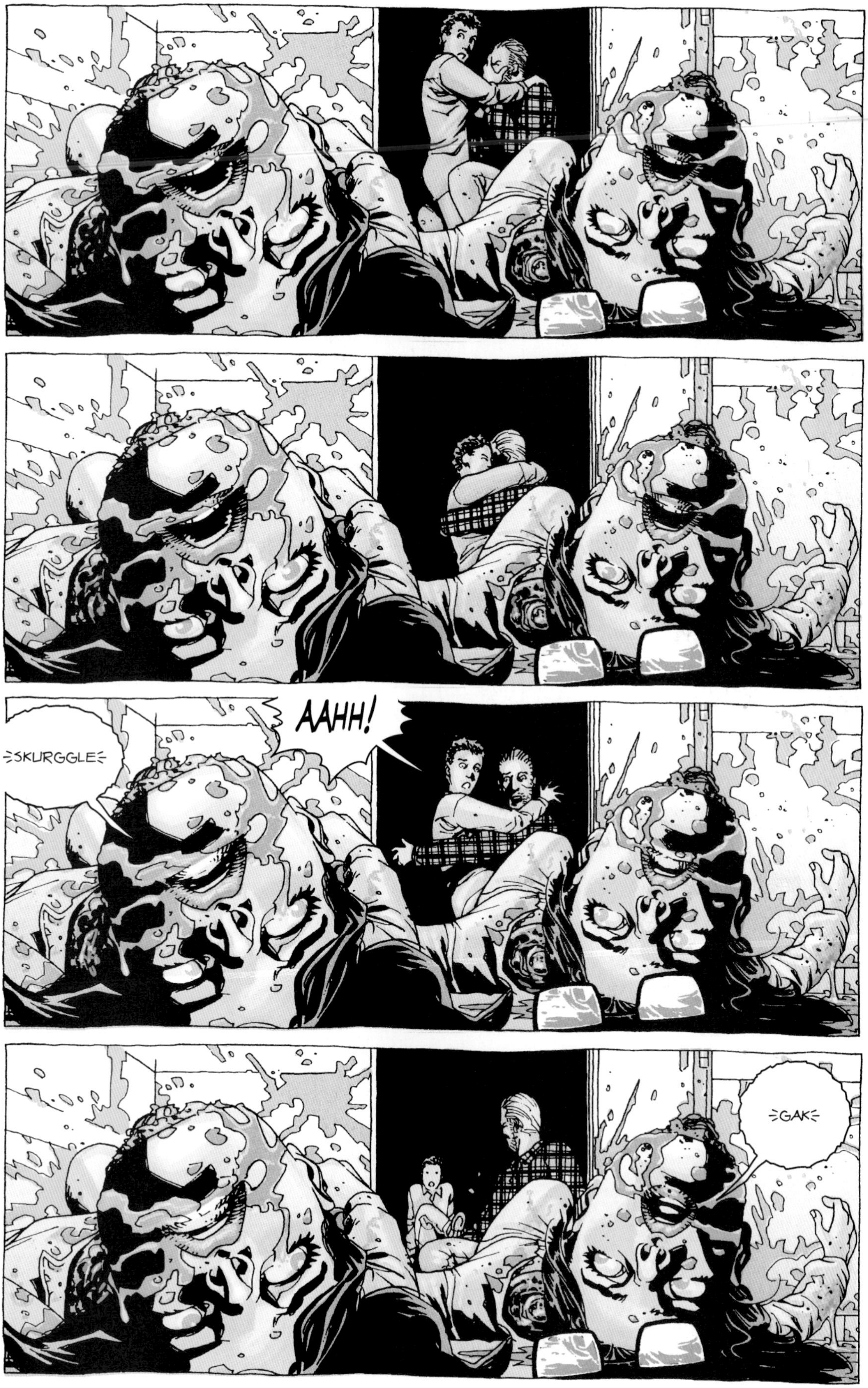

SKURGGLE
AAHH!
GAK

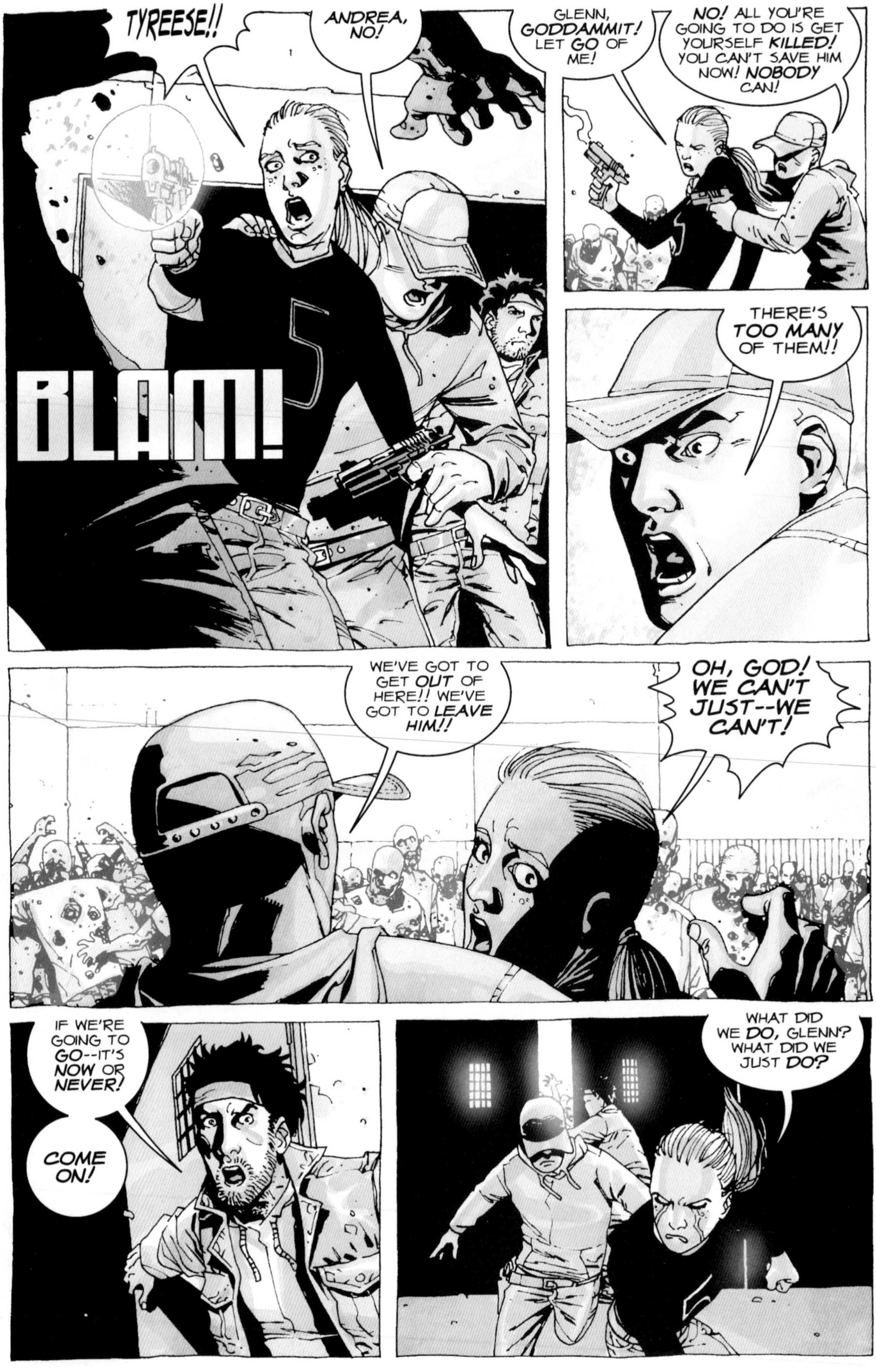
TYREESE!!
ANDREA, NO!
BLAM!
GLENN, GODDAMMIT! LET GO OF ME!
NO! ALL YOU'RE GOING TO DO IS GET YOURSELF KILLED! YOU CAN'T SAVE HIM NOW! NOBODY CAN!
THERE'S TOO MANY OF THEM!!
WE'VE GOT TO GET OUT OF HERE!! WE'VE GOT TO LEAVE HIM!!
OH, GOD! WE CAN'T JUST--WE CAN'T!
IF WE'RE GOING TO GO--IT'S NOW OR NEVER!
COME ON!
WHAT DID WE DO, GLENN? WHAT DID WE JUST DO?

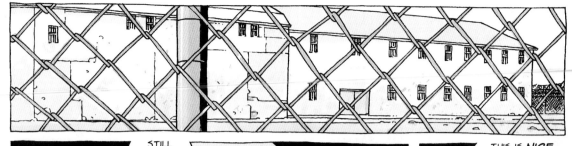

STILL WORRIED ABOUT RICK?

A *LITTLE.* I'M TRYING NOT TO *THINK* ABOUT IT, ACTUALLY.

SORRY.

SO IT WAS NICE OF DALE TO OFFER TO WATCH THE KIDS SO WE COULD CLEAN UP...

YEAH...

THIS IS *NICE* ISN'T IT? I STILL CAN'T GET OVER THE FACT THAT THIS PLACE STILL HAS *RUNNING WATER.*

I *SERIOUSLY* DOUBT THE WATER IS *TREATED* MUCH AT THIS POINT. IT'S STILL COMING TO US, BUT I DON'T THINK IT'S *CLEAN* ENOUGH TO DRINK WITHOUT BOILING.

UH-HUH.

IT DOESN'T *STINK,* THOUGH... SO I DON'T MIND SHOWERING IN--

AAAIIIEEEEK!!

I'M *SORRY! I'M SORRY!* I DIDN'T KNOW ANYONE WAS IN HERE! I *SWEAR!*

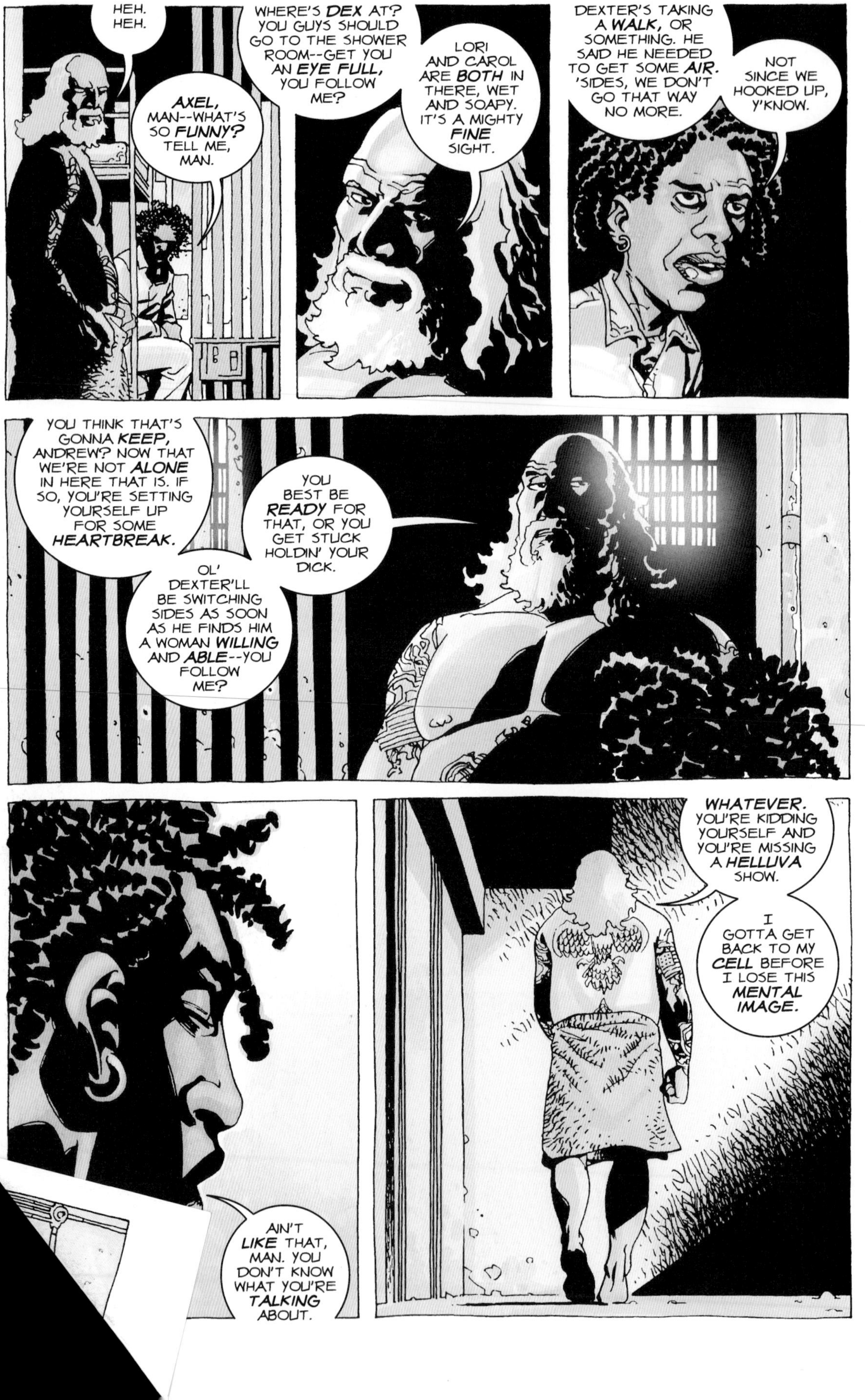
HEH. HEH.
AXEL, MAN--WHAT'S SO FUNNY? TELL ME, MAN.
WHERE'S DEX AT? YOU GUYS SHOULD GO TO THE SHOWER ROOM--GET YOU AN EYE FULL, YOU FOLLOW ME?
LORI AND CAROL ARE BOTH IN THERE, WET AND SOAPY. IT'S A MIGHTY FINE SIGHT.
DEXTER'S TAKING A WALK, OR SOMETHING. HE SAID HE NEEDED TO GET SOME AIR. 'SIDES, WE DON'T GO THAT WAY NO MORE.
NOT SINCE WE HOOKED UP, Y'KNOW.
YOU THINK THAT'S GONNA KEEP, ANDREW? NOW THAT WE'RE NOT ALONE IN HERE THAT IS. IF SO, YOU'RE SETTING YOURSELF UP FOR SOME HEARTBREAK.
OL' DEXTER'LL BE SWITCHING SIDES AS SOON AS HE FINDS HIM A WOMAN WILLING AND ABLE--YOU FOLLOW ME?
YOU BEST BE READY FOR THAT, OR YOU GET STUCK HOLDIN' YOUR DICK.
AIN'T LIKE THAT, MAN. YOU DON'T KNOW WHAT YOU'RE TALKING ABOUT.
WHATEVER. YOU'RE KIDDING YOURSELF AND YOU'RE MISSING A HELLUVA SHOW.
I GOTTA GET BACK TO MY CELL BEFORE I LOSE THIS MENTAL IMAGE.

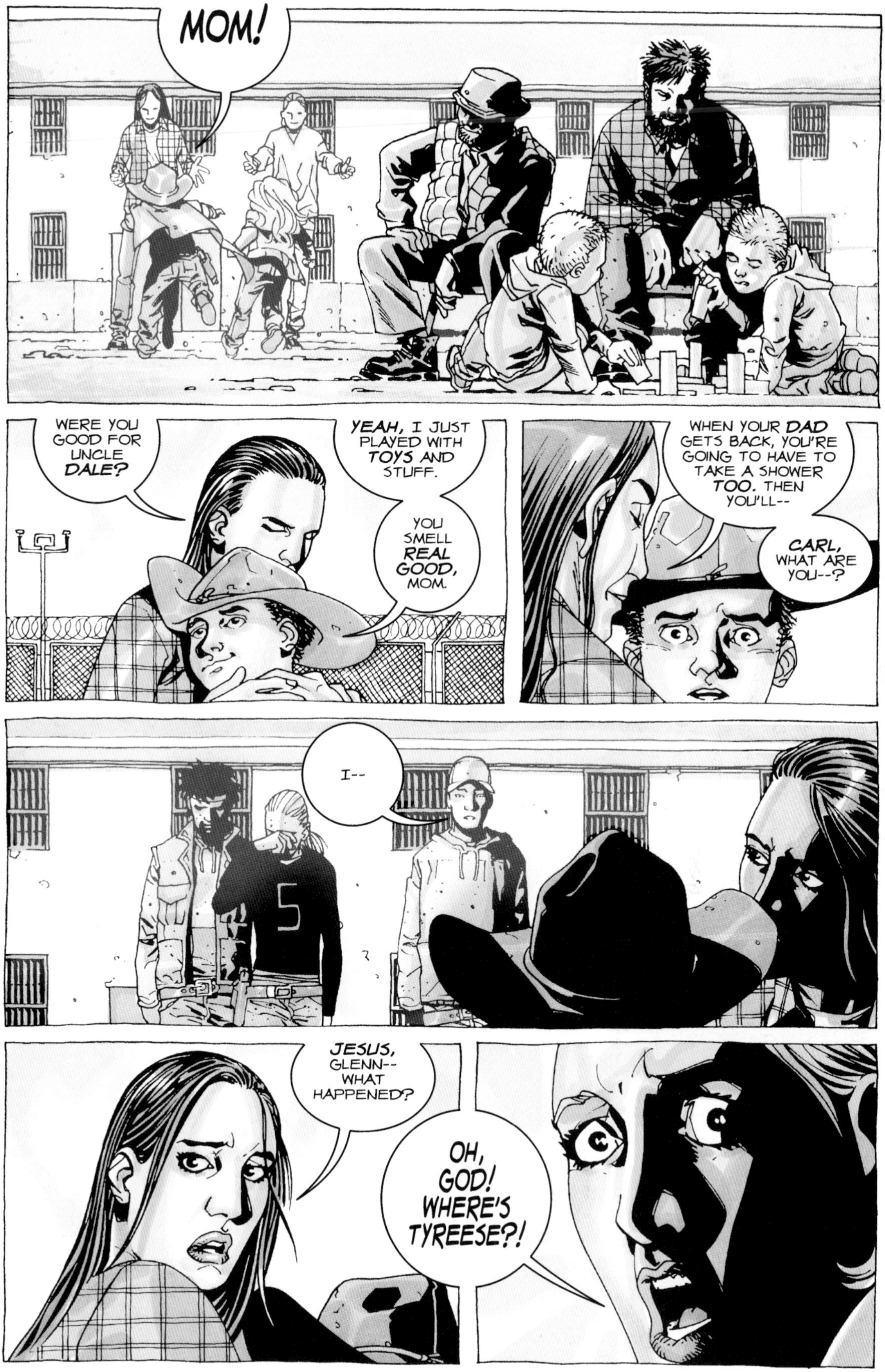
MOM!
WERE YOU GOOD FOR UNCLE DALE?
YEAH, I JUST PLAYED WITH TOYS AND STUFF.
YOU SMELL REAL GOOD, MOM.
WHEN YOUR DAD GETS BACK, YOU'RE GOING TO HAVE TO TAKE A SHOWER TOO. THEN YOU'LL--
CARL, WHAT ARE YOU--?
I--
JESUS, GLENN-- WHAT HAPPENED?
OH, GOD! WHERE'S TYREESE?!

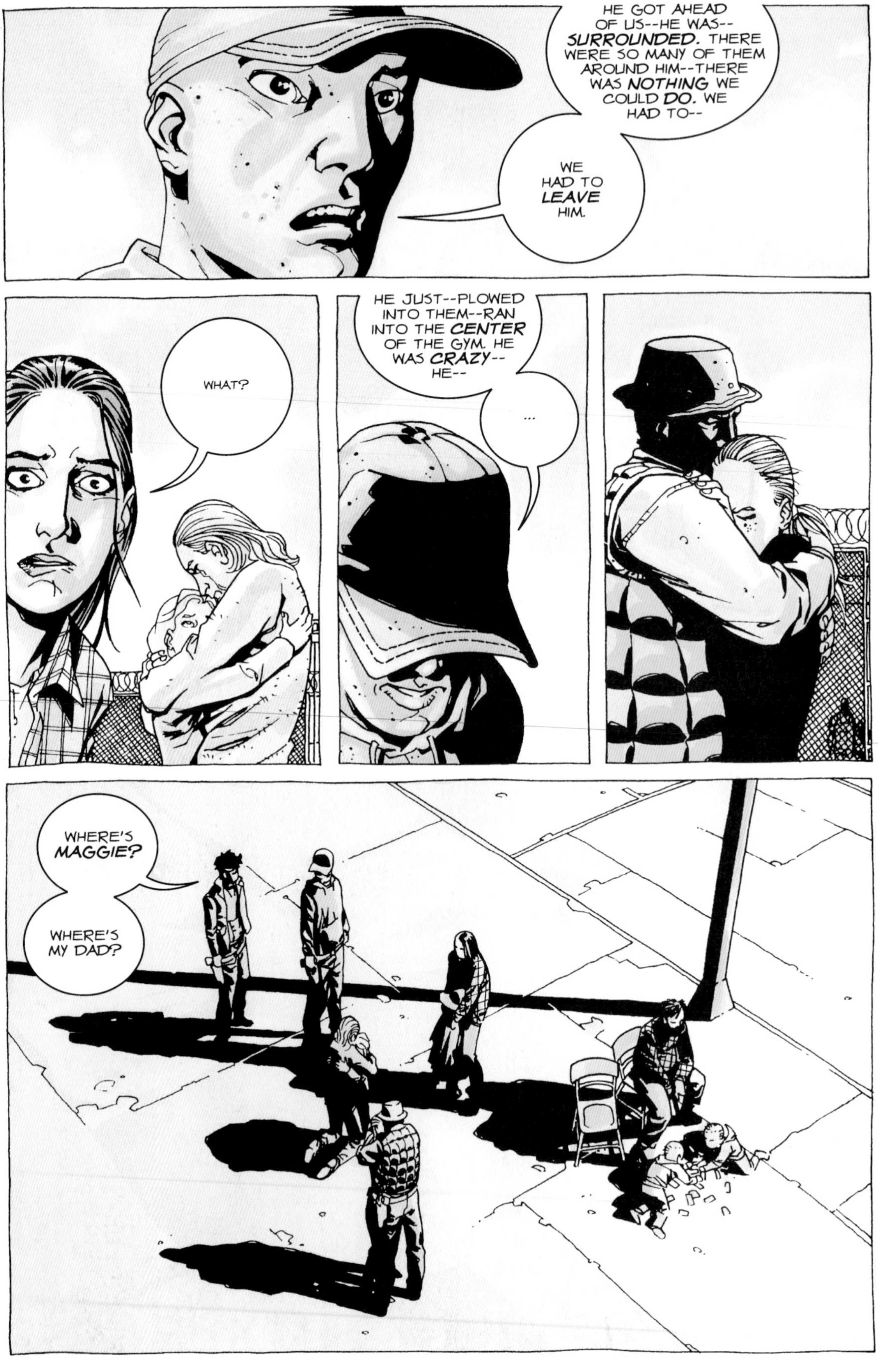
HE GOT AHEAD OF US--HE WAS-- SURROUNDED. THERE WERE SO MANY OF THEM AROUND HIM--THERE WAS NOTHING WE COULD DO. WE HAD TO--
WE HAD TO LEAVE HIM.
WHAT?
HE JUST--PLOWED INTO THEM--RAN INTO THE CENTER OF THE GYM. HE WAS CRAZY-- HE--
...
WHERE'S MAGGIE?
WHERE'S MY DAD?

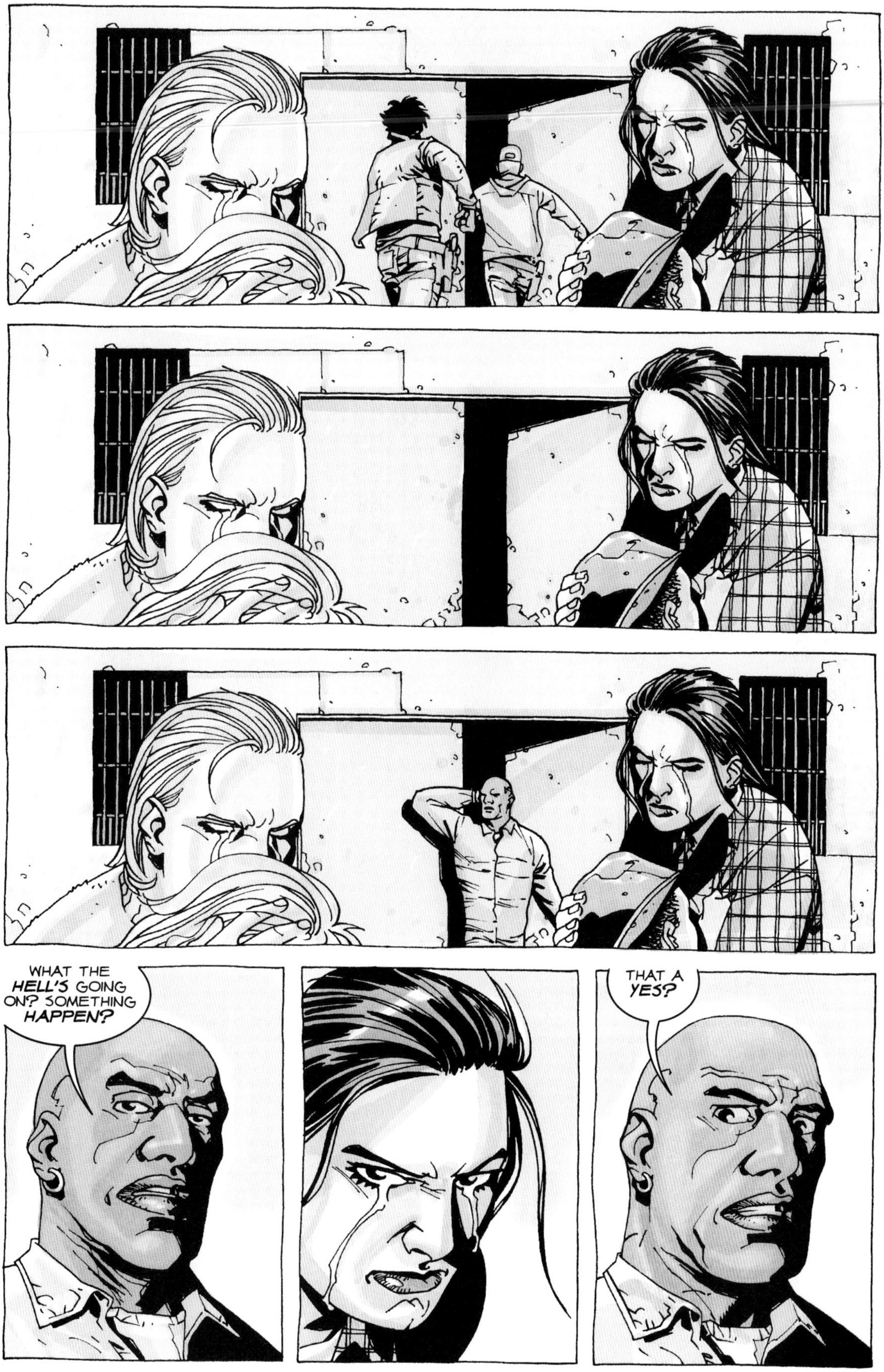
WHAT THE HELL'S GOING ON? SOMETHING HAPPEN?
THAT A YES?

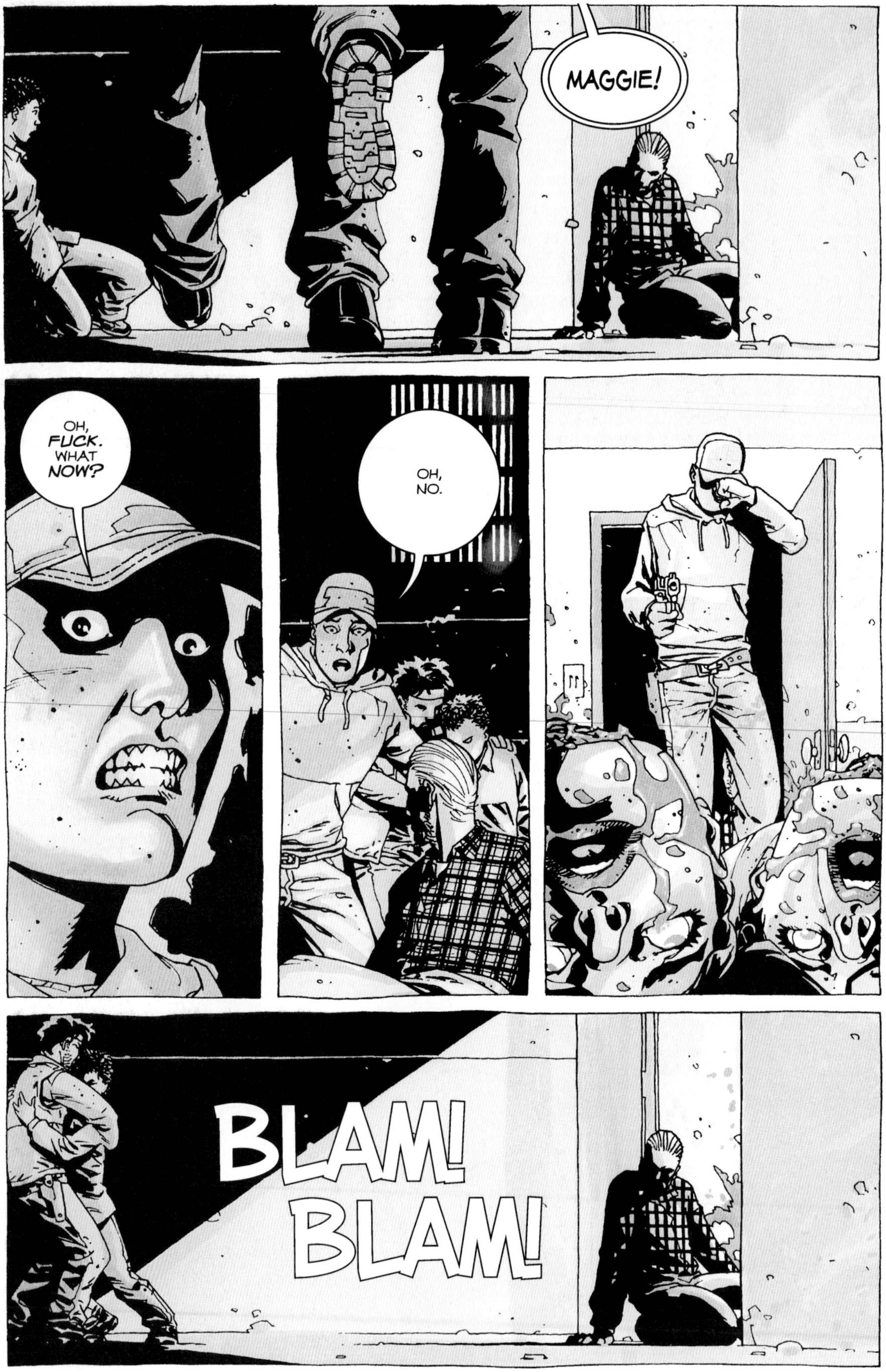
MAGGIE!
OH, FUCK. WHAT NOW?
OH, NO.
BLAM!
BLAM!

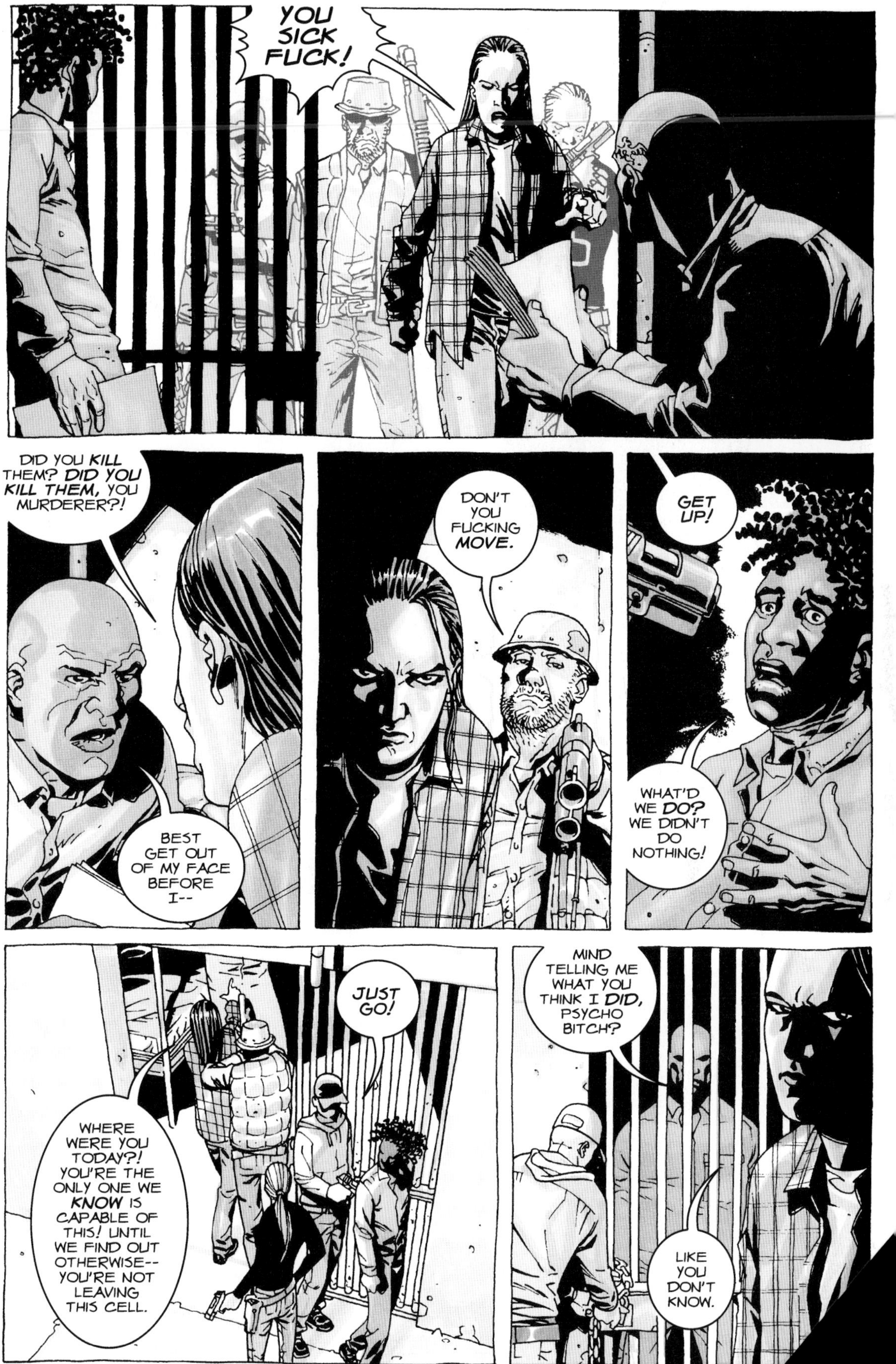
YOU SICK FUCK!
DID YOU KILL THEM? DID YOU KILL THEM, YOU MURDERER?!
BEST GET OUT OF MY FACE BEFORE I--
DON'T YOU FUCKING MOVE.
GET UP!
WHAT'D WE DO? WE DIDN'T DO NOTHING!
JUST GO!
WHERE WERE YOU TODAY?! YOU'RE THE ONLY ONE WE KNOW IS CAPABLE OF THIS! UNTIL WE FIND OUT OTHERWISE-- YOU'RE NOT LEAVING THIS CELL.
MIND TELLING ME WHAT YOU THINK I DID, PSYCHO BITCH?
LIKE YOU DON'T KNOW.

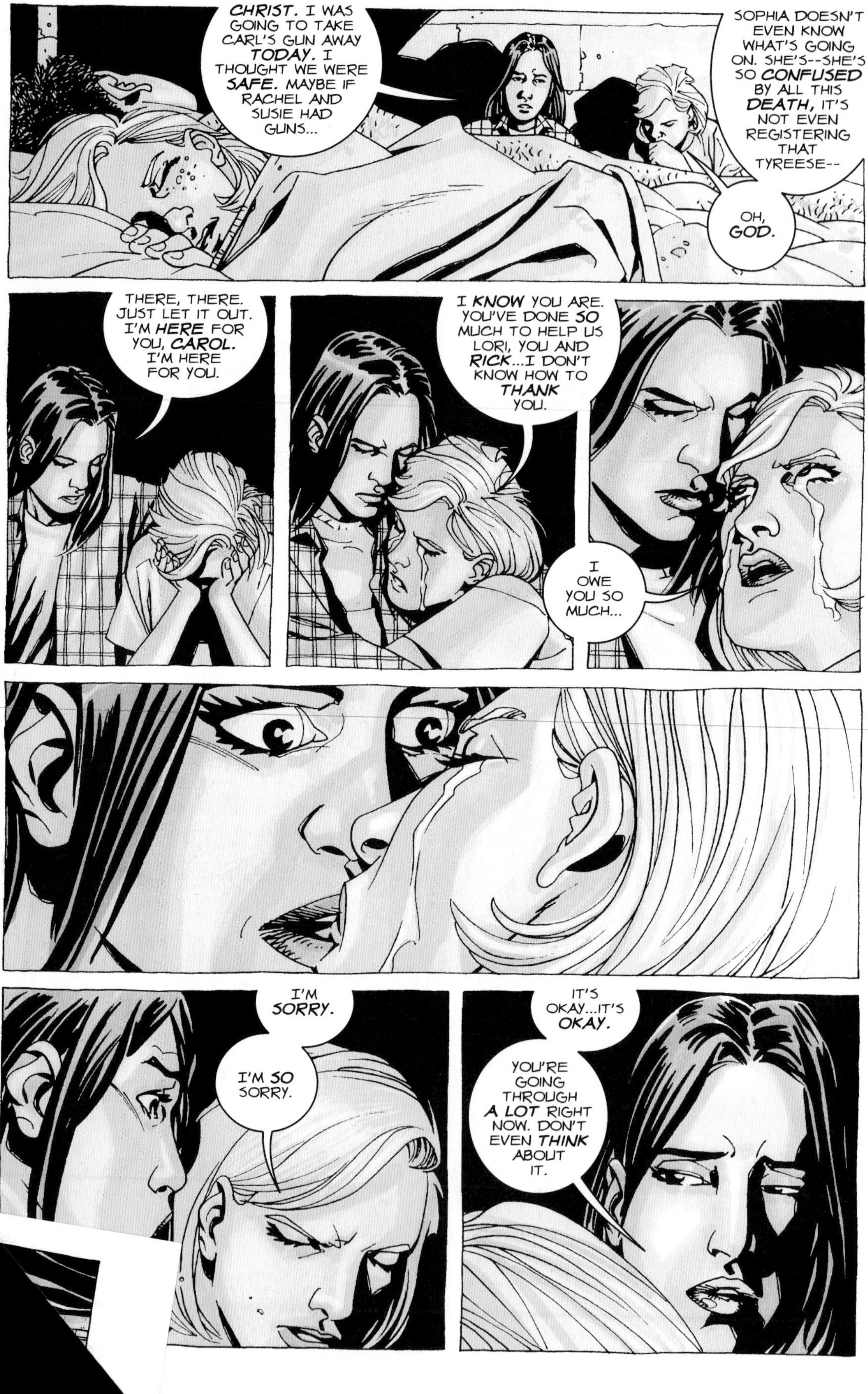
CHRIST. I WAS GOING TO TAKE CARL'S GUN AWAY TODAY. I THOUGHT WE WERE SAFE. MAYBE IF RACHEL AND SUSIE HAD GUNS...
SOPHIA DOESN'T EVEN KNOW WHAT'S GOING ON. SHE'S--SHE'S SO CONFUSED BY ALL THIS DEATH, IT'S NOT EVEN REGISTERING THAT TYREESE--
OH, GOD.
THERE, THERE. JUST LET IT OUT. I'M HERE FOR YOU, CAROL. I'M HERE FOR YOU.
I KNOW YOU ARE. YOU'VE DONE SO MUCH TO HELP US LORI, YOU AND RICK...I DON'T KNOW HOW TO THANK YOU.
I OWE YOU SO MUCH...
I'M SORRY.
I'M SO SORRY.
IT'S OKAY...IT'S OKAY.
YOU'RE GOING THROUGH A LOT RIGHT NOW. DON'T EVEN THINK ABOUT IT.

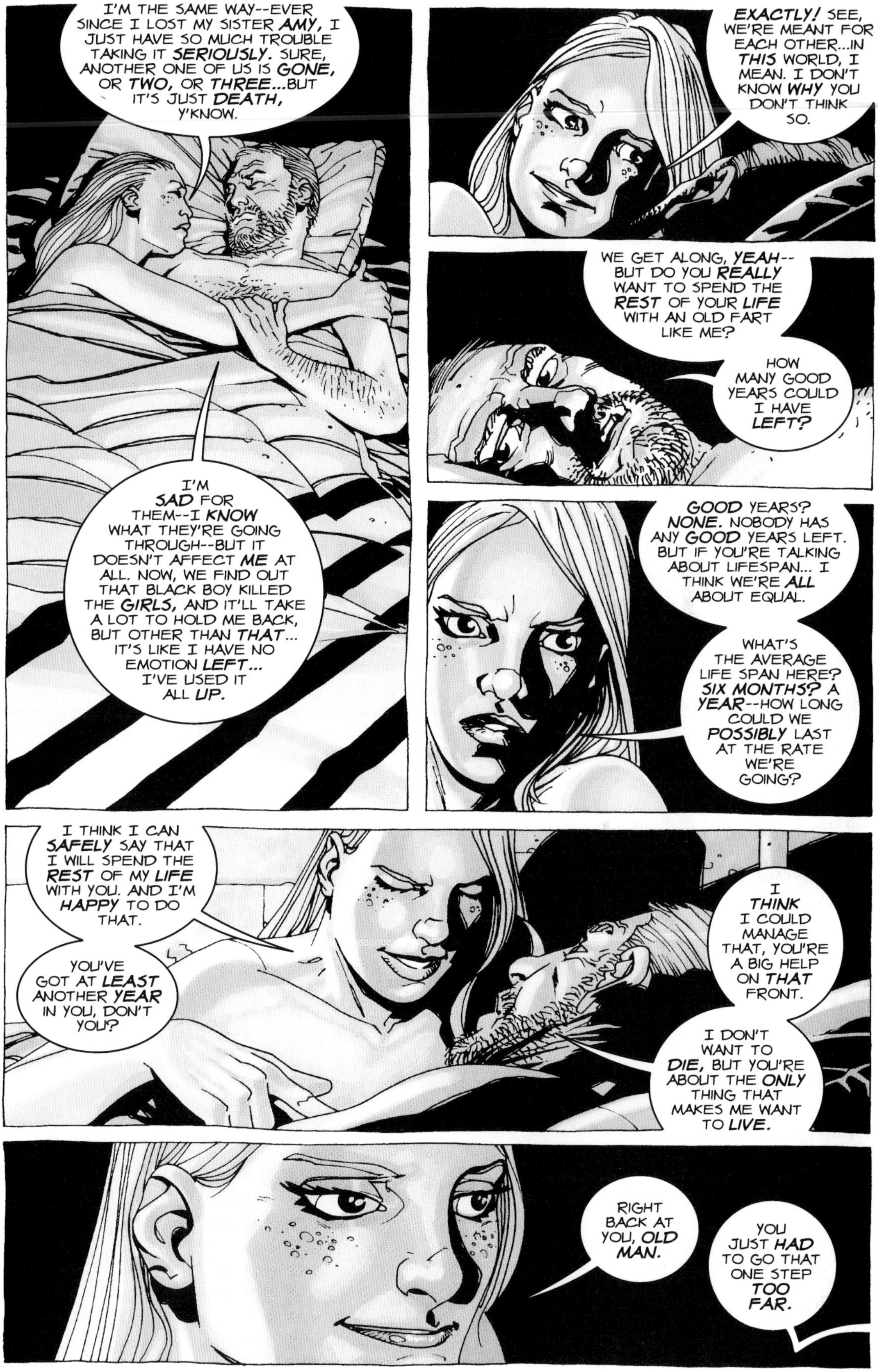
I'M THE SAME WAY--EVER SINCE I LOST MY SISTER AMY, I JUST HAVE SO MUCH TROUBLE TAKING IT SERIOUSLY. SURE, ANOTHER ONE OF US IS GONE, OR TWO, OR THREE...BUT IT'S JUST DEATH, Y'KNOW.
I'M SAD FOR THEM--I KNOW WHAT THEY'RE GOING THROUGH--BUT IT DOESN'T AFFECT ME AT ALL. NOW, WE FIND OUT THAT BLACK BOY KILLED THE GIRLS, AND IT'LL TAKE A LOT TO HOLD ME BACK, BUT OTHER THAN THAT... IT'S LIKE I HAVE NO EMOTION LEFT... I'VE USED IT ALL UP.
EXACTLY! SEE, WE'RE MEANT FOR EACH OTHER...IN THIS WORLD, I MEAN. I DON'T KNOW WHY YOU DON'T THINK SO.
WE GET ALONG, YEAH--BUT DO YOU REALLY WANT TO SPEND THE REST OF YOUR LIFE WITH AN OLD FART LIKE ME?
HOW MANY GOOD YEARS COULD I HAVE LEFT?
GOOD YEARS? NONE. NOBODY HAS ANY GOOD YEARS LEFT. BUT IF YOU'RE TALKING ABOUT LIFESPAN... I THINK WE'RE ALL ABOUT EQUAL.
WHAT'S THE AVERAGE LIFE SPAN HERE? SIX MONTHS? A YEAR--HOW LONG COULD WE POSSIBLY LAST AT THE RATE WE'RE GOING?
I THINK I CAN SAFELY SAY THAT I WILL SPEND THE REST OF MY LIFE WITH YOU. AND I'M HAPPY TO DO THAT.
YOU'VE GOT AT LEAST ANOTHER YEAR IN YOU, DON'T YOU?
I THINK I COULD MANAGE THAT, YOU'RE A BIG HELP ON THAT FRONT.
I DON'T WANT TO DIE, BUT YOU'RE ABOUT THE ONLY THING THAT MAKES ME WANT TO LIVE.
RIGHT BACK AT YOU, OLD MAN.
YOU JUST HAD TO GO THAT ONE STEP TOO FAR.

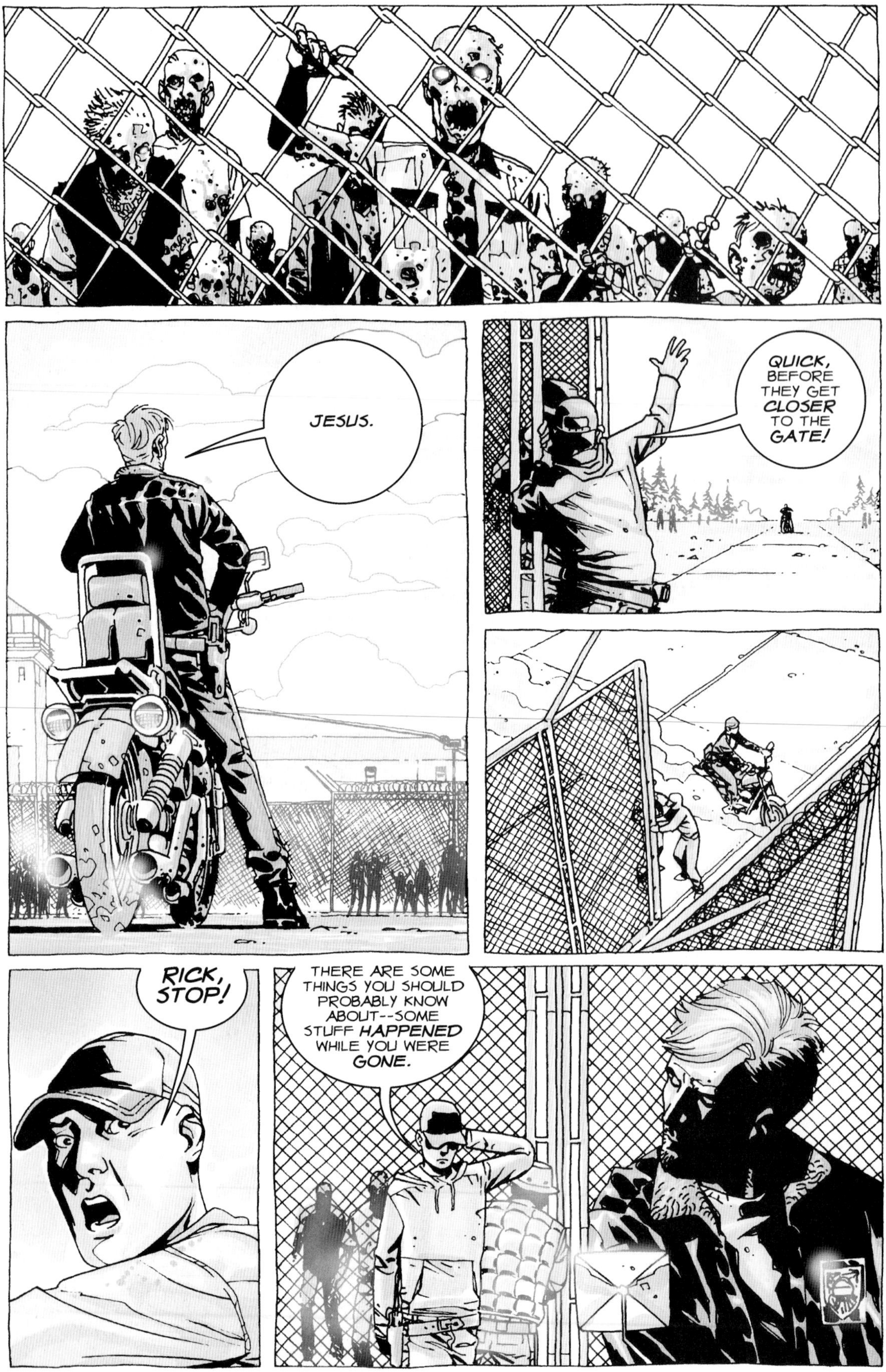
JESUS.
QUICK, BEFORE THEY GET CLOSER TO THE GATE!
RICK, STOP!
THERE ARE SOME THINGS YOU SHOULD PROBABLY KNOW ABOUT--SOME STUFF HAPPENED WHILE YOU WERE GONE.

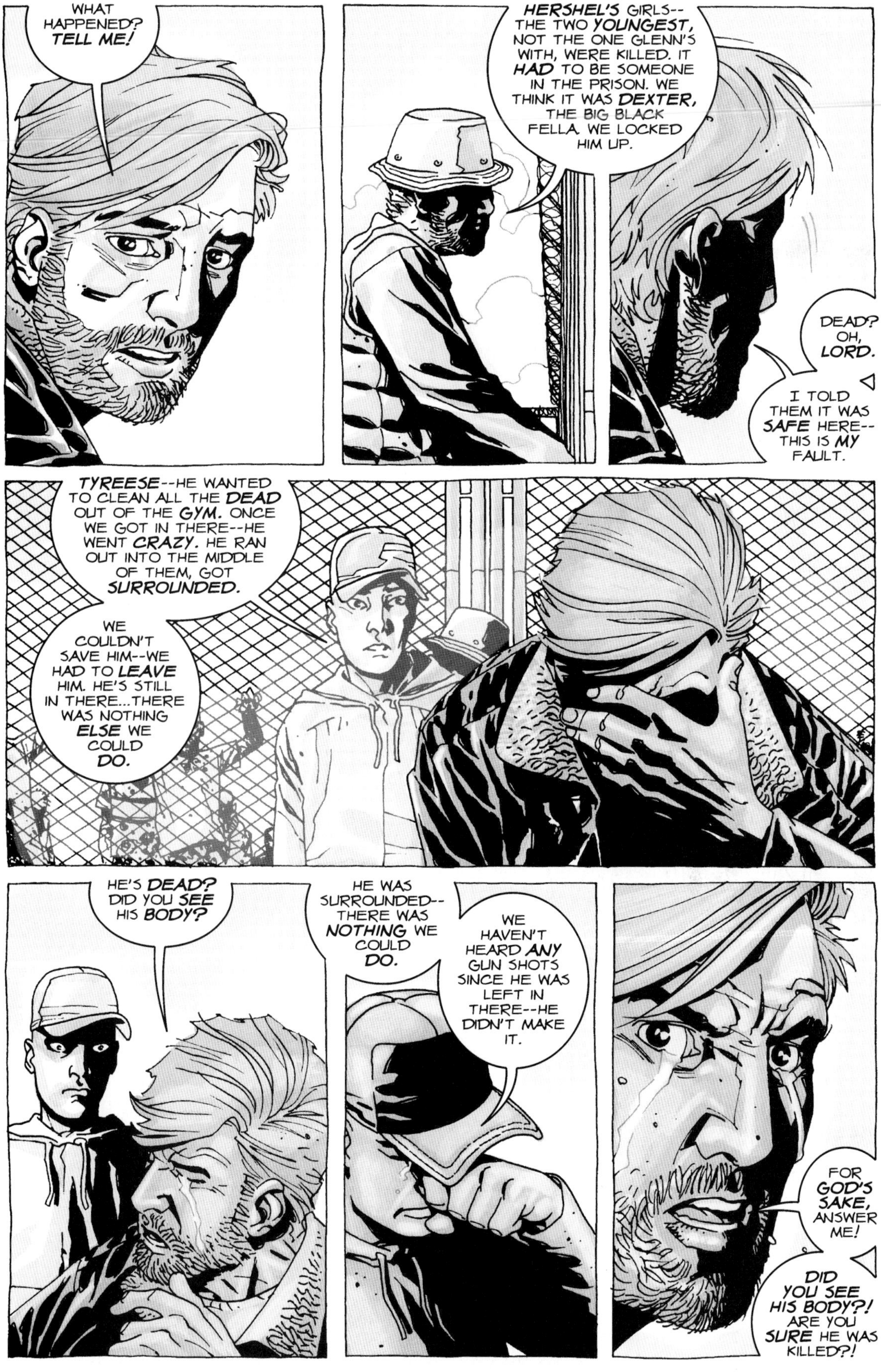
WHAT HAPPENED? TELL ME!
HERSHEL'S GIRLS-- THE TWO YOUNGEST, NOT THE ONE GLENN'S WITH, WERE KILLED. IT HAD TO BE SOMEONE IN THE PRISON. WE THINK IT WAS DEXTER, THE BIG BLACK FELLA. WE LOCKED HIM UP.
DEAD? OH, LORD.
I TOLD THEM IT WAS SAFE HERE-- THIS IS MY FAULT.
TYREESE--HE WANTED TO CLEAN ALL THE DEAD OUT OF THE GYM. ONCE WE GOT IN THERE--HE WENT CRAZY. HE RAN OUT INTO THE MIDDLE OF THEM, GOT SURROUNDED.
WE COULDN'T SAVE HIM--WE HAD TO LEAVE HIM. HE'S STILL IN THERE...THERE WAS NOTHING ELSE WE COULD DO.
HE'S DEAD? DID YOU SEE HIS BODY?
HE WAS SURROUNDED-- THERE WAS NOTHING WE COULD DO.
WE HAVEN'T HEARD ANY GUN SHOTS SINCE HE WAS LEFT IN THERE--HE DIDN'T MAKE IT.
FOR GOD'S SAKE, ANSWER ME!
DID YOU SEE HIS BODY?! ARE YOU SURE HE WAS KILLED?!

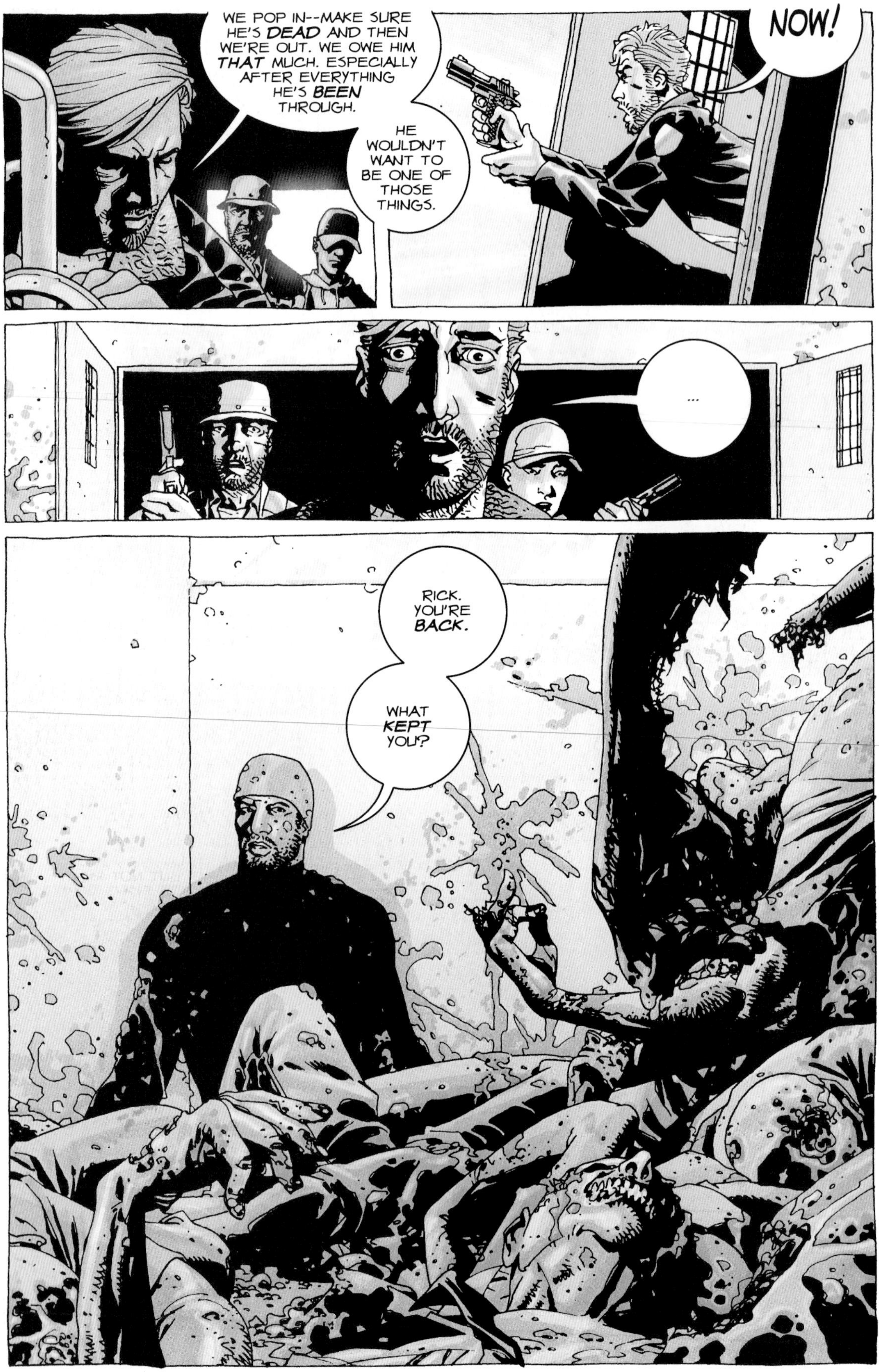
WE POP IN--MAKE SURE HE'S DEAD AND THEN WE'RE OUT. WE OWE HIM THAT MUCH. ESPECIALLY AFTER EVERYTHING HE'S BEEN THROUGH.
HE WOULDN'T WANT TO BE ONE OF THOSE THINGS.
NOW!
...
RICK. YOU'RE BACK.
WHAT KEPT YOU?

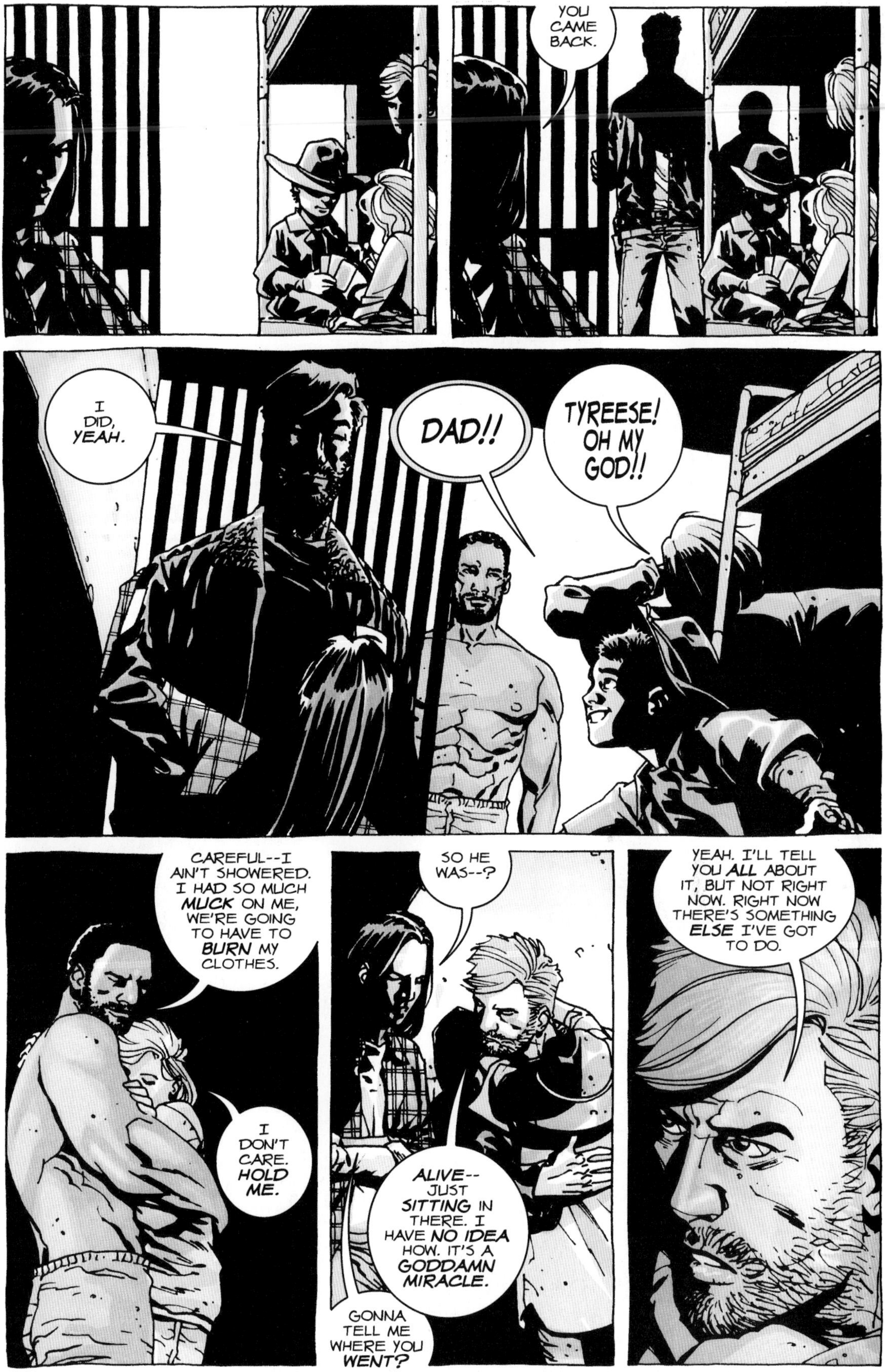
YOU CAME BACK.
I DID, YEAH.
DAD!!
TYREESE! OH MY GOD!!
CAREFUL--I AIN'T SHOWERED. I HAD SO MUCH MUCK ON ME, WE'RE GOING TO HAVE TO BURN MY CLOTHES.
I DON'T CARE. HOLD ME.
SO HE WAS--?
ALIVE-- JUST SITTING IN THERE. I HAVE NO IDEA HOW. IT'S A GODDAMN MIRACLE.
GONNA TELL ME WHERE YOU WENT?
YEAH. I'LL TELL YOU ALL ABOUT IT, BUT NOT RIGHT NOW. RIGHT NOW THERE'S SOMETHING ELSE I'VE GOT TO DO.

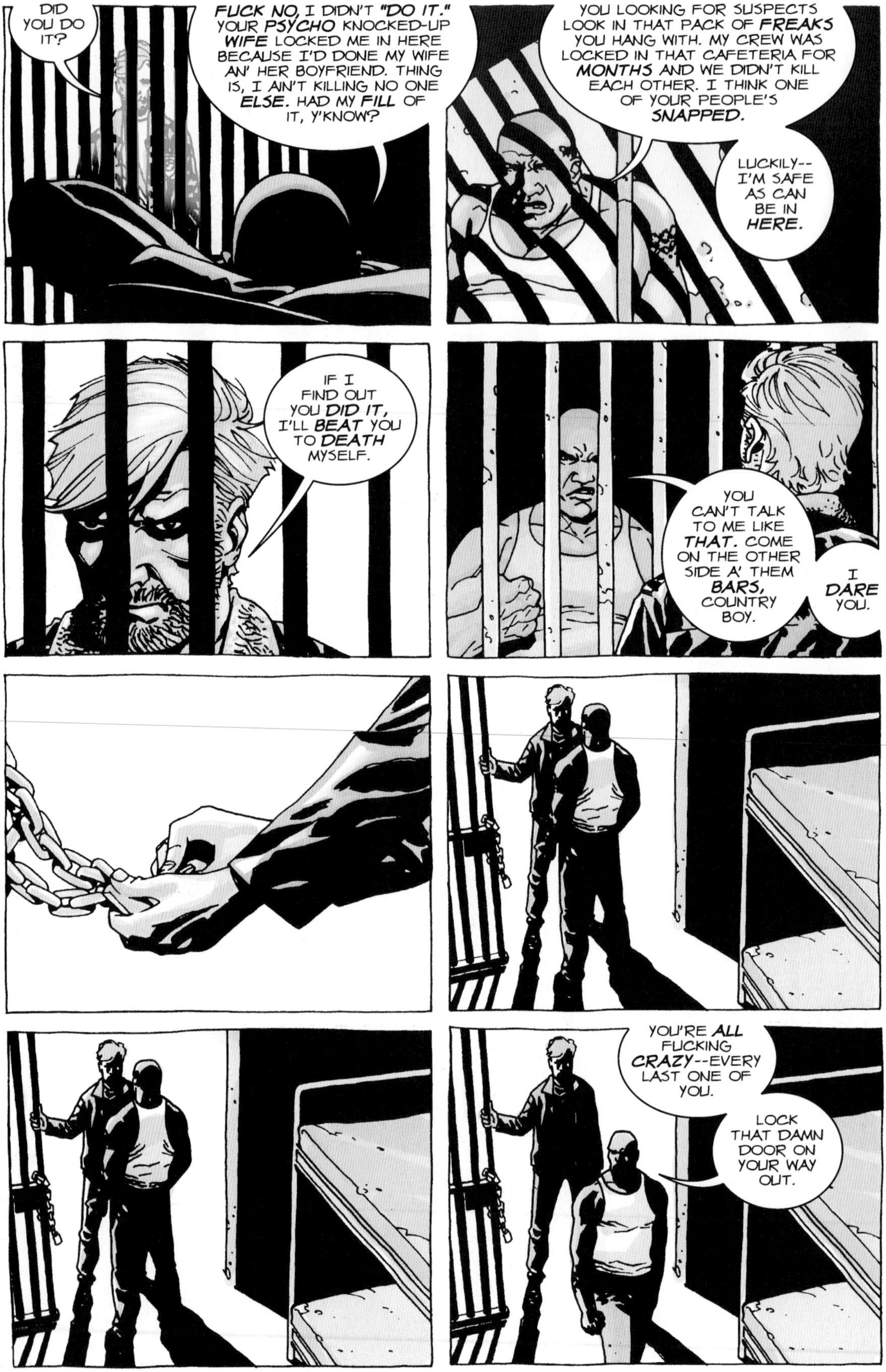
DID YOU DO IT?
FUCK NO, I DIDN'T "DO IT." YOUR PSYCHO KNOCKED-UP WIFE LOCKED ME IN HERE BECAUSE I'D DONE MY WIFE AN' HER BOYFRIEND. THING IS, I AIN'T KILLING NO ONE ELSE. HAD MY FILL OF IT, Y'KNOW?
YOU LOOKING FOR SUSPECTS LOOK IN THAT PACK OF FREAKS YOU HANG WITH. MY CREW WAS LOCKED IN THAT CAFETERIA FOR MONTHS AND WE DIDN'T KILL EACH OTHER. I THINK ONE OF YOUR PEOPLE'S SNAPPED.
LUCKILY-- I'M SAFE AS CAN BE IN HERE.
IF I FIND OUT YOU DID IT, I'LL BEAT YOU TO DEATH MYSELF.
YOU CAN'T TALK TO ME LIKE THAT. COME ON THE OTHER SIDE A' THEM BARS, COUNTRY BOY.
I DARE YOU.
YOU'RE ALL FUCKING CRAZY--EVERY LAST ONE OF YOU.
LOCK THAT DAMN DOOR ON YOUR WAY OUT.

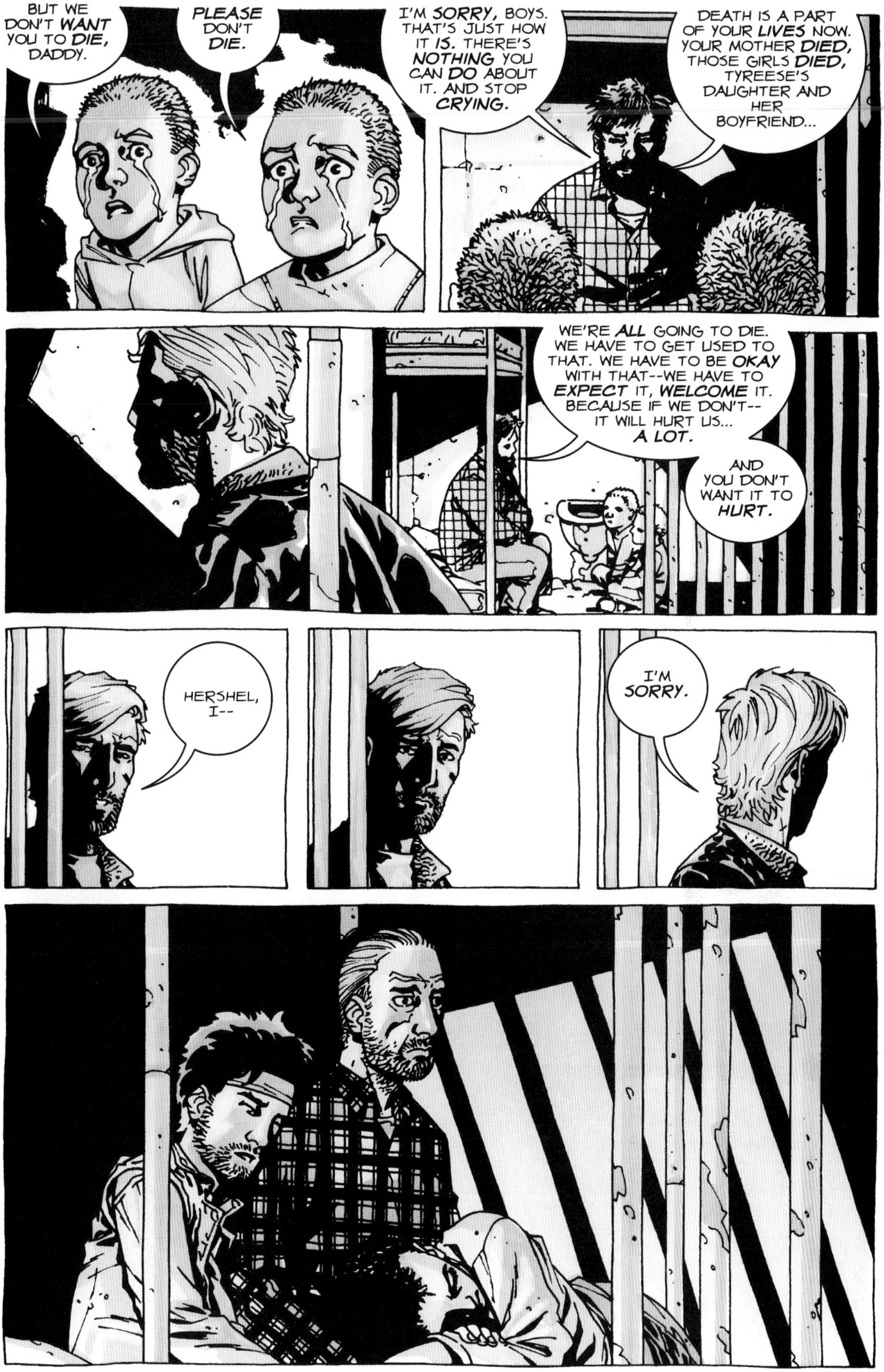
BUT WE DON'T WANT YOU TO DIE, DADDY.
PLEASE DON'T DIE.
I'M SORRY, BOYS. THAT'S JUST HOW IT IS. THERE'S NOTHING YOU CAN DO ABOUT IT. AND STOP CRYING.
DEATH IS A PART OF YOUR LIVES NOW. YOUR MOTHER DIED, THOSE GIRLS DIED, TYREESE'S DAUGHTER AND HER BOYFRIEND...
WE'RE ALL GOING TO DIE. WE HAVE TO GET USED TO THAT. WE HAVE TO BE OKAY WITH THAT--WE HAVE TO EXPECT IT, WELCOME IT. BECAUSE IF WE DON'T-- IT WILL HURT US... A LOT.
AND YOU DON'T WANT IT TO HURT.
HERSHEL, I--
I'M SORRY.

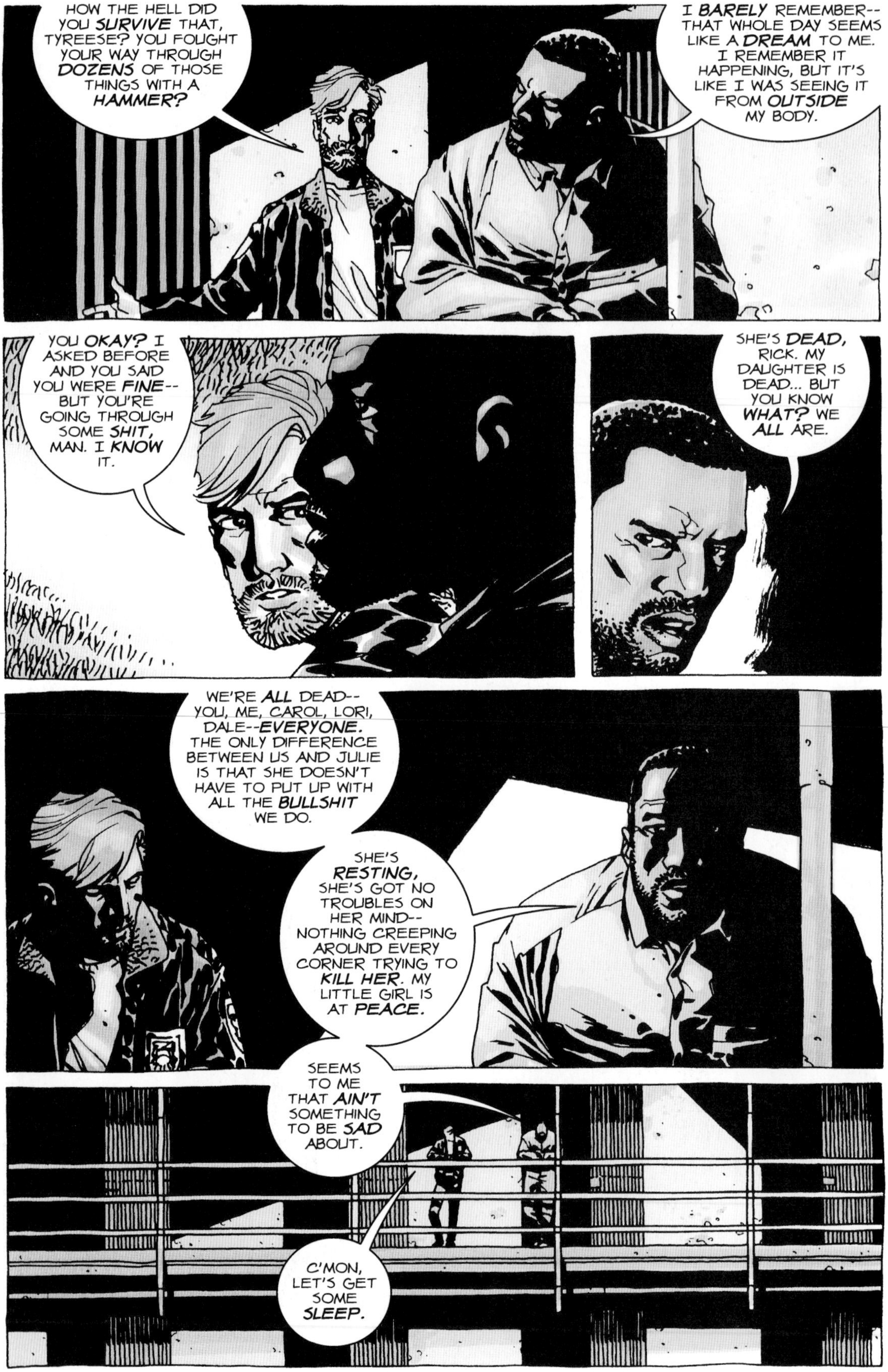
HOW THE HELL DID YOU SURVIVE THAT, TYREESE? YOU FOUGHT YOUR WAY THROUGH DOZENS OF THOSE THINGS WITH A HAMMER?
I BARELY REMEMBER-- THAT WHOLE DAY SEEMS LIKE A DREAM TO ME. I REMEMBER IT HAPPENING, BUT IT'S LIKE I WAS SEEING IT FROM OUTSIDE MY BODY.
YOU OKAY? I ASKED BEFORE AND YOU SAID YOU WERE FINE-- BUT YOU'RE GOING THROUGH SOME SHIT, MAN. I KNOW IT.
SHE'S DEAD, RICK. MY DAUGHTER IS DEAD... BUT YOU KNOW WHAT? WE ALL ARE.
WE'RE ALL DEAD-- YOU, ME, CAROL, LORI, DALE--EVERYONE. THE ONLY DIFFERENCE BETWEEN US AND JULIE IS THAT SHE DOESN'T HAVE TO PUT UP WITH ALL THE BULLSHIT WE DO.
SHE'S RESTING, SHE'S GOT NO TROUBLES ON HER MIND-- NOTHING CREEPING AROUND EVERY CORNER TRYING TO KILL HER. MY LITTLE GIRL IS AT PEACE.
SEEMS TO ME THAT AIN'T SOMETHING TO BE SAD ABOUT.
C'MON, LET'S GET SOME SLEEP.

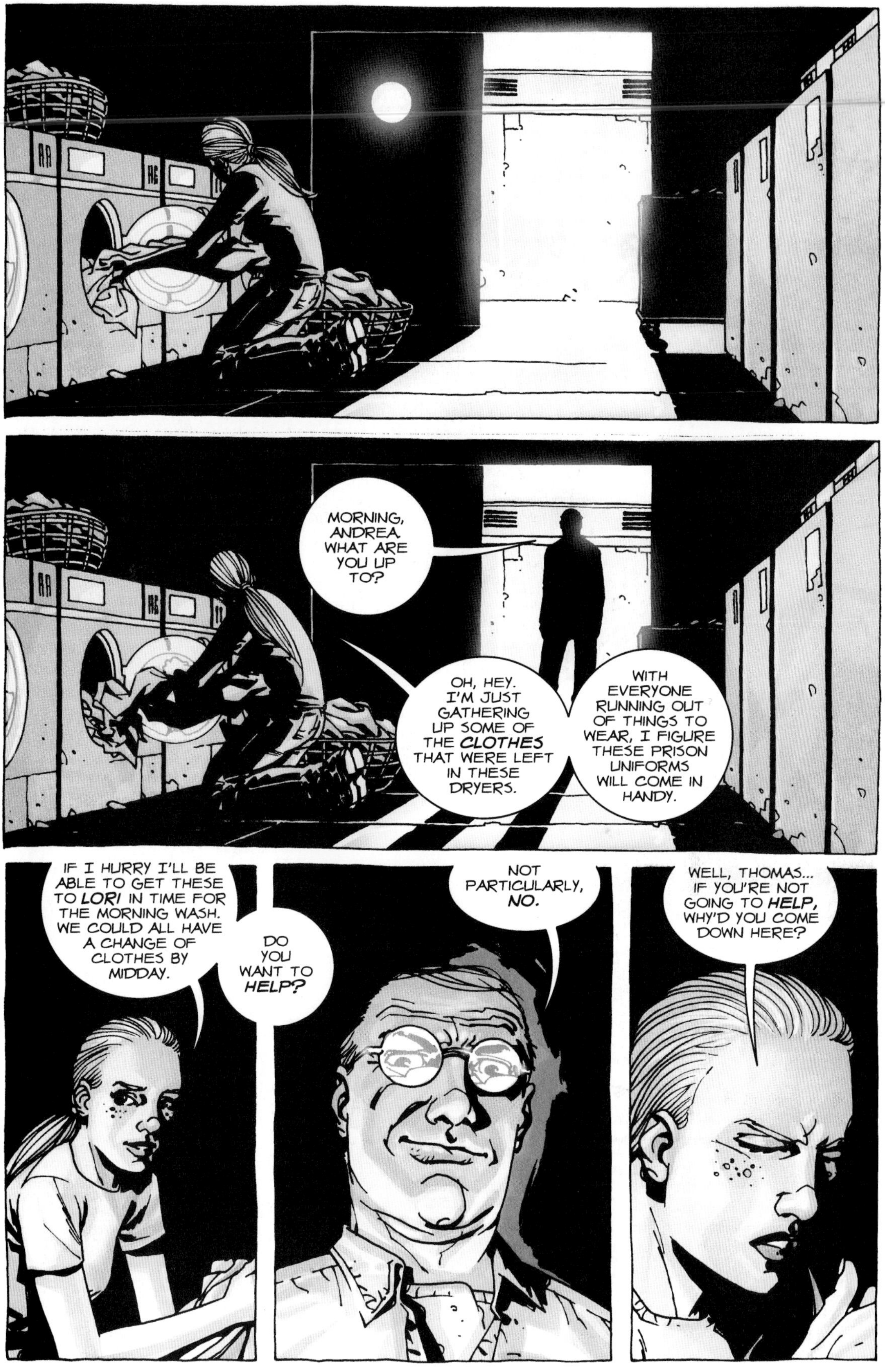
MORNING, ANDREA. WHAT ARE YOU UP TO?
OH, HEY. I'M JUST GATHERING UP SOME OF THE CLOTHES THAT WERE LEFT IN THESE DRYERS.
WITH EVERYONE RUNNING OUT OF THINGS TO WEAR, I FIGURE THESE PRISON UNIFORMS WILL COME IN HANDY.
IF I HURRY I'LL BE ABLE TO GET THESE TO LORI IN TIME FOR THE MORNING WASH. WE COULD ALL HAVE A CHANGE OF CLOTHES BY MIDDAY.
DO YOU WANT TO HELP?
NOT PARTICULARLY, NO.
WELL, THOMAS... IF YOU'RE NOT GOING TO HELP, WHY'D YOU COME DOWN HERE?

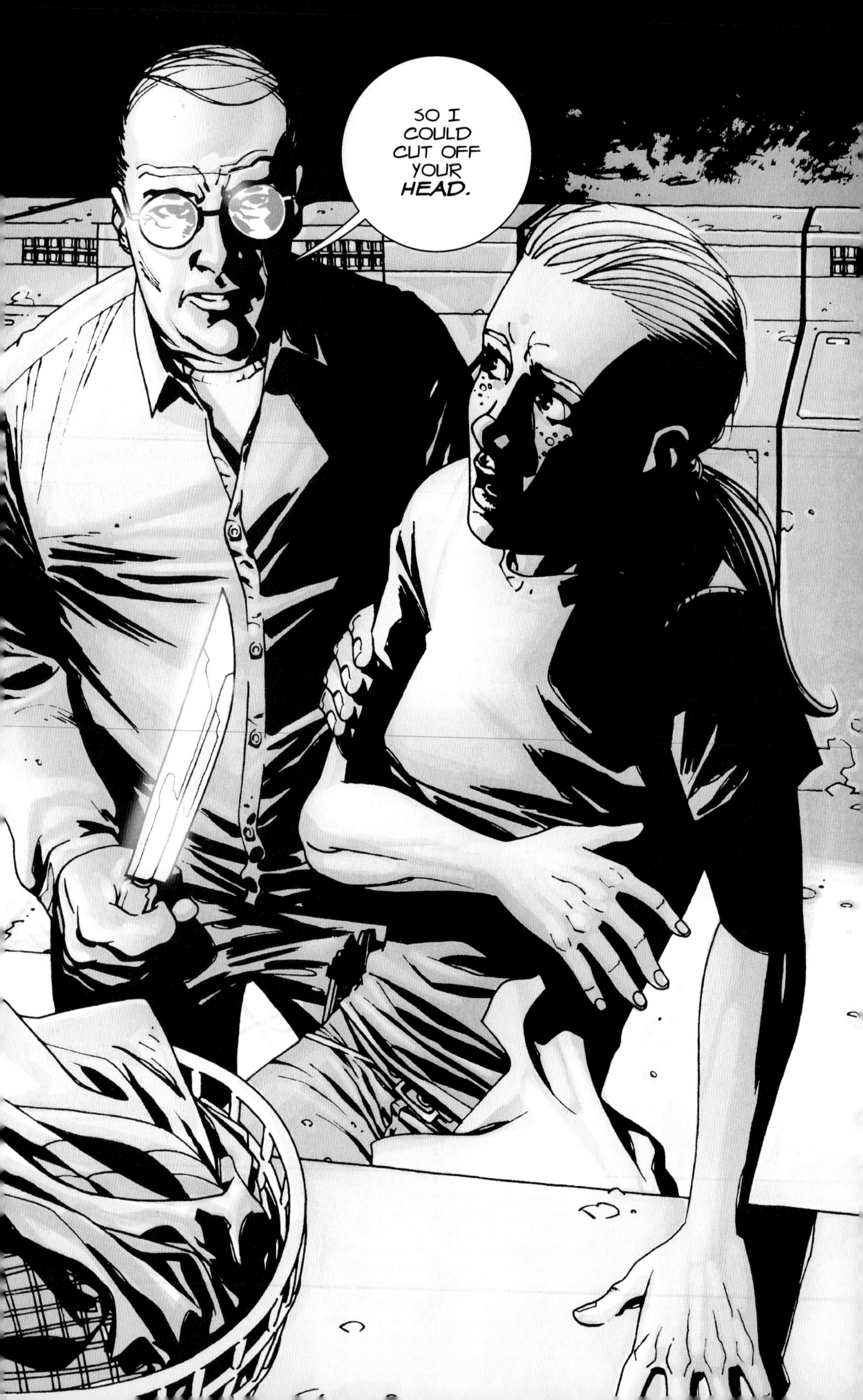
SO I COULD CUT OFF YOUR HEAD.

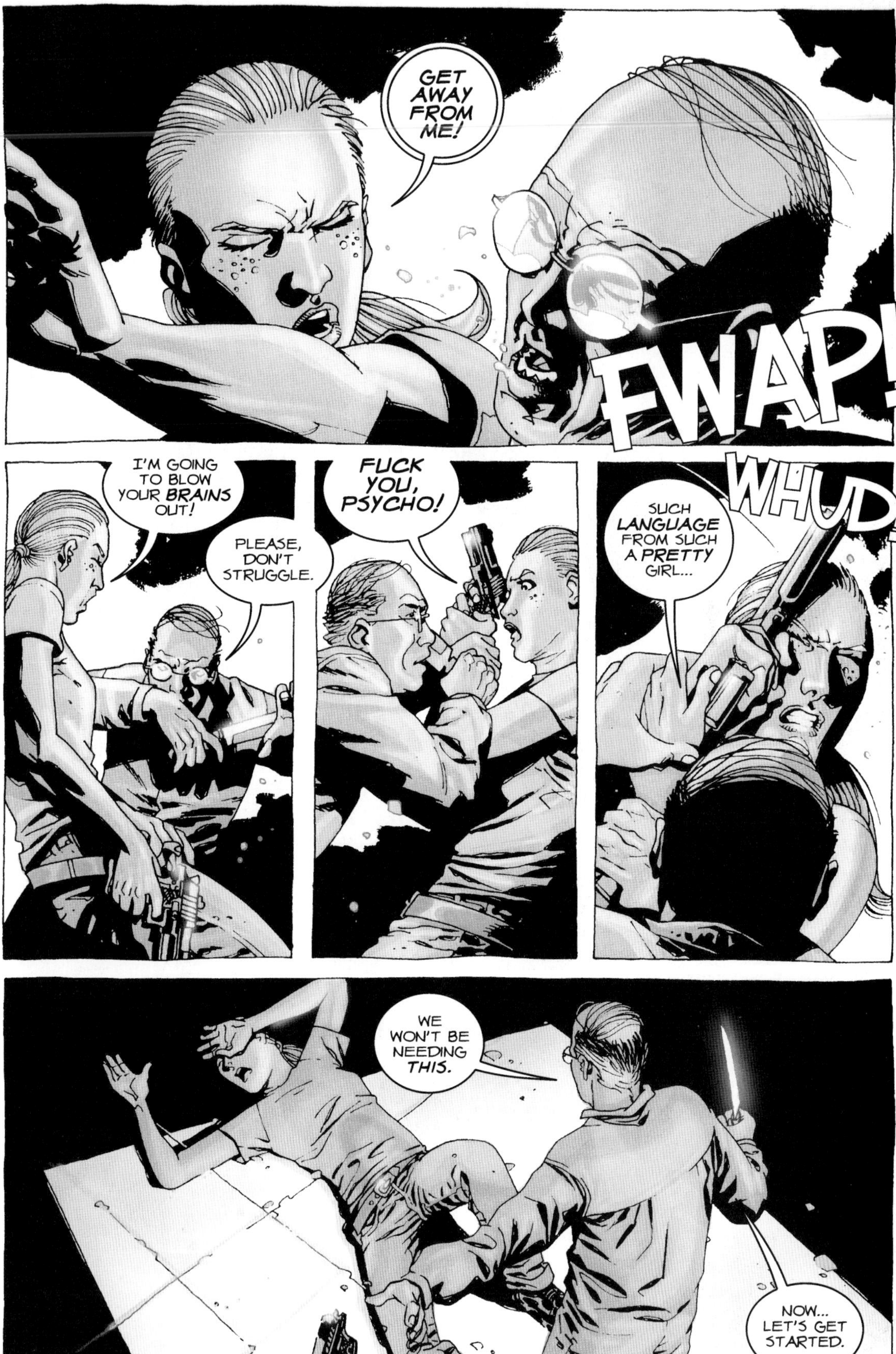
GET AWAY FROM ME!
FWAP!
I'M GOING TO BLOW YOUR BRAINS OUT!
PLEASE, DON'T STRUGGLE.
FUCK YOU, PSYCHO!
WHUD!
SUCH LANGUAGE FROM SUCH A PRETTY GIRL...
WE WON'T BE NEEDING THIS.
NOW... LET'S GET STARTED.

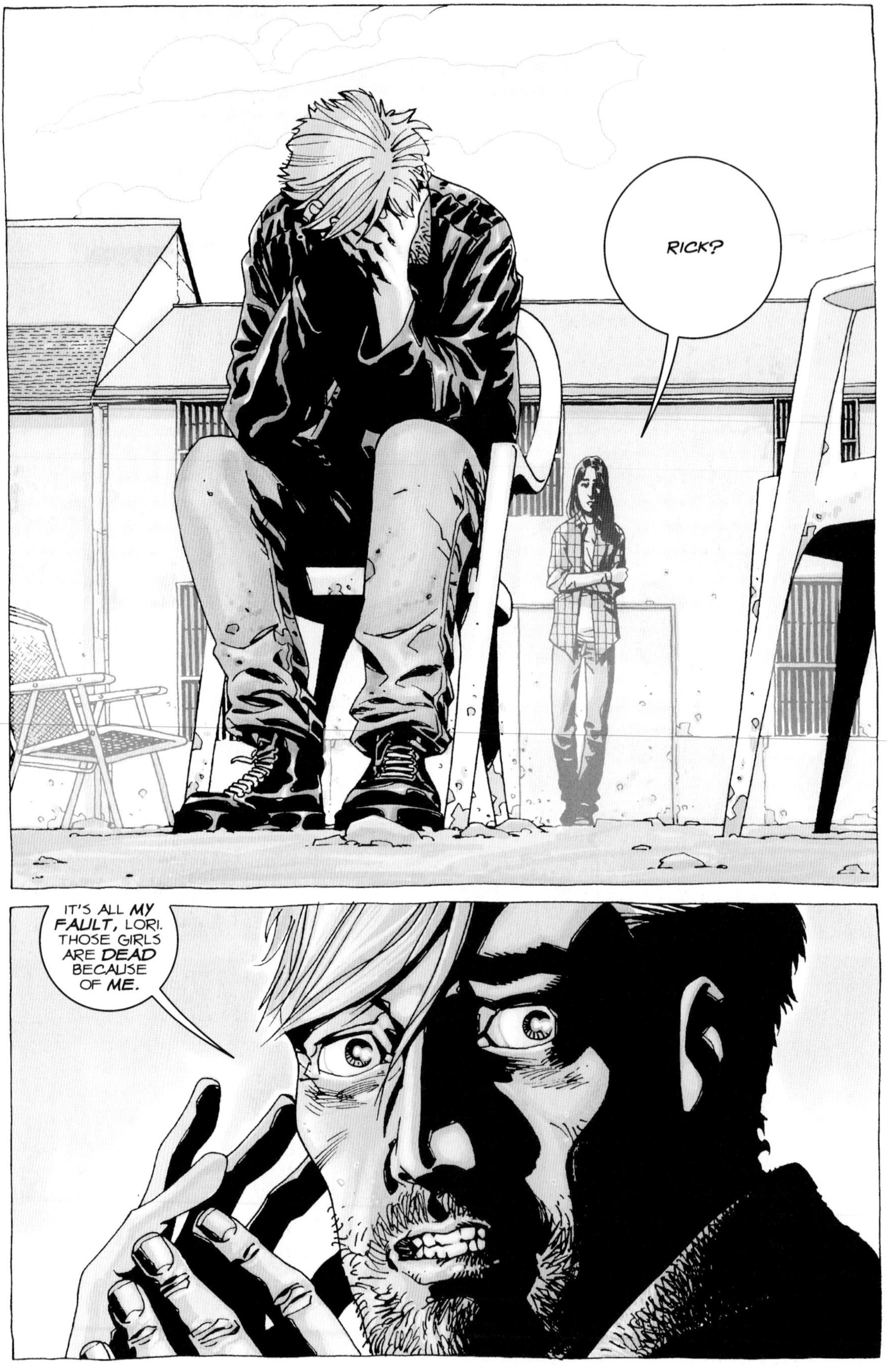
RICK?
IT'S ALL MY FAULT, LORI. THOSE GIRLS ARE DEAD BECAUSE OF ME.

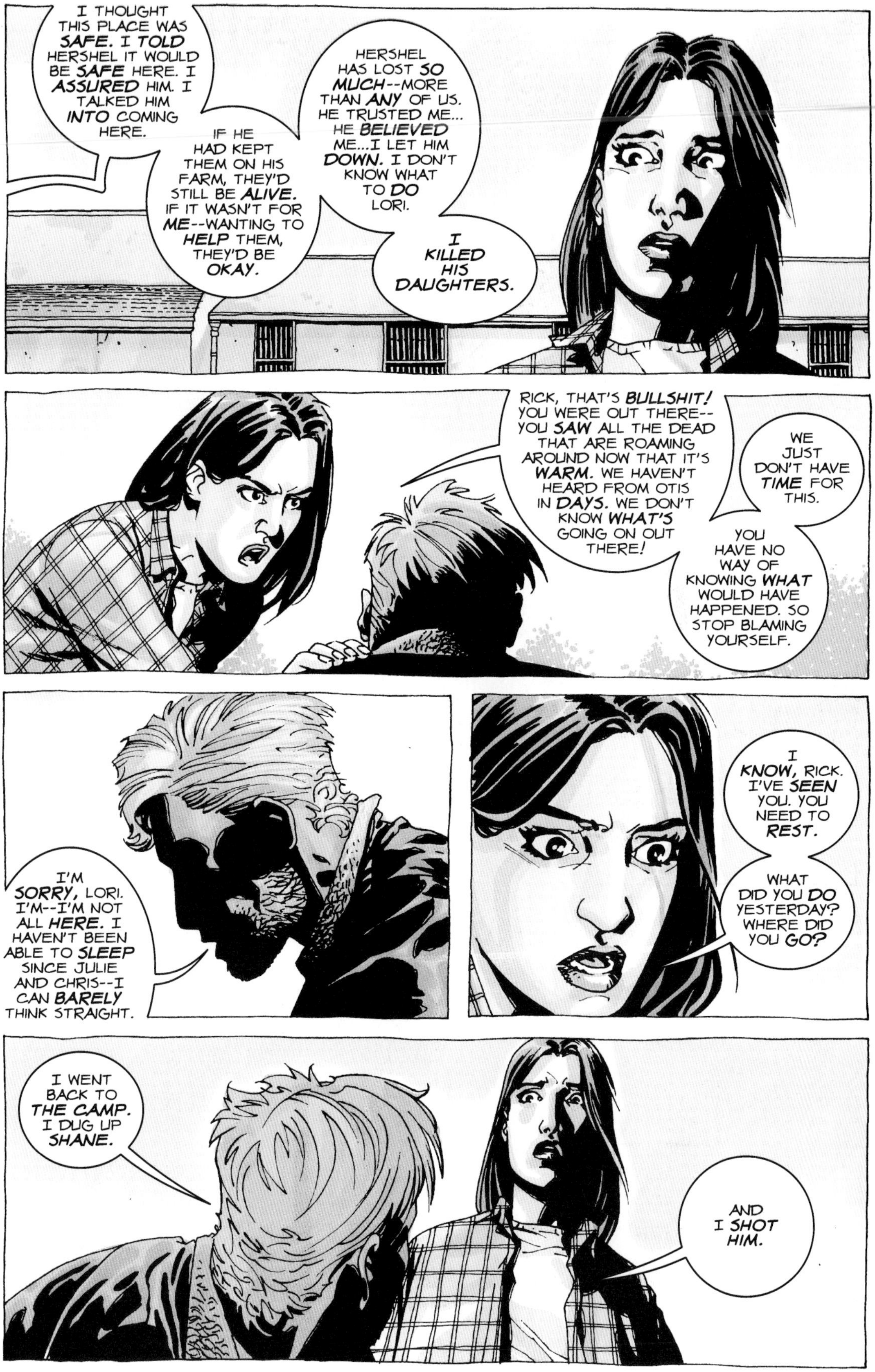
I THOUGHT THIS PLACE WAS SAFE. I TOLD HERSHEL IT WOULD BE SAFE HERE. I ASSURED HIM. I TALKED HIM INTO COMING HERE.
IF HE HAD KEPT THEM ON HIS FARM, THEY'D STILL BE ALIVE. IF IT WASN'T FOR ME--WANTING TO HELP THEM, THEY'D BE OKAY.
HERSHEL HAS LOST SO MUCH--MORE THAN ANY OF US. HE TRUSTED ME... HE BELIEVED ME...I LET HIM DOWN. I DON'T KNOW WHAT TO DO LORI.
I KILLED HIS DAUGHTERS.
RICK, THAT'S BULLSHIT! YOU WERE OUT THERE-- YOU SAW ALL THE DEAD THAT ARE ROAMING AROUND NOW THAT IT'S WARM. WE HAVEN'T HEARD FROM OTIS IN DAYS. WE DON'T KNOW WHAT'S GOING ON OUT THERE!
WE JUST DON'T HAVE TIME FOR THIS.
YOU HAVE NO WAY OF KNOWING WHAT WOULD HAVE HAPPENED. SO STOP BLAMING YOURSELF.
I'M SORRY, LORI. I'M--I'M NOT ALL HERE. I HAVEN'T BEEN ABLE TO SLEEP SINCE JULIE AND CHRIS--I CAN BARELY THINK STRAIGHT.
I KNOW, RICK. I'VE SEEN YOU. YOU NEED TO REST.
WHAT DID YOU DO YESTERDAY? WHERE DID YOU GO?
I WENT BACK TO THE CAMP. I DUG UP SHANE.
AND I SHOT HIM.

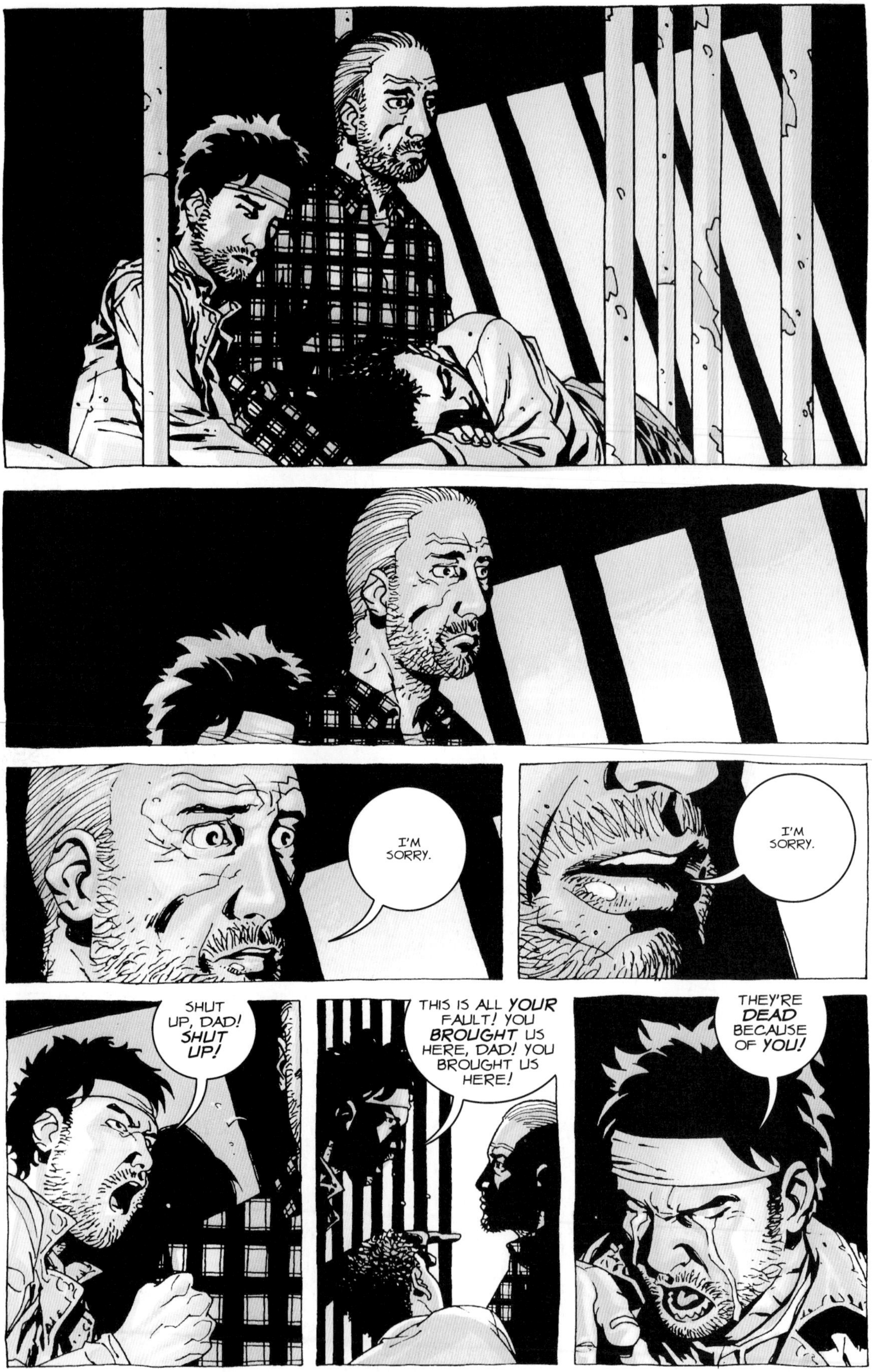
I'M SORRY.
I'M SORRY.
SHUT UP, DAD! SHUT UP!
THIS IS ALL YOUR FAULT! YOU BROUGHT US HERE, DAD! YOU BROUGHT US HERE!
THEY'RE DEAD BECAUSE OF YOU!

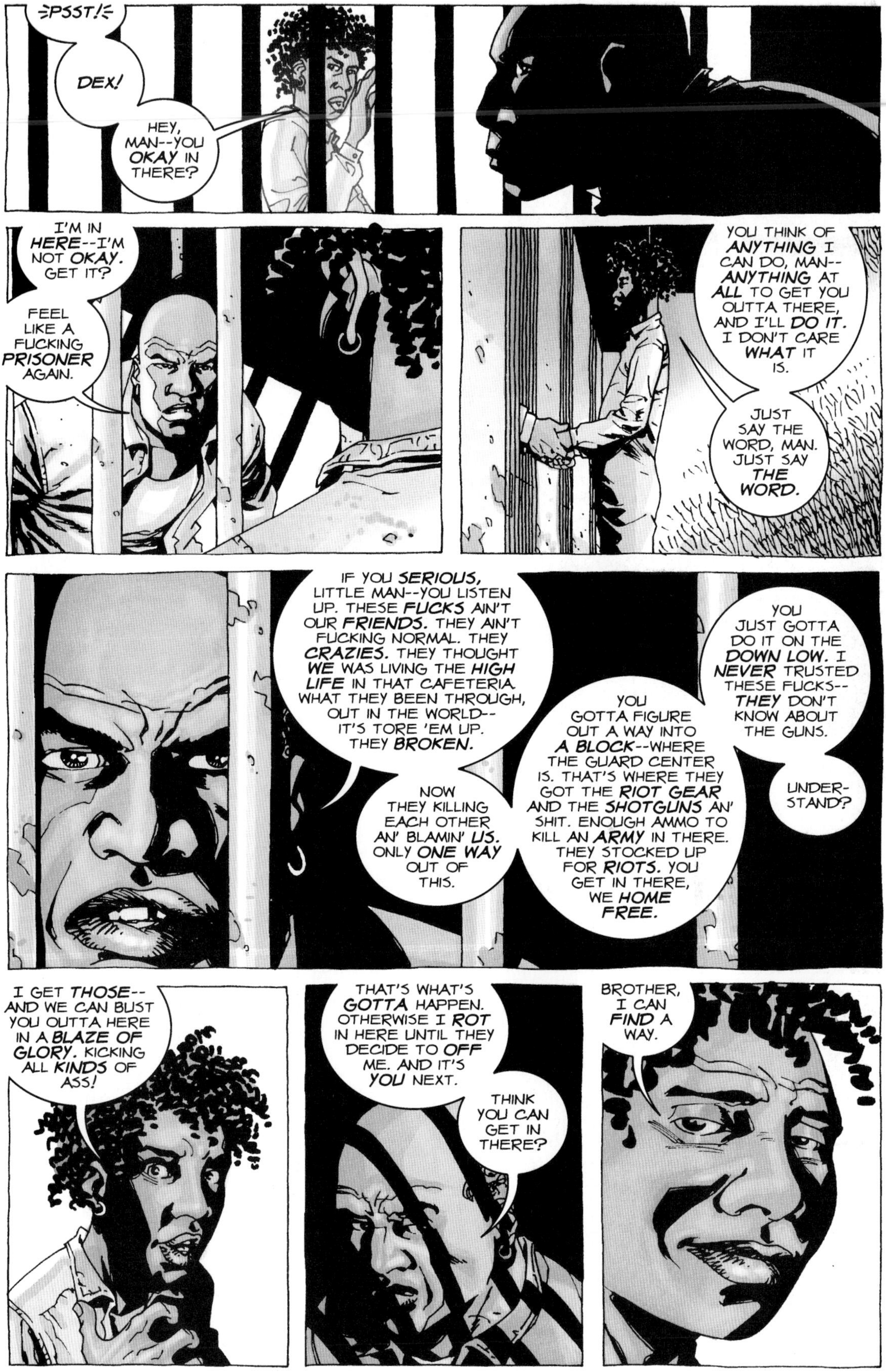
PSST!
DEX!
HEY, MAN--YOU OKAY IN THERE?
I'M IN HERE--I'M NOT OKAY. GET IT?
FEEL LIKE A FUCKING PRISONER AGAIN.
YOU THINK OF ANYTHING I CAN DO, MAN--ANYTHING AT ALL TO GET YOU OUTTA THERE, AND I'LL DO IT. I DON'T CARE WHAT IT IS.
JUST SAY THE WORD, MAN. JUST SAY THE WORD.
IF YOU SERIOUS, LITTLE MAN--YOU LISTEN UP. THESE FUCKS AIN'T OUR FRIENDS. THEY AIN'T FUCKING NORMAL. THEY CRAZIES. THEY THOUGHT WE WAS LIVING THE HIGH LIFE IN THAT CAFETERIA. WHAT THEY BEEN THROUGH, OUT IN THE WORLD--IT'S TORE 'EM UP. THEY BROKEN.
NOW THEY KILLING EACH OTHER AN' BLAMIN' US. ONLY ONE WAY OUT OF THIS.
YOU GOTTA FIGURE OUT A WAY INTO A BLOCK--WHERE THE GUARD CENTER IS. THAT'S WHERE THEY GOT THE RIOT GEAR AND THE SHOTGUNS AN' SHIT. ENOUGH AMMO TO KILL AN ARMY IN THERE. THEY STOCKED UP FOR RIOTS. YOU GET IN THERE, WE HOME FREE.
YOU JUST GOTTA DO IT ON THE DOWN LOW. I NEVER TRUSTED THESE FUCKS--THEY DON'T KNOW ABOUT THE GUNS.
UNDER-STAND?
I GET THOSE--AND WE CAN BUST YOU OUTTA HERE IN A BLAZE OF GLORY. KICKING ALL KINDS OF ASS!
THAT'S WHAT'S GOTTA HAPPEN. OTHERWISE I ROT IN HERE UNTIL THEY DECIDE TO OFF ME. AND IT'S YOU NEXT.
THINK YOU CAN GET IN THERE?
BROTHER, I CAN FIND A WAY.

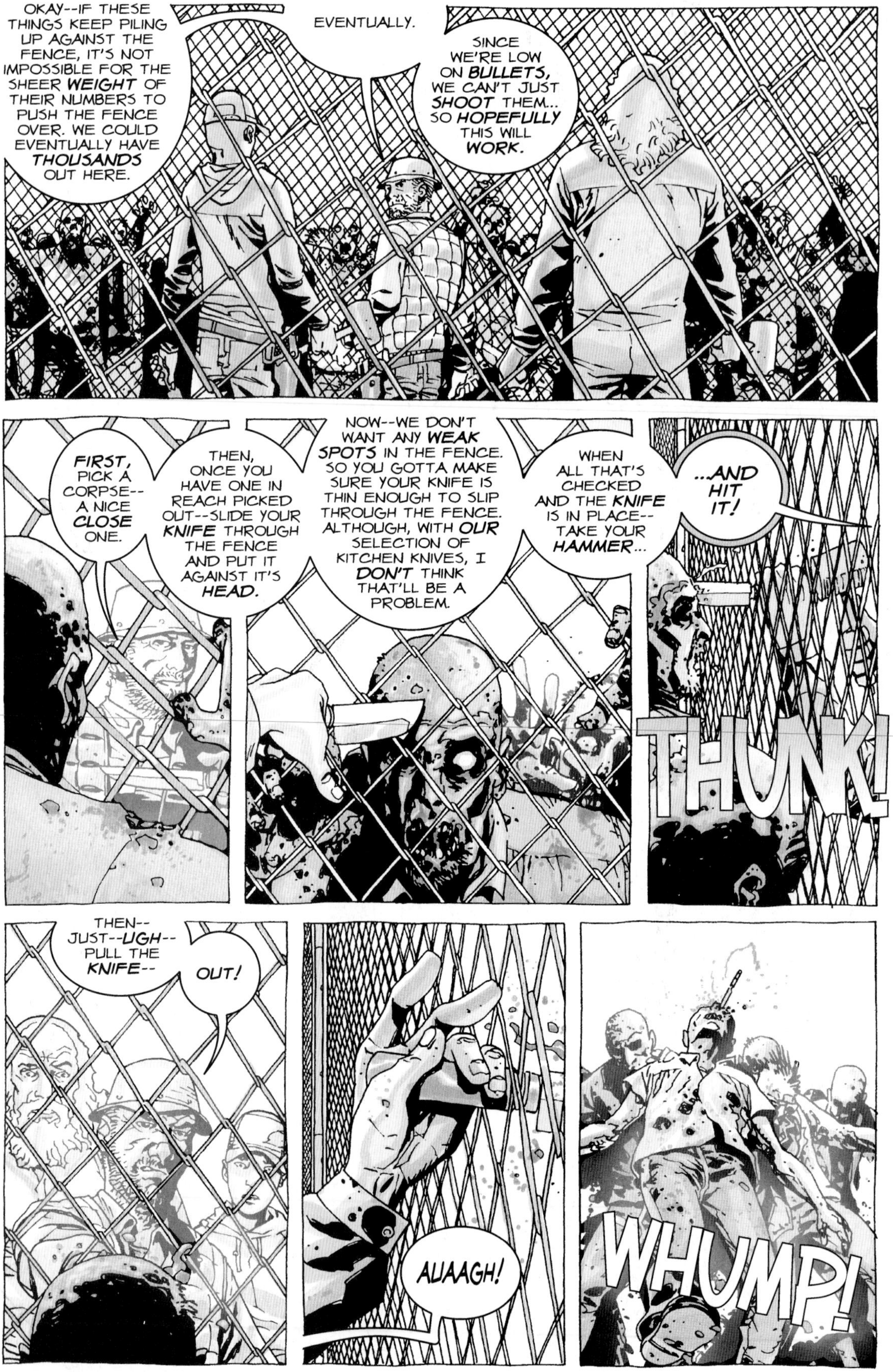

OKAY--IF THESE THINGS KEEP PILING UP AGAINST THE FENCE, IT'S NOT IMPOSSIBLE FOR THE SHEER WEIGHT OF THEIR NUMBERS TO PUSH THE FENCE OVER. WE COULD EVENTUALLY HAVE THOUSANDS OUT HERE.
EVENTUALLY.
SINCE WE'RE LOW ON BULLETS, WE CAN'T JUST SHOOT THEM... SO HOPEFULLY THIS WILL WORK.
FIRST, PICK A CORPSE-- A NICE CLOSE ONE.
THEN, ONCE YOU HAVE ONE IN REACH PICKED OUT--SLIDE YOUR KNIFE THROUGH THE FENCE AND PUT IT AGAINST IT'S HEAD.
NOW--WE DON'T WANT ANY WEAK SPOTS IN THE FENCE. SO YOU GOTTA MAKE SURE YOUR KNIFE IS THIN ENOUGH TO SLIP THROUGH THE FENCE. ALTHOUGH, WITH OUR SELECTION OF KITCHEN KNIVES, I DON'T THINK THAT'LL BE A PROBLEM.
WHEN ALL THAT'S CHECKED AND THE KNIFE IS IN PLACE-- TAKE YOUR HAMMER...
...AND HIT IT!
THUNK!
THEN-- JUST--UGH-- PULL THE KNIFE--
OUT!
AUAAGH!
WHUMP!

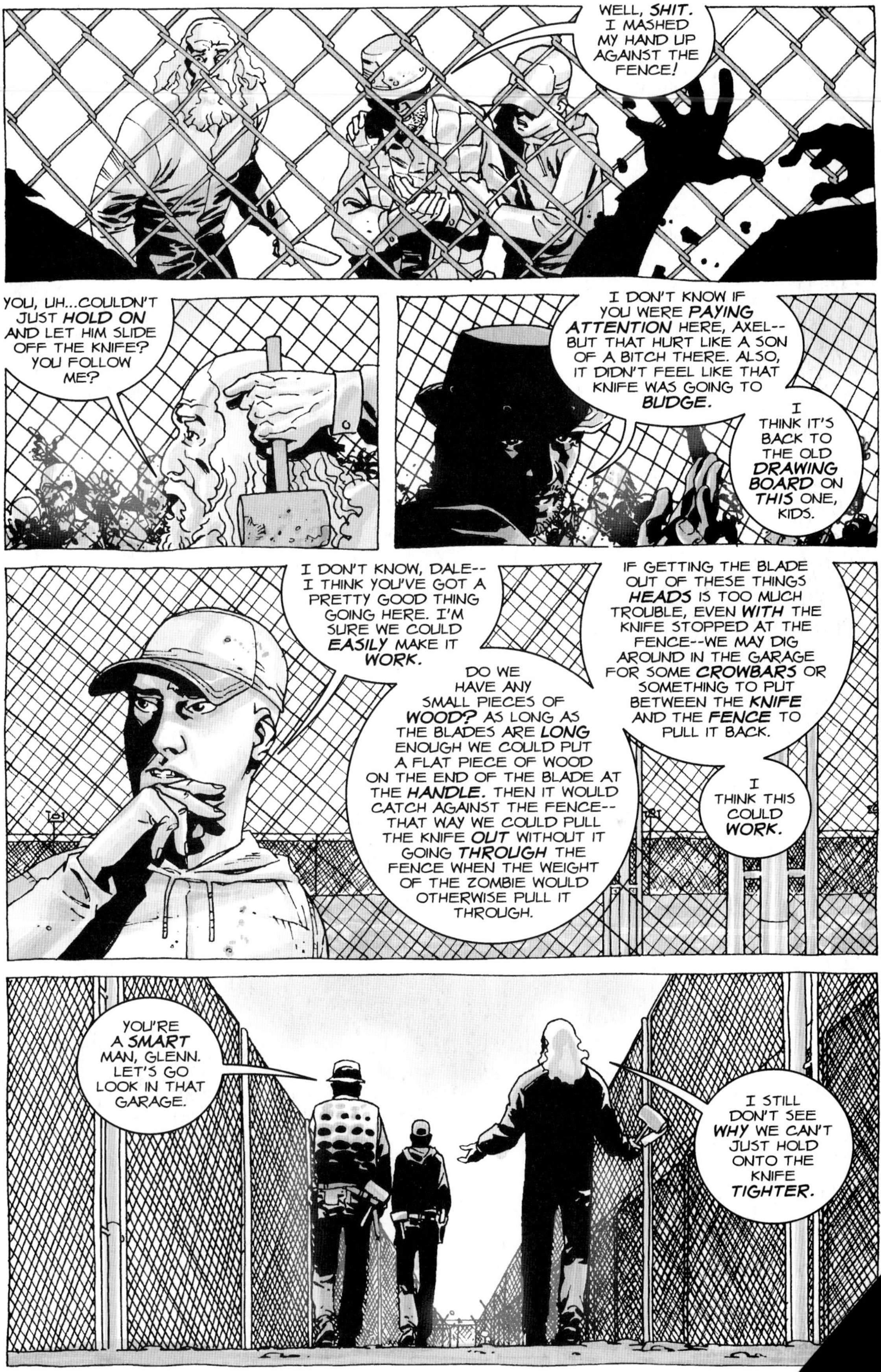
WELL, SHIT. I MASHED MY HAND UP AGAINST THE FENCE!
YOU, UH...COULDN'T JUST HOLD ON AND LET HIM SLIDE OFF THE KNIFE? YOU FOLLOW ME?
I DON'T KNOW IF YOU WERE PAYING ATTENTION HERE, AXEL-- BUT THAT HURT LIKE A SON OF A BITCH THERE. ALSO, IT DIDN'T FEEL LIKE THAT KNIFE WAS GOING TO BUDGE.
I THINK IT'S BACK TO THE OLD DRAWING BOARD ON THIS ONE, KIDS.
I DON'T KNOW, DALE-- I THINK YOU'VE GOT A PRETTY GOOD THING GOING HERE. I'M SURE WE COULD EASILY MAKE IT WORK.
DO WE HAVE ANY SMALL PIECES OF WOOD? AS LONG AS THE BLADES ARE LONG ENOUGH WE COULD PUT A FLAT PIECE OF WOOD ON THE END OF THE BLADE AT THE HANDLE. THEN IT WOULD CATCH AGAINST THE FENCE-- THAT WAY WE COULD PULL THE KNIFE OUT WITHOUT IT GOING THROUGH THE FENCE WHEN THE WEIGHT OF THE ZOMBIE WOULD OTHERWISE PULL IT THROUGH.
IF GETTING THE BLADE OUT OF THESE THINGS HEADS IS TOO MUCH TROUBLE, EVEN WITH THE KNIFE STOPPED AT THE FENCE--WE MAY DIG AROUND IN THE GARAGE FOR SOME CROWBARS OR SOMETHING TO PUT BETWEEN THE KNIFE AND THE FENCE TO PULL IT BACK.
I THINK THIS COULD WORK.
YOU'RE A SMART MAN, GLENN. LET'S GO LOOK IN THAT GARAGE.
I STILL DON'T SEE WHY WE CAN'T JUST HOLD ONTO THE KNIFE TIGHTER.

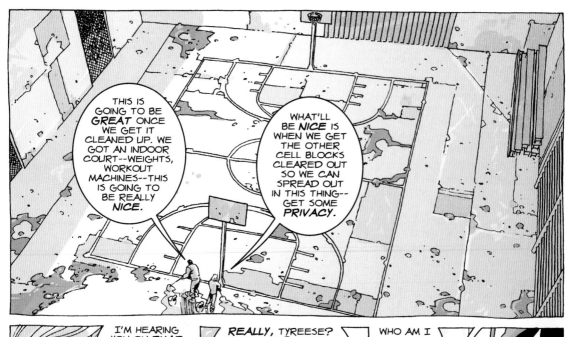

THIS IS GOING TO BE *GREAT* ONCE WE GET IT CLEANED UP. WE GOT AN INDOOR COURT--WEIGHTS, WORKOUT MACHINES--THIS IS GOING TO BE REALLY *NICE*.

WHAT'LL BE *NICE* IS WHEN WE GET THE OTHER CELL BLOCKS CLEARED OUT SO WE CAN SPREAD OUT IN THIS THING-- GET SOME *PRIVACY*.

I'M HEARING YOU ON *THAT* FRONT, CAROL-- I'M ABOUT *DUE* FOR SOME *ALONE* TIME.

REALLY, TYREESE? IS THAT *SO?* ALLEN IS WATCHING SOPHIA--AND THERE'S A *CLEAN* SPOT ON THE *FLOOR* BACK THERE--LOOKS *REALLY* COMFY.

WHO AM I TO DENY A WOMAN WHAT SHE *WANTS?*

JUST BE *QUICK* ABOUT IT--THIS FLOOR IS *COLD*.

YOU BE QUICK. I'M GOING TO TAKE MY *TIME*.

YES, SIR.

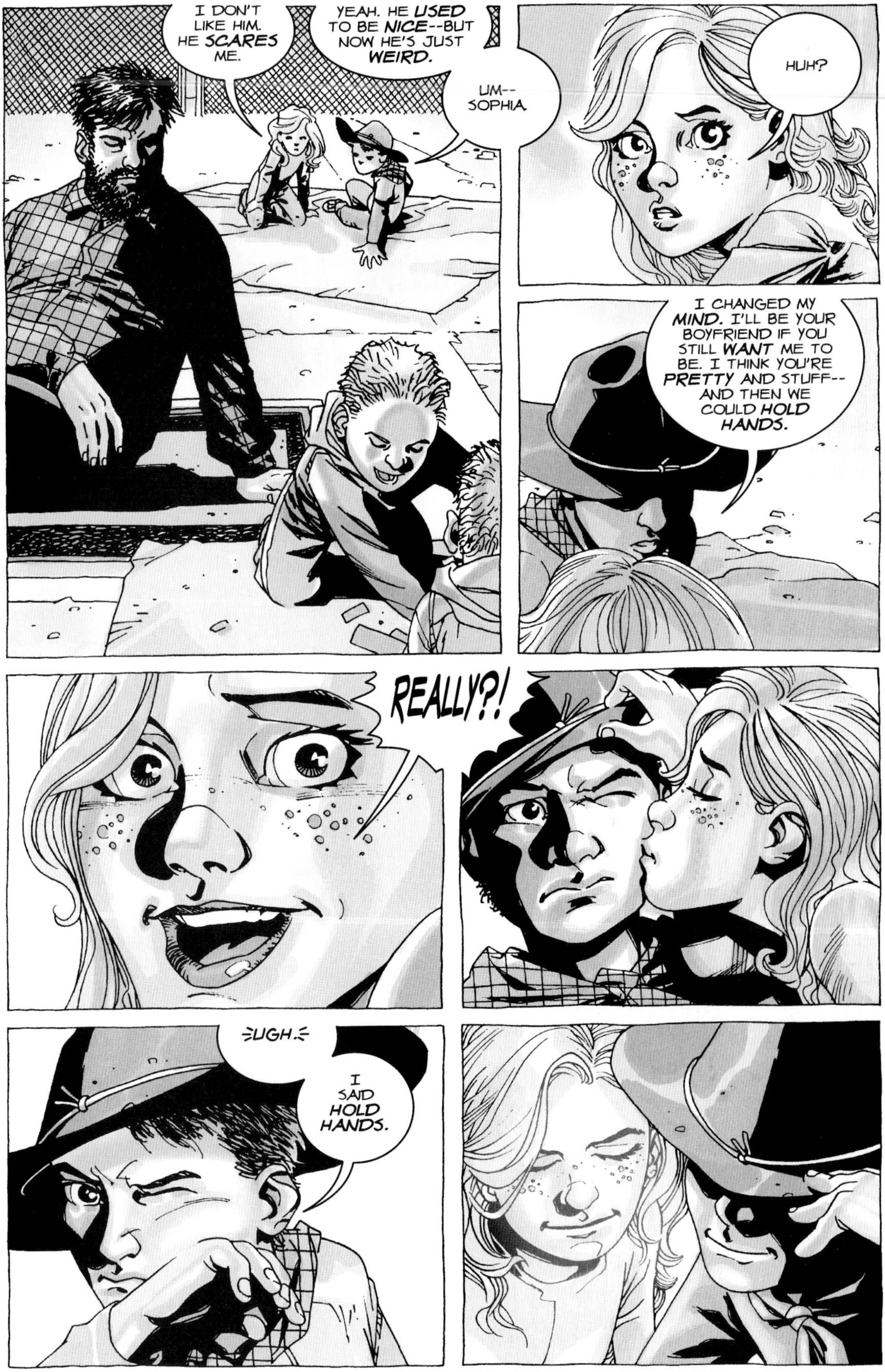
I DON'T LIKE HIM. HE SCARES ME.
YEAH. HE USED TO BE NICE--BUT NOW HE'S JUST WEIRD.
UM-- SOPHIA.
HUH?
I CHANGED MY MIND. I'LL BE YOUR BOYFRIEND IF YOU STILL WANT ME TO BE. I THINK YOU'RE PRETTY AND STUFF-- AND THEN WE COULD HOLD HANDS.
REALLY?!
UGH.
I SAID HOLD HANDS.

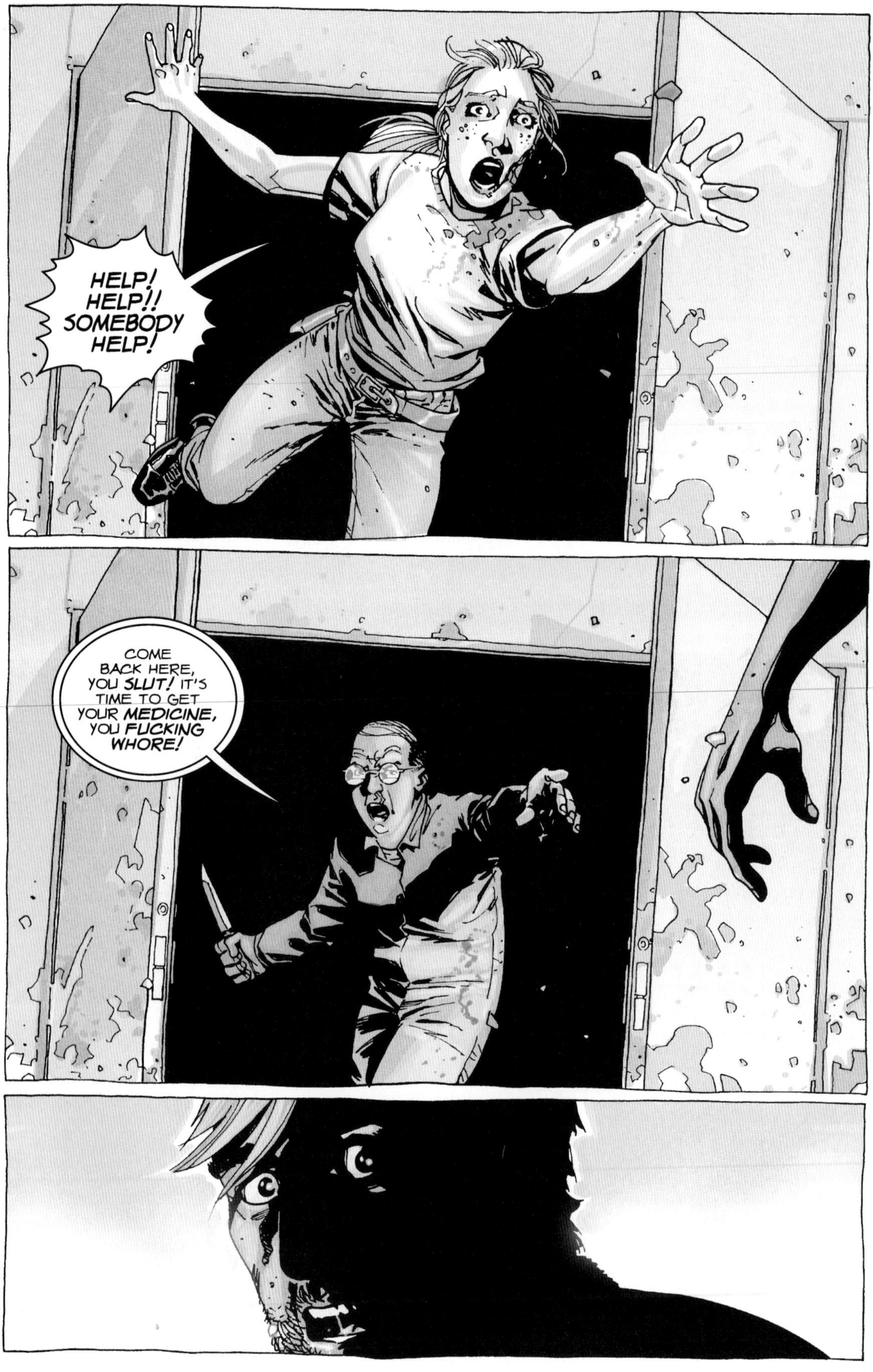
HELP! HELP!! SOMEBODY HELP!
COME BACK HERE, YOU SLUT! IT'S TIME TO GET YOUR MEDICINE, YOU FUCKING WHORE!

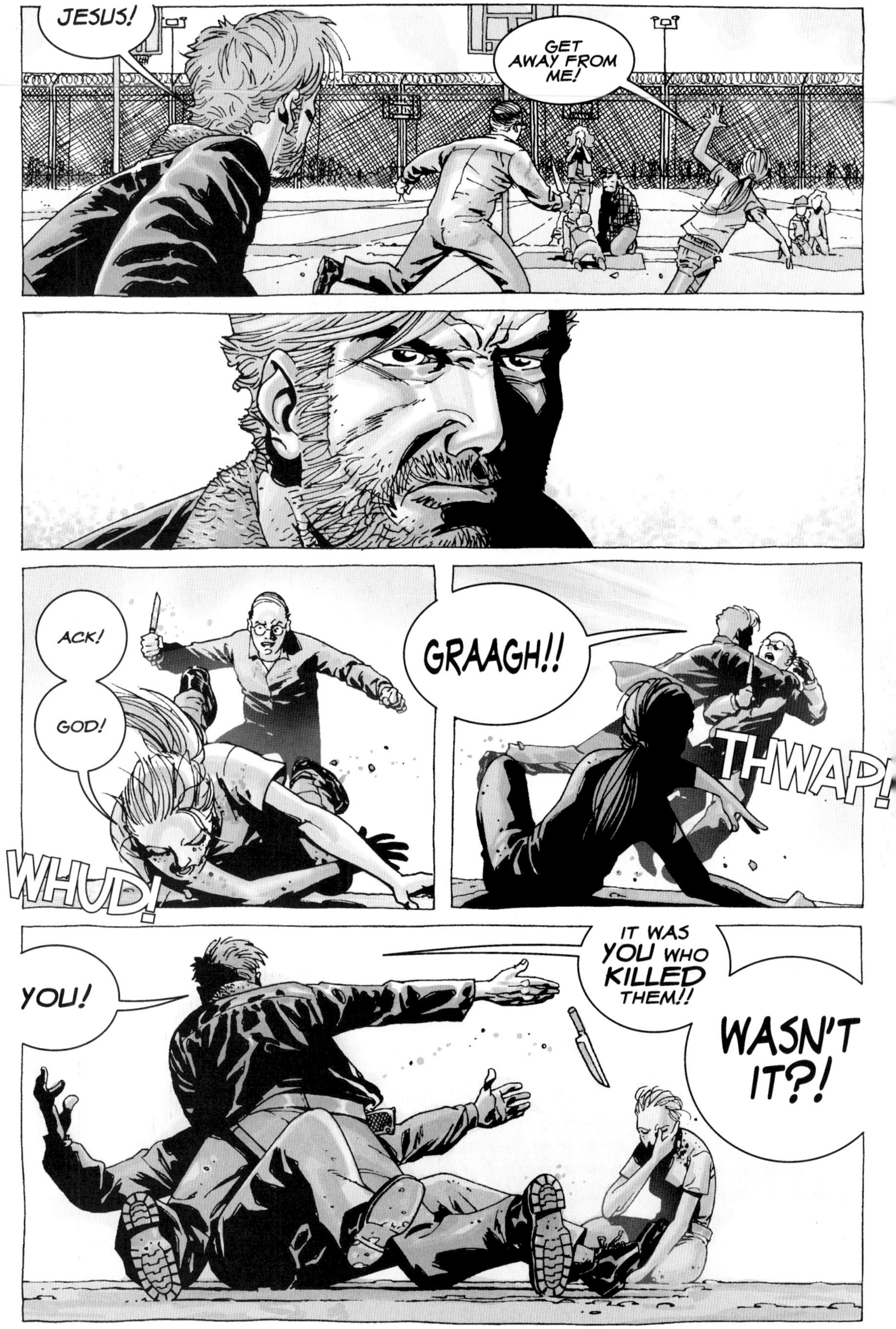
JESUS!
GET AWAY FROM ME!
ACK!
GOD!
WHUD!
GRAAGH!!
THWAP!
YOU!
IT WAS YOU WHO KILLED THEM!!
WASN'T IT?!

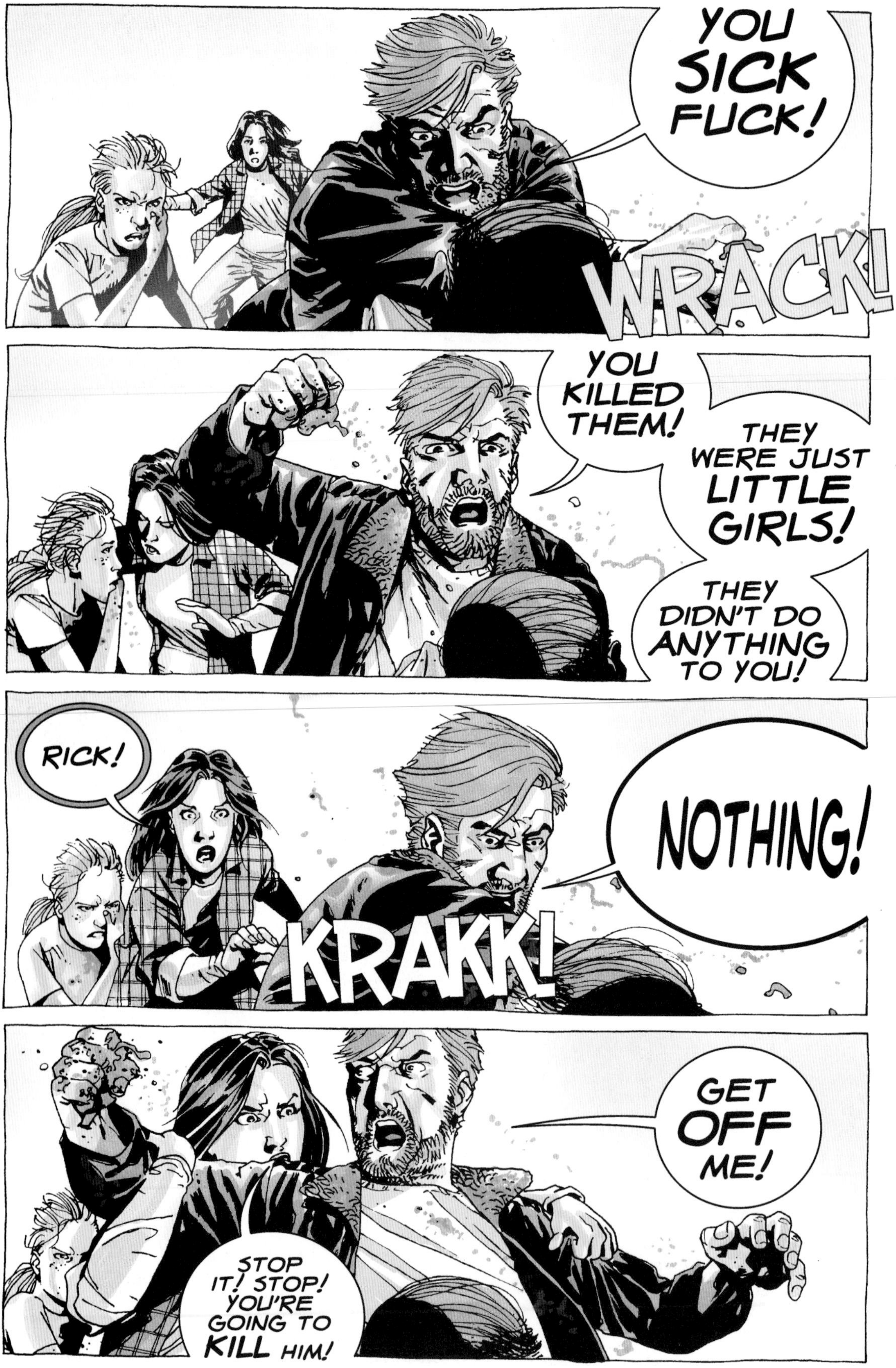
YOU SICK FUCK!
WRACK!
YOU KILLED THEM!
THEY WERE JUST LITTLE GIRLS!
THEY DIDN'T DO ANYTHING TO YOU!
RICK!
NOTHING!
KRAKK!
GET OFF ME!
STOP IT! STOP! YOU'RE GOING TO KILL HIM!

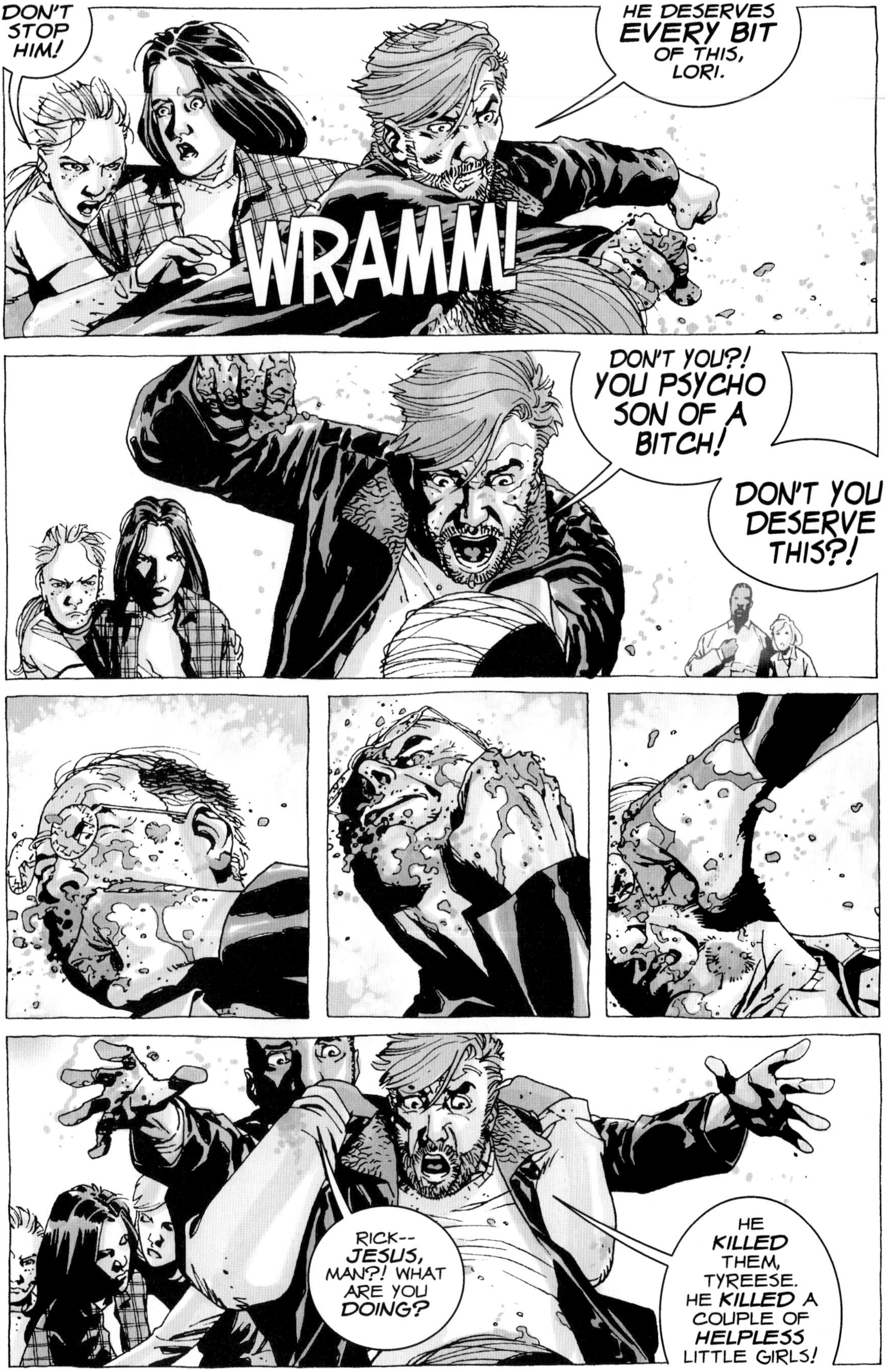
DON'T STOP HIM!
HE DESERVES EVERY BIT OF THIS, LORI.
WRAMM!
DON'T YOU?! YOU PSYCHO SON OF A BITCH!
DON'T YOU DESERVE THIS?!
RICK-- JESUS, MAN?! WHAT ARE YOU DOING?
HE KILLED THEM, TYREESE. HE KILLED A COUPLE OF HELPLESS LITTLE GIRLS!

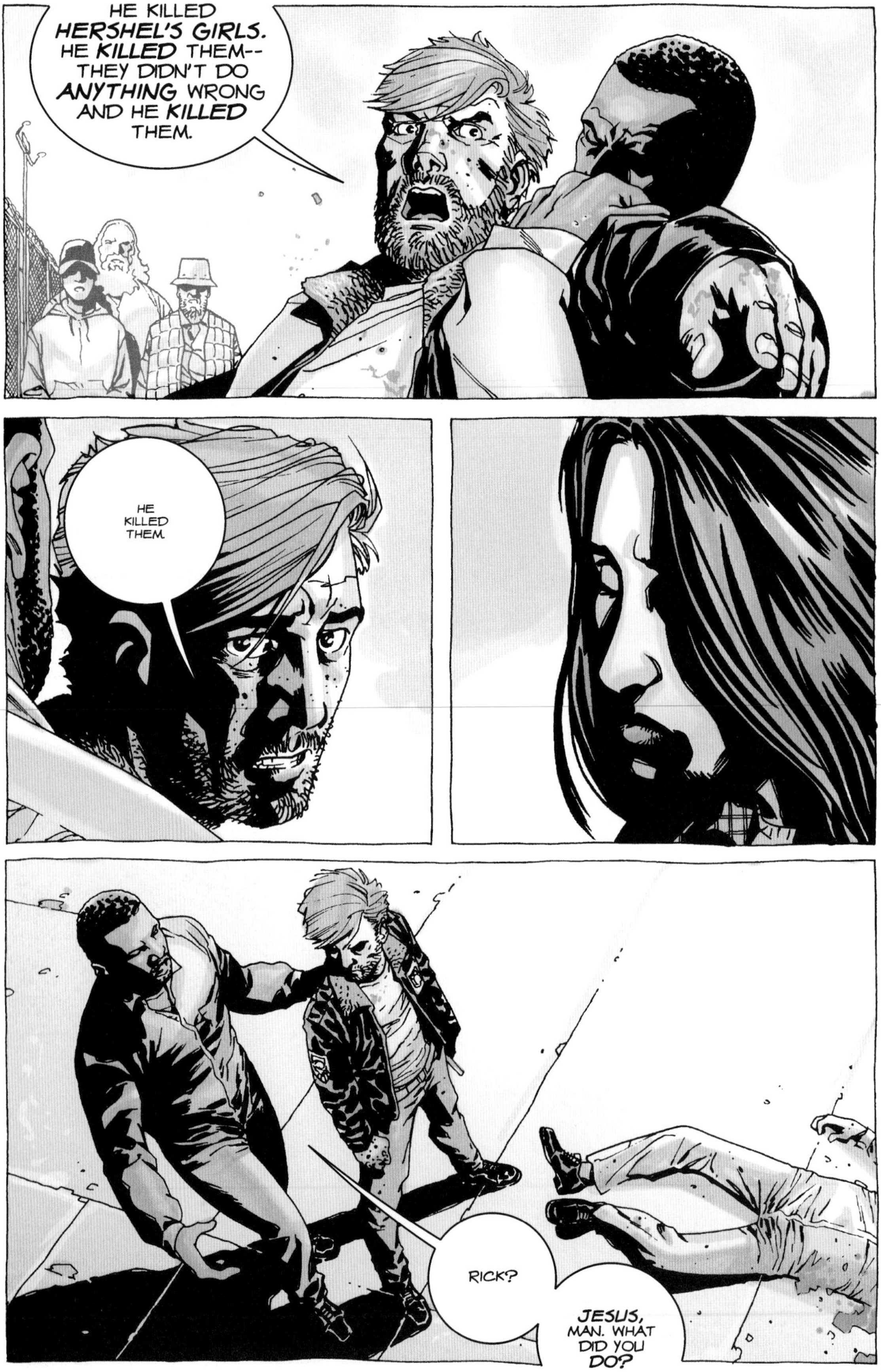
HE KILLED HERSHEL'S GIRLS. HE KILLED THEM-- THEY DIDN'T DO ANYTHING WRONG AND HE KILLED THEM.
HE KILLED THEM.
RICK?
JESUS, MAN. WHAT DID YOU DO?

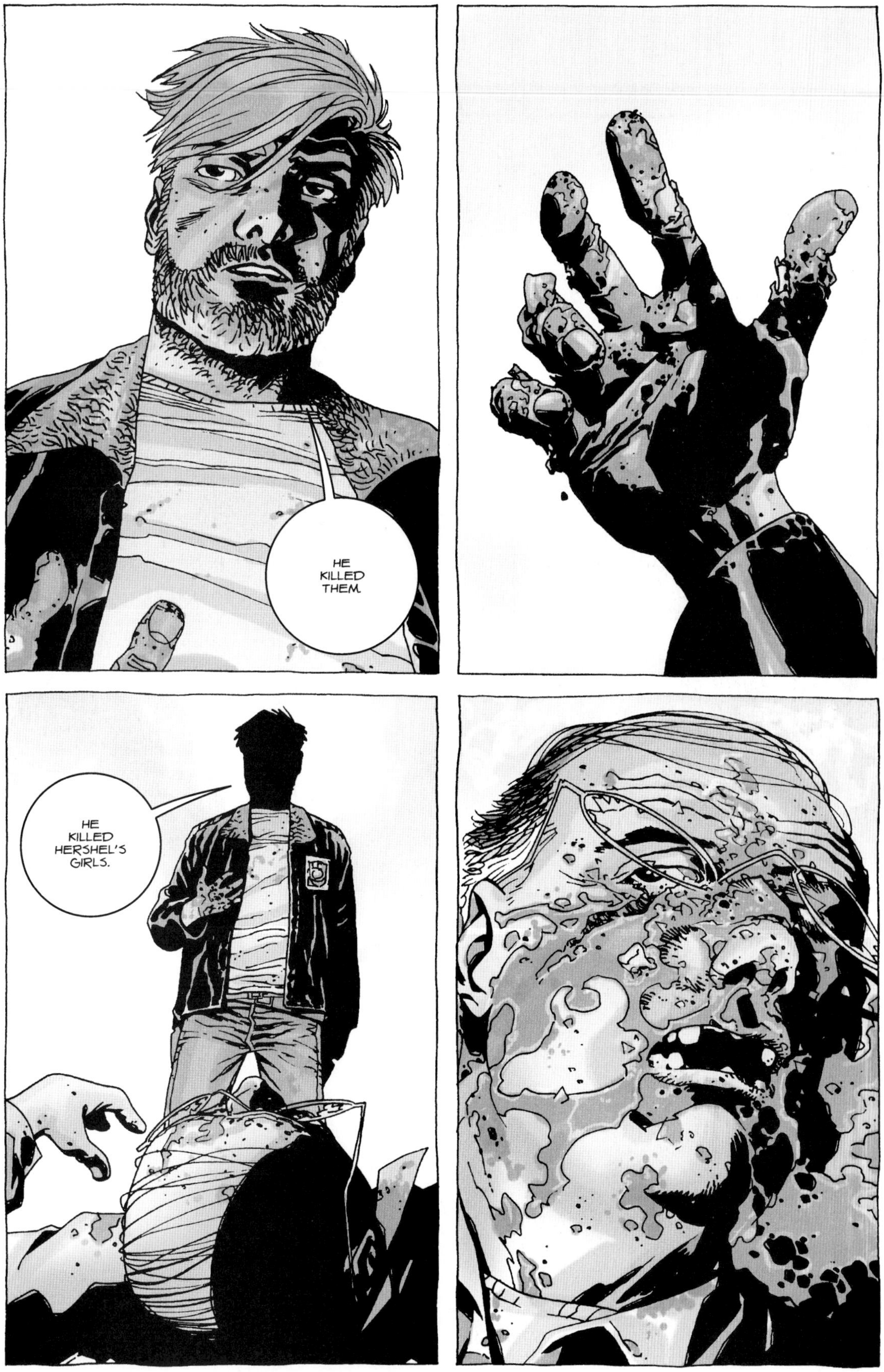
HE KILLED THEM.
HE KILLED HERSHEL'S GIRLS.

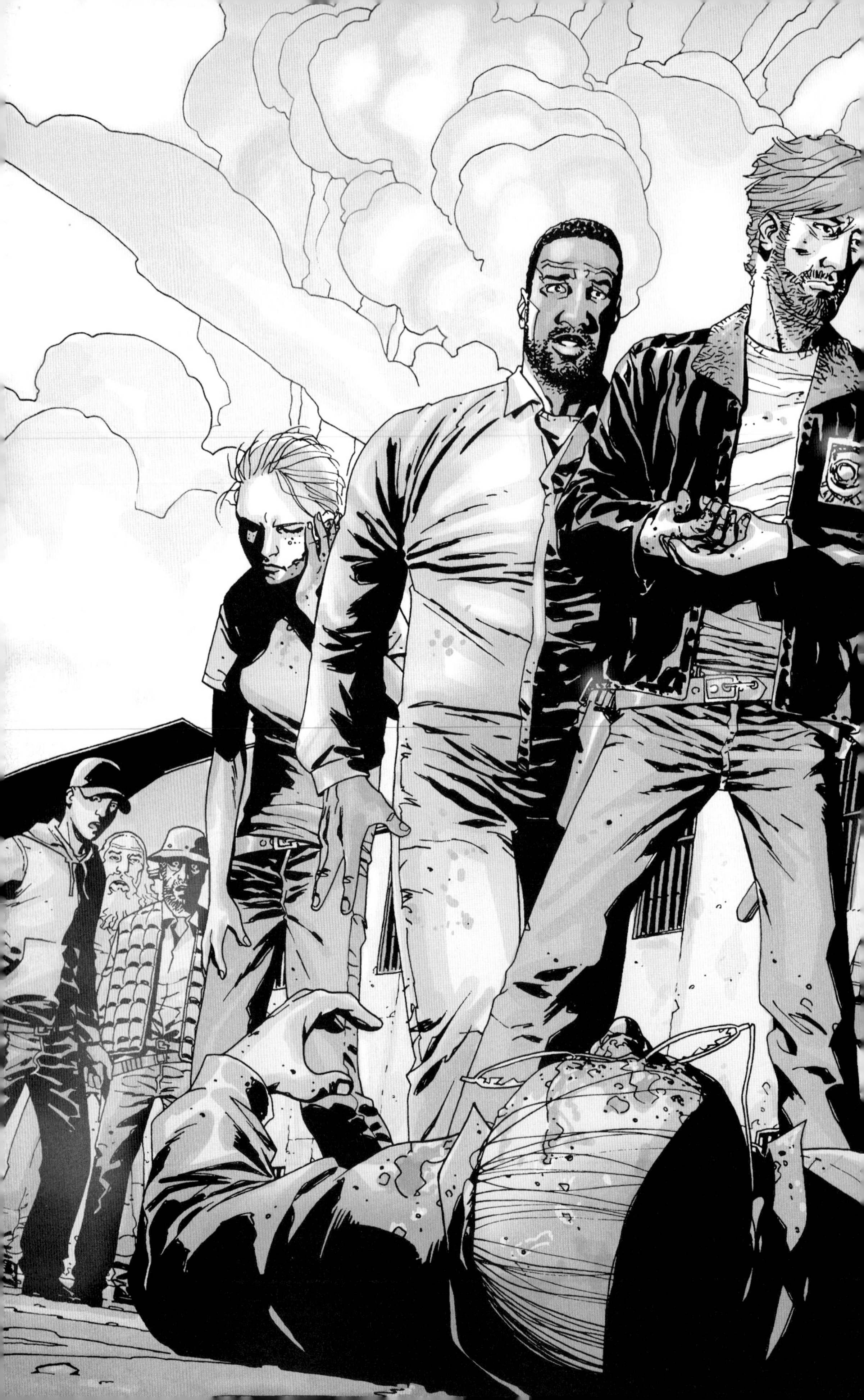

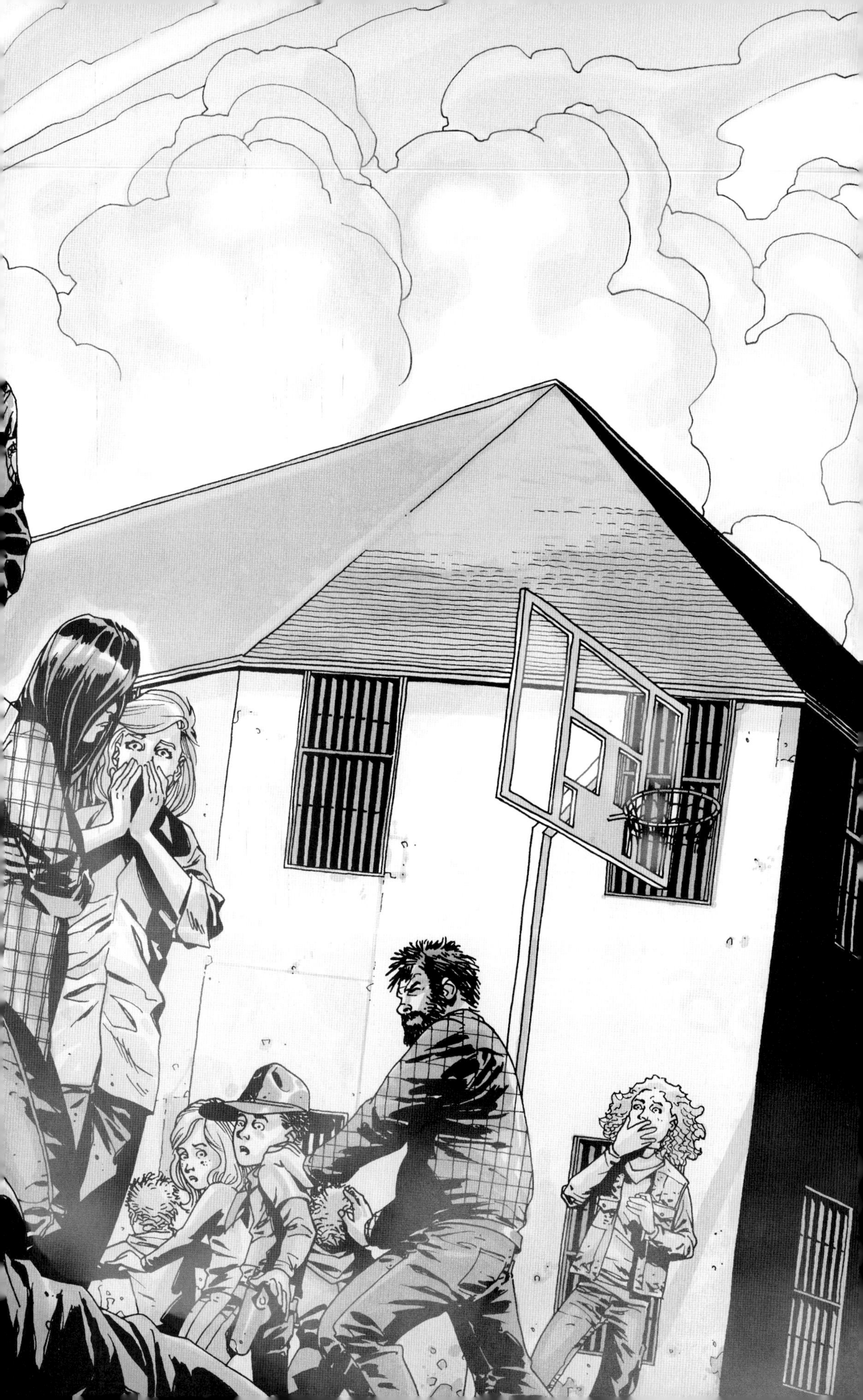

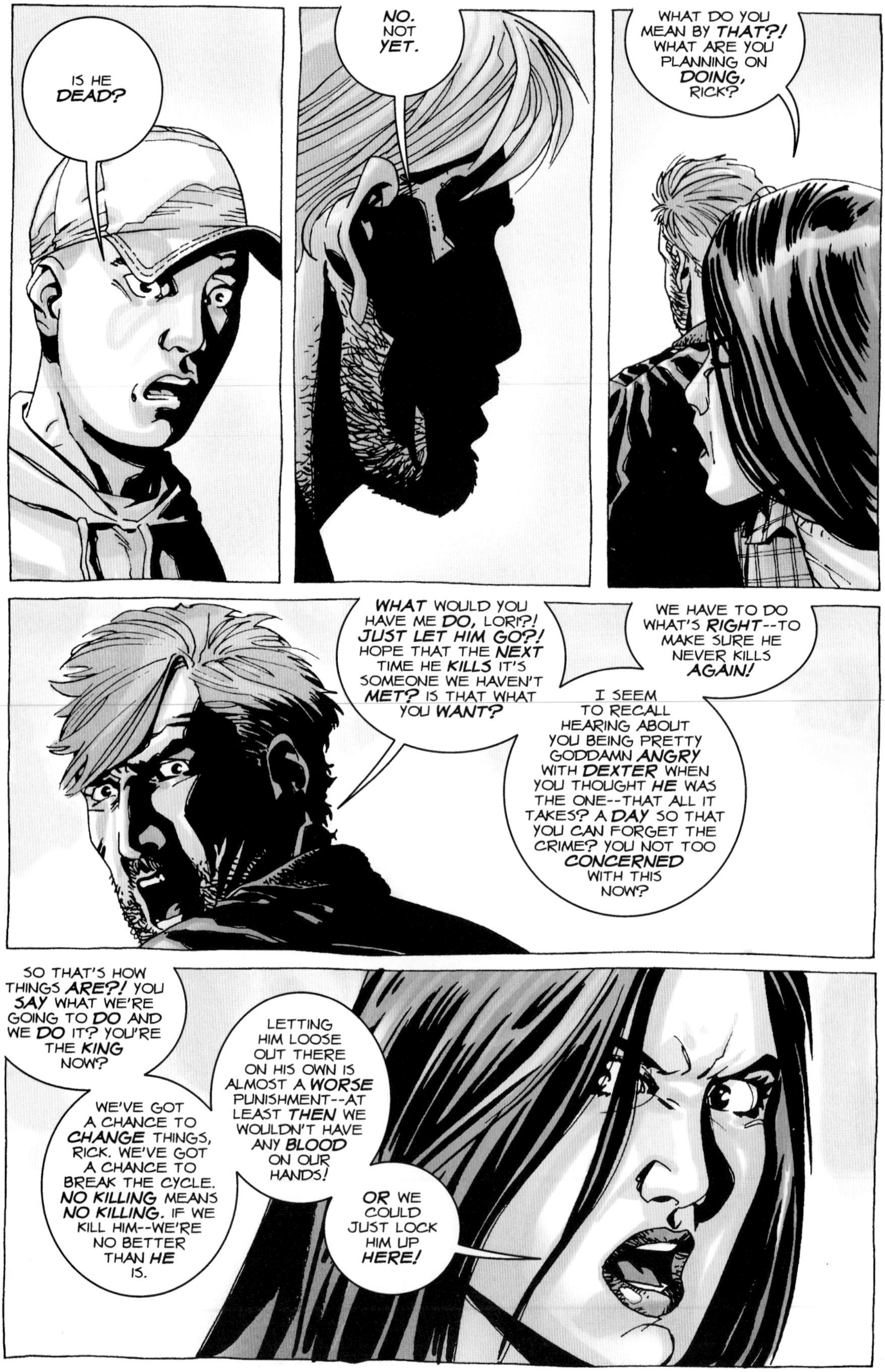
IS HE DEAD?
NO. NOT YET.
WHAT DO YOU MEAN BY THAT?! WHAT ARE YOU PLANNING ON DOING, RICK?
WHAT WOULD YOU HAVE ME DO, LORI?! JUST LET HIM GO?! HOPE THAT THE NEXT TIME HE KILLS IT'S SOMEONE WE HAVEN'T MET? IS THAT WHAT YOU WANT?
WE HAVE TO DO WHAT'S RIGHT--TO MAKE SURE HE NEVER KILLS AGAIN!
I SEEM TO RECALL HEARING ABOUT YOU BEING PRETTY GODDAMN ANGRY WITH DEXTER WHEN YOU THOUGHT HE WAS THE ONE--THAT ALL IT TAKES? A DAY SO THAT YOU CAN FORGET THE CRIME? YOU NOT TOO CONCERNED WITH THIS NOW?
SO THAT'S HOW THINGS ARE?! YOU SAY WHAT WE'RE GOING TO DO AND WE DO IT? YOU'RE THE KING NOW?
WE'VE GOT A CHANCE TO CHANGE THINGS, RICK. WE'VE GOT A CHANCE TO BREAK THE CYCLE. NO KILLING MEANS NO KILLING. IF WE KILL HIM--WE'RE NO BETTER THAN HE IS.
LETTING HIM LOOSE OUT THERE ON HIS OWN IS ALMOST A WORSE PUNISHMENT--AT LEAST THEN WE WOULDN'T HAVE ANY BLOOD ON OUR HANDS!
OR WE COULD JUST LOCK HIM UP HERE!

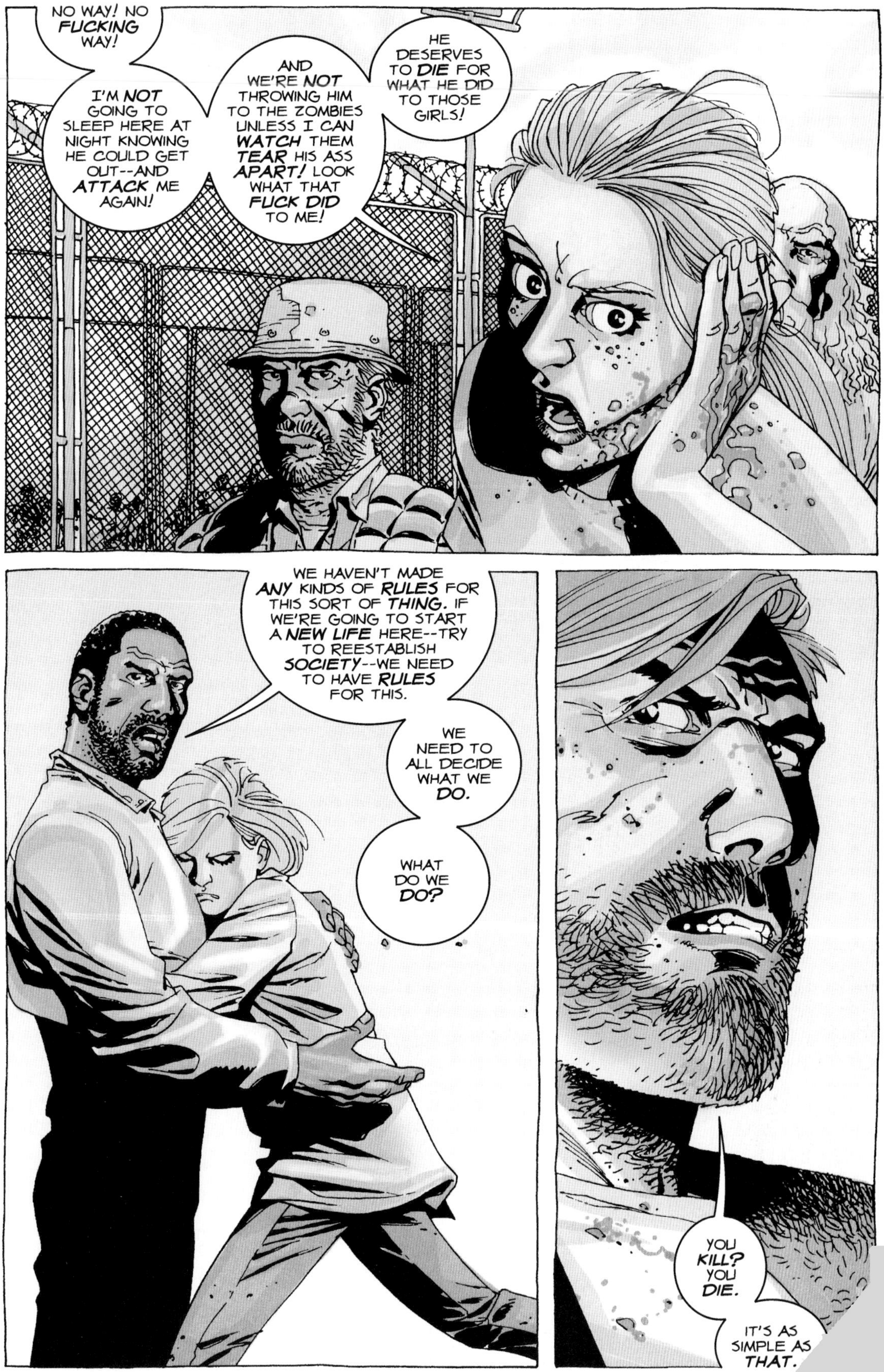
NO WAY! NO FUCKING WAY!
I'M NOT GOING TO SLEEP HERE AT NIGHT KNOWING HE COULD GET OUT--AND ATTACK ME AGAIN!
AND WE'RE NOT THROWING HIM TO THE ZOMBIES UNLESS I CAN WATCH THEM TEAR HIS ASS APART! LOOK WHAT THAT FUCK DID TO ME!
HE DESERVES TO DIE FOR WHAT HE DID TO THOSE GIRLS!
WE HAVEN'T MADE ANY KINDS OF RULES FOR THIS SORT OF THING. IF WE'RE GOING TO START A NEW LIFE HERE--TRY TO REESTABLISH SOCIETY--WE NEED TO HAVE RULES FOR THIS.
WE NEED TO ALL DECIDE WHAT WE DO.
WHAT DO WE DO?
YOU KILL? YOU DIE.
IT'S AS SIMPLE AS THAT.

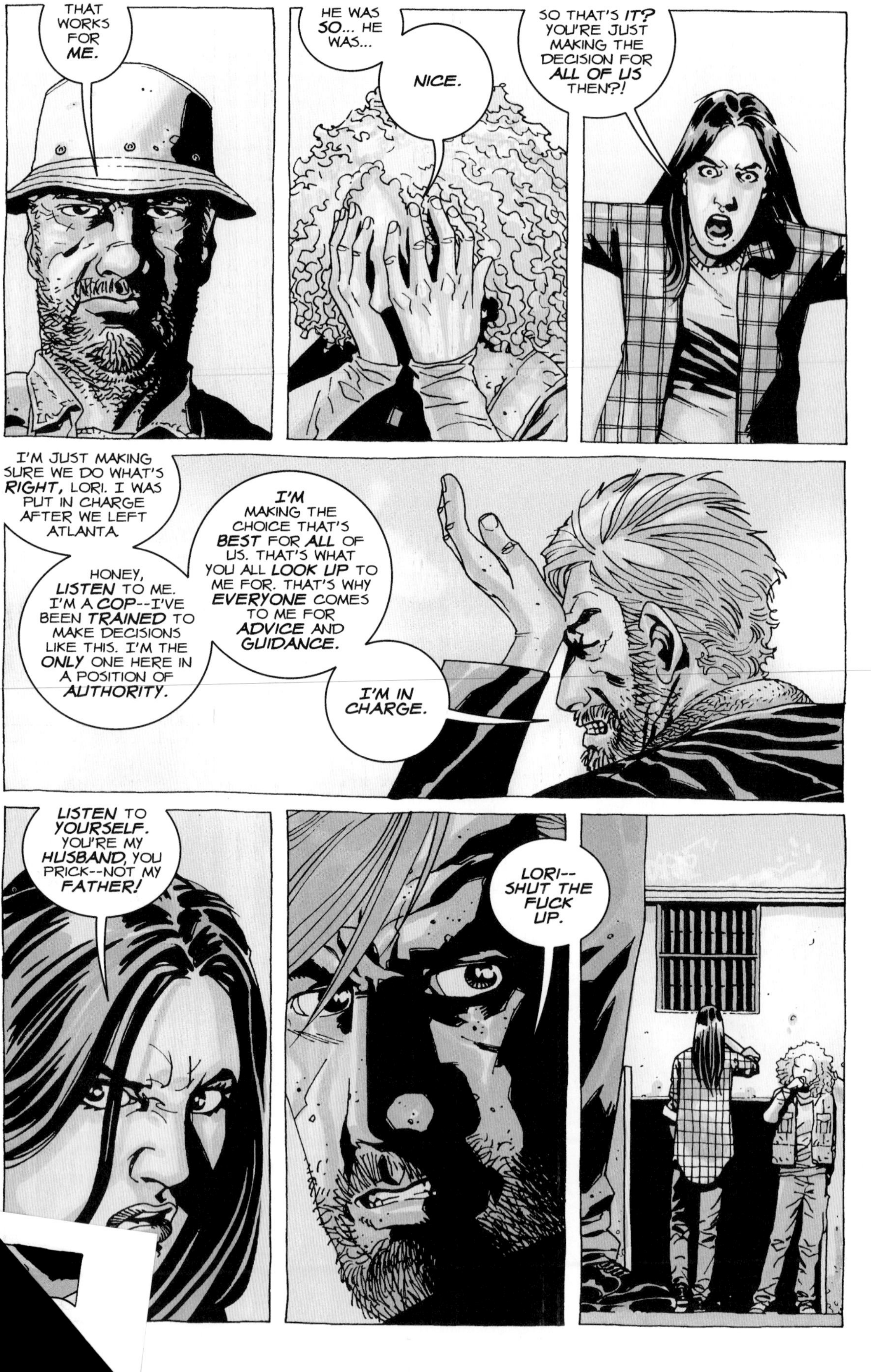
THAT WORKS FOR ME.
HE WAS SO... HE WAS...
NICE.
SO THAT'S IT? YOU'RE JUST MAKING THE DECISION FOR ALL OF US THEN?!
I'M JUST MAKING SURE WE DO WHAT'S RIGHT, LORI. I WAS PUT IN CHARGE AFTER WE LEFT ATLANTA.
HONEY, LISTEN TO ME. I'M A COP--I'VE BEEN TRAINED TO MAKE DECISIONS LIKE THIS. I'M THE ONLY ONE HERE IN A POSITION OF AUTHORITY.
I'M MAKING THE CHOICE THAT'S BEST FOR ALL OF US. THAT'S WHAT YOU ALL LOOK UP TO ME FOR. THAT'S WHY EVERYONE COMES TO ME FOR ADVICE AND GUIDANCE.
I'M IN CHARGE.
LISTEN TO YOURSELF. YOU'RE MY HUSBAND, YOU PRICK--NOT MY FATHER!
LORI-- SHUT THE FUCK UP.

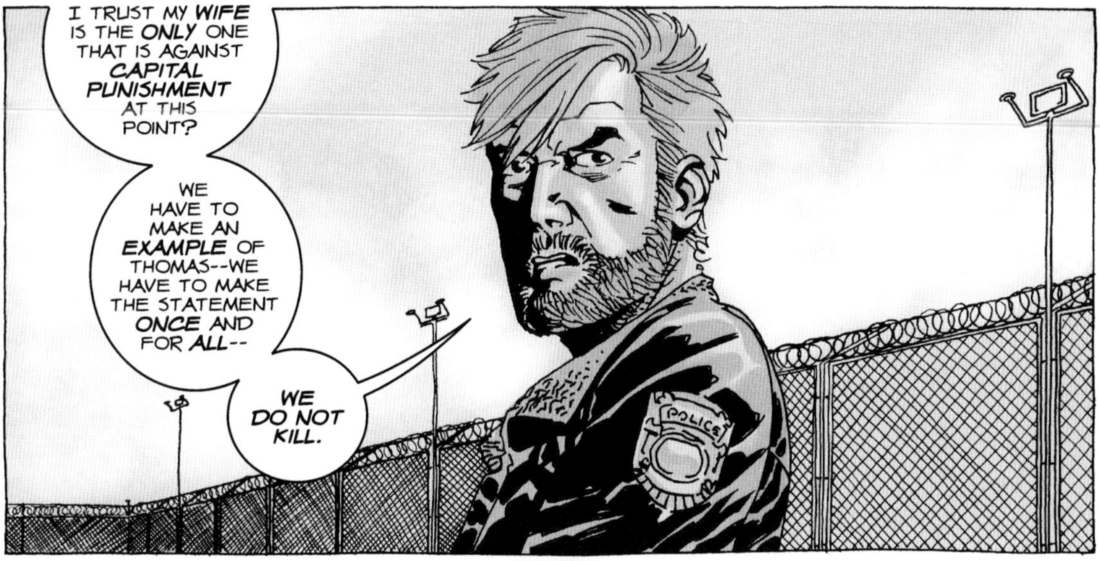
I TRUST MY WIFE IS THE ONLY ONE THAT IS AGAINST CAPITAL PUNISHMENT AT THIS POINT?
WE HAVE TO MAKE AN EXAMPLE OF THOMAS--WE HAVE TO MAKE THE STATEMENT ONCE AND FOR ALL--
WE DO NOT KILL.

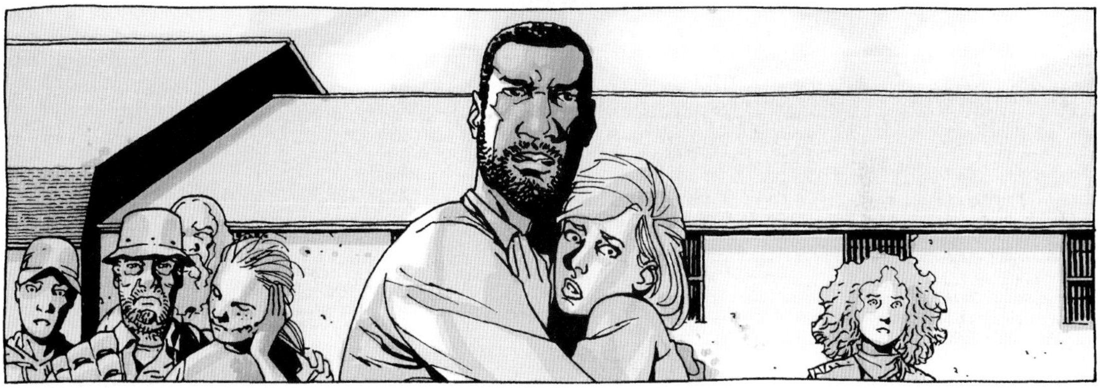

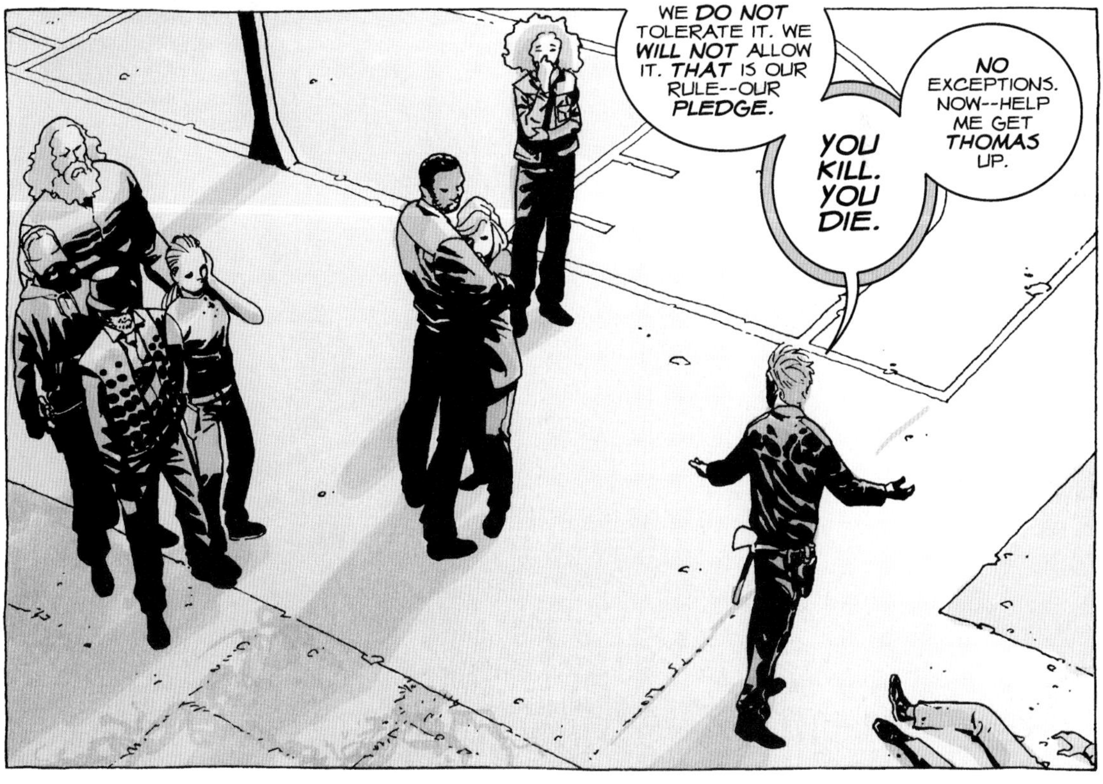
WE DO NOT TOLERATE IT. WE WILL NOT ALLOW IT. THAT IS OUR RULE--OUR PLEDGE.
YOU KILL. YOU DIE.
NO EXCEPTIONS. NOW--HELP ME GET THOMAS UP.

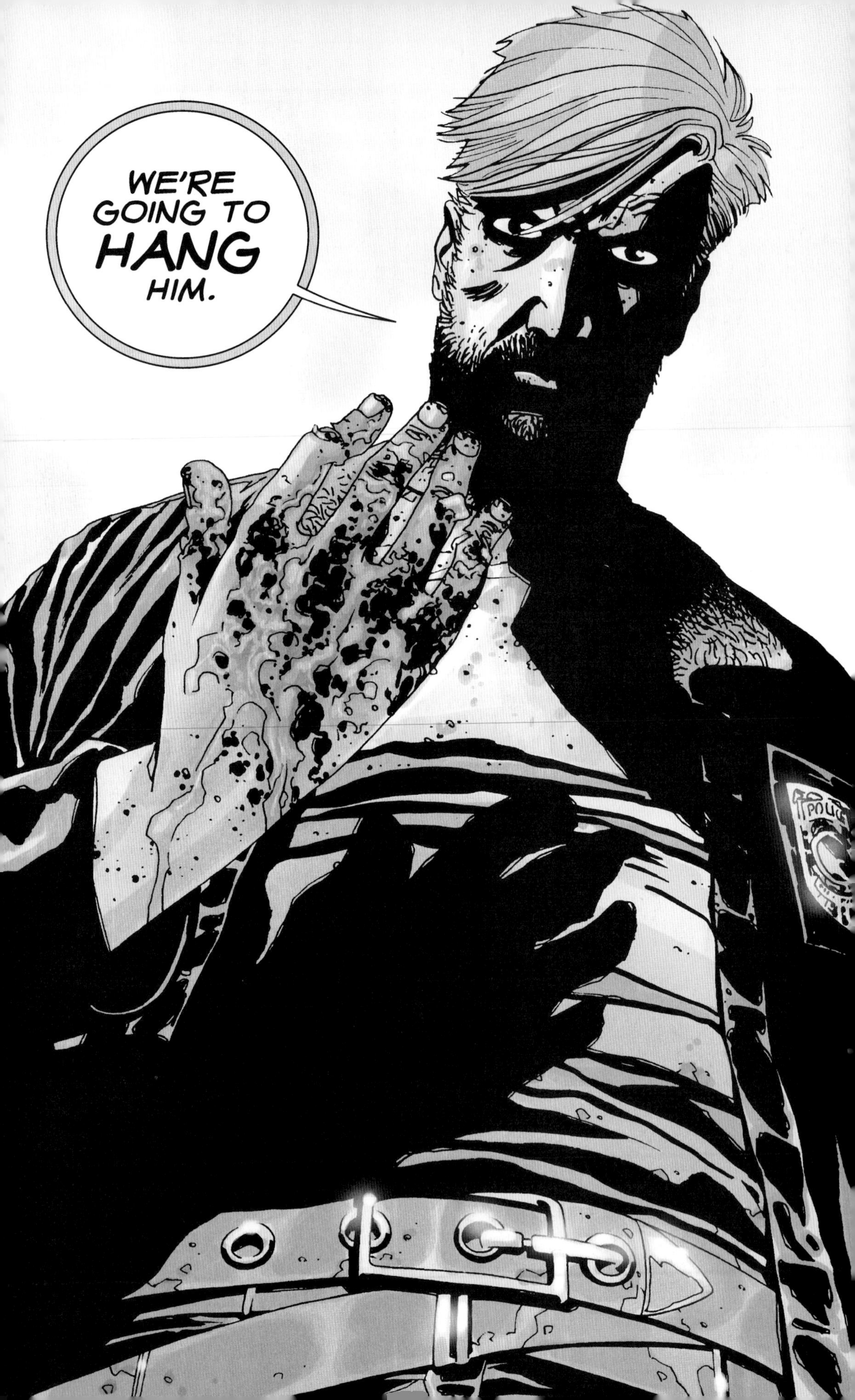
WE'RE GOING TO HANG HIM.

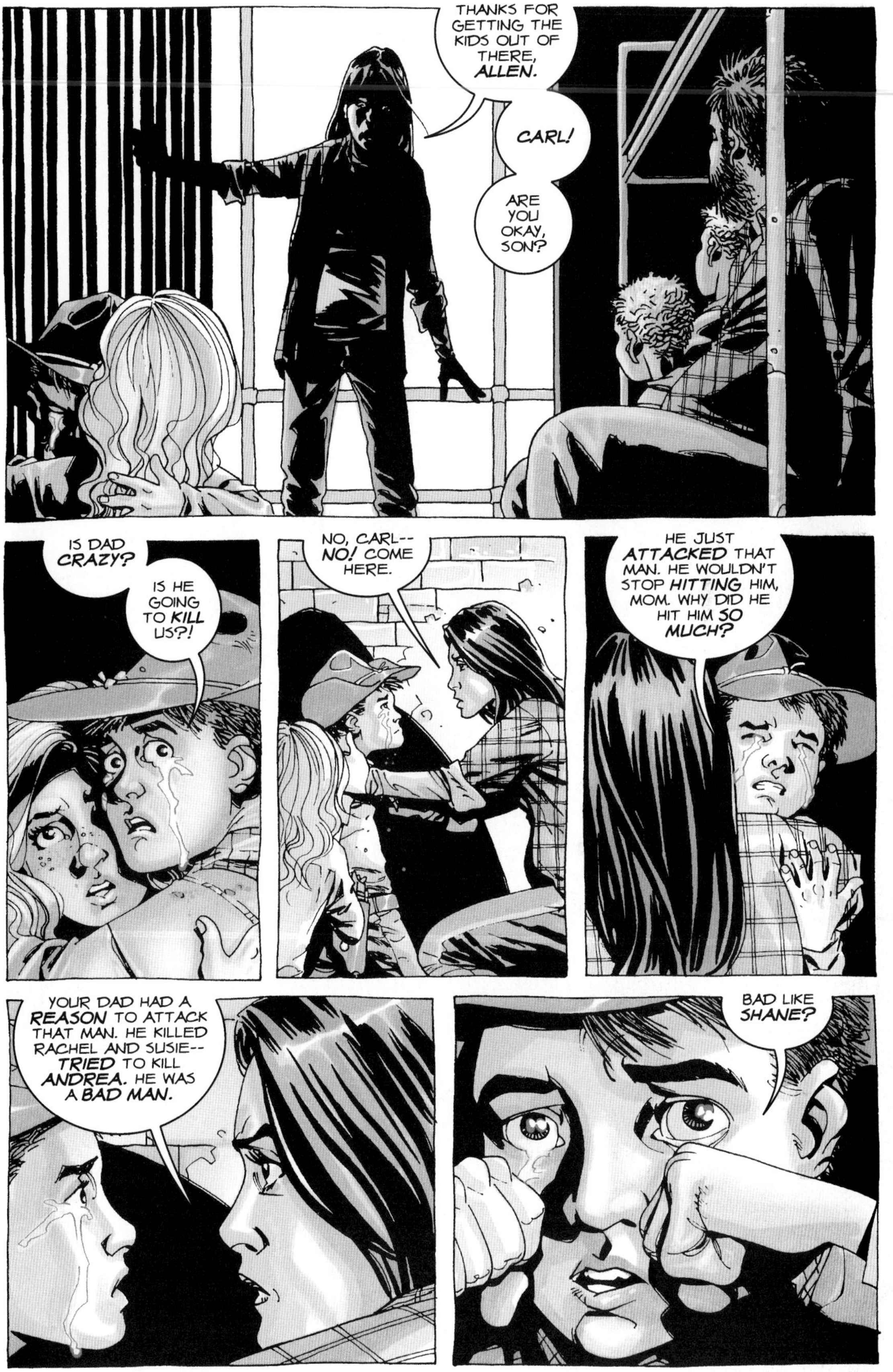
THANKS FOR GETTING THE KIDS OUT OF THERE, ALLEN.
CARL!
ARE YOU OKAY, SON?
IS DAD CRAZY?
IS HE GOING TO KILL US?!
NO, CARL-- NO! COME HERE.
HE JUST ATTACKED THAT MAN. HE WOULDN'T STOP HITTING HIM, MOM. WHY DID HE HIT HIM SO MUCH?
YOUR DAD HAD A REASON TO ATTACK THAT MAN. HE KILLED RACHEL AND SUSIE-- TRIED TO KILL ANDREA. HE WAS A BAD MAN.
BAD LIKE SHANE?

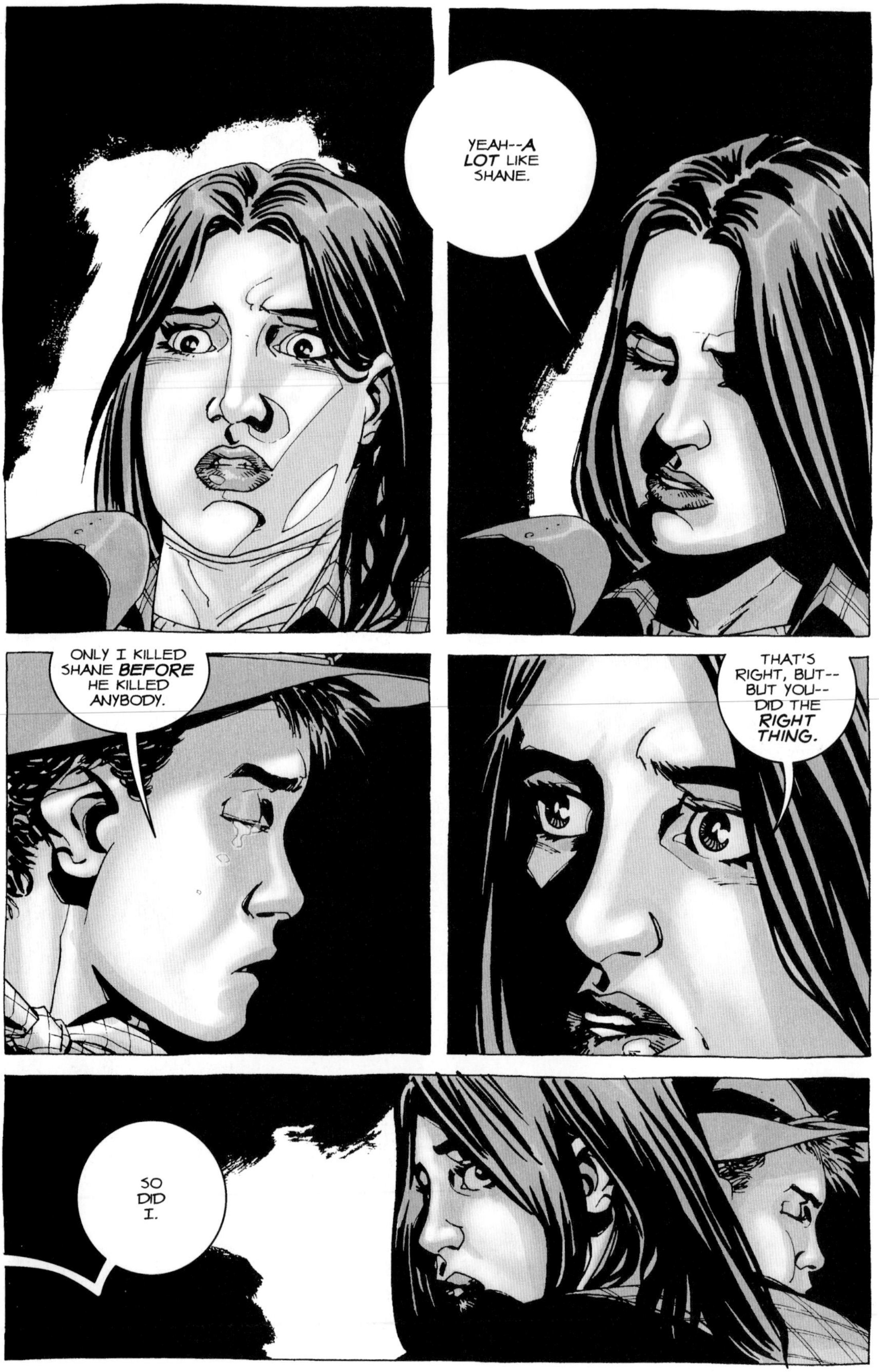
YEAH--A LOT LIKE SHANE.
ONLY I KILLED SHANE BEFORE HE KILLED ANYBODY.
THAT'S RIGHT, BUT-- BUT YOU-- DID THE RIGHT THING.
SO DID I.

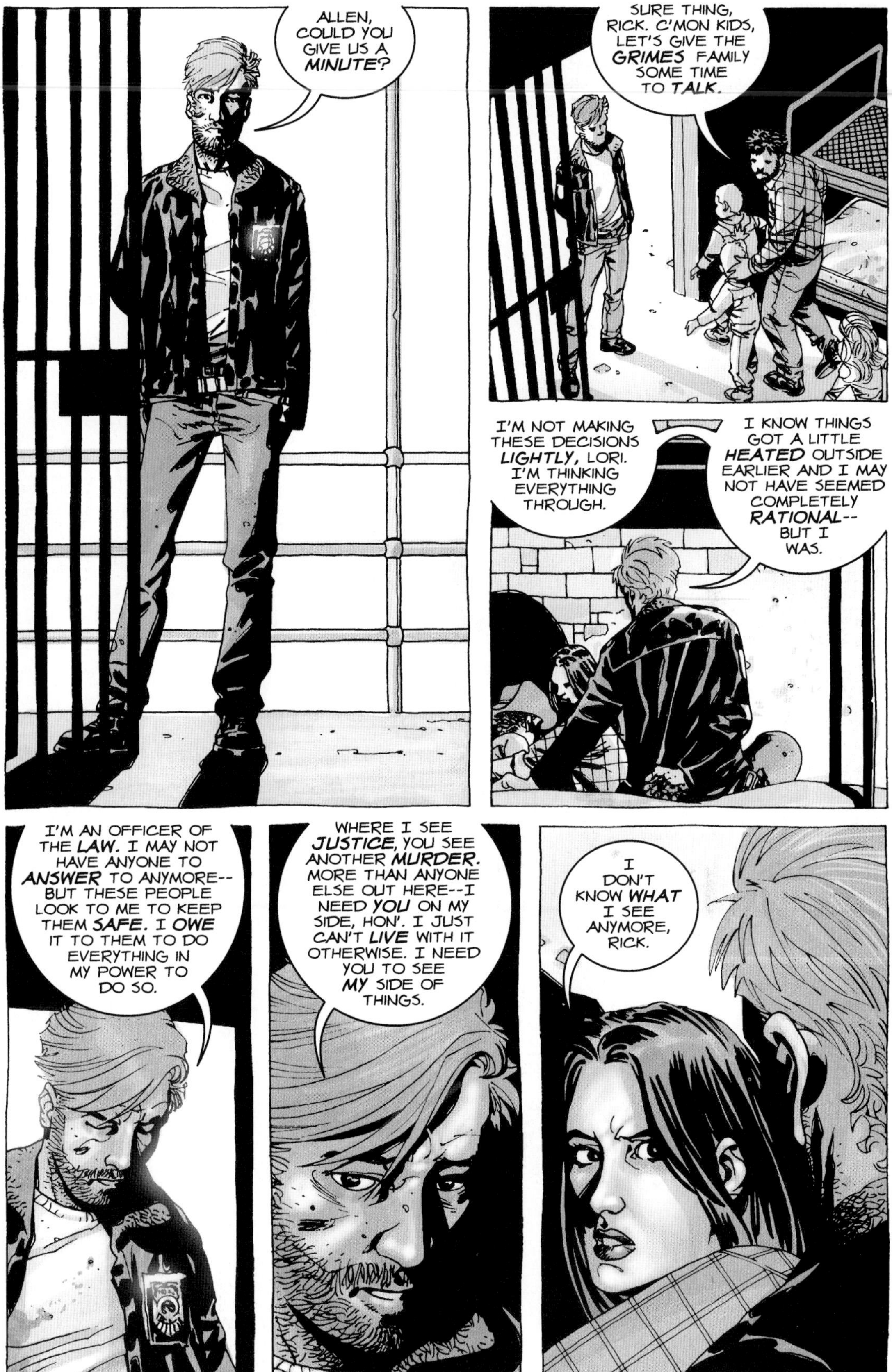
ALLEN, COULD YOU GIVE US A MINUTE?
SURE THING, RICK. C'MON KIDS, LET'S GIVE THE GRIMES FAMILY SOME TIME TO TALK.
I'M NOT MAKING THESE DECISIONS LIGHTLY, LORI. I'M THINKING EVERYTHING THROUGH.
I KNOW THINGS GOT A LITTLE HEATED OUTSIDE EARLIER AND I MAY NOT HAVE SEEMED COMPLETELY RATIONAL-- BUT I WAS.
I'M AN OFFICER OF THE LAW. I MAY NOT HAVE ANYONE TO ANSWER TO ANYMORE-- BUT THESE PEOPLE LOOK TO ME TO KEEP THEM SAFE. I OWE IT TO THEM TO DO EVERYTHING IN MY POWER TO DO SO.
WHERE I SEE JUSTICE, YOU SEE ANOTHER MURDER. MORE THAN ANYONE ELSE OUT HERE--I NEED YOU ON MY SIDE, HON'. I JUST CAN'T LIVE WITH IT OTHERWISE. I NEED YOU TO SEE MY SIDE OF THINGS.
I DON'T KNOW WHAT I SEE ANYMORE, RICK.

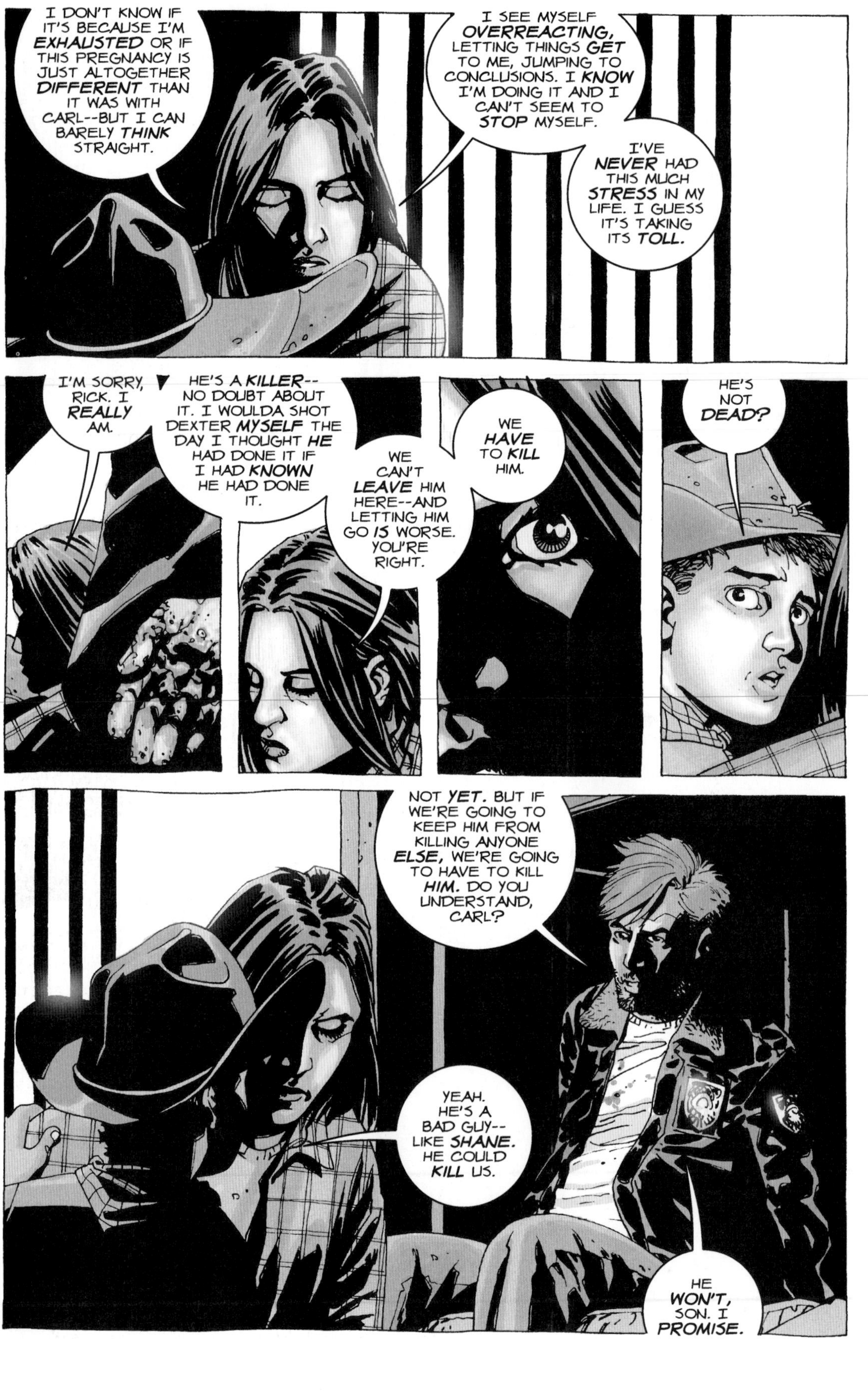

I DON'T KNOW IF IT'S BECAUSE I'M EXHAUSTED OR IF THIS PREGNANCY IS JUST ALTOGETHER DIFFERENT THAN IT WAS WITH CARL--BUT I CAN BARELY THINK STRAIGHT.
I SEE MYSELF OVERREACTING, LETTING THINGS GET TO ME, JUMPING TO CONCLUSIONS. I KNOW I'M DOING IT AND I CAN'T SEEM TO STOP MYSELF.
I'VE NEVER HAD THIS MUCH STRESS IN MY LIFE. I GUESS IT'S TAKING ITS TOLL.
I'M SORRY, RICK. I REALLY AM.
HE'S A KILLER-- NO DOUBT ABOUT IT. I WOULDA SHOT DEXTER MYSELF THE DAY I THOUGHT HE HAD DONE IT IF I HAD KNOWN HE HAD DONE IT.
WE CAN'T LEAVE HIM HERE--AND LETTING HIM GO IS WORSE. YOU'RE RIGHT.
WE HAVE TO KILL HIM.
HE'S NOT DEAD?
NOT YET. BUT IF WE'RE GOING TO KEEP HIM FROM KILLING ANYONE ELSE, WE'RE GOING TO HAVE TO KILL HIM. DO YOU UNDERSTAND, CARL?
YEAH. HE'S A BAD GUY-- LIKE SHANE. HE COULD KILL US.
HE WON'T, SON. I PROMISE.

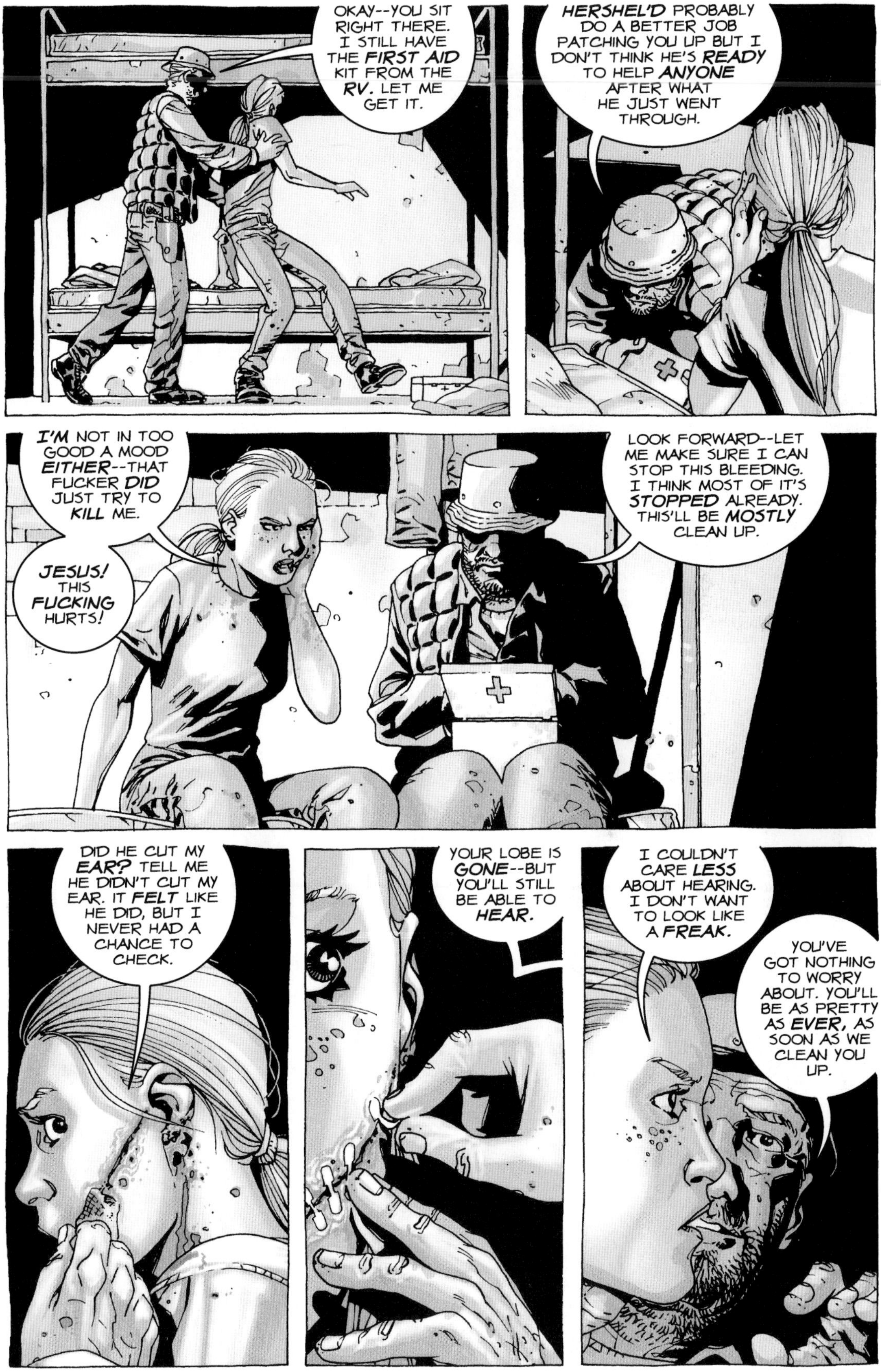
OKAY--YOU SIT RIGHT THERE. I STILL HAVE THE FIRST AID KIT FROM THE RV. LET ME GET IT.
HERSHEL'D PROBABLY DO A BETTER JOB PATCHING YOU UP BUT I DON'T THINK HE'S READY TO HELP ANYONE AFTER WHAT HE JUST WENT THROUGH.
I'M NOT IN TOO GOOD A MOOD EITHER--THAT FUCKER DID JUST TRY TO KILL ME.
JESUS! THIS FUCKING HURTS!
LOOK FORWARD--LET ME MAKE SURE I CAN STOP THIS BLEEDING. I THINK MOST OF IT'S STOPPED ALREADY. THIS'LL BE MOSTLY CLEAN UP.
DID HE CUT MY EAR? TELL ME HE DIDN'T CUT MY EAR. IT FELT LIKE HE DID, BUT I NEVER HAD A CHANCE TO CHECK.
YOUR LOBE IS GONE--BUT YOU'LL STILL BE ABLE TO HEAR.
I COULDN'T CARE LESS ABOUT HEARING. I DON'T WANT TO LOOK LIKE A FREAK.
YOU'VE GOT NOTHING TO WORRY ABOUT. YOU'LL BE AS PRETTY AS EVER, AS SOON AS WE CLEAN YOU UP.

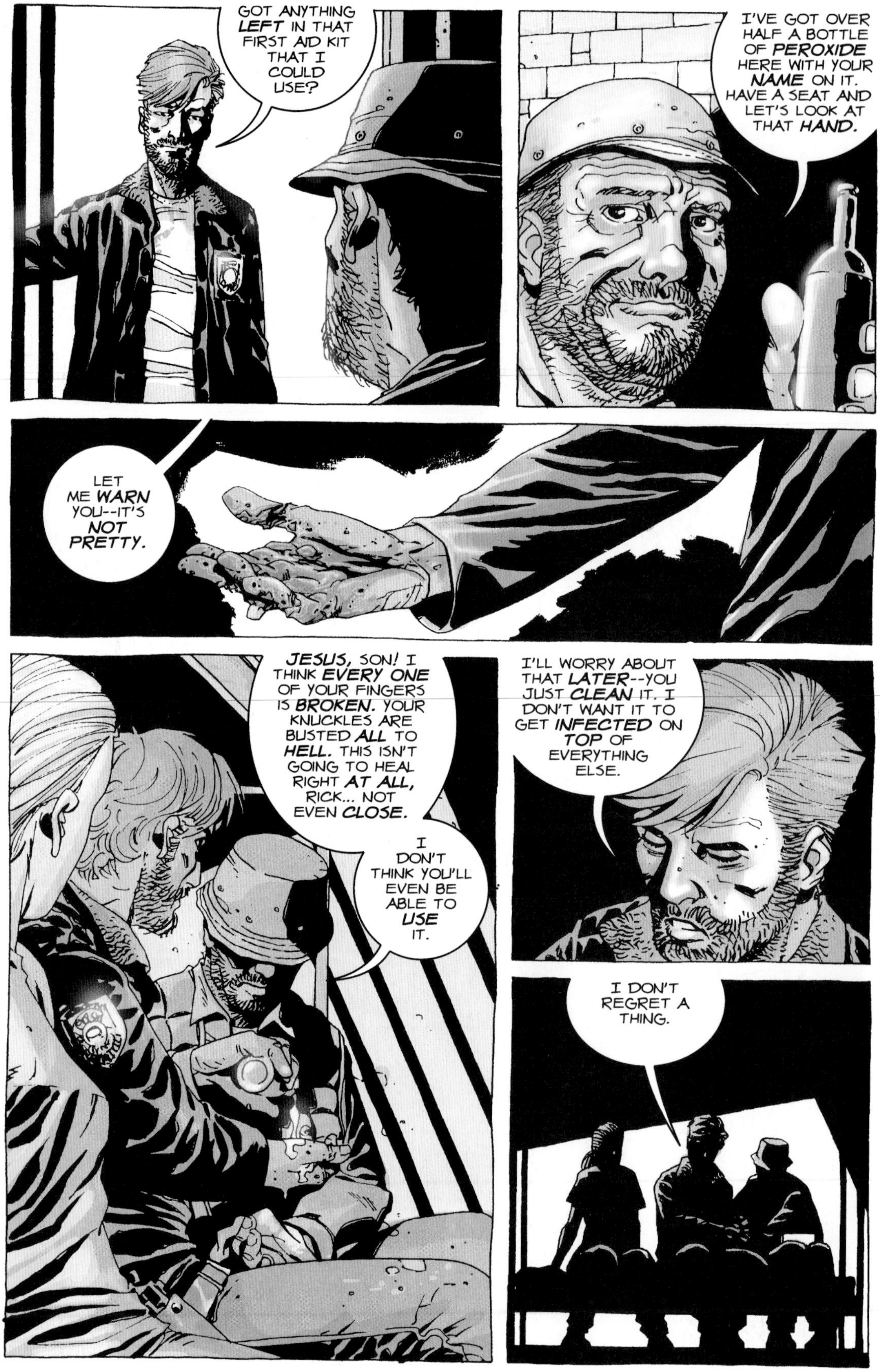
GOT ANYTHING LEFT IN THAT FIRST AID KIT THAT I COULD USE?
I'VE GOT OVER HALF A BOTTLE OF PEROXIDE HERE WITH YOUR NAME ON IT. HAVE A SEAT AND LET'S LOOK AT THAT HAND.
LET ME WARN YOU--IT'S NOT PRETTY.
JESUS, SON! I THINK EVERY ONE OF YOUR FINGERS IS BROKEN. YOUR KNUCKLES ARE BUSTED ALL TO HELL. THIS ISN'T GOING TO HEAL RIGHT AT ALL, RICK... NOT EVEN CLOSE.
I DON'T THINK YOU'LL EVEN BE ABLE TO USE IT.
I'LL WORRY ABOUT THAT LATER--YOU JUST CLEAN IT. I DON'T WANT IT TO GET INFECTED ON TOP OF EVERYTHING ELSE.
I DON'T REGRET A THING.

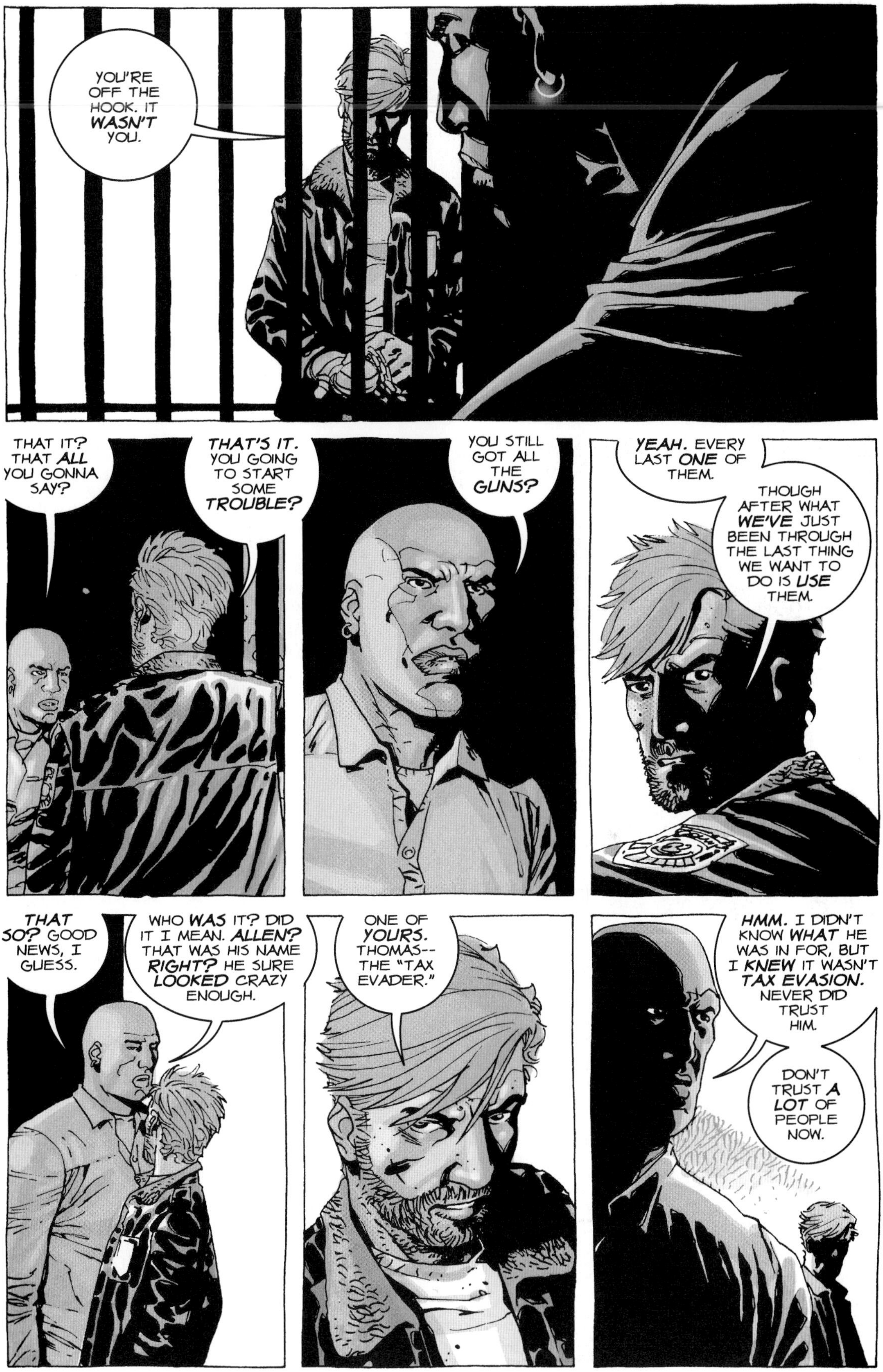
YOU'RE OFF THE HOOK. IT WASN'T YOU.
THAT IT? THAT ALL YOU GONNA SAY?
THAT'S IT. YOU GOING TO START SOME TROUBLE?
YOU STILL GOT ALL THE GUNS?
YEAH. EVERY LAST ONE OF THEM.
THOUGH AFTER WHAT WE'VE JUST BEEN THROUGH THE LAST THING WE WANT TO DO IS USE THEM.
THAT SO? GOOD NEWS, I GUESS.
WHO WAS IT? DID IT I MEAN. ALLEN? THAT WAS HIS NAME RIGHT? HE SURE LOOKED CRAZY ENOUGH.
ONE OF YOURS. THOMAS-- THE "TAX EVADER."
HMM. I DIDN'T KNOW WHAT HE WAS IN FOR, BUT I KNEW IT WASN'T TAX EVASION. NEVER DID TRUST HIM.
DON'T TRUST A LOT OF PEOPLE NOW.

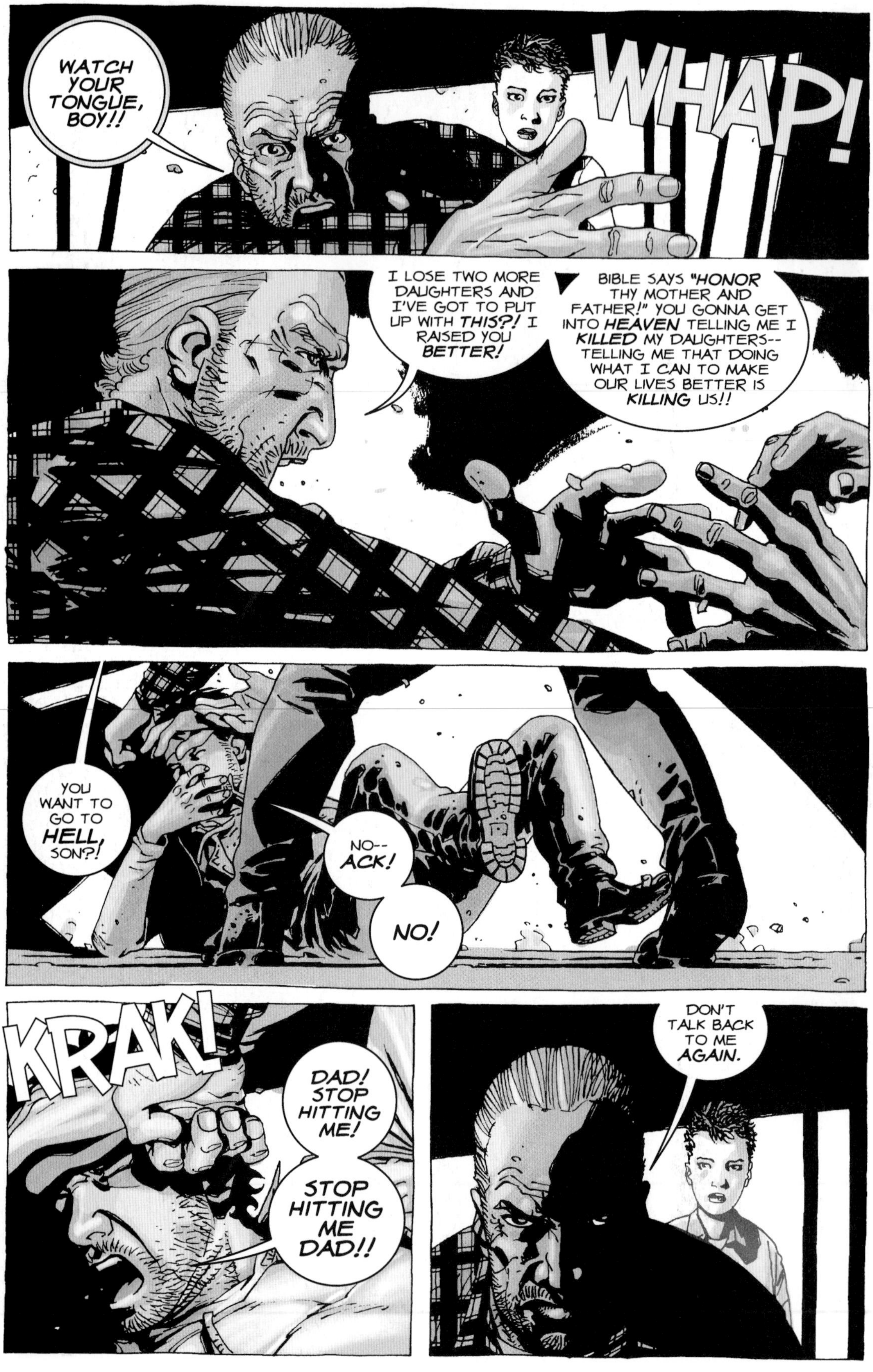
WATCH YOUR TONGUE, BOY!!
WHAP!
I LOSE TWO MORE DAUGHTERS AND I'VE GOT TO PUT UP WITH THIS?! I RAISED YOU BETTER!
BIBLE SAYS "HONOR THY MOTHER AND FATHER!" YOU GONNA GET INTO HEAVEN TELLING ME I KILLED MY DAUGHTERS-- TELLING ME THAT DOING WHAT I CAN TO MAKE OUR LIVES BETTER IS KILLING US!!
YOU WANT TO GO TO HELL, SON?!
NO-- ACK!
NO!
KRAK!
DAD! STOP HITTING ME!
STOP HITTING ME DAD!!
DON'T TALK BACK TO ME AGAIN.

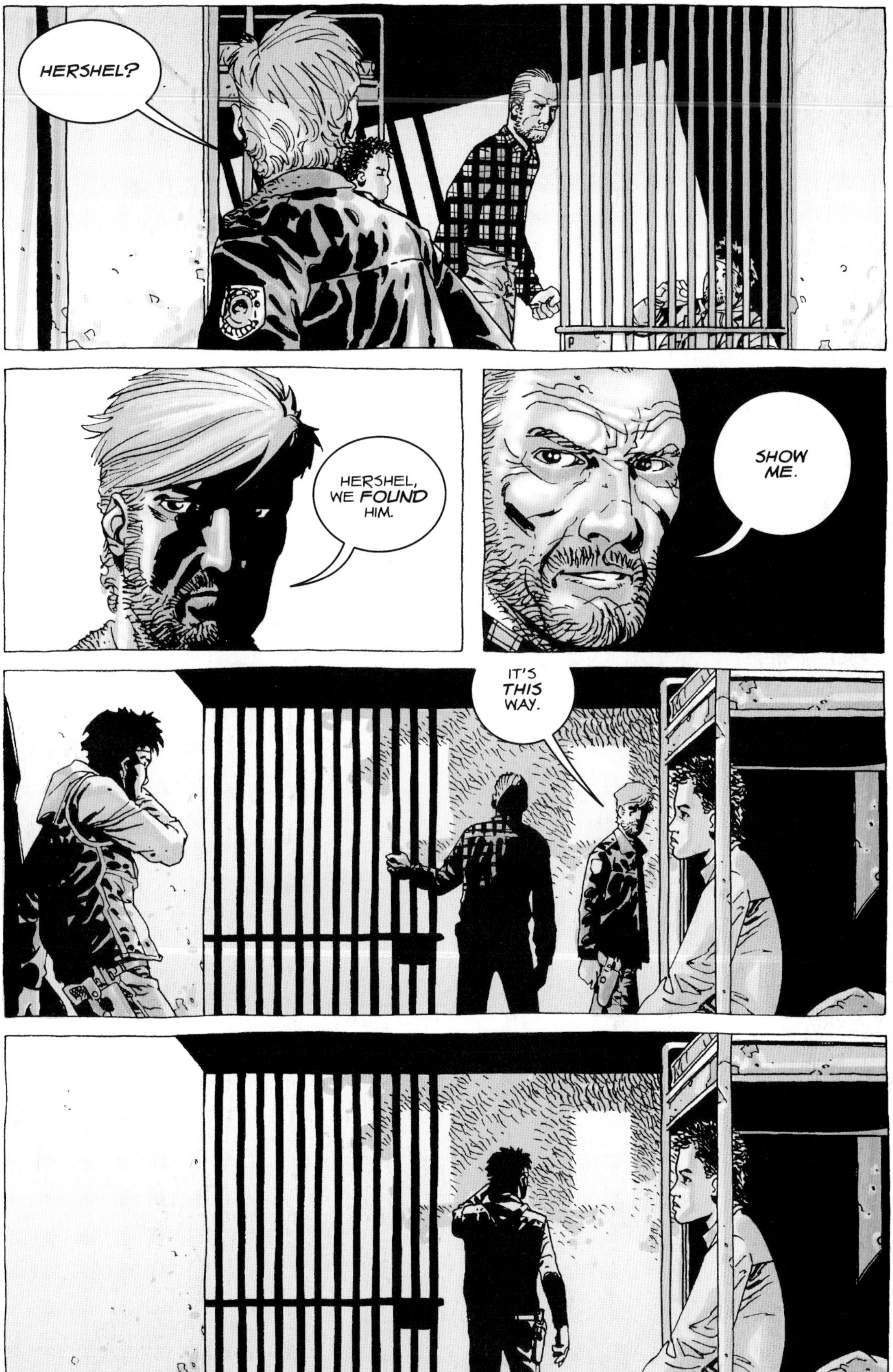
HERSHEL?
HERSHEL, WE FOUND HIM.
SHOW ME.
IT'S THIS WAY.

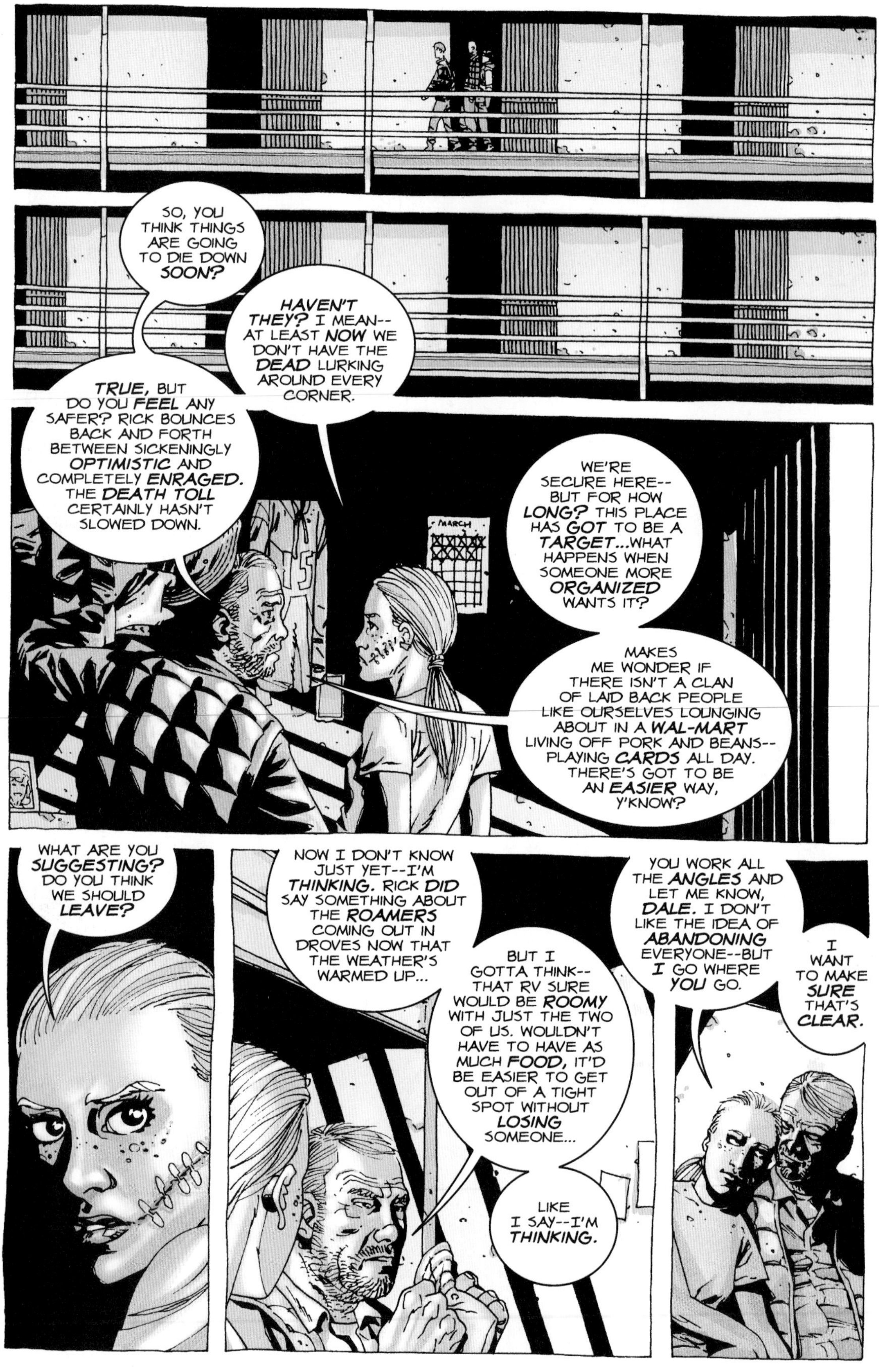

SO, YOU THINK THINGS ARE GOING TO DIE DOWN SOON?
HAVEN'T THEY? I MEAN-- AT LEAST NOW WE DON'T HAVE THE DEAD LURKING AROUND EVERY CORNER.
TRUE, BUT DO YOU FEEL ANY SAFER? RICK BOUNCES BACK AND FORTH BETWEEN SICKENINGLY OPTIMISTIC AND COMPLETELY ENRAGED. THE DEATH TOLL CERTAINLY HASN'T SLOWED DOWN.
WE'RE SECURE HERE-- BUT FOR HOW LONG? THIS PLACE HAS GOT TO BE A TARGET...WHAT HAPPENS WHEN SOMEONE MORE ORGANIZED WANTS IT?
MAKES ME WONDER IF THERE ISN'T A CLAN OF LAID BACK PEOPLE LIKE OURSELVES LOUNGING ABOUT IN A WAL-MART LIVING OFF PORK AND BEANS-- PLAYING CARDS ALL DAY. THERE'S GOT TO BE AN EASIER WAY, Y'KNOW?
WHAT ARE YOU SUGGESTING? DO YOU THINK WE SHOULD LEAVE?
NOW I DON'T KNOW JUST YET--I'M THINKING. RICK DID SAY SOMETHING ABOUT THE ROAMERS COMING OUT IN DROVES NOW THAT THE WEATHER'S WARMED UP...
BUT I GOTTA THINK-- THAT RV SURE WOULD BE ROOMY WITH JUST THE TWO OF US. WOULDN'T HAVE TO HAVE AS MUCH FOOD, IT'D BE EASIER TO GET OUT OF A TIGHT SPOT WITHOUT LOSING SOMEONE...
LIKE I SAY--I'M THINKING.
YOU WORK ALL THE ANGLES AND LET ME KNOW, DALE. I DON'T LIKE THE IDEA OF ABANDONING EVERYONE--BUT I GO WHERE YOU GO.
I WANT TO MAKE SURE THAT'S CLEAR.

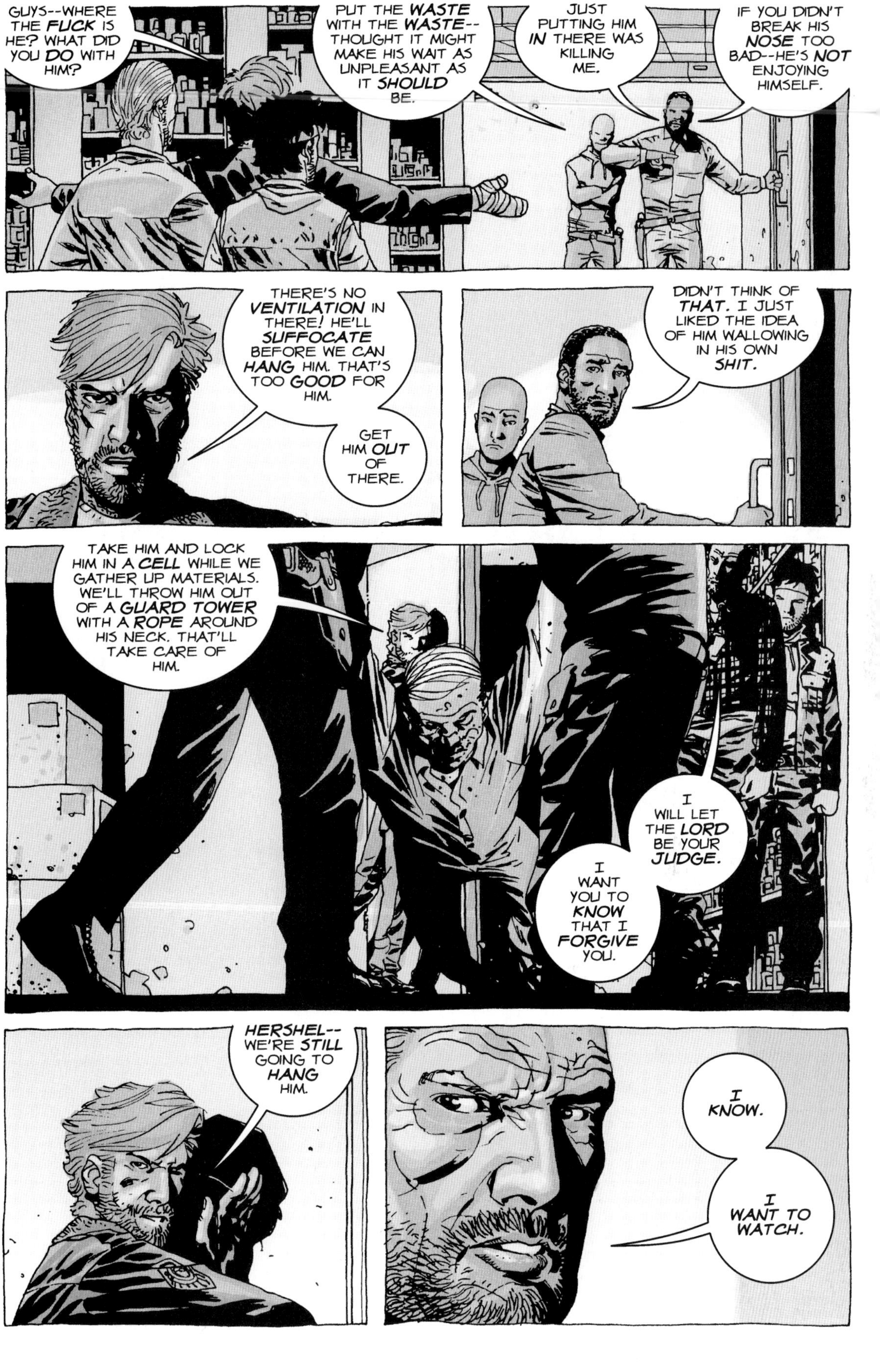
GUYS--WHERE THE FUCK IS HE? WHAT DID YOU DO WITH HIM?
PUT THE WASTE WITH THE WASTE--THOUGHT IT MIGHT MAKE HIS WAIT AS UNPLEASANT AS IT SHOULD BE.
JUST PUTTING HIM IN THERE WAS KILLING ME.
IF YOU DIDN'T BREAK HIS NOSE TOO BAD--HE'S NOT ENJOYING HIMSELF.
THERE'S NO VENTILATION IN THERE! HE'LL SUFFOCATE BEFORE WE CAN HANG HIM. THAT'S TOO GOOD FOR HIM.
GET HIM OUT OF THERE.
DIDN'T THINK OF THAT. I JUST LIKED THE IDEA OF HIM WALLOWING IN HIS OWN SHIT.
TAKE HIM AND LOCK HIM IN A CELL WHILE WE GATHER UP MATERIALS. WE'LL THROW HIM OUT OF A GUARD TOWER WITH A ROPE AROUND HIS NECK. THAT'LL TAKE CARE OF HIM.
I WANT YOU TO KNOW THAT I FORGIVE YOU.
I WILL LET THE LORD BE YOUR JUDGE.
HERSHEL--WE'RE STILL GOING TO HANG HIM.
I KNOW.
I WANT TO WATCH.

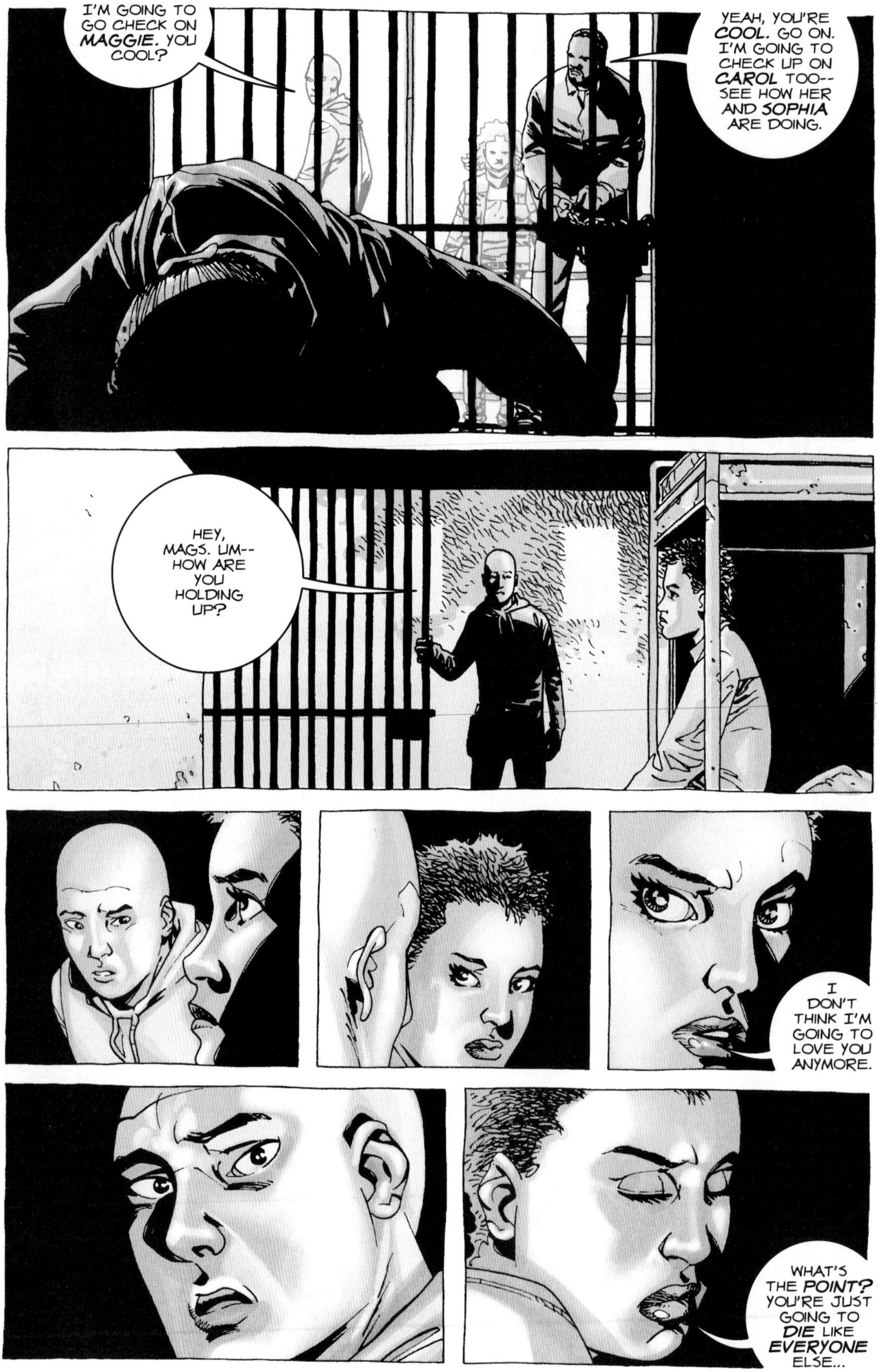
I'M GOING TO GO CHECK ON MAGGIE. YOU COOL?
YEAH, YOU'RE COOL. GO ON. I'M GOING TO CHECK UP ON CAROL TOO-- SEE HOW HER AND SOPHIA ARE DOING.
HEY, MAGS. UM-- HOW ARE YOU HOLDING UP?
I DON'T THINK I'M GOING TO LOVE YOU ANYMORE.
WHAT'S THE POINT? YOU'RE JUST GOING TO DIE LIKE EVERYONE ELSE...

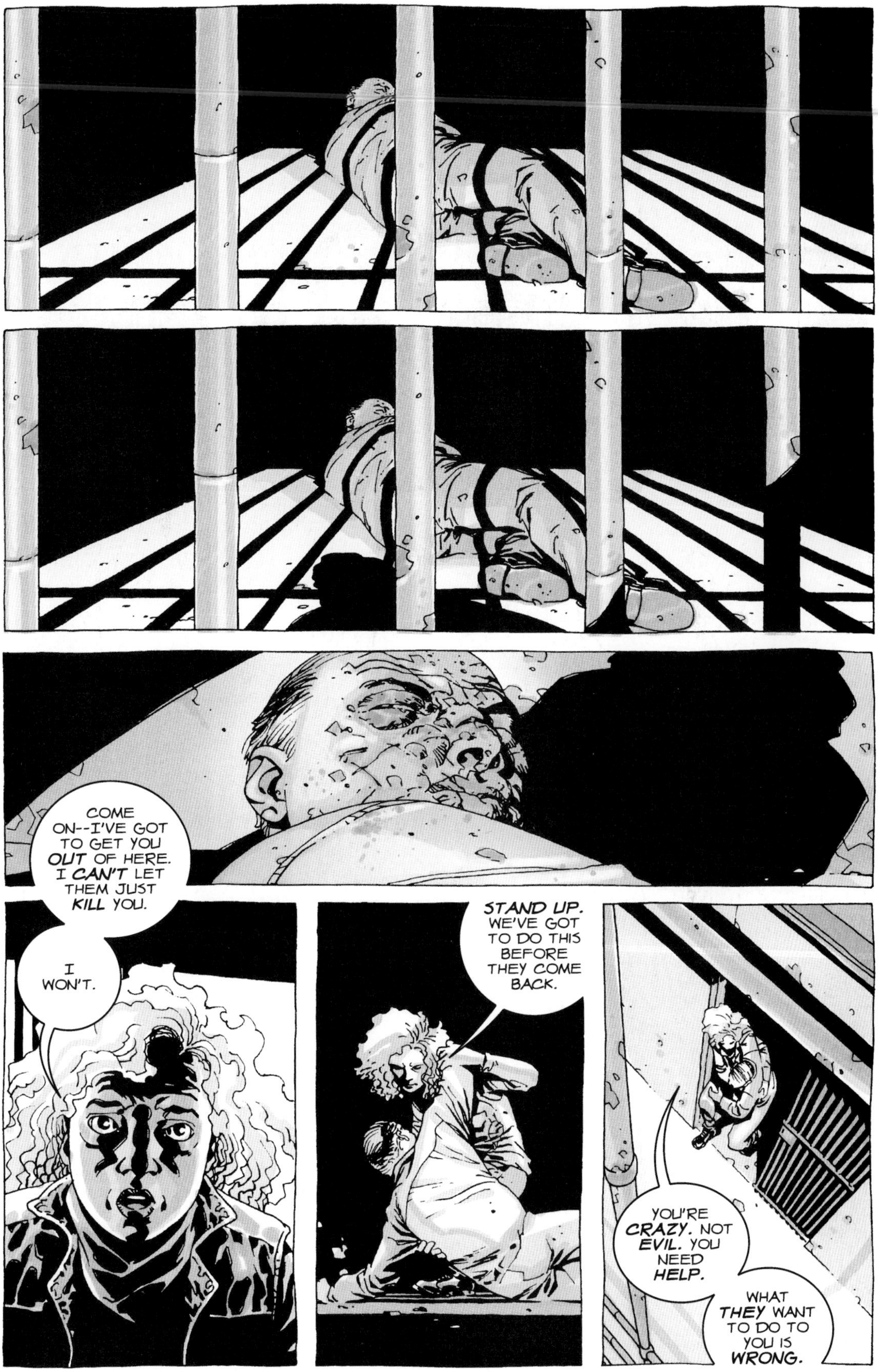
COME ON--I'VE GOT TO GET YOU OUT OF HERE. I CAN'T LET THEM JUST KILL YOU.
I WON'T.
STAND UP. WE'VE GOT TO DO THIS BEFORE THEY COME BACK.
YOU'RE CRAZY. NOT EVIL. YOU NEED HELP.
WHAT THEY WANT TO DO TO YOU IS WRONG.

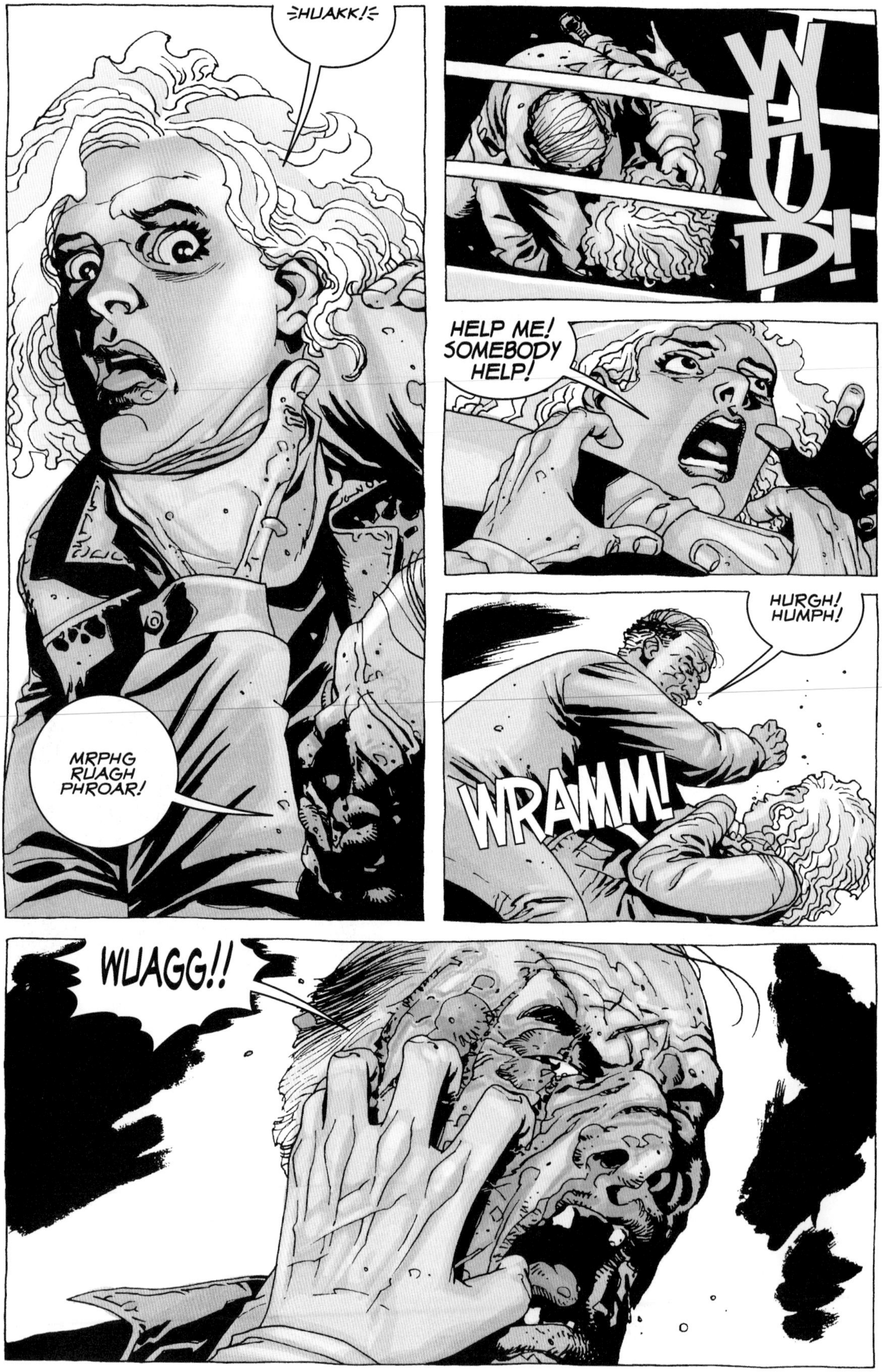
=HUAKK!=
MRPHG RUAGH PHROAR!
WHUD!
HELP ME! SOMEBODY HELP!
HURGH! HUMPH!
WRAMM!
WUAGG!!

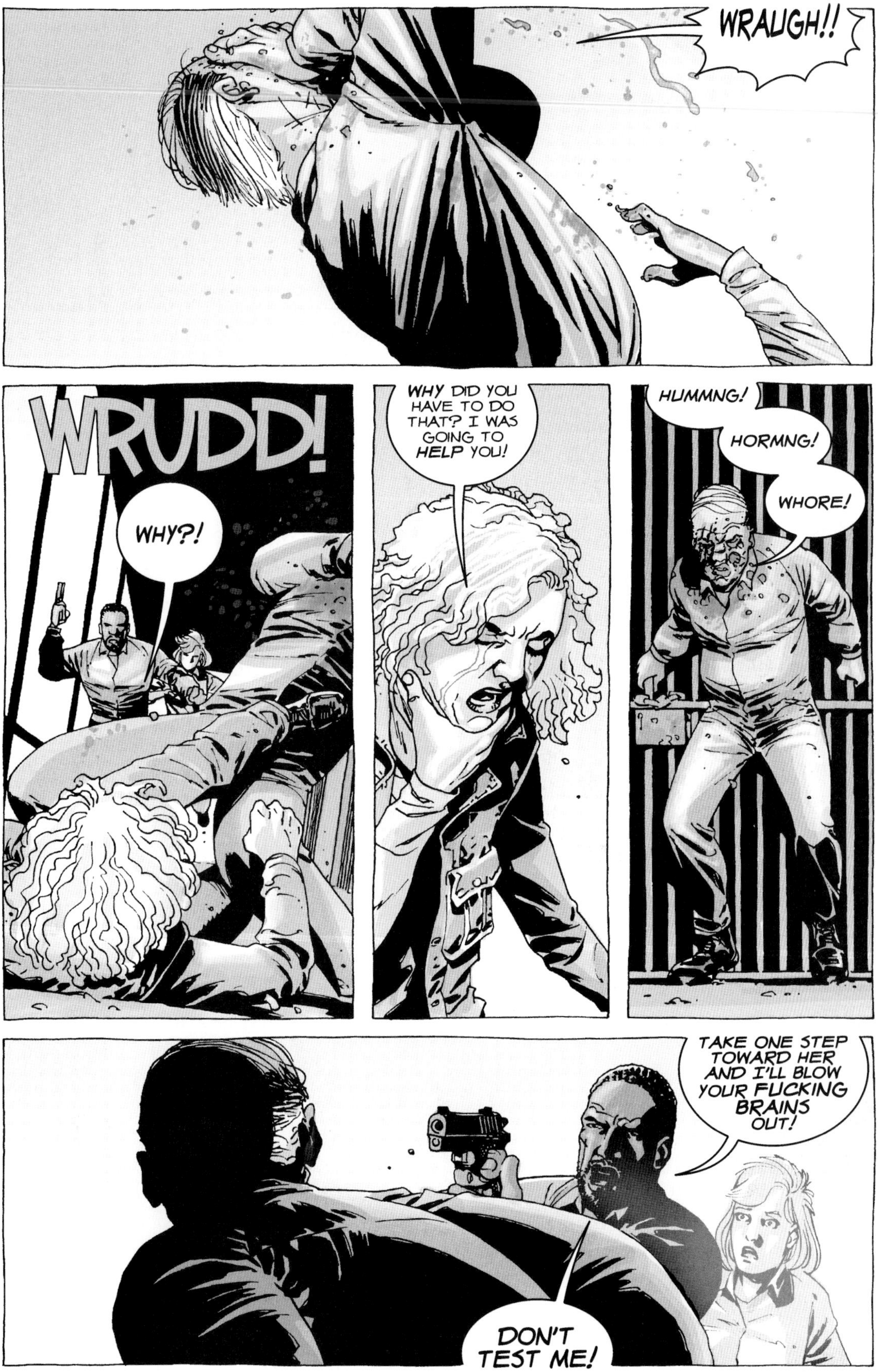
WRAUGH!!
WRUDD!
WHY?!
WHY DID YOU HAVE TO DO THAT? I WAS GOING TO HELP YOU!
HUMMNG!
HORMNG!
WHORE!
TAKE ONE STEP TOWARD HER AND I'LL BLOW YOUR FUCKING BRAINS OUT!
DON'T TEST ME!

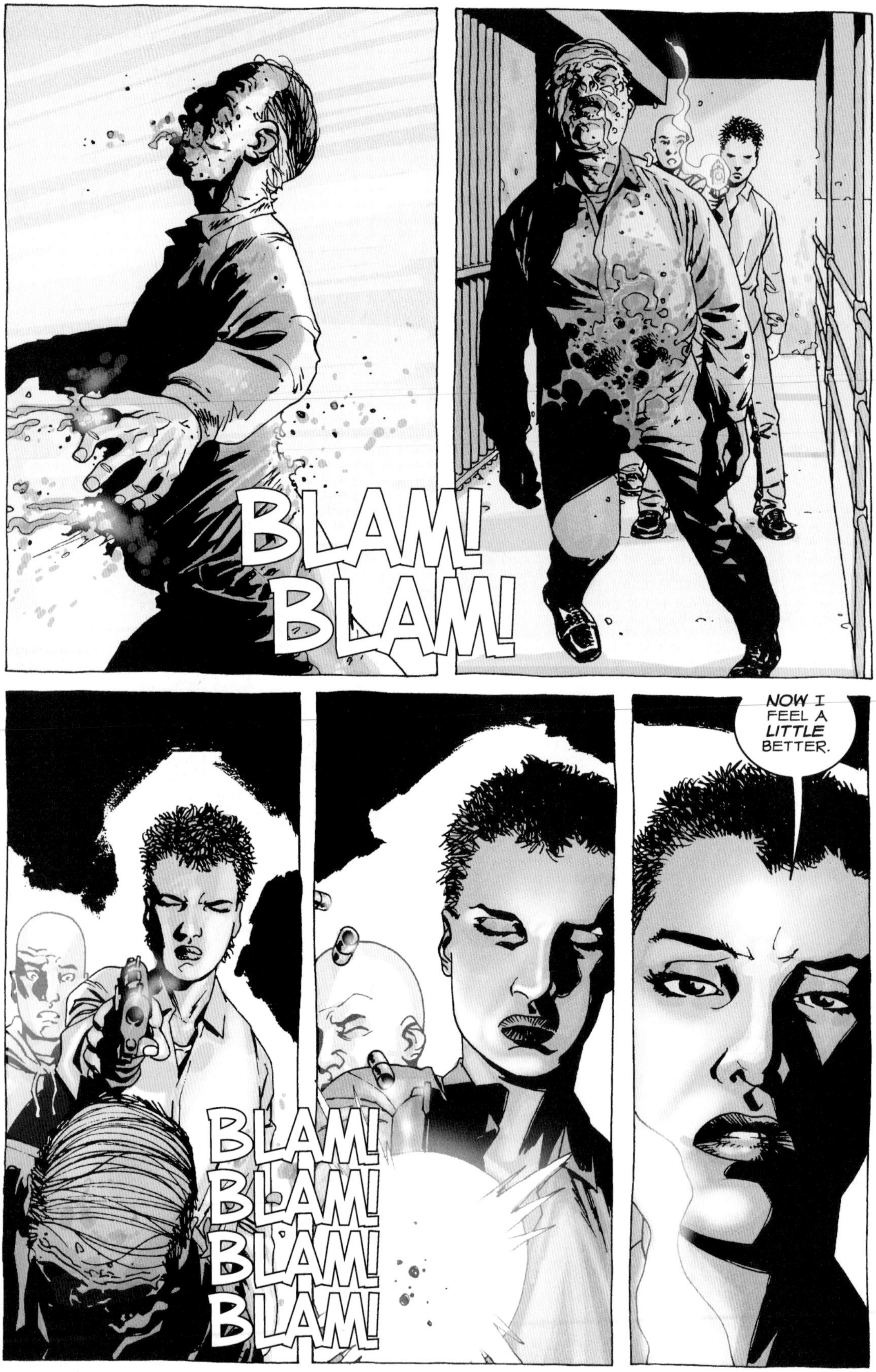
BLAM!
BLAM!
BLAM!
BLAM!
BLAM!
BLAM!
NOW I FEEL A LITTLE BETTER.

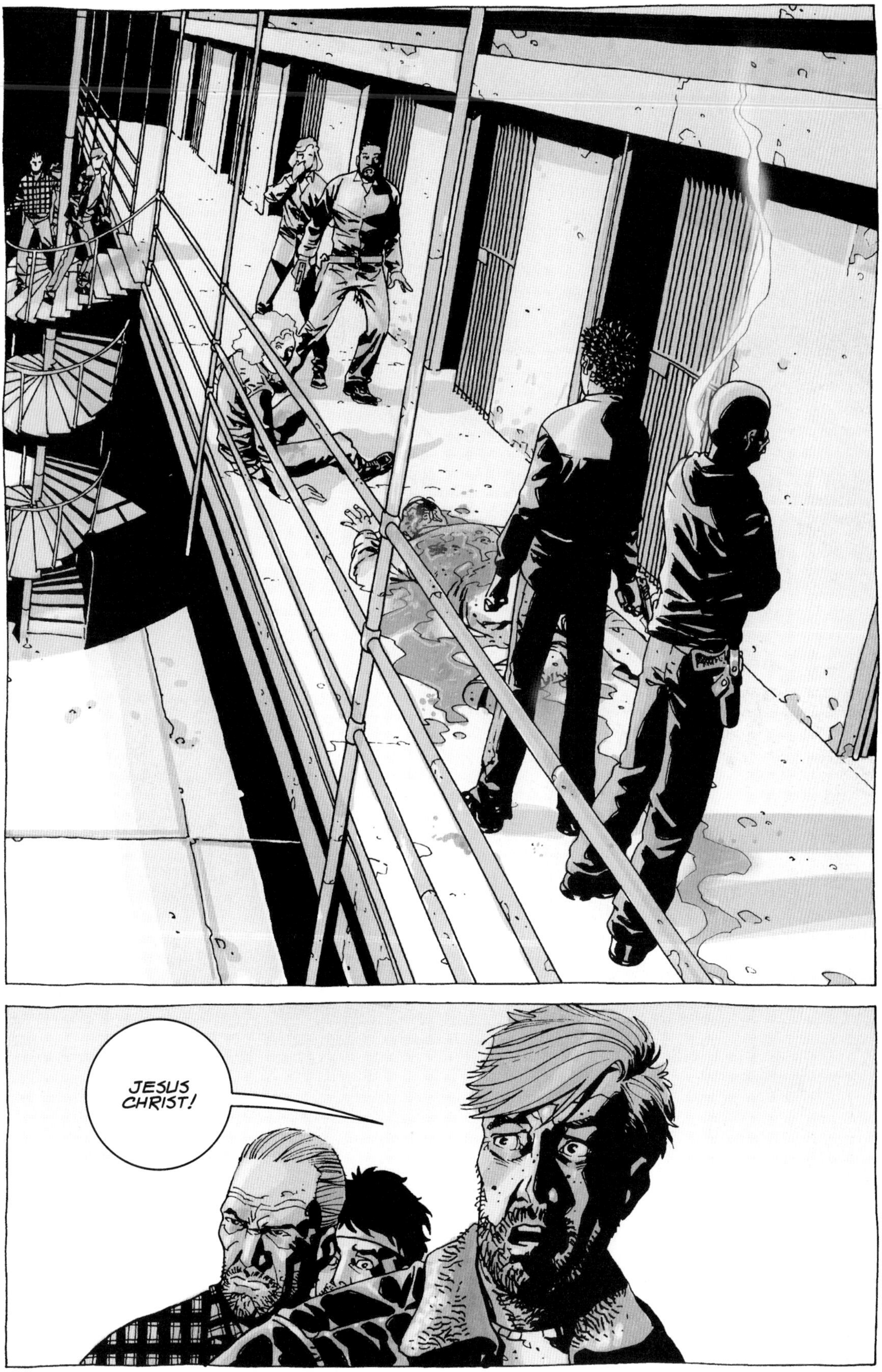
JESUS CHRIST!

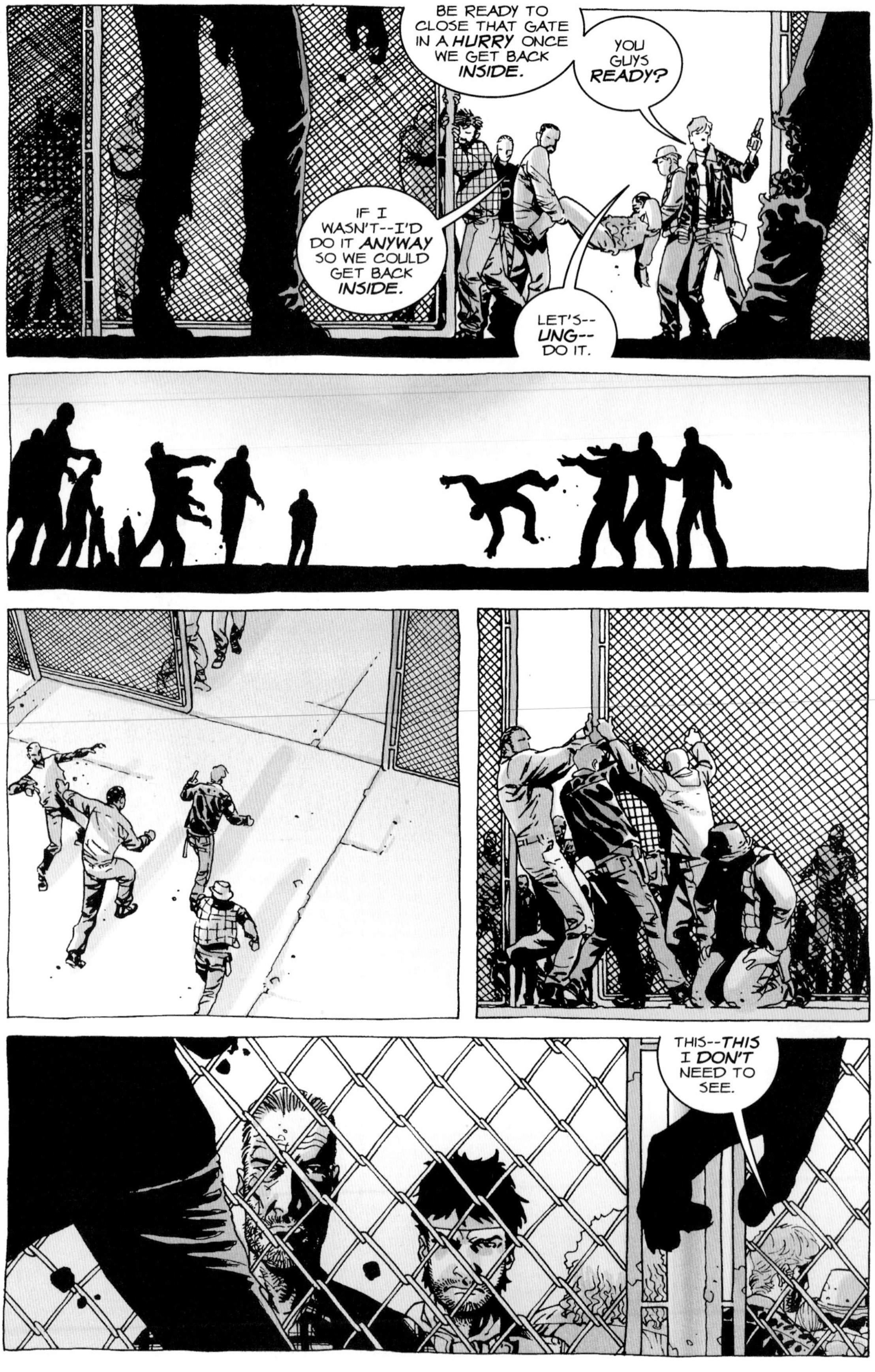
BE READY TO CLOSE THAT GATE IN A HURRY ONCE WE GET BACK INSIDE.
YOU GUYS READY?
IF I WASN'T--I'D DO IT ANYWAY SO WE COULD GET BACK INSIDE.
LET'S-- UNG-- DO IT.
THIS--THIS I DON'T NEED TO SEE.

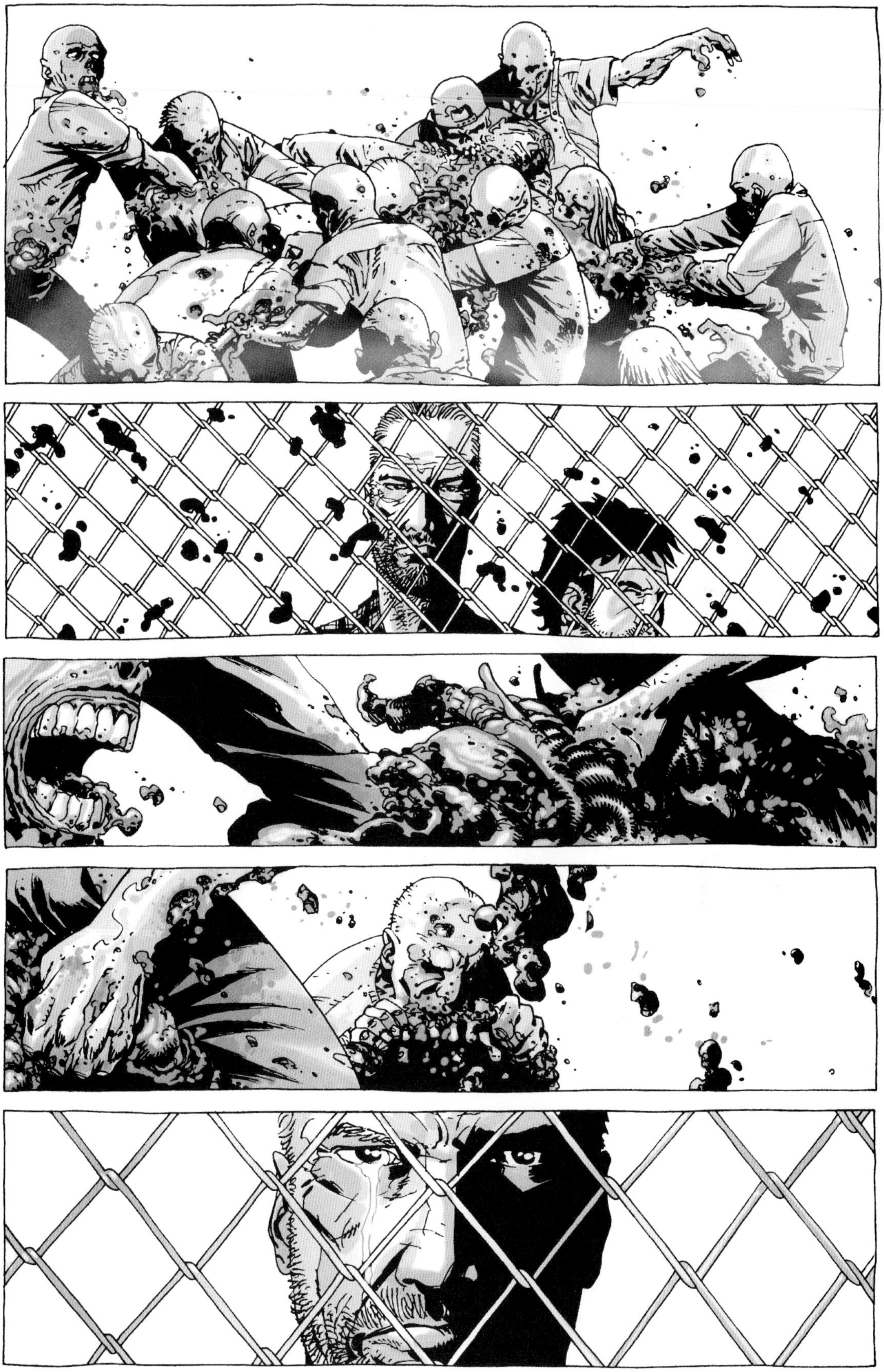

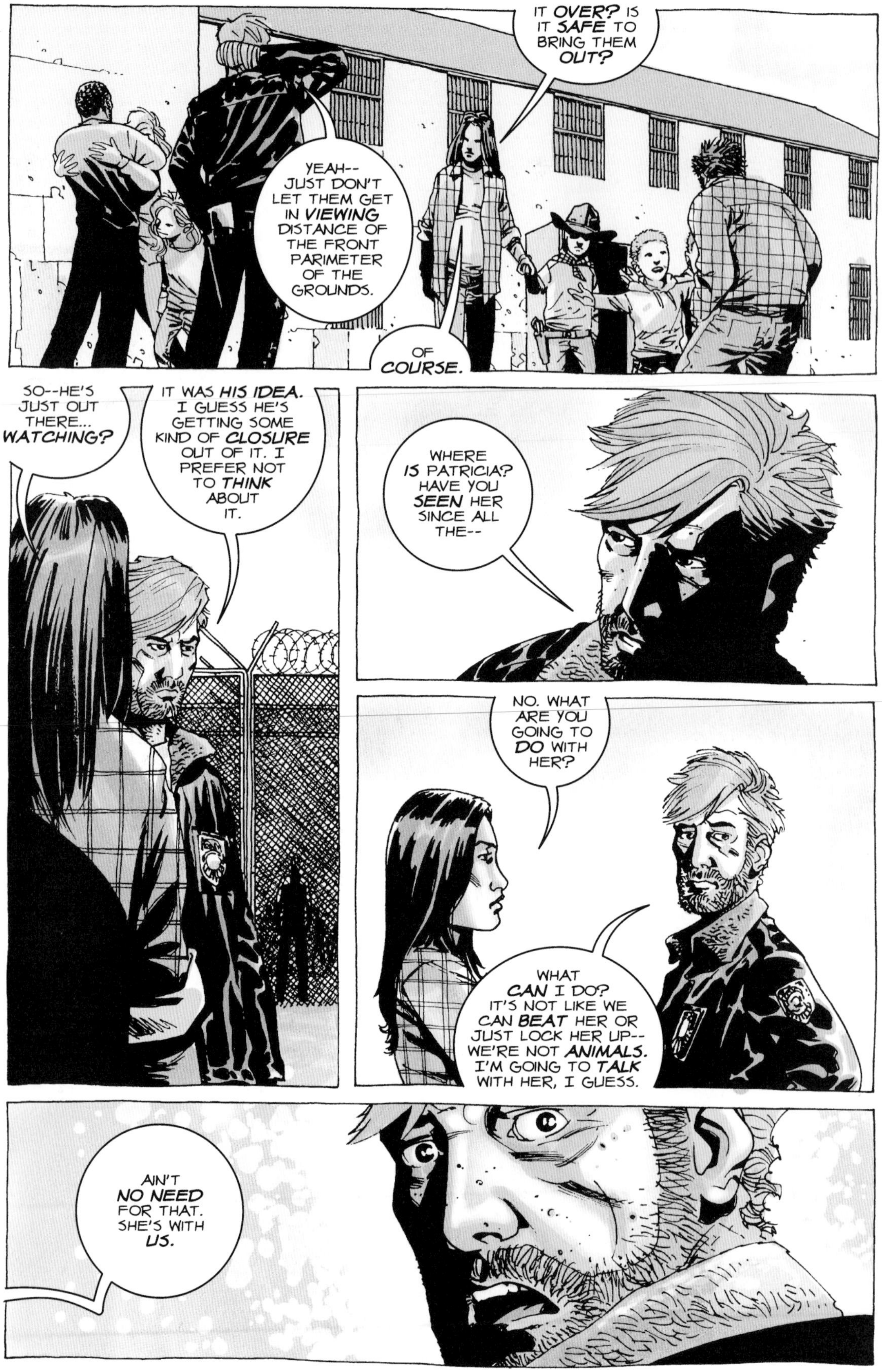
IT OVER? IS IT SAFE TO BRING THEM OUT?
YEAH-- JUST DON'T LET THEM GET IN VIEWING DISTANCE OF THE FRONT PARIMETER OF THE GROUNDS.
OF COURSE.
SO--HE'S JUST OUT THERE... WATCHING?
IT WAS HIS IDEA. I GUESS HE'S GETTING SOME KIND OF CLOSURE OUT OF IT. I PREFER NOT TO THINK ABOUT IT.
WHERE IS PATRICIA? HAVE YOU SEEN HER SINCE ALL THE--
NO. WHAT ARE YOU GOING TO DO WITH HER?
WHAT CAN I DO? IT'S NOT LIKE WE CAN BEAT HER OR JUST LOCK HER UP--WE'RE NOT ANIMALS. I'M GOING TO TALK WITH HER, I GUESS.
AIN'T NO NEED FOR THAT. SHE'S WITH US.

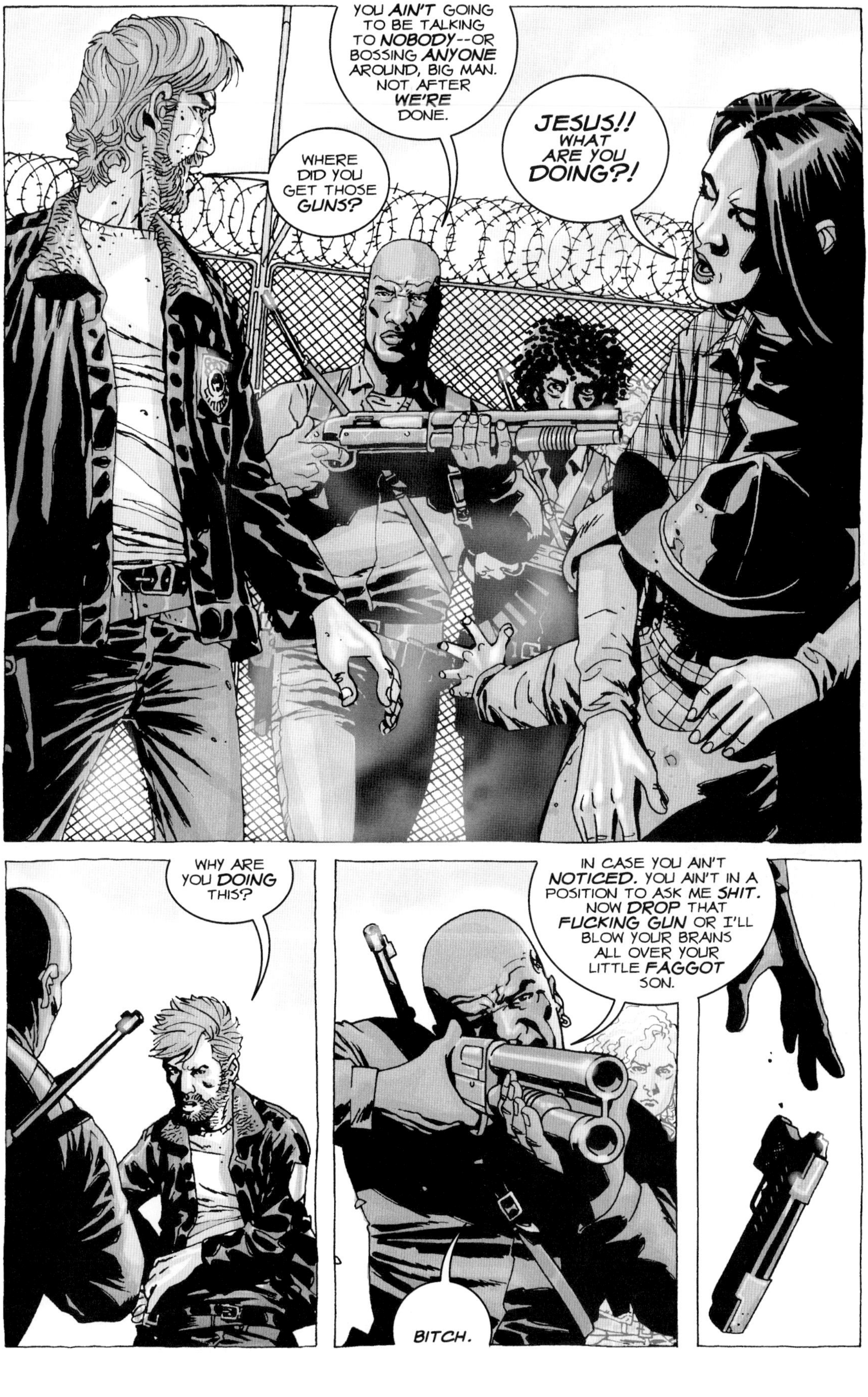
WHERE DID YOU GET THOSE GUNS?
YOU AIN'T GOING TO BE TALKING TO NOBODY--OR BOSSING ANYONE AROUND, BIG MAN. NOT AFTER WE'RE DONE.
JESUS!! WHAT ARE YOU DOING?!
WHY ARE YOU DOING THIS?
IN CASE YOU AIN'T NOTICED. YOU AIN'T IN A POSITION TO ASK ME SHIT. NOW DROP THAT FUCKING GUN OR I'LL BLOW YOUR BRAINS ALL OVER YOUR LITTLE FAGGOT SON.
BITCH.

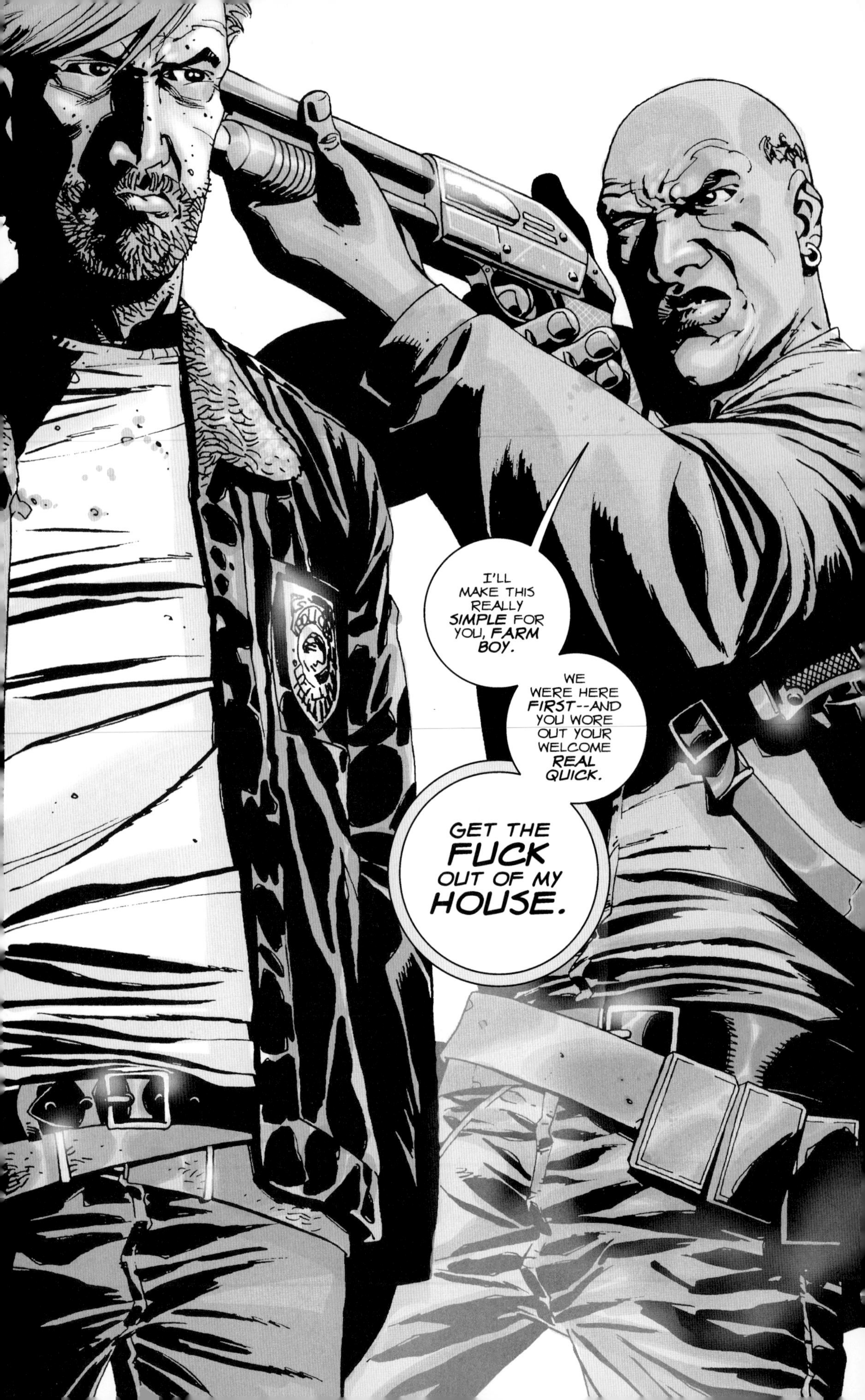
I'LL MAKE THIS REALLY SIMPLE FOR YOU, FARM BOY.
WE WERE HERE FIRST--AND YOU WORE OUT YOUR WELCOME REAL QUICK.
GET THE FUCK OUT OF MY HOUSE.

TO BE CONTINUED...

FOR MORE OF THE WALKING DEAD

TRADEPAPERBACKS

ROBERT KIRKMAN TONY MOORE
THE WALKING DEAD
VOLUME 1
DAYS GONE BYE

VOL. 1: DAYS GONE BYE TP
ISBN: 978-1-58240-672-5
$14.99
VOL. 2: MILES BEHIND US TP
ISBN: 978-1-58240-775-3
$14.99
VOL. 3: SAFETY BEHIND BARS TP
ISBN: 978-1-58240-805-7
$14.99
VOL. 4: THE HEART'S DESIRE TP
ISBN: 978-1-58240-530-8
$14.99
VOL. 5: THE BEST DEFENSE TP
ISBN: 978-1-58240-612-1
$14.99
VOL. 6: THIS SORROWFUL LIFE TP
ISBN: 978-1-58240-684-8
$14.99
VOL. 7: THE CALM BEFORE TP
ISBN: 978-1-58240-828-6
$14.99
VOL. 8: MADE TO SUFFER TP
ISBN: 978-1-58240-883-5
$14.99
VOL. 9: HERE WE REMAIN TP
ISBN: 978-1-60706-022-2
$14.99
VOL. 10: WHAT WE BECOME TP
ISBN: 978-1-60706-075-8
$14.99
VOL. 11: FEAR THE HUNTERS TP
ISBN: 978-1-60706-181-6
$14.99
VOL. 12: LIFE AMONG THEM TP
ISBN: 978-1-60706-254-7
$14.99
VOL. 13: TOO FAR GONE TP
ISBN: 978-1-60706-329-2
$14.99
VOL. 14: NO WAY OUT TP
ISBN: 978-1-60706-392-6
$14.99
VOL. 15: WE FIND OURSELVES TP
ISBN: 978-1-60706-440-4
$14.99
VOL. 16: A LARGER WORLD TP
ISBN: 978-1-60706-559-3
$14.99
VOL. 17: SOMETHING TO FEAR TP
ISBN: 978-1-60706-615-6
$14.99

HARDCOVERS

THE WALKING DEAD
BOOK ONE
a continuing story of survival horror.

BOOK ONE HC
ISBN: 978-1-58240-619-0
$34.99
BOOK TWO HC
ISBN: 978-1-58240-698-5
$34.99
BOOK THREE HC
ISBN: 978-1-58240-825-5
$34.99
BOOK FOUR HC
ISBN: 978-1-60706-000-0
$34.99
BOOK FIVE HC
ISBN: 978-1-60706-171-7
$34.99
BOOK SIX HC
ISBN: 978-1-60706-327-8
$34.99
BOOK SEVEN HC
ISBN: 978-1-60706-439-8
$34.99
BOOK EIGHT HC
ISBN: 978-1-60706-593-7
$34.99

COMPENDIUMS

The ultimate edition of The New York Times bestseller!
THE WALKING DEAD
COMPENDIUM ONE
Robert Kirkman • Charlie Adlard • Tony Moore • Cliff Rathburn

COMPENDIUM TP, VOL. 1
ISBN: 978-1-60706-076-5
$59.99
COMPENDIUM TP, VOL. 2
ISBN: 978-1-60706-596-8
$59.99

SPECIALTY BOOKS

THE WALKING DEAD
THE COVERS

THE WALKING DEAD: THE COVERS, VOL. 1 HC
ISBN: 978-1-60706-002-4
$24.99
THE WALKING DEAD SURVIVORS' GUIDE
ISBN: 978-1-60706-458-9
$12.99

OMNIBUS

THE WALKING DEAD

OMNIBUS, VOL. 1
ISBN: 978-1-60706-503-6
$100.00
OMNIBUS, VOL. 2
ISBN: 978-1-60706-515-9
$100.00
OMNIBUS, VOL. 3
ISBN: 978-1-60706-330-8
$100.00
OMNIBUS, VOL. 4
ISBN: 978-1-60706-616-3
$100.00

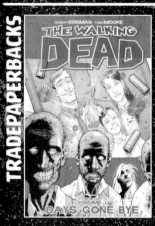

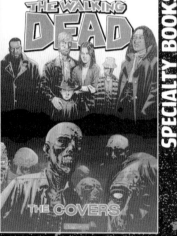